Sycamore Grove

K. Scott Fuchs

Published by K. Scott Fuchs, 2024.

SYCAMORE GROVE

First edition. September 17, 2024.

Copyright © 2024 K. Scott Fuchs.

ISBN: 979-8227971692

Written by K. Scott Fuchs.

Table of Contents

Dedicated to The Lord for being my hero, saviour, and truest friend. Thank you Heavenly Father, for always being there for me and saving me from myself.

To Miss Lee for being the dream that was, is, and will always be....

.

SYCAMORE GROVE

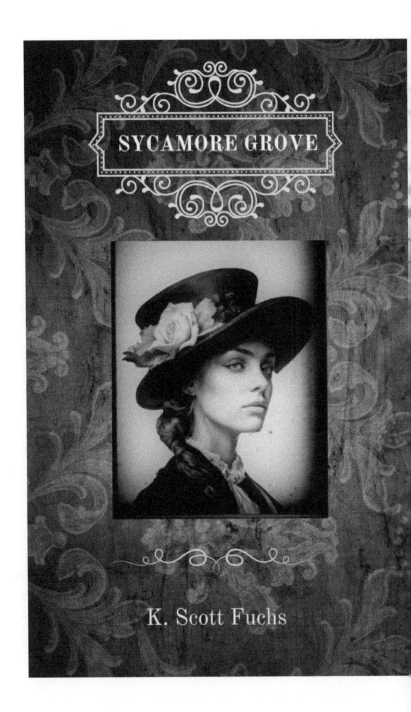

K. Scott Fuchs

PROLOGUE

There is no clarity, logic, or coherence – only ambiguity. I will likely forget that I wrote this; when I black out that's what happens - and I am on the verge of havoc. A point of no return, a terminus to a series of events that could have been misdirected and re-connected in my vast introspection. However, I must off-load this burden which is crushing, crunching, and bludgeoning me, everywhere that I go.

The time and date are irrelevant because it all feels the same to me. It's the same rain shadow casting its gloom upon the sunniest of afternoons. It drowns out the blue with a cold grey that chills my bones where I can never get warm. Why not face what has consumed you?

I wish I had the temperament to be virtuous; not proud and full of sin. Because I am like a butterfly trapped in a spiderweb, I can flutter my wings as vigorously as I wish but will I ever break free? Or will this darkness inject its venom finally and kill me? Acquiescing to this conclusion which seems inevitable, could grant me the serenity to let it pass. To fall to the bottom of that river which ambles beneath the aqueduct I have crossed. However, I choose to personify its character and follow its lead under the belief that the rocks, the crevices, bends, and turns all lead to some place that I could not conceive in the most intricate and exaggerated fantasies.

Is this my poetry? Where is my optimism? And where is my faith?! I don't know what lies ahead of me, five, ten, or even fifteen minutes from now. But I am lost! And it's gone late....

I started at one point and ended up here beside the still water with a vista of green rolling hills, roads leading to a quiet destination, and signs to a railway station. I could not recall its name, for it is replaced by the imminent threat, the thoughts of death, and my desperate escape, leading to these words scribbled on the back of a page I tore from a novel. Writing my own story that I can only touch and taste, the happy ending that eludes me. The romance floating through the air like the wisps of a dandelion blown by a child with haste; gliding along the stream like the geese beside me. They don't know where they are going, but they travel with intent; hopeful and elegant in their strides with such fluidity in their movements while I feel spasms in my knees.

Lord, please, take this from me...

There is a trembling in my fingers as my breaths become shallow. All I see is the blackness, the rage, the sorrow, and woe; it is coursing through my veins, it is a persistent clanging noise that makes me want to smash my face against the stonewall behind me. Perhaps I should have another smoke and take a deep breath. Let this diffidence and listlessness fade away into the nothingness I feel inside my soul before I rip this shit up and throw MYSELF in a hole!

I crinkled up this note and put it back in my pocket...

Part I

Ms. Temperance Lee of Marple

I.

My hands shook as I read the text etched on the screen of my phone.

Where are you?

How could I respond? My every thought fixated on the what if's and how I replied. I couldn't say where I really was. I couldn't tell him what I was about to do; then they'd know...

Audenshaw? Marple? Perhaps, I should write back: *Out for the day and you?* The last seemed to be the most viable option; or maybe I could say I went down to Leicestershire, so it ended there.

I hadn't seen Pete in a while, we had not spoken or seen each other since the day by the Roman Lakes when we were talking about Temperance; the day he suggested she wasn't what she appeared to be...

I looked up at the white brocade ceiling barely perceptible from the overcast skies pouring through the window. The walls knocked as if someone was all around poking their knuckles against the frame; as if they were inside and outside, at the same time. The wind howled and squealed, giving a voice to the phantom dissonance. My eyes glued back to the screen as my fingers trembled; I could hear my heart beating in my ears.

A knock again; this time it sounded like it was clunking against the front panel of the door; a tapping like that of a brass door knocker. I opened the door and no one was there. A brief gust of wind trickled across my face, shaking the oak trees that stood beyond the canal. I looked to my right and saw a man in a red coat, *Royal Mail* embroidered on the back, leaving a card at the door to the residence next door. The iron gate squealed as it opened and it hushed when the postman shut it behind him. He carried on walking up the lane toward the bridge over the canal, unaware of my existence or who resided where I was presently. His white headphones gelled into his ears and tucked beneath a white baseball hat as he continued his route.

I cannot recall a time when the mail arrived here whenever I was present; it was odd. I shut the door and put my phone back into my pocket. The rush of the wind transitioned into the sound of streaming water as I stepped into the kitchen. The cream tiles on the walls and the periwinkle paint above them seemed to glow with a warmth that gave it a unique cosiness. Temperance's long hair fell down the back of her cerulean dress, the navy skirt nearly dusting upon the ground. Temperance didn't know I was there and that is how I wanted it. Watching her in her daily tasks was a treat in itself. She was immersed in cleaning a dish, her hands nimbly holding the ivory while she ran the soap under the water to rinse it. I smiled and gazed at her with wonder, taken back by her beauty, basking in her soothing presence. I tip-toed behind her and threw my arms around her waist.

"So, two days to go before the big event." I kissed Temperance on the cheek, as she dried a wet dish and placed it on the rack.

"Last chance for you to get out..." She rebuffed with a witty smile, as she wiped her hands on a tea towel.

"Maybe you are right, perhaps I should make a run for it." I chuckled and she flicked some water at me playfully.

"Mong." She laughed and wiped her hands against a blue tea towel draped over a tarnished brass drawer handle.

I kissed the side of her head and ran my hands along her sides. "I wish you were my wife already..."

Temperance pressed her warm hand against my comparatively cold palms. "Tomorrow is going to seem longer than the total time, I've spent in this world..."

"About that, I was going to ask you..."

She turned off the tap, about-faced and pivoted her head to focus her sight on me. The blue of her eyes centred upon the words forming on my lips.

"Since we have tomorrow, I was wondering if we could take a drive..."

"Are you having a laugh?" She glanced down at blue ruffle which flowered from her flowing bodice. The white lacing in the collar and bustle complemented her fair skin and piercing gaze. "Custom dictates we aren't supposed to see each other before our nuptials..." Temperance pressed on the kettle.

"...yea but do you remember the plan?" I leaned my hands against the lip of the work top, sun broke through the clouds and came through the window, illuminating Temperance's skin.

"How could I not?" She smiled. "Is this another step in the scheme?" Her disposition grew serious. "...though this seems a bit eleventh hour in its conceptualisation..."

"Well we can go to Anglesey tomorrow and if you insist, we can spend the night in separate rooms..."

"Anglesey?" She crossed her arms. "That's miles away..." Temperance reached around to re-tie the bow on her back.

"I'll take care of that, my love..." I stepped behind her and assisted her.

"Ta..."

The sound of my tying the two bows around her back filled the kitchen as Temperance glanced out the window, until she finally broke the quiet. "How do you propose going to Anglesey when we are due in Knutsford the following morning?"

"...it's an hour's drive, Mama, we can leave at sun-up and have plenty of time..." I rubbed her back. "Plus, it's supposed to be warm tomorrow, perhaps we can catch some sun and go for a swim too while we are at it..."

"So, you wish to have a day out at the beach on the eve of our Wedding?" She turned around and lifted her lip, amused at the idea.

"The purpose of the journey is to take you somewhere that I feel will be a great blessing to our marriage and thereafter..."

"Anglesey, hmm..." Temperance eyed a packet of Seal bars on the oak corner table behind us. "...let me take a stab at it..." She placed her finger around her cheek and another her chin. "...the pilgrimage site, yea?"

"That's right..." I knew she could read minds but this didn't seem like a moment where she analysed what I was thinking. It was if she had a prior knowledge or familiarity with the location and I had merely rekindled the knowledge of its presence to her. "...have you been there before?"

"No..." She walked over to the table and took two Seal bars. "Shall I sneak you a bicky?"

"Sure..."

"I know of The Island of the Blessed..." Temperance placed three sweets upon the plate. "I have heard of countless stories of it wonders but I have been fearful to go as I have been haunted by the concerns of being damned..."

"Which you are not..."

Temperance only picked up the plate. I offered to carry it for her, but she softly brushed my hand aside and signalled for me to follow her into the front room.

"You must believe that." I followed her into the front room.

"Suppose I was to believe that, what do you wish to do exactly?" Temperance sat on the couch and placed the plate on the table.

"Pray together?" I sat beside her. "I think it will help in sorting out everything else that you were concerned about..."

Temperance unravelled the wrapper of one of the biscuits but had nothing to say.

"Why don't we give it a shot and see what happens?"

She bit into her biscuit and chewed for a moment, pondering what I was proposing to her. She dabbed her lips and peered over at me. "...Sure Chuck, our betrothal is already unconventional." Temperance placed the plate down. "...assuredly, visiting a Holy site will assuage any further need for superstition."

"My relationship with The Lord is not a superstition."

"I never said it was, treacle." She passed me a Seal bar encouraging me to join her.

"I'll sort out a hotel then..." I placed my hand over the green wrapping with a smile.

"Smashing..." Her eyes twinkled. "...although we will sleep in the same bed tomorrow, we have to maintain to some semblance of decorum."

"You can have the bed and I'll sleep on the floor. I just want us to do this before we get married..."

"...and should we go have a dip in the sea, don't be acting cheeky if I am in my swimming costume." She pointed at me and smirked.

The blood rushed to my head and adrenaline trickled through my veins. "Cheeky, how?"

"All touchy-feely and handsy..." The mist from the kettle hissed from the kitchen. "...we best save that for the wedding night..."

"Which swimsuit, are you taking?"

"The orange one..."

"The one with the little cutout area that shows your belly button." I pinched my arm.

"Of course..." She teased as she raised her voice.

"That's not fair...." I put my finger in my mouth. "And you know I despise orange for obvious reasons..."

"Blooming Georgia again..." Temperance rolled her eyes. "I'll be sure to wear it then when the Dawgs play the Gators." She smirked. "That way your odd abdominal obsession and your disdain for Florida will truly be at odds, alas you are forced to make a decision." Temperance chuckled.

"You are tempting me..."

"That's the whole point, plum." She replied confidently. "I suppose I could torment you and wear my Incredible Temperance costume too..." Another smirk firmed. "Or maybe, I'll just swim naked..." She threw at our arms and broke out laughing. "...Why have a peek, when you can see all of it?"

I started seeing spots like a dog in heat. "Well there is a lot to look at up, down, and around."

"Perv!" Temperance blushed as she smacked my shoulder. "You best behave as we are going to the Island of Blessed...." Temperance smirked as she bit into another biscuit.

In that moment, the hormones settled and the focus was no longer my physical passion and desires but the emotional mission I was proposing for the woman I love. "Wear the swimsuit on the wedding night..."

"Can do..." She smiled again. "...any other requests?"

"Both Incredible Temperance costumes too?" I raised my eyebrows.

"Both?!" She raised her eyebrows. "My, my, what are you planning to do to me?" She spoke seductively. "Are you going to ravage me for hours all through the evening?"

"You best believe it; it'll go onto the next day." I tapped her butt with a gentle affection. "Every part of your body for hours upon end." I licked my lip and smirked. "There won't be anything left of you when I am done."

"Really?" Temperance drew her lips close to my ear, her breaths sensual and enticing. "I am not typically all for that talk but that sounds orgasmic...." She spoke seductively into my ears. "...It'll be hard to resist you when you are in a suit and tie, but I get you after it." Her tongue escaped her lip and grazed my ear. "But please don't take your shirt off at any point until we are wed." The kettle started to hiss in the background. "...That might be a bit too much for me to withstand...."

"Well it may get warm and these things happen..."

"And that black and white plaid flannel with the baggy black jeans and work boots." Temperance bit her lip as she looked at me seductively. "Winter hat and bubble coat included."

"And to think I thought you hated the winter hat and bubble coat..."

Temperance shook her eyes with a wry smile, she looked ready to pounce on me.

"As you know, it gets a bit cold by the coast and uh the boots are good for gripping the sand." I smirked at her.

"Is it going to be warm or cold?" Temperance regained her composure and shot me a maternal half-smile as if she were steering me clear from trouble but amused at the same time. "Make up your mind, will you?" The kettle hissed louder and turned over to bubbling. "Do us a favour then..." She glanced over at the kettle. "Cream and sugar in my cuppa please, darling, ta..." My beloved broke out in a chortle and pointed at me, as her she held herself with laughter.

"Sure." I tickled her sides and we playfully grappled each other until I pressed my lips against hers and hung on the kiss.

THE NEXT AFTERNOON, Temperance and I had exchanged the canals of Marple for the rocky beaches of Anglesey; we traded the view of Manchester in the distance for a dusty lane that was unadopted, leading through a thick wood of pine trees that finished at the car park beside a beach.

Hand-in-hand, Temperance and I made our way over the wooden planked footpath that crossed the dunes. We had a quick frolic and swim in the sea before we continued along the beachhead, the ripples of waves splashing not too far from us. The smooth sand had a gradient of light brown to dark where the tides had last met. Onward, we traversed a cobbled collection of sediment and sand; I held my beloved's hand as we passed by some jagged rock formations which had an obsidian-like glaze over their rough texture. There wasn't a cloud in the sky and the sun cascaded down upon the slightly rippled waters which meandered away from the shore. In the distance, the outline of the hills of Wales arched the horizon until all we could see was blue beyond it. In front of us, stood a small hut comprised of cream-coloured concrete. Beyond that a grassy hill which stretched out into the water, at the end of which stood a small white structure that looked like a buoy.

When we were together, Temp and I never stopped talking, there was always something to gab about as she would say. On this occasion, she was quiet. The sound of an occasion gull or splash in the distance would serve as the only dissonance. We were both still drying off from our brief dip in the water, my swimming shorts were damp and my t-shirt was off and hung around my neck. Temperance's skin was glistening in all the visible parts under her racerback orange swimsuit with a low back and neck, which she wore a lavender sarong over. After making our way across the sand, we arrived at the shack and were greeted by a map of *The Island of the Blessed* written in both Welsh and English.

"So, what comes next?" She put her hands on her hips and watched me from her eyes hidden behind the black lenses of her sunglasses.

I glanced at the map and saw a picture of a cross.

"The Cross..." I pointed at it, a faint breeze tossed a strand of her hair which was up, a heavy arrangement of auburn-cinnamon with barely any hairs below her ears.

The sun shined on Temperance's skin which glistened from sweat and water. She reached into my backpack and removed some sunblock. Temperance walked under the hut and applied the cream to herself, lathering herself in it until her skin shined. Her body language was tense and her anxiety was palpable.

"...it's going to be alright, my love." I walked into the hut and put my arms around her. She rested her head against my shoulder. I rubbed her lycra-clad abdomen, running my fingers over her skin where the small ovular opening in her swimsuit exposed her navel and some of her toned core. Her stomach was supremely strong yet soft and feminine, it was a marvel to behold.

We took our time heading up the hill and took in the view, it was something out of a storybook. Water surrounded the island on all sides, and to our left was a large panorama of the hilly landscape which brought every chisel and curve of the coast into visibility. At the base of the hills across the water, a small town was set upon its rise; a collection of white and red houses and buildings scattered in green.

On the other side of us, smaller hills with a white manor house beset amid the smooth emerald rise. Ahead of us, a cross was set upon the top of the hill, erected at its highest point. I led Temperance to the path toward it and helped her over a small break in a stone fence. We scaled the sand-dusted incline until The Cross was only feet in front of us. The wind had started to gust more forcefully, as we were now above the dune that protected us from the gales in our approach.

"Let's go before The Lord and place our hands at its feet."

Temperance did not follow me as I took the first few strides.

I looked back at her and noticed her shoulders hunched and her posture tense and upright. "What's wrong?"

"This is as far as I go..." She lowered her sunglasses. "I cannot touch that as it would be no different than if I had been doused in Holy Water..."

"The Lord loves you." I took two steps toward her. "He wants to set you free not imprison you..." I stroked her arms with tenderness.

"Yes, but with respect to the circumstances surrounding my present situation...."

"All you have to do is believe and trust in Him..." I placed my around her back.

"I do trust Him but I will touch it after we are married, perhaps then His love for you and your kinship with Him will be bestowed upon me."

I held her tighter and pointed at The Cross. "That right there is a symbol of His love for you." I drew my other hand to her cheek and grazed the back of it with my hand. "Receive it and do not be afraid..." I smiled at her. "You are a beautiful human being, Temperance. I'd be more concerned about me being condemned..."

Temperance did not react to the compliment nor the remark; her eyes became engrossed with the relic. She looked like a little girl in a toy store that could not afford the thing that she really wanted. *If she only could*...her eyes watered as her breaths became more laboured.

"Would you pray before it and ask for His love and His blessing?"

She nodded with confidence. "I will kneel and clasp my hands."

I took her hand and we walked together to the base of The Cross, ascending the steep hill which was comprised of sand and sediment.

"The words I trust will be better said by you..."

"Just speak what is on your heart, my love..." I threw my shirt onto the ground. "I don't want you to get your knees dirty..." I smiled at her and she beamed back at me for a moment, distracted by my gesture until she placed one knee down with a glare of apprehension. It wasn't a matter of her not having faith, it was a visceral fear that she was rejected. If only, I could make her realise that The Lord was not like that of her biological father. He would not abandon her; He does want her; she is precious to Him; and He knows her heart. This was a prayer that I was praying silently as she dropped her other knee and bowed her head.

"We may very well fall down the hill...." She joked with a hint of nervousness in her voice.

"We won't..." I placed it around the small of her back. "I will hold you and kneel behind you as I do so..." I watched as Temperance clasped her hands. "I will touch The Cross with my other hand, the only one at risk of falling is me..." I dropped to a knee. "But because of our most wonderful Father in Heaven, I am upright."

The steepness of the grade of the hill yanked on my back but I dug my knees into the rough terrain and placed one hand firmly around my beloved's abdomen, pressing her tight against me as my other arm extended toward the granite base of The Cross. For a moment, I took in the roar of the wind, the faint splash of the waves against the rocks below, and the feeling of Temperance breathing in my arms.

"Heavenly Father, Lord of Lords, King of Kings, we come before you today and give thanks for your unfailing love, mercy, forgiveness, and your many great blessings. We give thanks to you for this day and the blessing of being able to come before you together in this time and this place to lay our hearts before you. I thank you for Temperance...."

Temperance started to tremble as I continued in my prayer.

"...I thank you for the blessing of encountering her and falling in love with her. I pray tomorrow that our union is one that will honour and glorify you. For you are love and because of your love, we are here today; to give thanks to you..."

I heard Temperance sniffle and let out a faint breath, though my eyes were shut and firmly wrapped around her stomach, I could tell by her trembles and the slightest of jostles that she was weeping. The instinct to protect her and comfort her was within me, innate to me as if it were something I was always meant to do, thus my arm wrapped ever snugger around her ribs and my hand pressed tight against her midsection. It seemed that the tighter I held her, the more settled she would become.

"I pray you forgive us of our sins, the ones that we have committed in our hours of weakness and the ones that we do not know that we commit. I pray Lord that you will restore us and strengthen our hearts, our minds, and our souls through your Holy Spirit."

Temperance pressed her hand toward mine.

"...Lord I pray you bring us together as one flesh, in all that we do. Everything that we do Lord, may it be together. May we be unified in you; bound in you; and our spirits rooted in you, as our truth and saviour...."

I felt Temperance press my hand harder against her. My eyes opened for a moment to see her other hand erected toward the sky, signalling her participation and engagement with the prayer.

"...For the good days and the bad; in the moments of difficulty or the moments of joy, whether we walk, run, climb, or swim, may Temperance and I do it as one. We pray for your blessing and countenance upon our marriage, in Jesus' name...." I held Temperance firm against me. "...and Father, I pray that Temperance knows how much you love her. That she has a father and that is treasured by you."

Temperance's cries became obvious but I did not stop.

"Only you Lord, can create something as marvellous as her and I thank you every day Father for her. I wish I could be half the person that she is..."

Temperance's sniffles muffled over the wind.

"...Amen."

"Amen..." Temperance joined me.

"The Lord is great, honey" I helped her to her feet and embraced her tight as she burrowed her head against my chest. "I love you so much...."

"I love you too..." She sniffled and pressed her lips against my chest before resting her head in my embrace. We remained embraced until the blue of the sky transitioned into a light purple. We started our journey back toward the car, our hands intermeshed as we were once again silent in conversation. There was no need for chit-chat, what weighed heavy on Temperance's mind and my own spoke louder than any word or verse could articulate.

The sun had quickly dashed across the sky making its way toward the faint horizon line as we descended the very path. "So how are you feeling, my love?" I squeezed her hand as we passed under a large stone formation that arched overhead.

"Much better now, my dear." She swung our arms with a smile. "I can hardly wait until tomorrow." Her smile glistened like the orange of her swimsuit in the fading sun. Though her eyes hid behind her sunglasses, I felt the jubilance radiate from them; my eyes fixed upon hers as we passed along the path until we arrived at the small hut. The sound of the sea quickly over took both our loving gaze and the sight of the shelter. In front of us, we saw nothing but the white foam of the water separating us from the beach we walked upon when we came.

Temperance and I looked at each other.

"It appears that we are cut off, Honey Bee...." I glanced over at a sign in the hut that read *"High Tide at 18:15, leave at 15:45 or risk being trapped on the island until the waters recede."* I pointed at the sign. "It will be pitch black by the time we wait this out..."

"Well, you did pray that we walk, run, climb, and swim together as one." Temperance glanced out at the water. "Looks like we have achieved all that in one day..." She chuckled; a smile broke from my face as I looked up to the sky, acknowledging The Lord for his sense of humour.

"I guess we are off to a good start then."

"Indeed..." Temperance glanced at the water and removed her sarong. "We'll have to swim it..."

"I'll keep you close as that water looks a bit cold and rough..." I clutched her hand.

Temperance shot me a look. "Have you had a dip in the River Thames?"

"I can't say that I have..."

"Between the filth and powerful tidal currents, this is having a bath comparatively speaking..." She tossed the sarong on the rocks. "At least we came prepared..."

I smiled back at her and glanced at the sun now ducking below the horizon.

"I'll race you!" She bolted for the water and I felt a tug as our hands never let go of one another. Temperance glided through the water like a mermaid whilst I kept my head down and pushed through.

When we emerged from the water, the frosty air descended upon us and dried us en route to the car, Temperance used her electrolytic powers to generate heat to keep us warm until we arrived. All in all, we made it back to our hotel in high spirits and had a laugh about it.

II.

I t was an early summer evening, just before dusk. My beloved and I strolled through the open evergreen-coloured wrought iron gate under the golden-inscribed words Ashton Gardens. We traversed a wide footpath canopied under oak trees and edged by a series of metallic matte benches. Our arms cuffed, ice cream in our hands.

My beloved pressed the tip of her white parasol against the concrete with each step she took. Her matching bonnet clung to her long copper-red hair as her ivory muslin gown and long bustle dragged behind her. Marigold ribbons from the back of her hat and her red scarf tied over a gold brooch flicked in the breeze. My black suit jacket barely moved, keeping both the white shirt beneath it and the grey tie draped over, remaining stationery.

A gentle breeze blew across the still park which was followed by the faint chirps of birds. Murmurations of starlings danced overhead, wafting in the deep pastels of blue as they departed the beachhead of St. Anne's or maybe even Blackpool which was just a mile north of us. We followed the footpath past the cenotaph and a children's play area until the aroma of rose petals tickled our noses.

"I got to tell you, Mama." I scratched the shadowy stubble on my face with my free hand. "We are getting a lot of looks and I am sure it has nothing to do with my tie...." I glanced at Temperance and as usual, found myself in awe of her beauty. "...I am willing to bet all eyes are on you, looking afternoonified as you are."

"You are always so creative with your flattering remarks; they never cease to amaze me." Temperance flexed her arm latched in mine. "However, I insist they are revelling in you." She smiled at me as she twirled her parasol. "So much has changed, yet so much has remained the same." She swabbed her tongue through a pink scoop of ice cream at the top of her waffle cone. "Shall we go have a look?"

"Lead the way, my lady." I kissed her cheek and took her hand.

The rose garden was a world unto itself. We passed through a narrow path that was embraced on both sides by two Victorian-aged stone gate bases with circular caps. Water running into a fountain was the ambient soundtrack, as it poured from a stone fountain of the Greek goddess Iris. On our left and right, roses of all different colours and sizes were set in grass patches. A series of stone footpaths extended from a circular junction that all converged around the fountain. We made our way toward the benches that lined the periphery of the garden, my beloved occasionally asking me to hold her ice cream as she cupped a flower and delighted in its scent.

"This is like a trip back in time for me." She closed the parasol. "I can recall so many instances I've wandered through here alone and wondered if that's how it shall always be..." Her eyes peered at me with joy twinkling in them. "...this rosary is the same as it was, the day it opened." Temperance smiled as she looked at the large villas that stood beyond the park in St. George's Square, all dated to the nineteenth century with the distinguishing characteristics of sashed bay windows, Flemish brick bonding, ornate gables, octagonal shape, and turret structuring to draw the eye upward toward steeply-pitched slate roofs with signature finials. "Absolutely remarkable, how this has withstood the test of time."

"Victorian engineering for you." My eyes gawked at her from head to toe, as I took her parasol.

"Why do I have the sudden inclination you are not referring to the masonry?" She blushed.

"If you take care of something..." I placed my arm around her as she sat and took her hand. "...I think, it can last forever."

"Like us?" Temperance licked her ice cream.

I pushed a plastic spoon into one of the blue scoops of the bubble gum ice cream. "Definitely, my love." I patted her thigh and snuck her another quick kiss on the cheek.

Scott Joplin's *Heliotrope Bouquet* started to play as the Victorian gas lamps in St. George's Square turned on. Lights had illuminated around the rose garden, sprinkling white light on the trellis near the entrance and exits of the rose garden.

"Is that Scott?"

"Indeed, it is!" Her voice rose with excitement. "How idyllic!" Temperance's eyes twinkled against the lightning. "...they must have known Joplin is your favourite composer."

"Who's they? I couldn't help but feel a sense of anxiety given the oddity of the coincidence; it seemed too surreal to be true. My thoughts grounded once Temperance began to speak.

"The caretakers." She said.

"But where is the music coming from?"

"They must have installed those portable outdoor speakers that you can hide in the hedges." Temperance swam the plastic spoon into one of the blue scoops in my cup. "Another innovation of the digital age..." Temperance nibbled on the spoon to clear it of any ice cream. "Would you like a lick?" She giggled and pushed her cone near to my lips.

"Strawberries and cream, a classic choice..." I licked the cone. "...for a classy lady." I winked at her. Temperance broke a smile as she feigned pushing the top swirl into my nose before she continued to attack my ice cream, eating rather voraciously.

"You are a hungry gal today."

"I've been eating for three." She cracked a laugh and watched for my reaction.

"You are a strong woman, you got to keep your energy up." I smiled back at her. "So, what is this big news that you have to tell me?" I dabbed a small puddle of ice cream formed at the cupid bow of her smile. A stray strand of hair danced in a gentle breeze as she watched a family walk by on a footbridge that bypassed the garden.

"Did you know I did song and dance in the old North Pier theatre in Blackpool?"

"I recall." I stroked the stand of her hair. "In 1904, right?"

"You remembered." My beloved nodded with a smile. "It was a good bit of fun, wearing fancy dress and pretending I was a sailor girl."

"Fire the cannon, honey."

Temperance saluted me with a cheeky smile and proceeded to whistle a cadence from an Irish step street dance routine.

"So, do you still have that costume too?" I winked at her and put another spoonful of ice cream into my mouth.

"Naughty boy." Temperance batted her eyebrows. "Enough with that malarkey, we did that whole charade when we got married and tore each other to bits."

"How could I ever forget that?" I sat back and bulged my eyes. "Still, I don't know how the sailor girl get up would compare to the Incredible Temperance costume though..." I poked her rib to elicit a squeal from her. "Cause my wife looks ridiculously hot in it..." I kissed the dome of her head.

"Well when you see her, you should tell her..." Temperance placed her hand on my chest. "If you haven't already, of course..." She chuckled and moved her head away.

"Yeah, I'll let her know." I pecked her lips. "Have you seen her?" I glanced around the garden and drew my hand to my eyebrow.

"Temperance?" I dog-whistled. "Where are you, Honey Bee?" I called out loudly.

Temperance pushed into me playfully. "You are flippant, you." She stroked another strand of hair back. "Thinking back about that night and the days that followed, I will unfortunately have to postpone wearing such costumes for the foreseeable future. It's akin to a second layer of skin and I reckon it will tear given the state of me." Temperance bit into her waffle cone as her ice cream scoop finished.

"The state of you?" I placed my hand over hers. "Is everything alright, Mama?"

Temperance finished chewing and waved her hand through the floral air. Satie's "*Je te veux*" came on.

"I adore this piece..."

I placed my cup of ice cream down on the bench beside us. "Would you like to dance?" Heat rushed to my cheeks as I stood up.

She beamed and extended her hand to me. I pressed one hand behind her back and my other to her waist. My beloved placed one hand on my shoulder and placed her head against my chest. We danced at a slow pace, swaying back and forth with the melody.

"So, tell me what's going on..."

She moved her head from my chest, her blue eyes locking on mine. "Do you remember the look on the vicar's face when we walked each other down the aisle?" Temperance laughed as she blew electric sprites into the air, creating the illusion of shooting stars falling around us.

"How could I forget?" I stroked her hair with a brief laugh. "It was as if he never saw anything like that before."

"Indeed." Temperance had a glow about her. "I am equally amazed you took my surname as your own."

"My surname was horrible as it was." I kept my arm around her waist, eyes locked upon hers as we continued to slow dance. "Though I did it primarily because it has special meaning to you and you were also doing me a favour..."

Temperance broke a smile. "It was truly a supernatural evening..."

"It was." I looked down at her as we continued to dance slowly. Instinct told me that there was more that still needed to be said. "So, is that what you wanted to tell me?"

"I don't know how to put this." Her eyes wandered upward to the sky and then toward the lights that surrounded the garden, her next words forming carefully on her lips. "It's been months now, since we have been married and had the miracle." She swallowed and paused... "When you were freed from that horrible wretch..." Her eyes started to water up, tears quickly filled mine thereafter at the sight of it.

"All great blessings and miracles thanks to The Lord." Said, I.

She seemed overwhelmed and that energy was cast upon me, filling me with a relentless anxiety that scourged through me, I could hear my heart pounding in my ears.

"Well, The Good Lord has blessed us with another miracle..." A smile burst from her lips "...I am with child."

My jaw dropped, as the dancing came to an abrupt halt. I pressed my hand against my chest and let out a sigh of relief. A smile wildly unfurled across my face.

"Twin girls..." A tear escaped from her eyes. "...identical twin girls..."

It was truly unreal, a world with Temperance in itself was full of wonder, now there would be two more of her in likeness, nuanced with the many traits that make their mother all the more enchanting.

It didn't feel real, it was something out of a movie; a dream; a novel. I wondered if it was like this for everyone who was blessed to enjoy such a miracle.

Tears fell down my cheeks. "Two more of you, Praise The Lord." I threw my arms around her and kissed the side of her head. "I love you so much, Mama."

"I love you too, Butterscotch." She embraced me tight.

"I can skip with joy through these streets." I held Temperance against me. "This is the greatest news I could ever hear but I thought after the test..."

"I have known for some time now..." Temperance looked down. "I should have said something sooner but I feared telling you, I am sorry..."

"There is no need to apologise, my love." I rubbed her back. "But why on Earth would you be afraid to tell me?"

"Because my father didn't want me and I reckon I was filled with an irrational trepidation subconsciously as to how you would take it..."

My euphoria was briefly overcome by a pervasive sorrow that she feared such an event happening to her. Temperance didn't deserve that now and she didn't deserve to live with such a dark and shadowy precept ever. However, things had changed and for that, the ecstasy soon returned and barrelled across every inch of my body. "Honey bee..." My hands rubbed against the curve of her cheek. "You are very much wanted. And I wanted..." I stressed the word wanted emphatically. "...to have a little girl, just like you..." I embraced her tight as tears trickled from my eyes. "Praise The Lord, I have two..." My hands cupped around the muslin of her arms. "I told you I am always going to take care of you and we will take care of them." I smiled at her. "These girls are going to have the best parents ever." I let out a chuckle as my eyes glanced down to Temperance's midsection. "Now, it all makes sense." I placed my hand over her abdomen. "Your increase in appetite and the dresses not fitting..."

"...and why I've been icky in mornings and spent all the bleeding time in the toilet..." She placed her hand over mine. "In a blink, the lasses will be kicking..." Temperance smiled. "...and though I am not showing at the present, I will soon grow a huge belly too..."

"You will be all the more gorgeous, my queen." I stroked her hair as another tear trickled down my nose. "These girls will idolise you for the noble, beautiful, virtuous, strong, and courageous woman you are."

"And us ladies will be privileged to have the most wonderful, affectionate, and devoted husband and father." Temperance ran her thumb against my eyes to blot my tears.

"We have to get up to the Golden Mile and play some skee-ball to mark this occasion."

"We must darling, we must." Temperance giggled. "And we can have a go on some of the amusements in the penny arcade, too..." She clapped her hands.

"But before that..." I pulled my beloved in for another deep and passionate kiss.

SOME MONTHS HAD PASSED since that night in St. Anne's when Temperance revealed she was pregnant with the girls. Temperance was seven months pregnant and at times the cramps and many changes that came with the pregnancy became daunting for her. Though she was endowed with supernatural talents, she seemed to tire quicker and easier; she was just like any other woman navigating the rigours of child-bearing. Gratefully, I was always able to be there to tend to her and take care of her. I admit though that

I was not used to seeing her slowed down; nor was she settled with that notion either.

I placed my arm around Temperance's back and walked with her into the front room, my palm firmly pressed to the back of her lavender blouse. Her stomach bulged through the cotton; her steps were slow and gingerly in comparison to how she normally moved. There was a reason why I called her "Honey Bee", as the affectation was not just a term of endearment but also a reference to how Temperance could move with such pace and efficiency whilst exuding grace and gentleness like a honey bee. Temperance had a talent for making busy, darting around, and all the while demonstrating such profound attention to detail; it was one of the many things that I love about her. There have been times I would stand back and watch her move, admiring her seamless ability to multi-task with such fluidity, speed, and organisation as she juggled concurrent tasks with a smile on her face, humming a tune, or singing a hymn.

"Here we are, my dear." I kept my hand around her back and took her other hand, as she slowly sat upon the lime-coloured couch.

"Goodness, me." She sighed; a smile quickly broke to her face. "It won't be long now until they've finally arrived."

I placed my hand over the bulge and she placed her hand over mine. "Praise The Lord..." A kick tapped against my finger. "Wow..."

"And that's only one of them." Temperance chuckled; I plucked a plate of digestive biscuits from the table which sat next to our two empty tea cups. She watched as the plate moved closer to her in my hand and plucked a milk chocolate biscuit from the plate. "Ta".

"We never figured out what we are going to name them..." I placed the plate back down on the oak coffee table.

"I was named on the day of my birth, so I believed it would come to us in the moment..." She bit on the biscuit.

"I had an idea though..."

She held the biscuit between her thumb and pointer, as she bit into the biscuit, glancing at it as she found the taste pleasurable.

"Temperance..."

Her eyes enlarged to signal she had my attention as she swallowed before speaking. "Yes?" She smiled.

"No, I want to name our daughter, Temperance..."

"Oh..." She placed one knee over the other and brushed down her skirt as she looked away. "Well, which one?" My beloved turned her head to look back at me, as she chuckled.

I shrugged my shoulders.

"Shall we flip a coin to decide which one of the two gains my namesake?" She smirked and rolled her eyes. "Imagine the agro, if we were to name one after me and not do so with the other, it would be profoundly miserable." She had another nibble.

"We can name them both Temperance and give them different middle names."

She shook her head as she chewed.

"It's the traditional thing to do and obviously quite common in your time."

Temperance licked some melted chocolate off of her finger.

"...and most importantly I want to honour you."

She waved her hand to disregard the notion.

"So, this displeases, my wife?"

She pressed her hand to mine. "It's very kind of you and I am honoured." Temperance stroked my fingers. "However, it's the twenty-first century..."

I raised my eyes at that response.

"Our daughters should have their own identity..."

"So, did you have a name in mind?"

"Henrietta..."

"That's wonderful..."

Temperance nodded and took another bite of the digestive.

"How about Grace?"

She paused and chewed once.

"Henrietta and Grace?"

"That's my second given name, I see what you are trying to do..."

"It is also by the grace of The Lord that we are having these two wonderful bundles of joy..."

Temperance smiled and finished the rest of the digestive, wiping her hands. She reached for a glass of water on the table, I attempted to grab it but she stopped me. After she took a sip, she placed the glass down and looked over at me. "My mother said the same thing when I was born..."

"So, you like it?"

"I cannot contest the sentiment..." Her blue eyes shimmered in a beam of sunlight as she glanced at me. "...how about for a second given name?"

I nodded. "Why don't we call one of them, Elizabeth Grace?"

"Elizabeth?" She looked at me with coy out of the corner of her eye.

"On the day we met, I told you that is one of my favourite names."

"That much is true..." Temperance looked ahead, revisiting that first encounter on a brisk autumn day on the canal that meandered just beyond our home.

"Plus, it's your mother's middle name too..."

Temperance raised her hands in acquiescence. "That was a well-formed discourse and superb argument..." She tapped my hand. "Very well, then..."

"And what shall Henrietta's middle name be?"

"Anne." The name escaped Temperance's lips, as if it were waiting to emerge.

"For Anne Bronte?" I cracked a silly joke.

"I knew you would say that." She chuckled. "No disrespect to your favourite author but I was paying tribute to where I told you that I was pregnant and where our daughters were first conceived." Her pulse started to throb through me. "...St. Anne's." She licked her lips. "When we made love on the beach under moonlight.". I could feel my heart start to beat through my chest as I recalled the evening, we made love under the stars with the sound of the waves crashing behind us. Though the air was chilly, it was surprisingly still and the passion of the moment drenched us in sweat and heat that could not escape our bodies.

"That was when we first consummated our marriage actually." She gasped. "...you could feel the electricity in the air, I still feel it now...." Temperance waved her hand.

I placed my hand on her stomach and locked eyes with her; I ran my hand up her blouse and drew close to her before pressing my lips against hers and clutching her cheek. Temperance grasped the back of my head and exerted force as the kissing engaged deeper, before she pulled back and pressed her forehead to mine. "This is how large families get started..."

We both shared a laugh.

"I want you to do something for me...."

"Anything...." I rubbed the bulge of her stomach.

"I know things are changing but don't stop writing." She leaned her head on my chest. "...in fact, I think you should explore it more and get yourself out there."

"Honey Bee, we are about to have two daughters."

"Come off it, butterscotch." My beloved raised her hands. "You rap over *Stoptime Rag*, write poetry, and have composed countless stories..."

"I don't know, my love..." I shook my head briefly. "I hate all the politics and I don't want to be around the alcohol with the bad environments...."

"You can choose the venues that are right for you. I wouldn't have you legless in some boozer, you can do readings at a library." My beloved reached for a glass of water to take a brief sip "The important thing is you share your art with the world." She looked up. "He gave you a gift, use it."

I smiled.

"And I'll be there to support you." She looked into my eyes. "We all will..." Temperance smiled. "Henrietta and Elizabeth would be inspired to see their father do what he loves."

"Thank you."

"You are a great writer, far more talented than I...."

"I don't know about that, Mama." I rubbed her back. "But what about you? You sing beautifully, I would encourage you to do the same."

"It's just a bit of fun, Butterscotch." She glanced out the window at the setting sun. "I am fairly secure in the fact that I wish to be a housewife and a homemaker. At this point, I'd be contented in educating our girls and overseeing the daily chaos."

"But I am going to help you with that..."

"I know you will." Temperance took another sip of water. "And I know that you will tell me that you can work from home as you have done and I could tell you that I have more than adequate savings to support ourselves, but you wrote that novel about me and how we first met." Her eyes widened. "It's quite a story and a beautiful piece of literature, it would be an utter shame if no one ever heard it." Temperance looked down at the floor. "Darling, you must publish it." Temperance took my hand and glanced ahead, pensive and lost in the many thoughts racing through her head. "Why should your abilities remain a secret, as well?" My beloved looked up at me with watery eyes; Sorrow and pity filled her. I ran my thumb under her eye to catch her tears and pulled her back into my chest, stroking her hair gently as we both sat in the shadowy stillness. And then a thought flashed across my mind.

"Do you think the girls are going to have your powers?"

Temperance moved her head and raised her eyebrow, squinting as she dove into a deeper cycle of thought. A smile formed on her face again followed by concern, then back to joy, on towards alarm then confusion and a final return to happiness; all seemed to form and dissipate in her complexion. Like passing storms and swells over a vast and open ocean.

"We'll just have to wait and see..."

III.

I remember the first day I set my eyes on Sycamore Grove for the first time. It was a house that looked like a place you would find my beloved; it had the same refinement, class, and mystery that she had. The pointed roof and the turrets of the house mirrored the elegance of Temperance when she wore her hair up under a decorative hat, its cream-coloured hooded windows matched her porcelain skin, the green accents matched the bodice she wore on the day we purchased the house, the sky behind it matched her eyes.

It reminded me of a house I once saw near Goostrey on a day that was far less delightful. Still now, I remembered a picture centred in the front room of a former lady of the house, someone that Temperance may have known personally at one point; someone that bore a semblance to her. At one point I dreamed of what it must have been like to live such a life, now I was living it.

Sycamore Grove was just as Temperance imagined it would be; a place where we would be surrounded by fields for miles where it would only be us and our love. The house hid behind a hedgerow and iron-wrought gate that concealed the drive. It reminded me of Lime Hall in Marple where Temperance was a governess but even more remote, tucked away on a small country lane that led to another lane that led to another road back to Goostrey in one direction or Twemlow in the other. The house was only a fifteen-minute drive from Knutsford, forty minutes from

Manchester or Liverpool without traffic, and an hour from Birmingham but none of those places were even a thought. The large capstone with etched Sycamore Grove reminded you of where you were and the solitary house's only friends were a large weeping willow tree in the front garden and a large sycamore tree behind it in the back garden. The nearest neighbour was a quarter or half a mile down the lane. It was easy to pass by Sycamore Grove unnoticed, as there were many ash, elm, and oak trees that lined the lane, extending their branches over the hedgerows that narrowed the lane.

We moved in months just after our daughters were born and the conversation that we had over the names soon became a distant memory. All our priorities were tossed into a tailspin the day our daughters came. The two of us were working around the clock, bathing, feeding, nursing, and settling our girls to bed. Lest we forget that Temperance had to recover from rearing two girls and though her constitution and dexterity were superhuman, she nonetheless needed to catch her breath for a couple of days after that experience. I had never seen her so fatigued; it was as if a part of her had severed from her and Hetta and Bet were different iterations of Temperance, with the same vim, vigour, and energy that she had.

Not before long, two years had passed from that same conversation when Temperance was seven months pregnant, and we thought it was a matter of weeks. I couldn't recapitulate all the events that forged together between then and that late summer eve thereafter, that would be a novel unto itself.

I found myself sitting with my feet reclined on the couch in our front room. My baby daughter Henrietta slept on my chest, her dark auburn hair trailing across the white 4 of my red Georgia Bulldog jersey. Her little hand wrapped around my neck, as her breaths expanded and contracted against me.

"The Bulldog defence is as good as it gets. This is a football team that has put up historic numbers..." Commentary filled the room from the speaks of our television set, a flat and thin black device with a light that piqued brilliantly in the dim room.

"Butterscotch." My beloved called out to me.

"Yes, my love."

"I best go put little Hetta down with her sister." She stepped into the sitting room. Her hair fell down her back and toward her breasts taut in a lemon bustier. She wore a white hoop skirt, yellow armbands, and a matching white bow in her hair.

"She's sleeping." I stroked Henrietta's hair. "I'll bring her up after the Dawgs score a touchdown."

"Them again..." My beloved glared at the television.

"You say it with contempt."

"That's because they inspire your antics which are contemptible." She threw her hand on her hip. "How did you manage to source the match?"

"Streaming." I glanced up at her. "duh..."

"And here come the Dawgs to take the field." The television accentuated.

"Let's go." I pointed at the television at the sight of the Dawgs running out from the tunnel through the smoke onto the field.

"Hen, oh Henri, Henrietta." I sang with the Georgia fight song "Glory Glory". Her eyes beamed open with a large smile.

"Oh dear, you are going to stir her." My beloved stepped over urgently. She halted when Henrietta let out a giggle and a big smile.

"She loves it." I pat the couch. "Right, my beautiful?" I rubbed my nose against Henrietta, she laughed and rested her head back on my chest. "Papa." I kissed her head and stroked a strand of her hair.

"And following the Bulldogs, the Georgia Tech Yellow Jackets..."

"Booooooo." I shook my head at Henrietta and she cringed. "Good girl." I kissed her forehead. "She already knows...."

"Polluting our daughter's mind, are you?" My beloved snickered. "I best start the tea." I grabbed her hand as she turned to go back to the kitchen.

"Plop down next to me, my love, I ordered us a Chinese."

She looked down at me and curled her fingers in mine.

"We both cook all the time. I got you the beef satay you like." I rubbed her knuckles. "Along with some soup and other appetizers..." Her hands started to vibrate.

"Half-chips, half-rice, and curr...

"And curry...." I smiled as I interrupted her.

"When did you do that?"

"Well I didn't know if you knew this, my love, but we are no longer in the Victorian times." I chuckled. "I know you are from there but we can use the phones now to get that stuff up and running..."

"Bravo, I thought you were nearly as old as I, chap. Jolly good show, you have modernised yourself a bit." She giggled and slapped my wrist, playfully. "Something came for you in the post today..." Temperance scuttled off and came back to the couch and handed me an envelope already opened.

"So, you read it already?" I looked up at her with a smirk, as I held the envelope in my hand.

"It's addressed from the Cheshire Society of Authors." She brushed off her skirt and sat beside me. "I can't help having a nosey with such an exciting correspondence." Temperance looked down at me as I held the envelope. "As you do..."

"As you do..." I bantered.

"As you do..." She smiled referencing an inside joke between us. "Go on and read it, then..."

I held Henrietta against me and removed the letter slowly. As I read it over, my eyes bulged at what was written.

"What does it say?" Temperance clapped the palm of her head excitedly.

"It's an invitation to read my poems at The Bogbean." I put the letter down on the coffee table. "In a month's time."

"Darling, that's wonderful." She leered at me. "You are going to do it right?"

"Perhaps, I can dazzle them with my gobbledegook." I chuckled.

"Do we have to have a natter about how you are a gifted writer and orator?"

"I don't know about all that, my love..." I blushed.

"Believe in yourself, a bit more, please." She quickly sat on my lap and put her arm around me. "I'll be there for you." She kissed my cheek. "And so, will the poppets, alright?" Temperance rubbed my hand gently.

"It says here that apparently, I submitted a manuscript to them in the summer?"

Temperance raised her hands and shrugged her shoulders. "I confess..." She opened her hands. "I did it."

I broke a smile and directed my attention back to the game briefly.

"I anticipate a few more replies..."

"Honey Bee, how many places did you reach out to?"

Temperance clenched her teeth and bit her lip. "I must have posted about a dozen or two lots of queries."

I let out a brief laugh, admiring her industry and grateful for her thought but this was the last thing that I was thinking about. "I appreciate the support, but in all reality, I can't be doing this now..."

"Why not?" She rose to her feet. "You can and you should..."

"We have the girls to look after..."

Temperance always tried to build me up and make me feel safe, it was unlike anything I had experienced previously, the rigours of enduring tyrants that always wanted to tear me down; the persistent gauntlet of not knowing that they would be there the next day or when they would turn their back on me. My beloved was steadfast and true, I knew she always had my back. I never had to run after her nor did I have to cover up and absorb an onslaught of mockery and derision. She was a safe place I could run towards with her arms open to hold me gently and nurture me when I felt weak or overwhelmed. Temperance has always been a faithful companion and a best friend; she was always there to lift me. At this moment, I didn't want to think about my writing, I just wanted to be there for her, which meant more to me than my own personal wants and needs.

Temperance soon returned to the room with five more envelopes of contrasting colours in her hand. She sat beside me and placed the stack of them on my lap. "Have a look at those...."

"What is all this?"

"Two more opportunities for you to read your work aloud, a letter from a publishing house who express interest in progressing negotiations further, and evidently you're wanted to give a lecture in London on Victorian literature and creative writing..."

"Wouldn't the last thing be your speciality?"

Temperance made a face and shrugged her shoulders with indifference.

"I appreciate all this, I do..." I adjusted Henrietta in my arms. "...but why?"

"Because though we spoke about it previously, you clearly would never have a go at it." Temperance's eyes glanced down at the stack of envelopes. "Thus, I had to do something about it..."

"But I would have put myself out there..."

She shook her head. "You are very much fixated on the three of us."

"Is that a bad thing?"

"No, my love." She rubbed my shoulder. "But our daughters should see their Daddy at their best and I want you to have every dream of yours come true."

I looked at Temperance for a moment, her sincerity came through her eyes that I had forgotten about the game. I was focused on her and all the thoughtfulness that she put into this effort. Who cared about Georgia when there was her? Winning her heart was truly winning a championship that cannot be defined in prose or any form of precursory literature.

Her eyes remained unmoved, squinting slightly as her vision was glued to the correspondence that she had saved.

"I want the same for you, Mama." I took her hand.

"Well..." She exhaled and sighed for a moment. "...there is one thing I had hoped to do."

I glanced at her, urging her to tell me.

"Something I haven't done for a while..." Her head lifted as her eyes focused on a log on the fireplace.

"Nursing?"

She didn't respond.

"Is it charitable work?" I ran my hand up and down her sleeve as I inched closer to me with Henrietta asleep on me.

She didn't respond again, this time a purple sprite of electricity formed at her fingertip before it ignited the log. The glow of the fire and the television set illuminated our faces in a tapestry of blue and orange.

"It was a bit draughty in here..." Temperance rested her head against my shoulder and nuzzled up to me. "It's cosier now..."

"Do you want to tell me what it is?"

Temperance's eyes darted toward a pink bow resting on the bookshelf next to her mother's portrait. Typically, she tied it around her throat in the past when she was wearing her Incredible Temperance costume, but she was serious...was that what she was considering?

She squinted, deliberating over how to answer until the sight of Henrietta stretching her little hand across my chest to her caught her attention.

"Perhaps when they are a bit older...." Temperance glowed at the sight of our fussy little girl mewing to her.

"But I just said the same thing..."

"The difference is you're ready..." Temperance smiled. "I am not." She looked down at Henrietta again. "But when I am, you'll know..."

IV.

As time marched on, I received more offers to recite my work around Cheshire and the area of interest soon expanded across the country. I self-published a few copies of the novel and very it quickly gained a lot of attention. Some of the queries and pitches that Temperance had put into circulation had come back and in the bookings of readings, I had engaged with a literary agent who was also integral in helping me promote my work. Now he wanted to take a step forward and formally facilitate the publishing process. His work as an agent and my enterprise collectively flourished nearly as rapidly as Henrietta and Elizabeth grew.

"Are you nervous?" Temperance fixed my collar. I looked around the car park, before my eyes scanned to our twin daughters asleep in the stroller, each tucked snugly under a white cotton blanket which had a purple horse embroidered into each.

I smiled for a moment and shook my head to acknowledge my beloved's response. "You beautiful handsome man!" She smiled widely; her ruby lips matched her flowering hat which poured with daisies from its white base. Her hair was neatly tucked underneath it.

The sunlight reflected off her white muslin blouse tucked into a long flowing navy skirt which was brought together with a black leather belt as she walked beside me. I pushed the pram, stopping under the signage for The Brown Cow – Warrington. I approached the entrance and held open the door for Temperance as she pushed the pram through. I placed my arm around the small of

Temperance's back and surveyed the cornucopia of red leather seats with marble-top tables.

A hand waved at us, and I acknowledged a middle-aged man in a blue polo shirt tucked into dark khaki slacks. He itched his salt and pepper hands as he adjusted his large black-frame glasses.

Temperance's heels echoed against the stucco tile floor as she pushed the pram whilst I walked ahead to clear the path for her to ensure she didn't bump into any chairs. The occasional sounds of chatter and utensils clinging invoking dissonances in the quiet morning environs of the eatery.

"Mick."

"Top man." He extended his hand and I took it. "I didn't know you were bringing your family with you."

"My wife and I deal with every important matter together." I rubbed her back. "This is my much better half, Temperance..."

She curtsied slightly. "An honour to earn your acquaintance".

"A pleasure." He snapped his fingers. "She's the one that the..."

"Book is about...."

His eyes glowed at the sight of our two angels, safely asleep.

"Aren't they lovely..." He opened his hand. "Let's move to a booth, then. I will try to keep this brief."

We followed Mick to the booth and sat across from him, the pram stationery at the edge of the table near to us. We ordered hot drinks and exchanged a few pleasantries before he opened up a black-and-white plaid briefcase to remove a multi-page document, which he slid across the table.

"Here are the royalty, non-disclosure, and copyright agreements for you to review." He took a sip of his espresso, lifting the small cup from the ivory white saucer.

"Thank you, sir."

I took the paperwork and removed it from the desk. Temperance put her arm around me and read the content, surveying every line. Once I was done reading, I would look at her, and she would nod back telling me to continue onto the next page.

"Should I ask him about this?" I glanced over at her, seeking her counsel on her make of terms in the contract which I found a bit opaque and questionable.

"No, sweeting, it's clear what it says; that all rights revert to the author..."

Temperance looked up at the agent who watched us both deliberate with a smirk on his face.

"Don't mind us, we're just working out all the details." I smiled.

"In addition to seeking her counsel, does your wife make the decision for you too?" He bantered.

"I usually let her do the talking." I looked at her and smiled. "She has a skill for negotiation and an agency about her."

"You always find new ways to flatter me, darling." Temperance chuckled and took a sip of her tea, curling her finger and her eyes scanned the contract.

"Mick, the woman is a bulldozer." I took her hand and grazed her wrist.

He laughed as Temperance waved her hand and pooh-poohed it. "I may be more poised but none are as dogged as this chum..." She smiled.

Mick laughed at Temperance's wit. "It's refreshing to see a man hold his wife in such esteem." Mick took off his glasses. "And if I may say Mrs. Lee, you certainly strike me as extraordinarily wise and articulate."

"Many thanks, sir." She passed me the contract. "In addition to his flattering remarks that is a wonderful advance and a remarkable distribution deal." Temperance closed the document and placed it in front of me. "All the details check out from my view." She nodded at me. "Sign it, lovey."

"Sign it?"

Temperance gave me a firm look and nodded again.

"How old are your daughters?" He glanced over at our stroller.

"They are more than two and a half, now." I shook my hand to indicate the grey period between two and three.

"Two and three-quarters as Ellie would say...." Temperance chimed in with a joke. "They are about to turn three, so they would insist."

"What are they called?" Mick passed me a shiny gold pen.

"Henrietta and Elizabeth."

"That's quite vintage and old-fashioned." He chuckled. "I like it, that's the way it ought to be."

I re-read the contract and all the details, as I got to the page after where the signatures are required. I saw an itinerary that saw book signings in Barcelona, Krakow, Paris, Vienna, Bratislava, Prague, Budapest, Berlin, Amsterdam, Eindhoven, Brussels, Antwerp, Bruges, Frankfurt, Cologne, Warsaw, Copenhagen, Malmo, Gothenburg, and Bern.

"These places in Europe. How does this all work?"

"Well over the summer, we can get you out to Europe for a few weeks and attend some events there to promote the book. And then in the winter, we can get you over to Australia." His accent deepened at the mention of the latter. "I'm from Melbourne originally, so we'll get you in there for sure but also Sydney, Canberra, Victoria, Adelaide, and perhaps both Auckland and Wellington in New Zealand."

I paused for a brief moment remembering the day I received the invitation letter to read my work for the CSA and how fast this all unfolded, it all materialised out of nowhere.

"That sounds exciting." Temperance tapped my hands with a smile on her face. Her glee could not be concealed.

"Well, that will be exciting for the girls, right?" I held the pen before I signed. "This has all gone so quickly, so we have to plan this out..."

Mick halted and clenched his teeth.

"We'd like to get you into the continent sooner than later, but I am sure we can sort something for Australia so Temperance and your daughters can join you."

"I am not going unless they can come with me." I put the pen down.

Temperance smiled at Mick and glanced at me from the corner of her eyes. *What are you doing?* That is what she really wanted to say. Her eyes rolled down toward the contract and subtly wrinkled her eyebrows, I subtly shrugged my shoulders back at her in response, affirming that I was resolved in my decision. Temperance tapped the contract as she cleared her throat.

"Butterscotch, it's only a couple of weeks. We can manage, we wouldn't want you to miss out..."

I looked at Temperance and then the girls. "Absolutely not." I shook my head and pushed the pen toward the centre of the table. "You know the deal, I go early in the day and come back late at night if need be." I looked up at Mick. "But at the end of the day, I sleep in the same bed as my wife."

"I appreciate your loyalty, my love." She put her hand over mine. "This is a massive step forward though."

"And I am only going to take it if we take it together." I put my other hand over hers. "We are not going to establish a precedent here and next thing we know, low and behold I am an absentee husband and father."

"It's a one-off book tour, toffee fudge." Temperance drew close to me.

"And you and the girls are the blessing of a lifetime."

Temperance leaned back momentarily; it was apparent that my comments moved her. "But we love you, we don't want to hold you back from such an opportunity."

"Thank you, Honey Bee but that's not necessary." I raised my hand and looked across at my counterpart. "Look, Mick, if it's financials, I'll contribute what I must to make it work or if it's timing we can coordinate a schedule to make it feasible." My face scrunched for a second "...but I am not doing it without her."

Temperance raised her eyebrows, glancing in the opposite direction. Her expression said it all, she wanted this so badly for me and was afraid I was going to miss the chance or blow it somehow. When I stroked her hands with tenderness and gentleness, Temperance soon abandoned propriety and fixed her steely gaze upon Mick to await his next move. My beloved sat up beside me, shoulder to shoulder, clutching my arm in a vivid display that she was standing beside me.

Mick smiled briefly. "I understand you are devoted to your wife and your daughters. It's quite admirable and to be frank, I expected that from you." He picked up the pen. "Sign the contract and we can at least get the distribution deal enacted and the advance in your account." Mick pressed the pen on top of the contract. "Those dates cannot be fixed until you sign anyhow. They are provisional, as it stands." Mick raised a steady hand. "These things change all the time."

"They come with me or there is no deal."

"Bon Bon, Mick never said anything to the contrary." She smiled. "He's a very passionate man, bless him..." Temperance waved her hands, delivering a well-time joke to ease the tension. "Just sign it, sweeting, it's tickety-boo".

"I haven't heard that saying in a while." Mick's eyes lit up at the euphemism.

Temperance nodded politely and then glanced over at me, bulging her eyes at me subtly to give me a silent signal to sign the paperwork. I looked over at her and then at Mick who adjusted his shirt, Temperance moving her head stealthy to maintain eye contact with Mick to offer a genteel smile.

I took a deep breath and relaxed in my chair.

"Honey Bee, we are going to the Gothic Quarter." I leaned forward and gripped the pen before I finally signed the dotted line.

"Congratulations." He extended his hand to me and then to Temperance, as we both rose to shake his hands.

THE SNOW FELL FROM the sky in bands, wafting downward as it landed on my shoulders and black woollen hat. Around me the field was coated in white; the elm, sycamore, and birch trees were draped in ivory. I blew into my hands, and a grey mist escaped into the air turning white as it ascended. I looked over my shoulder at the red wooden barn that glowed with lantern light. The candles gave it a homely feel from a different time when life was simpler. I brushed off my puffy wintry coat and looked across the field, the snow had started to slow and the clouds were starting to break. I could see the silhouette of a figure approaching, the outline sauntering towards me with the rein of a horse in hand.

Another colt neighed from inside the barn, adept to the prospect of his companion's return. The squall had passed, leaving the area coated in snow and ice to match the many stars visible in the clear night sky. The moonlight gave the surfaces a milky look. The figure came closer as I shook off my black boots and loose blue jeans. I started walking toward the figure, my boots muffling against the snow with each step that I took. I looked right and saw the faint glimmers of streetlights and houses nestled along the hills of Yorkshire below. We weren't terribly far from the Peaks, or

Sheffield, or the Dales. We were in a happy middle in between the three.

Finally, the outline and silhouette took form: it was my beloved. She had returned from her ride with a white pony trotting beside her. Her black satin gloves gently clasping the brown leather reins. The horse snorted white smoke as she exhaled smaller clouds of grey vapour. A deep violet woollen cape was over her head and flailed behind her, dancing in the wind. Some stray locks of her auburn hair escaped from beneath the hood; and her blue eyes were most distinct against her waxy and shiny porcelain skin which had dampened from the flurries. Temperance's crimson overskirt moved with each step she took over the snow, her steps far less pronounced as she crossed the field. Her strides were elegant, lady-like, and gentle and her boots against the snow echoed this. Below her shawl, an ivory white gown that hugged her bust and wrapped tightly around her midsection, accentuating her curves while clothing her in elegance. Gold embroidery was enmeshed into the bodice in the form of saint decals; the bodice had a shiny and glossy feel which was tight to her to complement the flowing skirt she wore, as well. Temperance looked breathtaking.

I gazed up at the stars once more and saw Orion's Belt. I smiled at the wonder and pondered how those celestial objects were so far away and yet they emitted a light that decorated the night sky. My eyes wandered across to Polaris which hovered just above Temperance as she continued onward to me. The North Star guided many travellers and Temperance in many ways guided me. She was the brightest star in my sky and reminded me I was never alone in this world when I felt lost.

"I am terribly sorry for my tardiness but this pony fancied a gallop." She halted with the horse following her lead. "I hope I didn't have you worrying too much..."

"I was going to look for you but saw you coming back." I took her hand.

"It was meant to be a brisk trot along the trail but my mate Alicia had a fright." She stroked the horse's head. "...fortunately, we didn't get caught in that squall...." Temperance whistled gently at Alicia to calm her. She neighed slightly as her black eyes fixed upon Temperance.

"We best get you settled in, my dear..." Temperance took my hand and we walked back toward the barn hand-in-hand.

I opened the door to the paddock and Temperance led the horse in before I shut it behind her as we exited. Temperance looked around the barn, scanning for a particular silver pal which she found in the corner.

"A mare always loves a carrot." She knelt down and reached into the pal. I came behind her and held her shawl so it didn't drag on the floor or get dirtied. "Thank you, darling..." Temperance threw the shawl around her once more to lift it off the floor as she scurried toward Alicia's stall.

"Would you like to feed her?" Temperance opened her gloved hand which had the carrot resting in its palm. "You best place it as I have here and let her take it from you..." I opened my hand as she placed the carrot onto my palm. I approached the stall as Temperance took my other hand, following close behind me.

My beloved made a clicking noise to get the horse's attention and she expediently moved toward the both of us. Alicia angled her head as she carefully clenched down on the carrot and took it from me.

"Good lass..." Temperance smiled.

"I knew you were good with horses, Mama but I've never seen you with them until now..."

"We haven't had any time away for leisure since before the girls were born." Temperance's eyes peered up at the oaken rafters and around the barn. "...it's so lovely of Scott to watch them for us for the weekend..." Her eyes set back on me. "...though I have my concerns for various reasons..."

"Henrietta and Elizabeth know to be on their best behaviour. Don't expect them to be starting any fires or lifting anyone's furniture that isn't theirs..." I removed my phone from my pocket to check for any messages on it: there were none. "...besides, we might as well make the most of this considering I don't know when we will be able to do this again..." I threw my arms around her and she held them against her stomach.

She inched her head and looked at me from the corner of her eye. "It's a gorgeous night, isn't it?"

A cold breeze filled the barn.

"The stars are out..." I moved my head forward and we shared a smile. I took Temperance by the hand and led her out of the barn into the field where the visibility was best. The snow had brought an ambient silence to all around, it was quiet and peaceful. The skies were clear and the stars were out around us. The only obstructions were our breath and faint chimneys and smokestacks letting out clouds of white, grey, and silver into the sky. The moonlight made her body glow in her white gossamer bodice along with her satin gloves. I returned to the barn, removed a long red quilt and wrapped it around her.

"Do you want to join?" She smiled slightly clutching the quilt with the side of her fingers. "We can enjoy the view together..." Temperance looked ahead at the town on the side of the hill, gazing at all the lights that twinkled in the night ranging from lights in houses to cars passing on a distant road wandering through the village.

"I rather look at you..." I smiled at her. "You look so beautiful standing there in the moonlight..." She turned around and her eyes sparkled at me. Our faces grew closer to each other until our lips met, and the kisses volleyed until it culminated with Temperance biting down on my lip. I put my arms around her waist and kissed her, making my way down her neck as my hands wandered up and down from her breasts to her stomach. She exhaled sharply and clutched my face with both of her hands as we embraced. We kissed deeper as my hand gripped her glute, and her hand started to work itself under my button-up shirt and towards my belt. Her warm hands reverberated against the hairs on my chest and midsection.

I wrapped the quilt around us as I undid the shawl and put it behind her on the ground, as we descended onto it. The snow and stars were all around us. Though the weather outside was frigid, the heat between our bodies kept it warm as our kisses steamed between the breaths from our mouths. I ran my hands under her skirt and rubbed her, she moaned with excitement as her nails dug into my back as she loosened my belt. We continued to kiss and press ourselves together until we were both naked and on top of one another. I ran my lips down her pale skin, over her nipples, down her stomach, and over her navel. She groaned as she squeezed the back of my head and bit on my earlobes. Though it was a cold night, we were drenched in sweat.

Temperance's eyes teared as we became one, her nails dug into the back of my neck as she gasped. I moved the quilt off of us for a moment as we engaged, pouring all of myself into her as she screamed. Temperance gripped me tight as we carried on, sharing exchanges of pecks and kisses throughout until I was pressed to her and massaging her bosom, squeezing her glutes, and rubbing her thighs as we continued to pummel each other. She clenched down on my shoulders with her hands and bit into me as she let out a groan when she climaxed. Her moans grew louder and louder as I soon followed in a similar cadence. We covered each other inside and out in bodily fluids until we both collapsed in each other's arms, the quilt wrapped around us. We briefly kipped under the stars, me still inside her until we were awoken by the faint cry of a horse from within the paddock.

V.

Everything continued to flash in a blur; I reflected the inertia of the events as I drove back from another book signing. What started as a memoir about my beloved wife had grown into its own life. And now time whizzed by like signposts on the very roads that I travelled, perhaps there was a way to slow it down.

I turned up the hedge-rowed lane toward our home passing the green fields, flowery meadows, and two fields of bluebells until I reached the iron gate of our drive. I stopped to open the gate and imagined Temperance and the girls sitting by the piano singing Beatles and Oasis songs together after my beloved lectured Henrietta and Elizabeth for the day.

I walked up the path toward the front door, the two locks unlatched, and the door opened. "Hello, my love." Temperance smiled and threw her hand on her hip, her blue eyes radiated life and peace. A purple spark flickered her from her open hand. She wore a blue silk halter-top gown with a plunging neckline and a gold ribbon that came together over the shelf of her dress. It hugged all of her curves and fell just above her knees. Her copper-auburn red hair curled and fell down her back and over her bust. Once again, Temperance's stomach bulged with a huge bump.

"If it isn't the most magnificent woman walking The Lord's green Earth." I beamed at the sight of her as my hands extended outward with the arrangements in both. "It's only appropriate that I bring flowers."

She placed her hand over her mouth from the delight, until her attention focused on her wedding ring. "I would have had that Holy Water for you." A tear trickled down Temperance's cheek.

"Oh, honey bun, please don't cry." I placed down the flowers and rushed up the steps.

"Tears of joy, bon-bon." She sniffled with a smile. "You look exactly as you were the day we wed in the chapel."

I swiped away her tears, threw my arms around her, and pressed my lips against hers. "And you are more beautiful every day, Mama." I stroked a strand of her hair back and wrapped my hand around her waist. "You are past 170 but more ravishing than ever." I patted her butt and kissed her shoulder.

"Would you prefer a wife more your age, dearie?" She chuckled.

"Are you mad?" I feigned an attempt at her accent and some of her sayings.

"You are getting better, Butterscotch." Temperance gripped me tighter as she laughed.

I pressed my lips against her cheek. "It would have been cool if I could control electricity like you too."

"Well you can't have everything now, can you?" She whispered with a smirk.

"I already do." I kissed her top lip. "I have you and our lovely daughters." I rubbed my palm against her face. "You, Hetta, Bet..." I moved my head down and kissed the bulge in her midsection. "And our little Georgiana." I kept my hand over her stomach and kissed her again until I felt a kick crash against my hand placed over Temperance's stomach. "There she is."

"She's saying hello to her daddy." Temperance looked down. "Our baby girl is a fierce ball of lightning..."

"Just like her mom." I kissed her forehead. "It's good to be back, I didn't even want to go..."

"I appreciate you wanting to look after me, but I assure you that the girls and I have everything covered."

"I am always going to take care of you..." I picked up a collection of roses. "just as you have with me..."

"We are best mates, right?" She smiled.

"More like soulmates."

"Indeed." Her smile grew wider.

I extended the flowers toward her. "Orchids, lavender, and roses for you, my rose."

"Thank you, my dear, these are spectacular." Temperance dipped her noses into them. "I'll fetch a vase for these." Her hair tailed behind as she stepped into the house, white and gold lad-chasers scattered across her strands. "Poppets, Papa is home".

I collected the two remaining arrangements, followed my beloved in, and locked the door behind me. Squeals and footsteps crossed the hall as our two girls scurried toward me from the kitchen. I knelt down and opened up my arms.

"Daddy!" Henrietta was the first to run into my embrace and plant a kiss. Her dark auburn hair trailed her in two long ponytails held together by white bows. Her navy blue dress seemed to move with her strides. She has her mother's blue eyes and face.

"Papa!" Elizabeth was not far behind with her long mahogany hair dangling down her purple day dress in the form of a thick plait. Like her sister, Bet has the same eyes, soft face, fair complexion, and porcelain skin. Her hair was in two plaits. She threw her arms around my neck and kissed me as well. I embraced both of them and picked them up off the ground,

"Hello, my beautifuls. Did you have a good day with Mommy?" I kissed them both on the mouth. They nodded and smiled as they kept their arms around my neck, pressing their lips against my cheeks at the same time.

"Good, I got you girls a present." I raised my eyebrows with a playful smile. I didn't take the dollhouse out of the truck yet as I wanted to surprise them.

"Really?!" They both squealed with excitement, I nodded once. "Thank you, Papa!" They looked over at Temperance and she smiled at them.

"You're welcome." Another smile escaped from me. "It's in the boot." I kissed both their noses and each giggled. "But before I go and get it, what did Mommy teach you?" My eyes shot up at Temperance who leaned against the wall toward our sitting room. An old piano stood behind her.

"Maths and geography." Henrietta gleamed.

"She also showed us how to sing *Good Day Sunshine*". Elizabeth reported. "Hetta played the piano."

"That's a song tailor-made for Hen."

"Mummy showed me how to fly." Henrietta glowed. "She should teach you."

"Your mother has taught me all sorts of things, Sweet Pea..." My eyes wandered to Temperance as she blew a kiss at me. "But how did she fly when she's pregnant with your little sister?"

"Mummy can do anything, Papa, you know that..." Henrietta smiled. "She's a superhero, after all."

"Henrietta, you are making me blush." Her cheeks went flushed.

Hetta drew close to Temperance and squeezed her left arm. "I am going to get muscles like you, when I get older, Mummy."

"And I'm going to make you another pretty pink cape that you can wear with your cool lilac costume." Bet beamed at Temperance. "You will look beautiful as you always do, Mummy."

"I will be sure to wear that cape on my adventures and you girls can be my sidekicks." She smiled at our daughters. "Stopping those rough lads on my own can be hard work. But I'll hardly break a sweat if I have my sweet little lasses there to help me."

"Can we have costumes too?" Henrietta's eyes lit up.

"Of course." She smiled. "All bespoke."

"I also brought you these, I collected the flowers off the ground. Lilies for Henrietta and carnations for Elizabeth.

"Flowers?!" They opened their arms and cradled their bouquets in their arms, their mouths open with excitement at the sight of roses and daisies. Both were full of rapture and said thank you more times than I could count.

"Who wants to tell Papa why we are going to place the flowers he so kindly brought us, by the window?" Temperance placed her hands over Elizabeth and Henrietta's heads.

"Because of photosynthesis." The answer escaped Henrietta's lips.

"Very good, Harriet." Tempie smiled. "However, it's important that you don't just shout answers even when you are enthused."

"Sorry, Mumma." Henrietta glanced down. "I fancy botany, that's all."

Temperance kissed the dome of her head. "It's alright. It's good to be eager but also important to exhibit good manners." She wrapped her hand around Hetta's cheek and stroked it. "Now, who wants to tell us what photosynthesis is?"

This time, Elizabeth raised her hand.

"Go on, Squeak."

"The flowers will take the carbon dioxide and use it as food and then give off oxygen as its waste, which we need to breathe."

"Very good, Elizabeth." Temperance raised her eyebrows and smiled with pride.

"Bets loves science." Hetta smiled at Elizabeth. "She should stick to math because she never adds up."

"Did you come up with that all by yourself, Bubble?" Elizabeth smirked.

"Clearly, you two are your mother's daughters." I smiled at both of them. "She has a catalogue of idioms and sayings..." I winked at Temperance playfully.

"Only second to you, of course, my nonpareil." My beloved replied.

"Mummy, can you teach me how to clap my hands and make lights go on?"

Temperance and I glanced at each other for a moment, surprised at the nature of the question. "All right then poppets." She hooked my arm and looked down at each of them. "Go fill up some jars of water and pop your flowers in them before you place them on the windowsill, please."

"Yes, Mother." Henrietta led Elizabeth to the kitchen, both clutched their flowers in their hands. "Thank you, Papa." Their voices trailed back down the hall.

"My pleasure, darlings."

Temperance's hands clutched my tie followed by a quick peck of the lips. I threw my arms around her waist and kissed her some more. Temp giggled as she pulled on the tie. "The ties that bind."

"Here we go with the puns."

"I have had to tie your loose ends before." Her eyes bubbled. "Though we have tied the knot, it appears you are also tied to my apron string."

I shook my head and started laughing. "You are a cheeseball, honey."

"Look, who's talking." She bantered.

I pulled her close to me and kissed her. "It's a part of your charm."

We stared at each other for a moment, the sound of the pipes running from the girls likely filling their jars broke the silence.

"Something odd occurred earlier..." Temperance looked back toward the bookshelf, the fireplace, and then the large window that let the sun into the sitting room. "I found Henrietta lying in a puddle of water but she wasn't febrile."

I took her hands. "It was warm earlier..."

"It wasn't sweat..." Temperance shook her head. "Pure water."

The pipes stopped running.

"She hadn't spilt anything or been near the sinks." My beloved looked back toward the front door for a moment. "And Elizabeth was scorching hot, as if she were a light, but she wasn't poorly either..."

"Maybe they have inherited a variation of your powers?"

Temperance's eyes gorged at the notion.

"We can't write it off..." I gazed down at the fairness of her skin and her soft and flawless complexion. "It was a possibility." I noticed some faint hairs rising near her wrists. "I mean look at what happened already..."

She peered at The Cross that was fixed to the wall over the piano. Though we conceived such a possibility, we were banking on such a possibility not being likely even if it was obvious that it would be the case. After all, when we married Temperance retained her powers and some incredulous things happened to me.

"Look on the bright side..." My thumbs rubbed her wrists. "...if they do have your gifts, it may finally be time to retire the bonnet and apron, wifey."

"Cheeky git." Temperance shoved me playfully.

I wanted to take her mind off what she was focused on. However, it was something that we would have to eventually deal with...the gifts. For the moment though, I was only worried about keeping a smile on her face.

"You want to start, Mama?" I poked her in the thigh to force a giggle from her.

"If you wish to be garrulous, I have two colleagues that would be happy to sort you out..." Temperance smirked and as carefully she tickled me without relent, forcing me down to the ground. "Poppets, Papa is being naughty..."

"Get him!" The girls ran into the room.

"The reinforcements have arrived." I braced myself.

Henrietta and Elizabeth wasted little time and jumped on me.

"That's it, poppets."

The girls let out squeals and giggles as they played. "Give up, Papa." Bet's teeth nipped into my shoulder. Her agility was remarkable.

"You silly, Daddy." Henrietta wrapped her arms around my chest, the strength behind it was unparalleled to what you would expect from a girl of her age.

"You are no match for us, darling." Temperance stroked her hair. Hen and Bet pressed their heads against her hips and midsection.

"I never thought I had a chance." I sat up and wiped the sweat away from my brow. "What are we feeding these girls?" I winked at them.

"Speaking of which..." Temperance reached down and pulled me up with minimal effort. "Tell them what the plans are for tea, dear."

I chuckled as I brushed myself off. "Ladies, since it's a special occasion and you've been really helpful to Mommy, I am going to make you buffalo chicken pasta for dinner tonight."

Our daughters cheered, each hopping on the balls of their feet once.

"What's the special occasion, Papa?" Bet pressed a finger to her lip.

"That the four of you exist." I smiled at Temperance, gazed at her belly, and then our daughters, who all looked toward me visibly moved by my remarks. Henrietta and Elizabeth said nothing but came forward and both hugged me, I threw my arms around them and kissed them both before I released them and they turned to look at their mother.

"And we are really happy that you exist." Temperance smiled at me. "...right, poppets?" Both nodded enthusiastically and smiled at me, rushing forward to embrace me again.

"If Papa is making the buffalo chicken pasta..." Hetta turned to look at her mother. "Can you make that pudding again, Mummy?" She clapped her hands enthusiastically.

"For afters?" Elizabeth chimed in, matching her enthusiasm and glee.

"I will do but you girls must finish your reading and put your toys away." Temperance placed her hand on her hip. "If you do, Summer Pudding, it is my little berries."

Henrietta hugged Temperance's waist. "We'll make sure the bedrooms are spic and span."

"Excellent, my loves." Temperance rubbed Hetta's head. "Now your father and I are going to have a lie down for a tick and then we'll sort out tea."

"I have a question before we go..." Henrietta gleamed. "Where did you and Mummy go when you got married?"

"The moon." I smiled and Temperance glowed back at me.

"How did you get there?" Elizabeth threw her hand at her hip. "Did Mummy put on her tights and fly you there?"

"We took a zeppelin, right?" I raised my eyebrows toward my beloved.

"We did indeed and it had a fantastic view of the stars..." She leaned down and kissed our daughters on the tops of their heads. "...you could nearly reach out and touch them."

"And if you do a good job for Mommy, perhaps we'll take you one day..." I smiled at them.

"That's right, poppets." Temperance rubbed Henrietta and Elizabeth's faces. "I'll fly us there."

"Will you really?" Hetta looked up with wonder.

Temperance smiled and nodded.

"We will wipe all the sides and work tops in the scullery too then." Bet exclaimed with enthusiasm, gleaming at her mother.

"Sparing us the mangle." She smiled. "For that effort, there will be extra custard with your puddings."

"Thank you, Mummy!" Our daughters hugged her.

"My pleasure, my sweetings. Thank you." Temperance embraced them tight and kissed them all on their heads. "Such lovely girls, you are." She glowed as she watched Elizabeth and Henrietta travel up the stairs.

I came behind Temperance and put my arms around her, watching the spectacle as I pressed my lips against her cheek. "After they're off to bed, we can put on a fire, and listen to some music." I swayed with her for a moment. "Unless you need me to do some errands for you?"

"Ta, darling..." She sighed. "With this being our third, I thought I would have gotten the hang of this by now..."

"Well whatever I can do to help, I am at your service, my lady." I scooped Temperance into my arms coaxing a giggle from her. We never took our eyes off each other as I carried her to the couch. I placed her down on the couch and propped two vermillion plush pillows behind her head. I scuttled in behind her and made sure she had room to be comfortable. I placed my arm over hers which held the bulge from her stomach and pulled down a black quilt which was folded over the crest of the sofa cushions.

I took her hair clip out of her hair and stroked it as I let it down for her before I pressed my head against hers.

"Comfortable?" I yawned and gently let her hair flow over her chest in thick waves of cinnamon-auburn.

She nodded and brushed her head against mine, I kissed her and we cuddled until we finally drifted off to sleep.

"MUMMY!"

Temperance and my eyes opened at the same time. My heart raced at the loud screech that pierced through the quiet.

"Yes, lovey?" My beloved replied, the more composed of the two as she threw off the quilt and sat up.

"You see Bet, she wasn't outside." Henrietta's voice carried from the top of the steps. I moved the quilt to the floor as Temperance reached for her hair clip and threw her hair up. The girls scampered down the stairs, each of our daughters had contrasting reactions; Elizabeth looked impressed and Henrietta alarmed.

"Is everything all right, my darlings?"

"Did you use your powers, Mummy?" Elizabeth glowed at Temperance.

"Can you teleport too?" Henrietta squinted.

"Teleport?" She chuckled. "We were having a kip." Temperance stroked the side of Henrietta's cheek.

"I saw you in the street just now, Mumma." Bet smiled. "But you had done your hair and looked all Fancy Nancy."

"It wasn't Mummy." Henrietta's eyes bulged with an uneasiness.

"What do you mean, sweetheart?" I took her hand.

"It was..." Hetta glanced around the room until she focused on the corner bookshelf beside the piano before she pointed at the picture of Temperance's mother, Abigail.

My beloved and I looked at each other for a moment, unsure of what to make of the claim or how to respond.

"Nana?" Temperance let out a nervous laugh. "I am sorry poppets but your Nan is in a very special place right now..."

"She may have come back from there."

"It's okay, Hetta, Papa is here now." Elizabeth squeezed Henrietta's fingers. "He'll protect us."

"My goodness, Bubble." Tempie sighed. "You look as if you have seen a ghost."

"I may well have done, Mummy." Henrietta clutched my hand. " That is why we came for you and Papa." She started to cry.

"My beautiful girls..." I reached down and picked up Henrietta and Elizabeth to place them both on my lap. "Mommy is right, there is nothing to be afraid of." I wrapped my arm around each of them and kissed them on the dome of their head. "I wouldn't let anything bad come near you, your sisters, or your mother. I will always make sure you are safe." I stroked her hair. "Maybe, it was someone who looked like her that was passing by."

"What if it wasn't?" Bet sobbed. "She stopped at the front of the gate."

"Squeak is right, she wasn't lost." Henrietta spoke with an urgency trembling upon her lips. "I watched that woman's every move, it was as if she had been looking for us..." She stared at the portrait of Abigail. "As if I could read her mind and hear her thoughts..."

A silence filled the room and a tension manifested that could be cut through with a knife. Temperance finally spoke to ease it. "Well let's not put the cart before the house."

"But Mumma, we are not dragging your dress through the manure." Hetta threw her hands out in protest, her eyebrows furrowed.

My beloved and I broke a smile at the remark, but Henrietta took affront as it appeared that she thought we didn't believe what she was saying.

"Papa, I know Mum can run through walls, do really cool flips, jump super high, and make electric butterflies, but I am telling the truth." Her hair wafted against my arms when she turned to look at Temperance. "It wasn't her..."

Elizabeth stood up and looked out the window. Our daughter froze as if she had gone into a trance until her hands waved and a smile broke from her face.

"Who are you waving at, Bet?"

"It's the lady again..." Elizabeth looked down at me. "She looks like she came from a painting in the Victorian room at the museum." Bet giggled and waved again. "She seems pretty nice, actually..."

Temperance and I stared at each other for a moment to validate what we were hearing and simultaneously both of us peered out the window onto the dusty country lane beyond the gate. Nothing was there, except for a crimson cloak blowing across the field...

VI.

"The baby is coming!" Temperance's face was drawn in agony. I clutched Temperance's hands as she screeched from the aching spasms.

"Ahuhhh!" Temperance screamed as she let out a series of rapid breaths. The lighting in the room had flickered and went dark for a moment before returning to its normal brightness.

"Girls!" I waved them forward.

Henrietta and Elizabeth stood vigil at the end of the bed, their little faces hanging on my every instruction as their blue eyes were consumed by their mother writhing. Henrietta and Elizabeth had joined at the hands; Hetta in a blue top with a white skirt and Ellie in a white top with a blue skirt; their hair both in pony-tails. "Can you get me the phone, please?"

"Yes, Papa!" Henrietta ran out of the room and Elizabeth followed her.

I'll call the ambulance; they'll be here shortly..." I rubbed her hands.

"Don't!" Temperance squeezed my hands as she clenched her jaw covered in a sheen of sweat. "It can only be you and I!" She could barely form words as she sat up and pressed her palms to the bed, cringing in pain. There were all sorts of bodily fluids scattered across the bedsheets, some red in tinge puddling from beneath Temperance. A lamp in the room blew out as purple sparks flew from it.

"I am losing control." Temperance cried out as she sat back in a pool of diaphoresis.

"Deep breaths my love." I held her hand. "You are doing great!"

"Bloody pro, me..." Temperance strained. "Ahhh!" She screamed as she pushed and clenched down on my wrist with her hand. Her grip was strong and nearly cut off circulation briefly to my arm. Vibrations filled my skin as it was warmed rapidly.

Another flash filled the bed area from near to Temperance: this didn't happen when the twins were born. Temperance was in control then and gave birth like she had done it a million times before. This time around, however, it was different. Her powers were unhinged and she was in despair and distress.

I held her hand and looked down, she had signs of crowning and her sky-blue yoga pants were only unravelled to her shins. "We are almost there, Honey Bee."

Henrietta and Elizabeth ran back into the room.

"Should I call the ambulance?" Hetta held the phone firmly in her hand.

"Please..." Temperance gasped and took hold of my hand. "We can't...."

I was reluctant to honour her wishes as I wanted to make sure she had everything she needed but I understood her concerns as lights were flashing everywhere in this house and there was a palpable fear that she could be found out.

"Hen, you can hold off for a moment." I smiled briefly at them. Henrietta clutched the phone with a look of confusion. "We don't want to unsettle your mother..."

Henrietta nodded and put the phone in her hand.

"Grr..." Temperance pushed.

"Bet, I need you both to carefully take Mummy's leggings off!" I spoke softly to reassure them. "But I need you to do it quickly, as your little sister is coming."

She nodded and got to work. Temperance grovelled as she pushed as Elizabeth gently took the leggings off of her, so she could spread her legs and be more comfortable. As the tumult ensued, the delivery went a lot faster than expected. In a matter of minutes, we were able to pull Georgiana from the birth canal and she cried on her first breath.

"There she is..." Immediately, I cut the cord and wrapped her in a blanket, tears flowing from me as I looked down at her shut eyes, little pink lips, and button nose. Though I could have held her there forever, I placed her in Temperance's arms. "Sweethearts, meet your baby sister..." Henrietta and Elizabeth joined Temperance at her side and looked over at the new life trembling in the white cotton blanket as she reached for her mother. Henrietta's eyes lit up and Elizabeth looked down at Georgiana with wonder. Temperance reclined in her bed, taking deep breaths as she cuddled our newest blessing against her breast.

"Do you want some water, Mummy?" Bet stroked her arm. Temperance nodded as she glowed at the sight of the child.

"It wasn't far different when Mother had I..." Temperance's eyes sparkled with life and joy as she smiled at Henrietta and Elizabeth who came back with a glass of water after she filled it from the pitcher on the nightstand.

"Here, Mummy." Bet poured the water into Temperance's mouth, so she didn't have to let go of Baby Georgiana. Bet put the glass down and drew closer with Henrietta. Both were in awe and they looked as they did on Christmas morning when they opened a present that they couldn't even imagine getting. Tears filled my eyes at the sight of the three of them immersed in Georgiana.

"It's the greatest day of my life, all over again." My head collapsed in my hands as I let out a cry before pressing my head to Temperance, my arm over Georgiana extended toward my other two daughters.

A COUPLE OF WEEKS PASSED and we finally got into the rhythm of a fourth lady residing in the house. Our daughters were wonderful toward their new baby sister, helping us feed her, wash her, and bed her. Henrietta and Elizabeth were eager to hold her and give her a bottle whenever they could. They also loved to tell her stories and attempt to make her laugh or respond to their antics. It was quite adorable, as that plump little ball with glowing green eyes and a warm smile seemed to ignite at the sight of her older sisters.

It was a cold late autumn eve and the house had drawn to a stand-still, Temperance lay on my lap shutting her eyes as she continued to recover from the pregnancy which took even more out of her compared to the twins. I delighted in running the entire house as she took her well-deserved reprieve but I too found comfort in taking a breather that evening. My beloved had our household run like a well-oiled machine and made it look effortless, I wasn't even half as efficient though I tried my best to be. Both of us sat quietly by the fire, my arm over Temperance's chest as she sprawled out on the couch whilst I had my feet up and reclined.

"The fire is going good."

A crackle and pop shouted over a knocking sound that came when the wind blew against the side of the house.

"Speaking of fire..." Temperance rested her hand against her head. "Are you aware they require volunteers at the fire station?"

"I never gave it much thought." I rubbed her once. "How did you find out?"

"It was posted on the county website." Temperance responded briefly with her eyes shut on my lap. Before I could even ask why or what she was doing on that website, she was succinct in her follow-up. "You should go for it."

I looked over at the bassinet that was outlined in shadows from the glow of the fire. Our baby girl was lying still under a grey woollen quilt. "Is that something I should be even thinking about at this point?"

"It seems like a piece of pie." Temperance waved her hand out. "From what I read on the job specs, you only respond if and when you can when the pager rings out" Temperance said, sitting up. "You are only expected to make a percentage of the alarms if you wish to receive contributions toward a pension, but it is still not rudimentary."

"It sounds like when I was back in New York."

"Well, job's a good un then." She chuckled. "Volunteer firefighter, it doesn't get more American than that..." Temperance rolled her eyes with jubilance.

"I am also a family man."

"You can be both." She smiled with warmth. "It's who you are, my love."

"But what if there is a fire in the middle of dinner or we were doing something with the girls?"

"You can answer that question better than I." Temperance stroked my cheek.

"Family, work, firehouse."

"All sorted then." She reclined. "We will make some adjustments from our end accordingly, as well..."

I remained imbued in thought about the demands that came with the role and the wider effect it could have on our young family. My reflections were interrupted by her chilled hands resting against my skin.

"I remember the first day we met, the mug you were wearing when you mentioned you had to give it up when you moved here." She shook her head and sucked on her thumb. "It was the only occasion that you weren't in good spirits that whole day."

"I was good the entire time, believe me. That was one of the best days of my life." I tilted my head slightly. "Don't pay any attention to the brooding."

"I've gotten used to it." She rolled her eyes. "To be fair, most of it has long been resolved. Temperance tapped my thigh. "...for both of us." She smiled. "Nevertheless, none can deny you are a volunteer at heart and you seemed eager to return to the fire brigade..." She opened her arms warmly. "I've thought much about that recently and now you can do it again..."

"You are very selfless, you know..." I rubbed her hands and smiled at her. "Between this and the whole writing thing..."

"And you have always selflessly devoted yourself to us." Temperance ran her finger along the side of my head. "Do as I say, that way I can gawk at you in uniform." She winked her eye and smirked. "If you'll indulge me when you are at home, naturally..."

"I think we can make that happen..." I chuckled. "I'll come in the house dressed ready to go..."

Temperance glanced over at me at me like I was a fresh piece of meat.

"...especially since you've been generous in feeding my whole Incredible Temperance obsession."

"Speaking of which, how would you feel if you saw me in that?"

"Is that a trick question?"

She shook her head.

"You are a bright woman, Mama, I take it the answer is obvious." I licked my lips which smacked with the pop of the fire. "Put it on now..."

Temperance shoved me and giggled. "I am serious, you spoon..."

"You mean like?" I couldn't catch my tongue. What could she mean? Was she talking about literally doing what she used to do?

Or was this some form of banter and teasing she often did to excite
and get a rise out of me?

Temperance raised her eyebrows and circled her hands to coax
me to speak.

"Papa!"

Both our eyes shot to the steps. Elizabeth and Henrietta's little
hands were wrapped around the oaken balusters, their eyes locked
onto us sitting on the couch. The twins looked like carbon copies
of themselves, the same hair as their mother and her piercing blue
eyes, the same pout on their pink lips. They were even wearing
the same red flannel pyjamas with a snowman pattern all across
them. Despite the many similarities, they could still be told apart
distinctly by their contrasting personalities.

"Yes, Hen." I looked over at Hetta whose wide eyes and soft
face reflected her gentle demeanour. My beloved argued that she
got that from me and though she looked like Temperance, her
disposition and her mannerisms were more similar to mine.

"I had a bad dream." Henrietta spoke with a tremor in her
voice. Her shoulders were tense and her lips were quivering.

"When Bubble told me, I got scared too, Papa..." Elizabeth
interjected. Though she was anxious, her eyes were always narrow
and bright, reflecting her inward confidence and determination;
an inheritance from Temperance uniquely gifted to Bet. Elizabeth
was less visceral in showing fear or anger, she was reserved and
steadier. However, Bet's lack of vigour in her voice reflected her
own intimidation.

I looked over at Temperance and started to sit up. "I'll
take this one..."

"Can we hug Mummy?" Hetta leaned her arms over the
handrail. "We just wanted to make sure she is okay." The concern

was sincere as both Elizabeth and Henrietta's eyes narrowed at the sight of her. I leaned forward and looked at Temperance.

She smiled and opened her arms. "Of course, you can, my loves..."

Henrietta and Elizabeth scuttled down the steps and made a straight line for Temperance.

"Nice and easy my dears, your sister is sleeping."

Henrietta and Elizabeth jumped into Temperance's arms and pressed themselves against her. "She's not hurt." Hetta pressed her arms across Temperance's abdomen and chest and Elizabeth soon followed. Temperance held them both tight and kissed their foreheads "Why would I be?"

"It's the dream." Henrietta wrapped her arm around Temperance's back and clung to her. "There was some man who was friends with Nana." Henrietta looked at Temperance for reassurance, shivering with fright. "Do you remember when she appeared?"

"That wasn't your grandmother, Harriet." Temperance smiled at her to reassure her. "And no man would fight me, Papa wouldn't let that happen." She directed her smile to me.

"Not a chance, Hen."

"But Papa wasn't there." Hetta contested with a look of alarm. "That was the problem!"

"Well, that's how you know it wasn't real, then..." Temperance reassured her with a gentle smile.

"Mummy looked like she does when she is a superhero but the man left her bloody..." Bet's eyes watered up, as she looked at me. "He was scary, he had red eyes and fangs..."

Temperance was jarred by the reaction; her strong aura had dissipated for a moment when her eyes looked away. However, she showed no emotion beyond that and wore a brave face, maintaining composure. She did this especially when she was around the girls.

"Did you dream this too, Bet?"

She shook her head with an urgency. "No, but that's what Henrietta said he looked like."

"He was well-dressed but it was hard to tell if he was stubby because it all happened so quickly..." Henrietta wept and embraced Temperance. "I didn't want to watch him hurt Mummy." Temperance shut her eyes and cradled our daughters against her as she soothed them and hushed them, returning to the nurturer and caregiver she was, seamlessly.

"It's just a dream, thank God." I rubbed Henrietta's back as she sniffled.

"That's what letting them read those penny dreadfuls before bedtime could do." Temperance ran her fingers through the top of Henrietta's hair.

I threw a few fingers out and shrugged my shoulders. "It sounds like another one of the tales that Henrietta wrote about you took on a life of their own." I ran my hand around Temperance's back.

"But Mummy always wins!" Henrietta spoke at length as she gripped Temperance's shoulders tight clear that she didn't want to let go of her. "And she was winning but the bad guy cheated and hit Mummy in the crotch and he kicked her loads."

"Oooh." Temperance gritted her teeth to embellish. "It hurts to get hit down there and then get kicked around a bit."

"Then he shot her with these spikes!" Hetta looked over at me with terror on her face. "Mummy doesn't ever lose though..."

"Did she lose?"

"No, Mummy blasted him with her electricity and then I woke up. But she looked really hurt though."

"The worst that ever happened in Henrietta's stories is Mummy taking a few hits but she shrugs them off." Bet kept her arm around

Temperance's neck as her eyes ambled across toward me. "...it's more for dramatic effect because Mummy would win easy every time if it were accurate."

We all laughed at Elizabeth's remarks.

"I hope it's nothing too bad..." Temperance smiled at both girls to divert their attention.

"You may get punched or kicked a few times but it's only in your legs, arms, or sometimes your stomach." Henrietta murmured. "...but it's only because we know you are tough and have muscles everywhere; those weak bad guys don't stand a chance..."

"Best make sure you go easy on me, for all our sakes..." She raised her eyebrows and glanced at the both of them. "...It will be hard for us to go stroke the deer at Dunham Massey if I am bruised up."

"We can have her win easy every time..." Henrietta sighed with relief. "I'd rather it be predictable and maybe even boring..." A smile came back to her knowing that the outcome would be controlled as she desired. "...but at least Mummy is fit and healthy!"

"Do it, Bubble!" Elizabeth nodded. "No one is as beautiful, tough, and strong as Mumma."

"Thank you, poppets." She stroked the underside of their chins before they both threw their arms around her.

"Can you read us a story before we go to bed?" Henrietta gently pressed her hand against Temperance's jaw.

"I knew they wanted something." I chuckled as I playfully grabbed Hetta's nose, eliciting a giggle from her. "I will do but after that, you have to go straight back to bed though." Temperance was stern yet soft. "We can't have you staying up late if we are going to swimming baths tomorrow..."

Both nodded in agreement and got comfortable on our laps.

"So, what shall we read my little berries?" Temperance put her hands together.

"Maude The Moth!" Elizabeth screamed out with her hands raised high. Henrietta crawled up on my lap with a book shaped like a moth with a watercolour cover. The moth had long brown hair and a golden body, it had two small white egg eyes with black dots and a squiggly smile that sometimes frowned. The creature's wings were brown with blue spots. Maude The Moth was written in script across the bottom, a discernible feature that caught both our attention as Bet handed the book to her mother.

Temperance looked at me and opened to the first page, I held the other end of the book so the girls could look at all the pictures, it was a joy to see their faces light up and eyes enlarge at all the images that stimulated them.

"There once was a moth named Maude who flew from house to house, she liked to eat lint and pieces of cotton lying on the ground. She always wanted to be a butterfly but was told her wings were too ugly, they were shrouded in brown." Temperance paused so they could look at the watercolour art of Maude hovering in with a smile on her face.

"Her wings had specks of blue in them, they were unsightly to others she knew, but still she wondered am I really a moth? Is it true?" Temperance continued and there stood an image of Maude with a frown as other butterflies flew away from her.

We turned the page and the image of Maude caught in a spider's web came into view.

"Then one day, Maude landed where a spider lay. Oh no! She exclaimed. This cannot be! I need to get away!"

Both girls, bit on their thumbs as we turned the page, our breaths jumped at the image of a big black spider but were relieved when its face was cordial and friendly, reminding us of Maude. Maude lay on her back and appeared frightened. Temperance's eyes squinted when she read the next few lines.

"Please let me go, I mean you no harm. I'm just an innocent moth and I am called Maude." Temperance feigned a look of concern from all the suspense.

"It's a pleasure to meet thee, I am called Tippie! A tarantula I am known and all creatures fear me!" Temperance put on an elderly voice to give the character a menacing undertone. "What a fascinating name..." My beloved turned the page. "Tippie is a nickname for Temperance, actually...."

"Mummy, is it you?!" Henrietta smiled as she pointed at the image.

"I am afraid not, darling." Temperance licked her fingers as she gripped the page to move on to the next one.

"Maude watched as the other butterflies flew toward the sun and in that moment, she didn't care she was stuck in the web that was spun. I'm so tired of being a moth, if you eat me, please do it quick. I'm fed up with these brown wings that make me look sick."

I held the book as we carried on to the next page.

"Maude you're beautiful just as you are. Don't ever for one second believe anything so far. I envy your ability to fly and soar in the sky. I am lonely on this web; it makes me want to cry."

"Aww..." Henrietta sighed at the image of Tipple's eyes trickling with tears.

"I would be your friend, Tippy, you seem misunderstood. Perhaps they both have us wrong, and we be what not we should."

The next image showed Tippy putting one of her eight legs on Maude's back in a comforting manner.

"Thank you, dear Maude, that means so much to me; but you do realise you are silly, can you not see?"

The final page had a picture of an open book of butterflies with a matching image of Maude in Tipple's possession. She had glasses on and Maude had a look of interest that matched our daughter's, her eyes enlarged; her face lit up with delight and wonder. Our daughters gasped in awe.

"You were never a moth, but a butterfly this whole time, Brown Argus to be precise. One of the rarest one can find and yet so you are lovely and nice." Temperance rubbed the girls' heads as they huddled together, clutching the quilt, their heads widened with anticipation and excitement.

"And so Tippie set Maude free and they became the best of friends, happy together on each and every adventure..." Temperance slowed down her cadence. "...THE END." She shut the book and placed it down on the coffee table.

"Yay." I clapped and encouraged the girls to clap; they tapped their hands with a sloppy delivery and slower cadence compared to mine.

"If you were a spider, Mummy, that's how you would be." Elizabeth spoke exuberantly.

"Thank you, treacle." Temperance chuckled and blushed at the kind remark. "Before we take you upstairs, does anyone want to share anything they learned from the story?"

Henrietta raised her hand, Temperance nodded slightly to acknowledge her. "It's important to be kind."

Temperance smiled and tapped Hetta's head. "Very good, Bubble." Elizabeth soon followed and raised her hand, before my beloved could say anything, the words escaped her lips as Temp glanced at her. "Don't judge things as they appear!"

"Very good, Squeak." Temperance's head pivoted back and forth between the two. "And another moral of the story is that we should see the beauty in others when others do not." Her eyes fixed on me. "You may just find a butterfly that everyone else said was a moth..."

"Or you may meet a tarantula that wants to be your friend!" Elizabeth's voice squeaked and Temperance broke a smile before her eyes scanned out toward the window. "Say, is it raining out there?" She raised her eyebrows.

I turned my head toward the window and noticed the droplets of water collecting at the stiles and sashes. "It looks like it, my love."

"I thought I saw some lightning too..." Temperance snapped her fingers and she was in her Incredible Temperance costume, the girls both gawked in amazement. "Should we open the door and have a look as we listen to the rain fall?" She picked up the girls off the couch and they took her hand as she ran toward the door. I kept my eyes on Georgiana who remained motionless with her arms sprawled out and head tilted to the left, unaware or undisturbed as Temperance opened the door and stood behind the girls. "There girls." She pointed to the left. Their heads pivoted. And from her fingertips a bolt of electricity flashed into the meadow beyond us to the right. A flash momentarily illuminated the sky.

"Woah!"

"Thundershowers, it appears."

She threw another bolt and clapped her hands.

The girls turned around and looked at her with wonder. Temperance leapt from the porch and the rain cascaded over as she stood with her palms point pointing toward the sky and purple, white, and pink electricity ascended upward toward the sky, turning the rain into a kaleidoscopic display of bubbles and sprites. Her body glistened from the water trickling down, her leotard and leggings clinging that much closer to her body as it shined from being wet. Her hair soon cleaved to her head as drops of water poured down her face and soaked her lips.

Temperance formed a pink and purple orb of electricity in her hands and walked towards the house until she reached the steps, the display brightened the girls' faces as they watched, and the energy morphed into a butterfly which fluttered its wings and travelled towards the girls before it evaporated into a heart before it reached them.

"Mummy, how do you make the rain look like that?" Bet's eyes were wide with wonder, reflecting the kaleidoscope of colours in the sky.

"Can you teach us how to do that one day?" Hetta looked up at her mother with reverence.

Temperance smiled softly, brushing a damp lock of hair from Bet's forehead. "Maybe someday, sweetheart. With these powers comes a lot of responsibility." She paused, her voice taking on a more thoughtful tone. "But the most important thing is using them to make the world a better place, even if it's just by making a rainy night a little more beautiful."

Temperance knelt down and embraced both other daughters who shut their eyes and rested in their mother's embrace. Each burrowing their heads into her with their arms wrapped tight around her back and waist whilst each of Temperance's gloved hands pressed into their hair as she held heads into her cleavage, resting her cheek over the domes of their heads.

As Temperance held our daughters, I felt a familiar warmth spread through my chest. It was moments like these that reminded me of the delicate balance we walked—between the extraordinary and the ordinary. Watching her with the girls, so powerful and yet so gentle, I couldn't help but think about the future.

VII.

Our girls' bedroom was a refuge where any girl could spend time scribbling secrets in a diary. On some days, we would find Henrietta writing or Elizabeth drawing with crayons at the white oak desk in the far corner, focused on every little detail that engulfed their bustling imaginations.

The walls of the room were painted in a gentle yellow that glowed from the early sunlight entering the room from the large bay window. White curtains danced in an occasional breeze as they hung above the two windows. Next to each window stood two brass candle holders which had long been vacant, the lighting coming from a white globe that descended from the ceiling fixed to it in a large brass ornamental fitting.

On the near side of the room tucked against the wall was a bed dressed in white floral sheets. The mattress sat atop an oak bed frame. On the bed itself between four fluffy pillows was a stuffed toy; an orange giraffe with a wide and friendly linear smile.

Across from the bed, a mahogany dresser with two smaller photographs of our two girls. Their soft facial features and warm smiles radiated from beneath their bonnets atop their heads, glowing against their black gowns. Another picture of Georgiana as a baby was placed next to them in a brass vintage frame, a black and white photograph with Gee's sparkling green eyes, chubby cheeks, and joyful smile as the central point of attention in the small oval image.

I put my hand into a cardboard box and removed a shiny white cylinder, fixing it to an erected tripod with another cylinder already placed in it. It was a telescope, bought for Hetta as an early birthday present. The moon – she often reiterated has 95% of its surface comprised of craters. Her fascination with Earth's sole satellite was the inspiration behind her wanting to take up piano to play *Claire De Lune*. I glanced into the oculus to see how the lens worked as my beloved kept our three tempests swirling around outside in the yard. The sound of laughter blew into the room over a gentle breeze.

I looked outside and there in our front garden; Temperance stood on the stone walk with Georgiana's hand in hers. My beloved wore a navy-blue cotton shawl over a white collared chemise, the look brought together with a blue bow wrapped around her neck and a copper cameo. From below the bodice, a long flowing ruffled pink skirt with a bustle at the rear. Her long auburn-cinnamon hair flowed down both sides of her face in volumes extending down to her breast and middle back. Her ruby lips were firm as her soft blue eyes watched the movements of the children; her soft porcelain skin shining gently in the afternoon sun. She held Georgiana's hand firm as she watched her sisters frolic with an innate curiosity that filled many toddlers and young children. Her eyes matched her mother's sunhat, her long auburn-cinnamon hair extending down her back over a white chemise that was tied together at her chest. A wheat straw skirt flicked in the wind landing just above her little black leather boots.

Elizabeth in a white dress with blue snowflake decals scurried around the lawn as she chased a white butterfly, two smears of black mascara over her cheeks to make a war paint. Her mahogany hair was plaited and down her back to prevent any distraction as she romped around. Henrietta in a similar outfit to Georgiana's wore her hair down in two pigtails, her eyes shutting as she smiled with glee diving into a pile of leaves.

The butterfly landed on Temperance's fingertips, resting on her and looking at her as she admired it, subtly fluttering its wings. The girls scurried over and looked at the creature with wonder, huddled together before it flew away; Elizabeth gave chase and Henrietta ran after Bet.

Temperance turned to look up at me, shooting a dignified smile at me that concealed the love that was bursting from her eyes. My heart warmed at the sight of her, she looked genuinely happy and at peace in the yard there with our daughters; I was overjoyed to see her as such. I waved at her and went back to checking the telescope lens again, before I looked around the room once more, recapping every event that led to this. A brief glow of sunlight filled the room as a smile unravelled on my face: it felt good to be at home, I never thought I would find it.

When I looked back to the yard, Elizabeth held Georgiana's hand and Temperance went missing. Henrietta crept around a pile of leaves until Temperance emerged from beneath the pile, sending a whirlwind of yellow, orange, and brown airborne as she let out a monstrous growl.

"Rahh!" She ran at Henrietta and she yelped, squeaking as she ran after Hetta, pretending to be a monster. "Roarrrr!" My beloved growled with a playful and silly tone as Henrietta ran but Temperance quickly tracked her down, scooping her up with both arms and smothering her with kisses. Elizabeth wore a brown fox mask over her eyes, watching on until she and Georgiana ran over to join the two. Temperance knelt down and removed the mask from Bet before she embraced both Gee and Bet, kissing them both with a nurturing maternal affection, holding their heads against her chest. As Temperance was knelt down Henrietta put her hands around Temperance's neck and rested her against her hunched shoulders. Temperance obliged and gave Hetta a piggy-back ride, moving her head to signal Bet to walk ahead with Gee.

I glanced over at the bookshelf, comprised of a matching mahogany filled with all sorts of children's books and novels, alike. On the third shelf, a mini globe and next to it a figurine which Temperance gifted to Hetta, a ballerina in a lilac skirt and porcelain skin in mid-spiral. Her hands extended outward and knees bent, small painted black eyes and smile with a hair colour painted to match all four women of the house. Next to it, was a gymnast in a lilac leotard and a more athletic build compared to the petite frame of the ballerina. The figure had a pink T on the back of its leotard and its flesh more detailed; it had blue eyes that matched the butterfly hair clip in its red hair worn up. Every curve and chisel of musculature evident in the crafting of this action figure; it was a miniature of my wife as Incredible Temperance. Bet always wanted a likeness of her mother and adored it.

Footsteps echoed through the hall as the girls entered the room followed by Temperance who now had Georgiana on her hip.

Hetta's eyes lit up at the sight of the telescope, her blue eyes accented by the freckles formed under them, her lips forming an o in awe. Hetta gasped and ran forward. "Wow!" She ran over to me and threw her hands around my waist, squeezing me tightly. "Thank you!"

Bet watched for a moment, happy to see her sister delighted but visibly sullen as she felt left out.

"You're welcome, sweetheart." I rubbed her head and put an arm around her. I looked over at Elizabeth and smiled at her. "Carrot, did you look behind you?"

Bet turned her head and her eyes locked onto a large wooden easel with a fresh piece of painting parchment fixed to it. On the base of the easel, a small collection of watercolour palettes with a fine black paintbrush, ready for use. Bet had the same reaction to Hetta, sprinting over toward it as she grazed her fingers over the glass window of the watercolour palettes. She loved to paint pictures of people and animals, capturing every fine detail to show the true personality of each of her subjects.

Bet abruptly about-faced and sprinted toward me, rushing into my arms beside her sister and pressing her head against my stomach. I knelt down and hugged them both, their eyes shut with wide contented smiles.

Temperance smiled warmly at me and then fixed her sights on our daughters, briefly adjusting Georgiana on her hips as she sucked on her thumb watching everything as it unfolded.

"Make sure you thank Mommy too, sweethearts." I glanced over at Temperance with a beaming visage. "She picked them out."

"Thank you, Mummy!" Both girls turned their heads, their little eyes enlarging with gratitude as they smiled at Temperance.

"You are very welcome, my little cherubs." She glowed at them and both left me to throw their arms around Temperance's hip, gripping her skirt as they rested the sides of their faces against her.

"We can take the telescope and look at the stars on the beach when we go next week!" Henrietta exclaimed.

"And I can paint the sea!" Bet followed with a visceral exuberance.

"I am going to make a sandcastle for you and Daddy!" Georgiana broke her silence, eliciting a smile from Temperance followed by a gentle tap of her cheeks from her mother's fingers.

"And I..." Temperance motioned her head to look down at both of them. "Will keep a diary of our holiday and write about everything we do!" She smiled at Georgiana. "That way we can always look back at our times together!"

"Like when you were in London, Mummy?" Elizabeth gazed up at Temperance.

Temperance's eyes flickered with a brief shadow of something—perhaps surprise, perhaps unease. The mention of London stirred memories she had tucked away, memories that were as intricate as they were bittersweet. She quickly masked her emotions with a warm smile, not wanting to let any lingering shadows disrupt the moment of joy.

"How do you know about that Squeak?" She glanced over at me. "Did Papa tell you?"

Bet emphatically shook her head. "I just know, Mummy...." A twinkle formed in her eyes. Temperance arched her eyebrow, glancing out in the hall with a bit of bafflement. "...and I've also seen that box that you keep a bunch of old things in."

"You haven't been in it, have you?" Temperance tensed up, caught on by the prospect of having to confront her past then and there.

She shook her head again avidly with more nervousness written on her face. "I was merely observing, Mummy." Elizabeth responded in a posher accent which broke a smile from Temperance as she ran her hand down the side of Bet's face affectionately.

"Mumma." Hetta gently tugged on Temperance's chemise which prompted her to re-direct her attention toward her.

"Yes, Bubble?"

"Can we ride on the donkeys at the beach?" Hetta looked up at my beloved.

It seemed that whatever worries she had about Elizabeth's mention of London had dissipated, reverting back to the gentle and affectionate mother she was just moments before. Temperance retained her modest smile and nodded once.

I ALWAYS ENJOYED TIME by the seaside, the water had a calming effect even if many events that I have chronicled near it have been blight and quarrelsome in my existence. I removed a boot and poked my toe into the precipice of where the tide gently met the wet sand, the chilled water kissed my toes before receding back from the beach.

To my left, several paces down the beach stood St. Anne's Pier, a shadow of its former self. A place that my beloved and I frequented in the infancy of our romance. Beyond it, the rusticated remains of an iron jetty from the original pier, a long-lost sibling from my epoch. It wasn't as I recalled it in the nineteenth century.

The skies were overcast, a collection of silver and grey clouds with a small breach of sunlight, the winds had picked up quite a bit, and the waters became disturbed as a result. As I surveyed the scene, I saw him. My precious husband, that lost soul I met on the canals, wandering onward to the water, passing the end of the pier heading toward the jetty.

"Even now is he wearing that silly Bulldog jersey..." I shook my head. "What's he like?" I put my boot back on and laced it up. "Butterscotch!" I yelled at him but there was no response. "The water isn't safe, my love." I held the edges of my skirt as I scurried along the sand, its aubergine cotton darkened at the edges from small splashes of seawater. My hair tossed behind me as the wind combed my pink muslin bodice, and the navy bow that descended from my neck over a turquoise brooch fastened at my collar. As I drew close, I could hear him singing Glory, Glory to Ole Georgia over the breeze as his boots stepped smacked into the water. There was a weight to his movements as if he was carrying something on his person.

"Dearest!" I called out to him but he ignored me. "Come back to shore!"

I was utterly perplexed as to what this man was doing. "What's he doing out there?" I uttered my thoughts aloud. "It's as, if he's on a one-way journey." A chilling idea entered my mind, this couldn't be what I imagined it to be.

"That's one way of looking at it..." A voice broke through the rush of the breeze.

I turned about and a man stood before me. He had silky white hair that wrapped around his head tucked under a khaki bucket hat. His hair was interwoven into a full and long resplendent beard. The man was dressed in matching white trousers and a gold sports jacket.

"Stripe me pink, you startled me!" I pressed my hand to my chest. "Who are you?" I inquired directly both in tone and in words.

"Your husband is a..." He itched his beard struggling with what to say next. "...dear friend of mine..." He watched as my dearest walked onward through the surf, the waves becoming larger and ferocious. "We've spoken of you previously."

"I am sorry but I cannot say I have ever met you before." My eyes squinted as I set my gaze upon him.

"You have." He nodded firmly; "I am a friend of yours, as well..." I raised my eyebrows at the audacity of his response.

"That's very kind of you." I turned abruptly to see where my darling was and his outline became smaller against the water, he had however gone stationery for the moment. He appeared ready to fall prostrate in prayer.

"This is not a happy day." The man looked sullen watching on. "He prayed vehemently about his strife before he set off..."

"From where?"

"It's irrelevant considering what he has planned."

"What's he going to do?" I threw my arms out as the terrifying notion filled me. "Lord in Heaven!" I replied with alarm. "Please don't be what I fear it to be!"

"I don't want it to happen as much as you do..." The man looked down and shook his head. "I've always been there for him..." He closed his eyes for a moment and when I looked out to sea, my beloved

head was titled toward the sky. My eyebrows wrinkled for a moment, confused as to what was going on and what possibly could be transpiring.

"What are you called?"

The man didn't answer, his eyes suddenly opened but he kept his watch on my dearest. "When you two were courting you had an argument which concluded with your expressing his desire to be gone..." He looked out to the sea. "Right before he proposed to you..."

"I was awful to him." I looked down for a moment. "I've never forgotten that and always attempt to shower him with love and affection."

"I remember he was drinking alone on the bench. He was torn up inside but I encouraged him to go back and speak with you."

"My Butterscotch is not from here and you don't sound like you are from round this way, either..."

"Do you wish to check my credentials, Tempie?" He spoke with authority as a smile filled his face. "With respect that is not of anyone's concern." He chuckled. "But as to our friend, he really loves you, you know..." This stranger character placed his hand under his chin. "His feelings for you remind me of a botanical garden in the midst of the spring bloom."

"I cannot idle whilst this unfolds." I glared at him with urgency pouring out of my eyes "...there must be a way to help him."

"Temperance, you don't exist in this reality."

"What?!"

An odd remark that was both harrowing and shocking, when I looked at the man seeking elaboration, the man held his hands out and looked at me unphased by my reaction.

"That's preposterous." I snickered. "And if I had more time to waffle, I would discuss the matter in greater detail but as you can see, I must do something!" I stormed off and walked towards the water. The sleeves of my dress blew in the wind as I walked in pursuit.

"*Before you go....*" *He called out to me.*

I about-faced and walked toward him, my bowed shoes leaving imprints in the sand. Around him, there were no footprints. A strange oddity as the entire beach was bereft of footprints from any party.

"*Do tell me if you still feel as if you are a curse to the world?*"

I might as well have transformed into a statue; I was frozen in place. This individual seemed to know my thoughts along with previous episodes of slander I directed toward myself. It was as if this were a dream within a dream.

"*I would say you are blessed...*" *He smiled at me.* "*...you have a lot of love in your heart.*"

"*I love him.*" *I pointed towards the water.* "*And I won't let him do this...*" *Tears filled my eyes.* "*I will go with him if I must!*"

"*That's what he needs.*"

"*Pardon?*"

"*Someone who will love him and nurture him in a way that you do. Someone who will be there for him like you are in spite of these troubles.*" *A smile returned to his face.* "*You two help each other in ways you do not realise...*" *A concern returned to his face.* "*However, you are wearing a puffy-sleeved dress with a full corset and petticoat.*" *He spoke to me as if I were his daughter and he was attempting to help and reason with me.* "*It's restrictive and not conducive in dealing with that rip current...*"

"*Fortunately, I have appropriate wardrobe should I fancy taking a dip.*" *I smiled and snapped my fingers, when I looked down a rose tint in all that I gazed upon, I was wearing pink goggle-like glasses over my eyes.* "*Astounding!*" *I lifted the goggles and noticed I was clad in an electric pink spandex bodysuit. I was perplexed, only my boots and gloves had gone lilac.* "*This is unique...*" *I adjusted the bow brooch around my neck and inspected my ensemble.* "*Quite sharp, as well, if I do say...*"

"It's a variation of what you like to normally wear in your many adventures." He took a sip of tea. "In this reality, you are Intemperance, not the Incredible Temperance."

"So, the villain then, am I?"

"Are you?" He smiled. "Should you comprehend how many lives you have touched with your kindness, it doesn't matter what you wear because you never weren't incredible, Temperance."

I put my hand on my hip, deciphering the riddles and parables of this fellow. I was fascinated given the timing of it all, as if the many questions and sentiments I had harboured had been reckoned with in this chaos, as well.

"But if you are planning to go swimming after him those goggles will help you see and if you are going to wear your patented costume, you might as well wear one that can act like a wetsuit." He picked up a travel mug. "Those leather leggings and the belt will weigh you down."

"I've swam in them just fine, before." I flexed my muscles to see how the suit contoured to every curvature of my body.

He took a sip from his mug. "Lest we forget that the water is bitterly cold."

"Then I shall kettle it." I spoke at length.

"You have a clever response for everything, don't you?"

"My dearest always said I was light on my feet." I briefly broke a smile at the thought of my Butterscotch's ability to argue with passion and eloquence whenever we did have disagreements or debates. In his tenderness, he yielded and always called me the clever interlocutor of us two.

The strange man was clearly amused at my reply.

"If you'll excuse me..." I started my march toward the water.

"Have you reconciled that you are still just a figment of his imagination in this reality?"

"What was once a figment of one's imagination has come to fruition; what once existed has since become a figment of one's *imagination." I spoke over the wind. "I can cite numerous examples that illustrate both axioms but the question is how one navigates these dynamics..."*

A big smile formed across his face. "And by who's power can you navigate said dynamics?"

"Contrary to what others want to lead me to believe in regard to my characterisation, I still hope and pray that by The Good Lord's grace, I can do such things." I looked out to the water and saw him fading into the horizon line as he became a smaller dot amidst the waves. "I pray it is so because I must utilise whatever channels necessary to save him..."

"Thankfully, you have always been the fiery type." The man nodded and smiled with approval. "And it cannot be solely attributed to your red hair." It was once again fatherly and as if he was waiting for me to say what I just said all along. "My shade is cinnamon-auburn, thank you." I smirked at him, sharing a brief moment of humour with him to distract from this daunting reality. I looked back out to the sea and I struggled to locate him. I looked to the pier, ah yes! I could see him from up there. Nevertheless, I would have to scale the ironworks to do so and then jump off and intercept him.

I felt his hand touch my wrist and looked back at him. "I just want you to know that you are very much loved." He looked out to sea. "...both of you are..." His hands warmed my hands and wrists. "...I told him that." He pointed at the sea. "And I know he would appreciate it if I did this..." The man pulled me in and embraced me tenderly, it felt as if he was hugging his long-lost daughter, his touch was gentle, affectionate, and very paternal. He held me and kissed my forehead. "We spoke about that as well..."

"Spoke of what?" A tear escaped my eye.

"That you never had a father..." His hand pressed against my cheeks to catch it. "But you do." He looked up to the sky. "And He very much loves you and treasures you, dearest daughter." Tears filled my

*eyes as he pulled the zipper up over my bust and smiled at me. "Never
think anything to the contrary." He placed his hands on my shoulders
and swiped away my tears. "How beautiful and remarkable you are."
I felt a mutual love and affection for this stranger as if I had always
known him and was happy to have been reunited with him.*

*"I have to go get him..." I moved my head toward the sea,
deflecting to cope with what I was hearing.*

*"Just know, if it were you out there, he'd be running after you
no matter what the circumstances were." He gleamed. "He would do
anything for you." A smile broke from his face. "He's already told me
that; you are everything he has ever prayed for, after all." He winked.*

*"Thank you..." I was completely at a loss for words, all I could do
was smile back at him hand-in-hand. "...If I may..." I curtsied and ran
off toward the pier. He smiled and watched on like a father watching
his daughter perform some incredible feat, glowing with an innate
pride and joy. It reminded me of my dearest when he watched Hetta
or Bet swing on the monkey bars or when they completed a drawing;
or when Georgie first learned how to talk or walk.*

*I glanced back once and the man waved at me to encourage me
on. When I reached the ironworks to the pier, I recollected on that
night so long ago when an adversary fell upon the rocks to his demise.
Today, my goal was to prevent such an event. But how? Could I touch
him? Would I be able to transcend and rip through the continuum?
I was going to go out and grab him, hopefully, he could feel my touch
or at that moment these parallels would be one like him and me. I
leapt and climbed through the iron beams, slippery and slick from the
rain. I continued to lift myself up, using my upper body strength and
flexing my shoulder muscles to carry on with my climb. I leapt from my
position to take hold of the railing on the deck with one and lift myself
upward. I strained as I lifted myself over the handle and rolled onto
the wooden bench affixed to the railing, before landing on my feet on*

the floor. A breath huffed from me, as I did so. I brushed off the back of my legs and my bum.

"My, my, this has changed."

The pier was smaller with green-roofed plasticine huts selling ice cream and sweets. They were all shut, there was no one on the pier but me. I looked ahead to the end of the pier and ran forward, the wind and rain pushing back against me and blowing my catsuit dry for a moment. I reached as far as I could and looked down from the top of the pier, below me the tide was coming in and crashing into the pier posts below it violently. I looked ahead at the remains of the old boat jetty; he had gone past it but still seemed to be on his feet where he stood. He was a decent way off. I lowered my goggles and made sure my hair was firmly placed up. When I stepped forward, I felt something brush against my foot in my right boot. When I reached in, I removed a pink pleather cap that could keep my hair at bay. I thought to myself, I sewed some little pink ears on it, it would be a mint Catwoman mask and a neat fancy dress idea for Halloween.

I put the cap over my head and jumped from the top of the pier, flipping beforehand to once again land on my feet softly in the shallow waters. A grunt escaped from my lips from the force of my landing. Electricity formed at my fingertips and I threw it ahead of me, warming the waters in a sprite of blue, pink, and purple sprinkles. The water crashed into me as I continued my trek toward him, a frigid blow to the ribs and breasts. I took a deep breath, put my head under water, and swam through the surf, it was far easier to navigate and cut through. I would also acclimate quicker to the temperature. When my head came above water, I shivered.

"Heavens, Butterscotch." A cold cloud of smoke came from my lips. "It's brass monkeys in here." I was able to walk still on the floor of the inlet and warm the water some more to make it not as cold. I could have waited for longer to increase the temperature but I wanted to

get to him. I took off my cap, unzipped my suit, stored it between my breasts, and carried on.

He wasn't far now. I pressed on, put my head back in the water, and swam some more before closing in on him. When I came out from the water, I stroked the strands of my hair back and called out to him.

"Butterscotch!"

No response, he stood there now idle in the surf. He looked unsure of what he was doing, just a lonely boy caught in the tides. The top of the white numbers 3 and 4 visible from his black Georgia jersey. It was a top that he gifted to me, I recalled the day and the championships that they had won, a day he said he had waited for but paled in comparison to any day he spent with me.

I had to bash on and I kicked my legs and flailed onward, letting out another cold breath followed by a grunt from the labour of navigating these rough and icy waters.

"Sweeting!" I called out to him again. I wasn't far behind him but all he did was flinch, as if he was unsure if he heard something or if it was all in his mind. When I looked ahead, I saw a massive wave coming our way. One that towered over the rest, a frightening kraken of a beast that would be written about in an epic. My darling looked up at it but he didn't budge.

He sang the lyrics to First Date by Blink 182, one of the songs we sang and danced to on our wedding night. We exaggerated every moment and hopped around on the balls of our feet like little children, frolicking together from the joy of our union. I wasn't a fan of the genre but the sentiment of the context behind the tune was most heart-warming.

The wave continued to close in; I ran through the water and reached for him. In that moment, I prayed that my hand didn't go through him but rather that I could touch him. I strained and tugged on the sleeve of his jersey. He looked behind him, his brown eyes looked perplexed and surprised, almost as if he had been meeting me for the

first time. I yanked him into my arms and held his head against my
breasts. Instinctively, I forced my lips against his head.

"You are safe now." I squeezed him tight and shut my eyes. He
embraced me tightly. A purple and pink assortment of sparks filled the
water for a moment as I heated the water to warm us. When I opened
my eyes, the wave was towering over us. When he saw it, his instincts
overtook him and his arms wrapped tight around me, shielding me
against him to protect me from the brunt of it. Even then and there,
his desire was my safety and well-being above his. However, I didn't
have to time to enjoy the fact I had gotten to him, that he was rescued,
or that his love for me was greatest of all. I envisaged and imagined an
exit from here, back to home. I looked behind us and saw a whirlpool
in the water, perhaps that was the way out.

"There!" I pointed and led us towards it as the wave started to fall.

"You first, Mama!" He stood behind me, positioning himself as a
rampart between the wave and me.

The shadow of the wave curled over us as I swam into the
whirlpool, our hands locked firmly together as if they were tethered to
one another, one flesh, an appendage of each other never meant to be
severed.

I WOKE UP IN THE MIDDLE of the night, sweat dripping
from my head. I breathed in and out, trying to catch my breath. I
looked to my left with a sigh of relief, my beloved was lying beside
me with her head on me and my arm still around her. Her head
raised as she smiled at me, sighing with relief.

"Darling, I had the most awful and frightening dream." She
pressed her head against mine and I held her against me.

"So, did I..." I held Temperance tight and put one of my hands
around the back of her head.

"Was there a rogue wave?" She raised her head. "I was in this cute pink suit..." She giggled.

I looked up at her and nodded, perplexed as to what transpired. "You looked really good in the pink suit." I embraced her. "You saved me."

"But when the wave came, you protected me." She kissed the side of my head.

"We are always there for each other." Blood rushed through me as I sat up. "Hopefully, I won't have to attempt to drown myself to see you in that outfit."

Temperance smacked my arm. "That's not funny." Temperance sat up and kicked off the duvet. "Please don't go on any shouts tonight with the fire brigade." She seemed nervous and on edge. "Stay with me..." She touched my hand.

I reached to the nightstand and turned off the pager and Temperance plucked it off from my hand to put it behind her. "Good..." She giggled. "...I can wear this for you all night, then." She snapped her fingers and she was in her pink costume.

"Oh wow, that's not even fair...." My eyes nearly popped out. "What?!" I took a deep breath to collect myself. "How did you do that?"

"I visualised it." She pressed her lips to mine. "I am delighted you like it."

"You look like Catwoman." I tugged on the zipper and pressed my lips to hers.

"Maybe I am her..." She batted her eyebrows and licked the side of my ear which instantly aroused me.

"Ehh..." I took a deep breath to compose myself. "...I think she wants to be you..."

She snorted to hold back a laugh and embraced me tight before her body grew stiff. When I looked down at her, she was staring up at the ceiling, her eyelashes fluttering with preoccupation.

"Do you think we imagined each other?" Her head pivoted towards mine. "So, we could save one another?"

I froze for a moment, haunted by the thought. At times, this all did feel too good to be true but I couldn't fathom a world without her, it seemed like a nightmare. I pressed my hand toward hers and she rubbed the back of my head before I lifted it. "I can tell you what's real..."

She raised her eyebrows.

"How important you are to me..." I ran my fingers up the side of her cheek and she shut her eyes for a moment, peacefully smiling at the sensual touch. "And how much I cherish you..." I held her face. "Not just as my wife but as a friend..."

She turned her head and smiled at me before she gently shut her eyes, carefully pressing her lips against mine. We continued to kiss and work our hands up and down each other. I started kissing her neck and reaching into her open cleavage, she started to breathe heavily and grunt as I plunged my head into her cleavage and kissed and sucked all over, ending with her nipples.

I pulled down on the zipper and started to kiss the areas of skin that were exposed. She moaned as I groped her and I licked the sweat from her abdomen, followed by swirling my tongue in her navel. I brought my hands down from her breasts, leaving her hard nipples erect from the caresses and strokes to focus on her tight abdomen. I massaged her love handles until they wandered down into her crotch, she started to moan from the rubbing and then my fingers penetrated her.

She moaned and sucked air as my hand soaked in her bodily fluids which poured from her. She groaned louder before kissing me and biting on my lip. "Ooh!" She grunted with pleasure, panting laboriously as I circled my fingers through her, my other hand massaging her bosom before it moved up her neck and cupped her face.

"Does that feel good?"

"Amazing..." She whispered breathily, as I pressed my lips to hers; our tongues danced as she threw off her sleeves and reached to take down my shorts. She bit my shoulder as my fingers soaked in her fluids. She forcefully exhaled and went limp, pressing her body to mine. I removed my fingers and licked them clean, tasting her as she convulsed from the orgasm. I rubbed my hands down her shoulders, over her lower back, and below her waist. We continued kissing and holding each other tight, I started squeezing and massaging her bum.

She pulled down my boxers as I pulled her suit down past her thighs, stroking her quadriceps as I did so as we continued to swallow each other in kisses. I ran my hands up her bum and put my fingers into her naval cleft, gyrating slowly as we continued to grind together until we were one and I felt her warmth. We both exhaled strongly and grinded, a soft and sensual intercourse as we traded kisses and moaned into each other's ears. The grinding intensified and was more forceful, we in turn got much louder. I smacked her bum and she clenched down on my neck as we pounded each other. I moved her hips up and down, reaching deep inside her as I nipped her neck and chest. She screamed louder and gripped my head, I pressed her down on the bed and exerted force, she cried out louder as the bed crunched into the wall; it was a sweat-filled, hot, and heavy euphoric ecstasy and we were about to both climax from it. Our hands joined as our fluids coagulated, exchanging kisses as we switched positions and I was making love to her from behind. The bed crunched louder against the wall until we were bathing in each other's sweat and bodily fluids. We both collapsed in each's other arms, still together as we gasped for air. The darkness was soon exposed by a light from the hall that suddenly entered the room as the door burst open.

"Mummy!"

"Bubble?" She swiftly pulled the duvet over us and we quickly disengaged, nervous that we had been caught in the act. I saw her shadow blur across the room, I took hold of Temperance and held her against me.

"Daddy!" Her little voice cried out to me; she was thankfully still unaware of what she had walked into.

"What's wrong, sweetheart?" I pulled the duvet over me and discretely pulled up my boxers and shorts.

"I've had an accident..." She sobbed at the edge of my mattress. Her hot breath was blowing against the back of my head.

"What kind of accident?

"...I wet my bed..." She sniffled. "I didn't mean to."

I glanced at Temperance as she covertly zipped her suit back up under the duvet.

Henrietta looked over with curiosity. "Why does it smell funny in here?"

"Don't worry about it, sweetheart..." I sat up and stroked the back of her head with my clean hand.

"I had a night terror..." She sobbed and started to cry. "...I was really scared." She clutched my arm. "I am sorry."

"It's okay, sweetheart..." I got out from under the duvet and looked over at Temperance who had pressed her hand to the sheet and then her groin. "Can I turn the light on?"

Temperance rolled the duvet over her and snapped her fingers; the lights went on.

"Why are you hiding under the blankey, Mummy?"

"Henrietta, one thing at a time, please..." I looked at her white flannel white night gown which was soaked and stained yellow around her stomach and thighs. "Come here..." I waved her forward and felt her pyjamas which were soaked and wreaked of urine. "What happened in this nightmare?" I smiled at her and kissed her cheek to console her.

"The wave..." Tears streamed down her eyes. "And you were really sad." She nodded her head. "You were in the sea and Mummy went in to help you and then a really big mean wave came..." She spoke really fast.

Temperance and I looked at each other with wonder. How did she have such clairvoyance? Was it another evolving power? We didn't have time to dwell on that as Hetta's tension engulfed us.

"It wasn't like Tsunami Tim..." Hetta spoke fast, referencing one of her favourite cartoon characters on Saturday morning TV.

"No, Tim would have tried to help us, right?" I smiled at her.

Henrietta nodded her head emphatically.

"It was just a dream, my dear." Temperance spoke softly. "...Papa and I are safe, you see?"

She clutched my wrist and threw her arms around me. I embraced her and ran my hands up and down her back.

"I am glad you are alright, Daddy." She kissed my cheek, the scent of urine gained strength. "I love you Hetta." I kissed the dome of her head and stroked her, before patting her bum which was still wet. "We are going to have to wash this, sweetheart." I picked her up and she put her arms around me. "Let's get you cleaned up and back to bed."

The mention of her going back to bed evaporated her smile and warm countenance. She was shifted into a gaze of worry, fear, and sorrow. Hetta started to shake, her eyes watered up as she trembled.

"Can I stay in here?" She sniffled. "Please..." The sob followed, the sight of which filled me with a desire to bring her back to the smiley little girl I had just embraced moments before.

"What do you think, Mumma?" I looked over at my beloved who glanced back at me. "Do you think we can let this little apricot sleep with us tonight?" I smiled at Hetta to bring her smile back. She looked over at Temperance who also smiled back at her.

"I reckon the occasion calls for it."

Her blue eyes lit up.

"But we are going to have to change you and bathe you first..." Temperance spoke firmly.

"Can you come with me, Daddy?" She looked up at me and smiled.

"You are a big girl, Skittle. You don't need me to bathe you, you are six years old..." I tried to respond as nicely as I could to my little girl. I didn't want her to feel like I didn't care or I was talking down to her.

"I need to make sure that you are safe, Daddy." She took my hand and pleaded. "I want to be able to see you and know you are okay..."

The poor girl was clearly spooked; her genuine concern for me was heart-warming and touching.

"And I appreciate that honey, here is what I can do..." I smiled and sighed. "...I'll sit on the floor and read a book." My hand went under her chin. "Okay?" Her head moved up and down with my hand as she smiled. "I am really touched by how much you care." I kissed her forehead and I got to my feet. She started to hop and skip on her feet and dancing to a rhythm with a big smile on her face, it was adorable. I joined in and made merry with her before her eyes peered around the room and lit up at the sight of a ladybird flying toward the light. Hetta ran after it to inspect it and marvel at it. She pressed her finger to her lip and saw that the small insect had flown onto a set of drawers.

"Allow me to let her out..." Henrietta released my hand for a moment to make her way toward the insect and put her finger on the drawer so the little red and black friend that she made, crawled onto her finger. Henrietta's eyes lit up in wonder as she gazed at the affable insect. Temperance smiled and opened the window beside her. Henrietta made her way to the window and on cue, the bug flew off into the night. "Farewell!" Hetta waved at it. "She said thank you and goodbye!"

Temperance chuckled as Henrietta skipped on the balls of her feet back to me.

"Let's go, princess." I took Hetta's hand and looked down at her, her smile squiggling across her face, her blue eyes sparkling with a combination of childish mischief and innocence, as she placed her hand in mind. Her hair was plaited and down her back over her white nightgown and socks, she looked like an adorable little doll. As I turned on the hallway light to lead Henrietta to the bathroom but she froze in her steps. She started holding her stomach and doubling over as if she had been kicked, moaning loudly as she did so.

"What's wrong, sweetheart?"

"I need to poo again." She grunted.

"Let's get you to the toilet." I pointed to the bathroom.

"No..." She held her stomach with both hands. "Now..." She squatted down; her body was soaking in sweat. Temperance ran over, she had put on a night gown without either of us noticing and had a red clay chamber pot in hand.

"Where did you get that?"

"You never know when circumstances call for such..." Temperance knelt down and reached under her skirt to pull down her undergarments before she placed the chamber pot behind her, stroking her hair and rubbing her back as she defecated in the pot. Hetta knelt over the pot as Temperance stroked her and massaged her stomach which proved therapeutic as it soon settled her. I watched with worry as Temperance nursed our daughter.

"She has loose bowels from being so wound up..." She rubbed her lip. "She needed to empty her stomach..." Temperance looked tenderly at our oldest daughter. "...it's the same reason why she wet her bed, her anxiety causes it..."

Henrietta looked at me with shame in her eyes.

"Don't be embarrassed, honey." I kissed her forehead. "It can happen to anyone." I got close to her face and smiled at her. "My anxiety has gotten the best of me many a times." I cupped both her cheeks as she smiled at me. "And I am an adult." I smiled at her. "...and it was over far less too." I made a funny face at her. "It wasn't anything extreme like a wave coming to get Mommy and me."

She looked at me attentively, her eyes sparkled with energy and innocence.

"There we are my little papillon." Temperance helped Henrietta up, fixed her undergarments, and nightgown. "All better..." She put down the chamber pot and rubbed her nose against Hetta's as she embraced her tightly.

"I'll sort this out too..." Temperance clutched the chamber pot. "And go check on Squeak and the baby whilst she is having her bath." Her footsteps creaked down the steps.

I took Henrietta for the bath and got her changed. Following that, I gave her a glass of water and a couple of salt crackers to keep her stomach settled. She had many questions to ask and I had answered her to reassure her. When she started to yawn, I carried her in my arms up the steps back to the bedroom. When we arrived, the sheets had been changed and the room was fresh. My beloved had also cleaned the sheets in her bedroom and laundered the soiled pyjamas. She managed to do all that without waking either of our two daughters who were asleep throughout the entire incident and get back under the duvet, awaiting our return.

Hetta jumped into bed and hugged Temperance. Then she jumped at me, I caught her and growled as I gave her kisses all over her cheek, Temperance also tickled her. Soon after, Henrietta settled and cuddled with my beloved and me. All the while, I wondered if Elizabeth or Georgiana (though she was too young to perhaps describe it as vividly as Hetta) had the same dream as I watched the both of them sleep for a while, grateful at the sight of them, before finally dozing off myself.

VIII.

I watched as the cigar smoke wafted into the air, drifting upwards like a grey cirrus cloud dancing toward a reunion with the white ones in the sky above. A crisp breeze rustled leaves and meandered through the grass, chilling the lukewarm Autumn afternoon. The sun columned on the downward slope ahead of us, making its way toward the horizon as dusk was only a couple of hours away, at most. One arm rested around my wife whose eyes glowed as our three daughters giggled and squealed chasing after each other in the field ahead of us, hovering around a large sycamore tree in the midst of the green expanse. Georgiana pursued her older sisters, Elizabeth kept trying to grab Henrietta, her arm draped in a lilac ruffled sleeve as her dark mahogany hair and red skirt blew in the wind behind her. Henrietta's white chemise glowed in the column of sunlight, raising the hue of her skin to a glowing temperature. Her hair was up and her blue eyes smiled at her sisters who chased after her, a lively smile matched her chemise and the laces of her polished black boots. She wore a long black skirt that draped behind her matching the bow tied around her neck; in many ways, she looked like my beloved as a little girl. Georgiana laughed as her strawberry blonde hair was in plaits, she wore a white sweater over a peach-coloured long-sleeve top and a long brown dress. She held her favourite doll Prudence in her arm, a doll with a squiggly smile and gentle green eyes like Georgie's, the hairstyle mirrored our daughter with two plaits to the side.

There was something different about Marple that day, though I had seen the green of the Memorial Park on a multitude of occasions. It didn't seem real, even if I could smell the grass and hear the breeze rustle the rope of the flag pole of Hollins Hall behind us. This notion seemed to consume my every thought and remove me completely from the previous reverie. I took another puff of the cigar and blew it away from my beloved's direction.

"What are you thinking about?"

I looked over at my beloved and saw she was reading the newspaper.

"I was recalling the night we made her..." My eyes followed Georgiana running across the field. Temperance rolled down the newspaper and smiled at the sight of our youngest daughter scurrying around. "It was as romantic as any night we ever had..."

"When it was just you and I in the paddock." A smile filled her face. "I am there now with you..." Temperance lifted the newspaper. "So how does it feel to be back in Marple?"

"I was actually just about to ask you that...."

"Well, I asked first." Temperance jeered.

"It was a wonderful idea to come up here for the day, Mama..." I took her finger and she squeezed mine. "Perhaps we should have never left..." I joked.

"We are only thirty-minutes-drive away, darling..." She answered in a more serious tone of voice as she turned another page and looked up to keep a watchful eye on her daughters, all the whilst they continued to scamper around the field. Occasionally, the bark of a dog or the whistle of a bird would harmonise with their laughter.

I took another puff and exhaled the smoke, looking up toward the clouds again. A strange unease settled over me as if the very air hummed with an invisible tension. The wind carried a whisper that I couldn't quite decipher.

Sitting there upon the bench, I recollected back to the aqueduct; meeting Temperance; the canal just at the end of the slope which leads out of the park; the old house; the canals; Mrs. Coleman; the churchyard on the hill...it all happened around me, it all happened here.

"We did great where we are..." I clipped the cigar and stepped on the smouldering ash. "I recall the first time I set foot in Goostrey... "I put the cigar away in a case. "It was just before I met you actually..." I flashbacked to a day when I was still under the duress of my former partner Rachel, who was relentlessly texting me about how I always made her miserable. Needless to say, the situation had changed dramatically.

"Finished already?" She looked over and me.

"Special occasions only, right?" I smiled at her and she smiled back, her blue eyes twinkled in the sun matching the colour of her cloak. "...Thinking about it more, I don't think it would have worked in your old house with the three of them running around."

"No, I don't suppose it would as we would all be on top of each other..." Temperance folded the paper on her lap and I could not decipher the date. "So, do you wish to tell me what you are really thinking about?"

"Am I that obvious?"

"It's as plain as day, I'm afraid..." She took my hand. "It's easy for me to know when the wheels in that head of yours are turning..." Temperance chuckled. "...it's never any different for you when the shoe is on the other foot."

"That's true..." A smile broke from my face. "I was just thinking about everything that has occurred over here, it's wild really..." My eyes focused on Georgiana who stopped and watched her sisters, as she bit on her thumb. "Do you remember the last time that we were here?"

Temperance looked at me with alarm.

"...when you were pregnant with Gee..."

"When we came to see Olivia..." Temperance's head slowly turned toward away. At that moment, it was my beloved who grew pensive whilst I was standing vigilant to comfort her. "...as you know this place and I have a deep-rooted history..." She looked down. "...are you truly surprised by the latest instalment in that tale?" She looked over her shoulder for a moment. "...because I still cannot speak of it..." Temperance swallowed shallow. "...even now..."

I squeezed her hand firmly. "...thankfully, I was there..." I looked out again at our daughters. "...to protect you and make sure you and the girls were safe...."

"And whilst I am grateful there wasn't any danger of that variety about..." She looked out at our children, as well. "...it was other things that gravely concerned me; concerns that I wish to relinquish as to go as far as blot them out of memory until you reminded me of their very presence here and now..."

"That was the last of it though, right?"

"I should hope so..." She glanced downward.

Silence filled the air as I glanced over briefly at the bowling green before turning back to our girls. "...do you know what baffles me?"

Her head raised as she focused on me.

"...how you have all supernatural powers and she can control electricity like you..." I pointed at Georgie.

"And ice as well..." She interjected.

"...and Bet can control fire like your mother apparently could..." My eyes scanned across to the final daughter. "...and Henrietta can manipulate water..." My head reclined. "...and they are all strong and athletic, but I haven't anything..."

"That's not entirely true...." Temperance lowered her head in my direction.

"I am just saying compared to four of you..."

"Feeling left out, are you?" Temperance chuckled. "Would you like to be able to zap someone and lift a boulder, is that it?" She patted my thigh with a playful push.

I shook my head without showing any form of amusement. "...I find it weird."

"How so?"

I moved closer to her and drew her closer to me with my arm around her. "...I've had dreams before where everyone else could do crazy things but I could not..." I stared out at a beech tree whose leaves danced in the wind and then onward to a red-brick Victorian house beyond it across the road. "...I felt that way before I met you..."

"That was the depression, Butterscotch..."

"But you don't think it's odd?" I looked at her and her blue eyes squinted as she gaped at me. "How it just skipped over me like that and went right to them...."

"Fluid bonding?" Temperance smiled, teasing me innocently in reference to our previous row over the subject before she pressed her head against my chest.

I held her against me and kissed the top of her head missing her bun of hair. "It's like I am living in one of those dreams ..."

Temperance moved her head back and grabbed my cheeks. "It is a dream, is it not?" She pressed her lips to mine" ...for both of us..." We locked eyes for a moment; A cold chill descended my spine, and a wave of vertigo splashed across my head whilst my back stiffened as if a wall of granite had extended from the bench behind me. The sensations shifted as my eyes shot toward our three daughters ascended the hill, holding each other's hands as they made their way towards us. A smile unfurled across my face and it grew wider as I glanced back at my beloved. I pressed my lips against her forehead and embraced her tightly.

I leered across the field at the red-brick Victorian house across the road and this time I observed all of the details, such as the black iron-wrought gate, it stood behind; in many ways, it was like our house; the same bowed windows with a large bay on the ground floor; the same gabled facades and balustrade friezes. Perhaps, a family lived there like we did, looking across the park at us. To them, we were just like any other family from a distance...

A spark flicked and water fell from the sky on an area of dry grass.

"Elizabeth!" Temperance yelled.

"We were watering the grass, Mumma." She protested and blew her finger.

"That's what watering cans are for..." Temperance's eyes moved toward Georgiana who dropped a hand full of ice.

"I am sorry, Mummy." Georgie's cheeks grew red.

Temperance looked at both Gee and Bet and smiled. Henrietta flanked them at stood with her arms behind her back.

"They are just being kids, Honey Bee..." I patted my beloved's hands.

"That's not that point..."

I got to my feet. "Are you guys done playing?"

The three of them nodded with a smile and all said "Yes, Papa" in sequence. "How about we take them for a scoop of ice cream?" I extended my hand to help my beloved to her feet, the girls exuberated behind us.

"One scoop." She raised her finger. "But no more funny business...". She smiled at the three of them.

They nodded in unison and smiled back; I placed my hand under Georgie's chin and she drew her head close to me.

"Daddy..." She looked up at me. "May I have two please?" She waved her doll in her hand "...so I can share with Prudie..." I chuckled at the innocence of Georgiana and rubbed her cheek.

"We'll figure it out, sweetheart." I placed my hand around her back and took my wife's hand. Henrietta took her mother's hand and Bet adjoined Hetta. Before we traversed the footpath toward the car park, I glanced over my shoulder at the house across the road, its outline oddly sharper than the rest of the scenery. A sudden, inexplicable chill swept through me, carrying a faint, mournful melody that made my heart race.

IT WAS A BRISK SPRING morning but there was a faint warmth hiding in the air, mingling with the sweet fragrance of blooming flowers. As we left Goostrey, the canopy of willow and elm leaves formed a green tunnel over the lane, casting dappled shadows on the fluorescent meadows below. The birds chirped merrily, delighting in the end of winter's cold grips, hopeful and joyful that no such time would ever come again.

My beloved sat on the far bleacher, one leg crossed off the other with her elbow resting on her knee cloaked in a black and white flower skirt. Her blue denim jacket lingered beneath a white shawl that she had wrapped around her to keep warm. Temperance was smiling and nodding at other couples who walked by, taking their seats on the bleachers, or standing on the side of the pitch to watch their girls play football as we did. I watched her move her head back and forth, her head swivelling in all directions, oscillating from the back of her bun held together with her blue butterfly clip to her side profile as her eyes fixed on the pitch.

"Here you are, my love." I extended one of two white foam cups to her. "Tea light and sweet..." Her crimson mittens gripped the outside of the cup. "...be careful it is a bit hot..."

"Cheers, darling." Temperance's glove swiped against my cheek as I sat beside her and placed my arm around her back.

"Would you like my coat?"

Temperance smiled and shook her hand. "Ta, love..." She opened the lip of her cup and took a sip. "There is our Georgie ..." Temperance pointed toward the pitch and amongst the clapping spectators, a club of seven-year-old girls all sprinted out onto the field in white jersey tops and red shorts with matching shin pads along with black cleats.

"It's crazy to think it was only a couple of years ago, she was a little thing running around with her doll in Memorial Park in Marple..."

"She has gotten bigger, hasn't she?" Temperance smiled at me before we both focused our attention back on the football pitch. "Come on, Giggle!" Temperance cheered as Georgie did a few jumping jacks and jogged in place for a moment at the edge of the semicircle. When she turned her back toward us as she stretched, I saw a black 27 on the rear of her top: my favourite number and one I wore when I played American Football in high school.

"She's wearing my number?" A tear filled my eyes, as I watched her check her plaited strawberry blonde hair to ensure it was snug.

"She was begging the poor coach for it because she insisted that she had to wear it for her Papa..." Temperance smiled as the whistle blew and the game started off. Whilst the rest of the crowd jumped into the game, I was still lagging behind moved by my little girl's gesture. This was the first time I learned of it. The haze broke when I saw Georgiana first touch the ball and pass it onward to the forward, splitting two defenders in a precision volley.

"Nice ball, sweetheart!" I clapped as Georgiana ran up the field to follow the forwards, maintaining discipline in holding her line as a Left Central Midfielder. For about five minutes the other team in green tops and gold shorts battled with our daughter's team for possession. The play was sloppy as would be expected in mini-football and a lot of balls floated out of bounds for throw-ins.

Georgiana took control of the ball and looked over at the stand briefly to see where we were; I noticed two black streaks of mud under her eyes as she let out a quick smile before she threw the ball into the play gently, running back into the action. The ball was passed down the side before another one of Georgiana's teammates who played right forward, kicked the ball long for a goal kick. The ball was soon kicked down the field and fell into a soft area between the young girls on both sides, bouncing toward a defender on Georgiana's team. The girl who sported #4 passed it to another gal who wore #15, she was a bit taller than Georgie and had long blonde hair in a ponytail. Georgie flanked her up the pitch and when two opponents closed in, she passed it to our little girl who got it on her right foot about twenty yards out. Georgiana dribbled for about five yards as two more defenders came in to close her down, Georgiana jerked her foot back and I stood up to watch as she extended her leg forward and kicked a rocket on a line which hooked toward the net. The ball sizzled through the air as the opposing goalkeeper dove for it, the ball bounced off the inside of the ivory post and into the back of the net, the force of the strike rattled the frame as Georgiana scored!

"Sweetheart!" I stood up and applauded, proud of my girl's goal. It was a thing of beauty.

"That's the one, Giggle!" My beloved stood beside me and clapped as we watched our daughter trot back to the semi-circle with her head down as her teammates all congratulated her with high fives and pats on the shoulder.

"That was a belter, that..." A gentleman sat two rows ahead of us in the bleachers glanced up at us. "I take it that is your lass?" He hunched his shoulders in a khaki denim coat, his bald head glowed under the rising sunlight.

I nodded my head.

"She's got a hell of a kick, her..." His shoes clanged against the bleacher as he chuckled.

"She gets it from her mom..." I winked at Temperance who playfully hit my arm in response.

"Don't listen to him..." Temperance smiled demurely at the man.

The teams once again lined up at mid-field as they did in kick-off and play soon resumed. The opposing club started with the ball and volleyed back and forth as they pushed into our side's third. Georgiana's head was on a swivel, watching their every move. One girl tried a cross but Georgie leapt forward and headed the ball onward, guiding it with the side of her head. The ball trickled down to the back line of the opposing team who then ensued to facilitate ball movement. Coaches on both sides gently issued instructions to each group of girls as they all communicated with each other.

Play carried on for a few more minutes but nothing eventful happened outside of a few passes and balls going back and forth, sometimes out of bounds. When Georgiana's team had possession, one of the defenders held the ball and I saw Georgiana motion her head to get her attention. The girl kicked the ball as hard as she could down the field and Georgiana started her run. In a dazzling spectacle, Gee started from behind two forwards on her team and sprinted down the pitch to collect the ball, Georgiana faked to step right and juked left which gave her an opening to turn on the jets. Three defenders gave pursuit to her but she was leaving them in the dust (or grass she was kicking up in her strides, in this case). Georgiana sped down toward the girl, her plait bouncing behind her with each step she took. It reminded me of re-watching Secretariat's Triple Crown win at Belmont Racetrack, as she was pulling away as she accelerated; a little girl version of *The Flash*. The goalkeeper started to make her way out of the net, Georgiana went to her right and faked a cut to the left, which sent the keeper down and she juggled the ball to her right to gently deposit it in the back of the net. Georgiana had her second goal and once again trotted back to the touchline.

Temperance and I roared in admiration of our daughter's accolades.

"I taught her those juke moves." I clapped. "...All those times you were telling us not to play football in the backyard..." I nudged Temperance's shoulder. "...it came in handy then..."

Temperance pooh-poohed and then laughed at me.

"Different form of football though..." Temperance chimed in. "One you wouldn't find much outside of America..."

"She'd be fantastic at that too..." I chuckled. "...she's built like a brick house and the girl can hit..."

"Funny you say that, considering I imagine you would encapsulate our Georgie in bubble wrap if you could." Temperance looked at me out of the corner of her eye as she replied with a sly wit, the double entendre aspect of her remark palpable in her tone of voice.

"What do you feed that lass?" The man yelled up to us with a smile on his face.

"Weetabix." Temperance coolly replied.

"She likes her pizza too..." I gave the man, a thumbs up and he laughed.

After the second goal, there was another ten minutes of play before we reached half-time. When play started back, Georgiana's team scored another goal and Gee got an assist. The opposing side was so focused on her that when she was fed the ball, she distributed it back to the girl who passed it her. The girl was wide open to take a shot which found the back of the net. As time moved on, the opposing team was awarded a penalty as a result of a rough challenge in the box. The score was now 3-1 and there were still 15 minutes to play.

As the match carried on, Georgiana and her teammates passed the ball around, resulting in a missed shot attempt. The flow of the game carried down to the other side but the other team never got a shot off and soon the wide-open style of play resulted in a swift counterattack which culminated in Georgiana's team earning a corner.

"Georgiana!" Her coach yelled out at her, she swung her around in attention. "Take the corner..."

Gee nodded and ran to the back post with the ball in hand, she wound up and sent a beautiful arcing ball into the box which her teammate #11 chested and kicked onto the net, the goalkeeper made a tremendous save but another corner came of it. Georgiana once again went out to take the set piece. Georgiana waved #11 forward to meet her and cupped her hand over her ear. The mahogany bun of her teammate bobbed to signal her cooperation. Georgiana passed the ball to #11 who passed it back to Georgiana; Gee then passed it on to another forward and she drove on the net, Georgiana supported her when the defence closed in on her taking the pass and backing her strong rear into her defenders to keep the ball away from her. Two of the girls at this point were trying to grip Georgiana's shoulder and grabbed her top, Gee dribbled the ball off her back heel between their legs and shrugged off both defenders as she sped onward onto the net, banking the ball over the goalkeeper, off the crossbar, and into the bottom of the goal. She shrugged off two girls that were all over her like they were dandruff, an epic feat of strength and athletic supremacy that would be astonishing for any athlete of any age; Georgiana was only seven. However, Georgiana this time around celebrated her hat trick with a handstand into a cartwheel and then into a somersault, landing in perfect form. Her teammates came rushing toward her to embrace her and congratulate her.

Temperance crossed her arms and looked at me with a speckle of concern and worry which seemed contrary to me who was regaling and cheering loudly. I was beaming with pride in what Georgiana accomplished, it's hard to do what she had done at any level and she made it look easy.

The match continued on and now the opposition had to throw the kitchen sink and send every ball downfield to try to get back into the game in desperation. The other team passed the ball around, clearly keeping the ball away from anywhere near Georgiana. After a couple of minutes of volleying, the Right Back on the opposing team elected to send a ball down the side to an attacking player, someone's little girl the same age with red pigtails and a very gentle disposition. Her eyes scanned with delight when she pursued the ball which would have potentially got her open to take a shot, Georgiana scanned the danger and took an angle to get there and as the ball got in, Georgiana slid into the grass, kicking up strands of loose leaves and pieces of mud to play the ball away and out of reach.

"Nice play, Gee!" I yelled to encourage her. In the midst of Georgie's attempt to defend, the girl innocent and unbeknownst tripped over Georgiana's sliding legs and fell onto the ground, her wrists hitting first followed by her chest. My excitement for my daughter soon transitioned into one of concern for the young girl. Temperance placed her hand over her mouth as the audience held their breath from the collision. Georgiana got back to her feet and swiped some mud off her legs and kicked out her spikes; the girl meanwhile was lying on the ground crying and sobbing. The referee blew the whistle.

When Georgiana looked over at the girl who was crying more loudly, she looked heartbroken and ready to cry herself; she was full of remorse. Georgie looked around at the field until her eyes fixed on a bluebell which sprung at the edge of the field. Georgiana sprinted over and plucked it from the ground, running back toward the girl who had an official checking on her. Georgiana kneeled down and handed her the flower; a smile filled her face as she delighted in the sight and scent, pressing it to her nose. Georgiana uttered some words to her, though they were not audible where we are, they could be read on her lips. "I am sorry, I don't want to hurt you." Georgiana extended her hand down and pulled her up to hug her. "Please don't cry..." could be read on her lips as the girl smiled at her and hugged Georgiana tighter, though they were both only seven years of age, there was so much that could be learned from this. Something most of the adults could take a lesson from. A series of "awws" came from around the pitch followed by a loud ovation to the show of sportsmanship and kindness. I tried to hold back tears but Temperance could not, we took each's other hands and looked upon one another. We both shared a moment of joy in knowing that our daughter is kind and considerate toward others, which we taught her was most important of all.

"Good lass!" A male's voice bellowed at the pitch. The gentleman that we were speaking to also raised his water bottle to us. We both nodded slightly, not looking to make a scene as wanted the focus to remain on Gee. We were supremely proud of her.

"I could care less about the hat trick..." I leaned into Temperance's ear. "...What she did there..." I pressed my hand against her chest. "That is all that matters..."

"Indeed." Temperance composed herself and dabbed her eye with a handkerchief, a simple nod and smile.

"Like I said, she takes after her mother." I pulled Temperance toward me and embraced.

"She has her Father's heart..." Temperance pressed the side of her head against mine.

The game continued on for about another five minutes until the referee blew the final whistle and the score was final.

Georgiana's team won 4 to 1: Georgie finished with three of the four goals. A gathering of white jerseys encircled at the half-line, jumping with glee and celebration that they had won. The bleachers and all that spectated stood and clapped, as each team made their way off the pitch, and so all in attendance went to collect their daughters.

I took hold of a cool bottle of water resting on the bench beside me and extended my hand to my beloved, she took it as she stepped down onto the grass.

"Thank you, Butterscotch." She grabbed my arm and walked alongside me as we made our way toward Georgiana. Georgie stood out on the pitch talking to that girl she tackled just before; the young lady had a bright smile on her face which was very much innocent and heart-warming like our daughter's. Georgiana looked over her shoulder and saw us approaching, she extended her fair sweat-drenched arm toward the girl to press her hands against her wrist and briefly hug her. Georgiana ran off and the girl waved goodbye to her, as she ran toward us.

I knelt down and opened my arms to Georgiana. "If it isn't Little Miss Messi..." Georgie ran into my arms and embraced me, pressing her lips against my cheek. She wreaked of sweat and her shin pads were grass-stained and muddy. "You were fabulous, honey..." I handed her the bottle of water and gave her a kiss on the head.

"Thank you, Papa." Georgiana opened the water and gulped it.

"Three goals, aye?" Temperance ran her hand through Georgiana's hair as she continued to down the water. "Not bad, that..."

Georgiana stopped to take a breath and swiped her brow clean of any water. "I just wanted to help the team win, Mumma..." She shrugged her shoulders with a smile and embraced Temperance.

"Well, clearly you did today, my dear..." Temperance chuckled and rubbed the back of Georgiana's head. When the two released each other, Georgiana dumped some of the water over her head.

"Georgiana, it's cold out here..."

"I'll keep warm, Mummy..." She wrung out the end of her white football top which clung to her from being dampened by the water. Georgiana lowered her top and raised her hand to snap her finger until Temperance grabbed her arm gently but with intent. "Not now, darling..."

"It's so I don't get any sweat or mud in the car..." Georgiana placed her hand on her hip.

Temperance shook her head again.

"Sorry..." Georgiana looked back at the girl who was she was talking to. She was still standing alone on the pitch looking onward, anticipating the arrival of whoever was supposed to come to get her. The little girl didn't seem overwhelmed but nonetheless eager to leave, she clearly didn't like to be standing out there on her own. Georgiana let her wet hair out of the plait, her long and thick strawberry-blonde locks fell down her back.

"I made a friend today!" Georgiana about-faced with a handful of hair. "She's called Hayley."

"I take it that is Hayley there?" I pointed subtly at the girl standing idle on the pitch surveying her roundabouts between glancing down at the ground. Georgiana nodded.

"That was very kind of you to help her up and show such good sportsmanship." I dabbed the black streak of mud under her eye that she clearly applied before the fixture.

"I didn't want to see her sad."

Temperance looked down and nodded with approval. "You are a good girl, Georgiana. You are very thoughtful of others."

"Thank you, Mumma." She curtsied slightly at Temperance and then directed her attention toward me. "Can Hayley come over and play?" Georgiana's voice squeaked with excitement. I smiled back at her and immersed myself in the blue of her eyes and how she looked just like my beloved; it was a spectacle and a wonder that I could not actually put into words. I was taken by the marvel of watching her grow into the young lady she had done. I found myself inundated in such sentimentality when I watched Henrietta play the piano or Elizabeth pass a vacuum over the carpet; even the subtlest of things made me reflect on how much they had grown. Georgiana was our last time to experience it. "She can meet Henna and Bets; I am sure she would love them..."

"We'll have to ask her parents' permission..." I motioned my head to Hayley's parents who finally stepped on the pitch. A woman in a long flowing black wool coat with shiny blonde hair fell on to her shoulder. A man stood beside her in a coat of a darker shade, his leather glove pressed against Hayley's back as she sipped on a juice box. "...but I think it sounds great." I glanced over at Temperance who was visibly apprehensive.

"I am sorry, Georgiana." Temperance adjusted her shawl. "I am delighted you have made a friend but I don't think we can have her over..."

Georgiana gazed up puzzled and when I saw her disappointment, I looked up at Temperance with similar dissension. "But why? They can play in the yard or..." I extended my hand outward. "...video games in the front room".

"You know why..." Temperance's remorse was evident in her look; she could barely make eye contact and it appeared as though she was reluctant to say no but had no other choice. "...especially after today..." She muttered; then the truth set in and I had to acquiesce.

"Did I do something wrong, Mumma?" Georgiana frowned.

"No, poppet..." Temperance ran her hand through Georgiana's hair.

"How about if we take them to Tatton Park and they can run around and look at the squirrels?" I interrupted with a suggestion; I didn't want to disappoint my little girl. "We can go get Hen and Bet on the way..."

"When it is a bit milder, perhaps..." Temperance was firm in her reply, her disposition committed to quelling any opposition from me.

Georgiana looked demoralised. "Hayley is shy and she joined football to make friends. She doesn't have many..." Georgiana's empathy and sensitivity were on full display. "I want to be her friend..." tears gathered in her eyes. "...can I stay in touch with her?"

Temperance smiled and stroked Georgiana's cheek. "Of course, you can..." A tear trickled from Temperance's eye down to the ground. Georgie scurried over toward Hayley with a beaming smile returning to her face.

"Don't run off so quick." Temperance yelled as she watched Georgiana scamper across the field.

"Sorry, Mum!" Georgie yelled back.

"I admire her vigour but she has a tendency to take off without even thinking about where is she going." Temperance placed her hand on her hip. We both watched as Georgie seemed excited to interact with her new friend.

"Are you sure, you don't want to re-consider?"

Temperance glanced down at the grass, a mix of shame, guilt, and sorrow had visibly consumed her. "I don't wish to discourage our daughter from socialising but you know what could happen..." Temperance looked up at me. "...she and this lass become more intimate and they start to share things with each other..."

"Isn't that the point, Temp?"

"Normally, yes...but..." Temperance turned her back and clenched her fist gently, the sun cascaded against her back. "...it's a different can of worms now..."

"You are worried that she will..."

"Yes." Temperance nodded to confirm what I was thinking, she had an uncanny way of finishing my sentences. We both did, our entire romance was marked by our ability to live in each other's minds.

"If you never shared your secret with me..." I placed my hand on her shoulder "...would we have her?" I motioned my head toward Georgiana who was in merriment and conversation with Hayley, her parents very much engaging with our youngest daughter. "Or Henrietta; or Elizabeth?" I took her hands into mine. "...would we have found each other?"

Temperance's eyelashes dropped in acknowledgment of my point. "It's different when you have children though, things can get far messier." Temperance looked out at Georgiana who waved back, Hayley joining her in the routine. "We are one nodding dog moment away from an unfathomable commotion." Temperance waved back with a smile.

"I thought that isolation isn't what you wanted for them?" I gazed up at the sky for a moment to see a passing jet streaking through the blue, the passengers drifting onward to a destination unsure of what perhaps they were even flying over. "I recall you saying you wouldn't wish that meagreness upon anyone..."

"It's to keep them safe, surely you understand that?" Temperance's answer was short and direct.

"I guess I let it go with Henrietta and Elizabeth because they always had each other but Gee is a few years younger...."

"And Georgiana will always have her big sisters too..." Temperance interjected.

"So, you are telling me that our girls are never supposed to be friends with anyone except themselves and us?"

"That's not what I am saying..." Temperance sighed.

"Then please enlighten me..."

"Very well, let's imagine for a moment that we take them to Tatton Park and invite Hayley over for tea. All goes well, right?"

I nodded.

"You and I can do our best to keep things under wraps but Elizabeth has a way of..."

"So, we give Hen and Bet a heads up that we have a guest..." I ran my fingers against the scruff on my cheek. "...they'll know the deal."

Temperance had clearly rehearsed and analysed every conceivable scenario as her responses were quick and comprehensive.

"What if one day Georgiana brings Hayley over unexpectedly?" A smile broke on Temperance's face. "She is an impulsive child and consumed by her curiosity..."

"We tell her to check with us first..." I let go of one of her hands to erect it upward to raise the point. "...which should be the case anyhow..."

"What if she tells Hayley that she is extraordinarily gifted and reveals the origins of these talents back to me?" Temperance's eyes grew larger. "What if she performs an exhibition, in her pink singlet, electricity at her fingertips, and all..."

"You sound like me now with the what ifs?" I delivered an untimely joke which didn't elicit a smile from Temp.

"Overthinking has merit on occasion." Her reply was cool and determined.

"Didn't you make her costumes?" I shrugged my shoulder. "...didn't you give her said pink singlet and lilac cape too?"

Temperance bit her lip, peering out of the side of her eye.

"She was enthralled by it and you stimulated her, right?"

"Yes, but this is different." Temperance re-established eye contact. "...this can lead to all sorts of possibilities that can utterly spiral." Temperance looked over at the girls who were now standing with her parents, both girls were waving us over. "I..." She gulped. "...we could be exposed..."

"Unless you decide to go all Incredible Temperance, throw on the old lilac and heliotrope yourself, and take Hayley with you to stop a robbery at a convenience store, I think she would think that any sensational tales that Georgiana tells her will just be Gee telling grand stories about her mother. She may the same about her mom for all we know."

Temperance fixed her attention on Georgiana.

"We can tell Gee to be mindful of what she does..."

Temperance bent her eyes down to pooh-pooh the notion as if it was more preposterous than anything previously discussed. "Conversation to be continued..." She took my hand and led me towards the pitch in the direction of Hayley and her parents. "We don't want to be rude..."

IX.

I stared into a drawer filled with a medley of ties—colours, patterns, and designs all blending together, unsure of which one to choose. I struggled with this whole notoriety thing, I was happy just for people to read my art and enjoy it, that's all I could hope for; however now, I was receiving an award in recognition of my work. My thoughts pivoted when I heard Henrietta and Elizabeth giggling, followed by Georgiana singing the chorus to *The Christian Life* by The Byrds. I placed my hand to my head and held back laughing, the girl had a way of being a riot even when she wasn't trying it.

My beloved entered the room wearing a lemon lace-bustier dress with short white sleeves that hugged her hourglass frame. Her hair fell down her chest toward her bust and back, tucked beneath a white floral hat with a purple violet. Her satin yellow skirt flowed around her hips toward the ground, accentuating her bell shape.

"Nearly time to go." She smiled at me. "I am taller than you, now." Temperance stood on her tippy-toes and drew her hand across over my forehead. "Three-inch heels will do the trick." She flicked her hat on the bed.

"If you won't wear the hat, I will." I winked at her.

"I will do, don't you worry." She took my hand and looked up at me. "To be fair, it would look better on you."

"Impossible..." I locked my eyes on hers. The blue of her irises burst with passion until she pressed her flips to mine. I grabbed her cheeks as I kissed her back; she bit down on my lip as we engaged deeper. I put my arms around her waist and she forced herself against mine. My beloved and I wrapped each other in our arms and fell upon the mattress, my hands swimming up her thighs as she gripped the back of my suit jacket. My hands soon followed up to her bosom as we kissed more, Temperance placed her hands on my backside and squeezed, as I massaged her bust further. She grinded against me further as I continued to grope her until she gasped and raised her hand.

"We should stop." She exhaled and I clutched the duvet hard, trying to control my urges. I took a deep breath and raised myself back off the bed. "We won't make it to the ceremony, at this rate..." Temperance sat up and brushed off her dress before I extended my hand to assist her to her feet.

"You do look stunning in that dress..." I smiled at her and took her hands. "...you look like a queen from a fairy tale."

"Cheers, Plum but I am your queen, my king..." She glowed with affection. "And as you are well aware, I cannot resist you when you are in a suit and tie." Temperance picked her hat up off the bed. "I know you fancy me in this dress, so that is why I wore it." She looked down at her white high-heels. "Just as I did when you were nominated Lieutenant, Lieutenant." She batted her eyebrows upon the second mention of the word.

"As you do."

"As you do." Temperance bantered back.

"As you do." I chuckled and gave her a peck on the lips before I reached into the closet to grab a red tie. I held it up to the sky blue/grey stripe tie I already wore.

She ran her hands against the collar to remove any creases and under my collar. "This one..." She removed a yellow tie from the closet. "...we can match." Temperance giggled. "Give us your collar...."

"Do you think Georgie will be alright will all of this?

Temperance removed my tie. "Presumably..."

"She can be quite vocal when she is in public." I squinted. "...it's because she gets overwhelmed like Elizabeth does."

"I'll place Georgeanne on my lap..." In record time, Temperance through a knot around the tie she selected. "Bubble and Squeak being there will be a great help..." Temperance pulled through the tie. "...not that they would miss this for the world, otherwise..." She clapped her hands. "There you are." Temperance ran her hands to my shoulder. "You look splendid, my love."

"Thank you, Mama." I kissed her cheek.

"My pleasure." Temperance glowed as her eyes watered up. "The girls and I are all very proud of you, we love you dearly." She smiled. "...I am so happy that your talent is recognised and that we all get to be there for it."

"I want you to read this before everyone else hears it..." I plucked three pieces of paper from the desk and handed it to Temperance.

Temperance read the first few lines and flipped another page. "It's your speech..."

I nodded.

"But I want you to read what I wrote about..."

Her eyes wandered and darted across all different places on the pages. Her brows raised and furrowed. "It seems that this entire composition is about me..." She looked over at me. "Read it to me, please...." I smiled. "...to be fair I am probably going to ad-lib most of it as you know I will get deeper into it." I drew to her shoulder and looked down at the speech.

"I am honoured to receive this award but think it would be unfair to accept it. This distinction is The Lord's and to Him should be the glory, He has been there for me every step of the way and I can never thank Him enough. He has been my rampart and my fortress through distress and through his mercies I stand before you today. I would also like to express my gratitude for His blessing me with a wife who deserves this honour more than I do. Indeed, Temperance inspired the story but she inspires me even now. From pillar to post, this is all her own enterprise. On the day I met her, she changed my life forever. As soon as I encountered her, I knew then and there, that she was my future. And from that point, she has been there to support me and help me confront my demons. And whilst I have endeavoured to do the same for her, my wife's might and majesty is far greater than mine. Let's call it what she really is: a heroine. Temperance is my heroine, as much as she is our daughter's.

She has endured far more than I could imagine and still carries herself with dignity, class, gentleness, and great strength. She sets an example in the littlest of things that are not only imparted upon our daughters but also upon me. Indeed, my wife is my best friend; she is my lover; she is my heart and my queen; she has sacrificed so much to enable me to pursue this ambition and she was the one who encouraged me to go after it even when I was unsure, perhaps even against my own will. My beloved sent out the queries, pitched my books to publishers, and publicised my works unbeknownst to me. As I said from beginning to end, she was there every step of the way and never faltered or took a step back. She was persistent and consistent, all the while sewing all the threads to keep our household together. She drives our family and I do not wish to speak of me today but instead share with you why she inspires novels and who is the woman that fosters the inspiration. The words cannot accurately convey all and the novel is only a preview into who Temperance is, only providing a brief glimpse into the magnificence and beauty that she is and possesses. I consider myself most fortunate and blessed to have her as a partner in life, and to observe her greatness in the subtlest of daily activities. Everything I had to endure and undertake to lead me to her was worth it and all the challenges we face do not compare to the love we share together. Temperance is my wife and a mother to the three greatest loves of both our lives: Henrietta, Elizabeth, and Georgiana, but she is also a talented nurse, teacher, mentor, friend, lover of animals, singer, songstress, gymnast, and she even has a knack for the sciences. Her understanding of thermodynamics is astonishing." She chuckled and waved the paper for a moment.

"That's lovely."

"There is more." I put my hands behind my back.

She re-configured her sights onto where she had left off. "...Temperance is also an angel who has blessed my soul. She has the talent to make everything better for those who surround her and do so with the utmost modesty, humility, and grace. As beautiful as she is, dressed up for this occasion, that is only a reflection of the person underneath the skin. Her beauty cannot be captured in words nor can my love for her be conveyed in sentences." Temperance's eyes welled up with tears. "What beautiful words..."

"None of this would have happened without you." I put my hands on her shoulder. "thank you." I pulled her in and embraced her. "For everything."

THE WHOLE RIDE HOME, Temperance was quiet as she looked out the window, glancing at all the trees as they passed by. I kept asking her if she was alright but she insisted that she wanted to retire from all the bustle of the day's events. However, when Hootie and the Blowfish's *Time* came on over the radio, I noticed certain lyrics seemed to invoke a reaction even if Temperance tried to hide it. I could see in the reflection of her in the window that tears were slowly descending down her face, her eyes were lost in a sea of melancholy and wistfulness. I attempted to console her but it was obvious she was trying to conceal her emotions from everyone, growing defensive, and assuring all that she was fine and 'rather fatigued'.

We arrived home and stepped into Sycamore Grove, Georgiana leading the way as she twirled and skipped about. Henrietta and Elizabeth followed, placing their gloves or hats on the side table before they marched onto the kitchen and the kettle, most notably. Temperance followed more sluggishly, followed by me shutting the door behind her.

As I took off my shoes, Temperance put her hands together and hunched her shoulders. Her pink scarf was still around her neck and down her back, as she looked into the dark front room. Temperance sauntered forward and sat on the couch, her hands still together as she placed them on her knees.

I walked into the front room and turned on the lamp beside her. She remained still and unfazed by the change in lighting, her eyes locked on the television but not actually looking at it. She was deep in thought and lost in whatever it was she fixated upon.

"My dear..."

She looked up at me briefly and said nothing.

"What's wrong?"

She shook her head briefly and expressionless.

I heard the girls laughing in the kitchen as the kettle hissed. The clacks of mugs and chatter filled the air. I peered back to focus on what they were doing but Temperance once again looked forward. It reminded me of when we were in Telford right after we married, consumed by some distant event that had since descended all around her.

Georgiana sprinted out of the kitchen, her long strawberry blonde hair trailing behind her as her maroon sweater blurred by with her blue skirt. Her white socks and pink shoes were the most distinctive features as she ran to the stairs. Georgie giggled as two mugs pressed against the worktops and two sets of footsteps followed. Elizabeth was followed by Henrietta.

"Girls..." I looked at Georgiana and then Bet and Hetta who passed in a blur of houndstooth and pink. "Let's slow it down please..." Georgiana had already gone up the steps whilst Henrietta and Elizabeth slowed as they gripped the handrail to follow their little sister.

"We're playing flash tag, Papa." Hetta exclaimed as she passed by.

Temperance's head pivoted when she heard the word flash tag. I was waiting for her to double down on the warning, but she only appeared mystified when she glanced at Henrietta. Hetta admittedly arched her eyebrows anticipating her mother guiding her actions which never came.

"And we can't let Giggle get away." Bet charged up the steps into the corridor.

Temperance looked back at the television again.

"Please be careful, ladies." I yelled up the steps.

"Yes, Papa!" A collection of Henrietta's and Elizabeth's voices echoed down the staircase.

I walked into the front room and sat beside Temperance, still unmoved or the least bit jostled by my presence or the girls' horseplay. Their footsteps echoed spread across the ceiling on occasion, a faint laugh or giggle reverberating through the carpet and floorboards down to join us.

"I cannot tell you how delighted I am that you received distinction for your work. I feel for you in such a way and I was overjoyed to be there." She sat back. "But I must confess, I am terribly envious of you." Her eyes finally wandered over toward the fireplace, a blue butterfly hairclip sat on the mantle twinkling in the moonbeam that came through the window.

"I was great once..." She looked down. "...some dare say I was incredible..."

"You still are..." I smiled at her and patted her thigh. "...I hope I made that abundantly clear in the speech..." I waved my hand around the room. "...though I do understand Georgie kept interrupting it when she was screaming Daddy, Daddy, Daddy and hopping up and down on your lap as she clapped her hands." I chuckled at the sweet affectations of our youngest daughter. Temperance however wasn't amused and appeared marooned in her own thoughts.

She drew her hand to her chin. "I wanted to be everything...." Tears filled her eyes and she started to sniffle. "But I am nothing..." She cried into her hands. My heart broke at hearing such overtures. I threw my arms around her but she didn't respond, she was immersed in her woe and tears. I could feel the warmth of tears drop onto my wrists.

"That's not true, my love." I could smell the salt of her teardrops. "Everything you see around us is because of you." I rested my head against her. "You are the one that's the voice of reason and puts everything right."

"Perhaps the roles have truly changed in more ways than one." She sobbed.

"Mama, as I have told you." I closed my eyes and listened to her breath. "Our daughters." I rubbed her rib. "The novel." I rested my head against her. "Why we were there today." I spoke softly. "All thanks to you." I held her as she trembled, my eyes started to fill with tears. "You inspired me and saw things in me that I could never see in myself."

Finally, I felt her hands pressed against my arm in a feeble attempt to hug me. She wanted to embrace me with the same love and affection as I had so tenderly, but she was filled with lament as if she had failed.

"Our girls are great women because they have you to follow." I held her tighter. "I am a better man because of you."

She sniffled and cried.

"Your achievements are not anchored to some arbitrary award. Your accomplishments are far greater! They span many centuries and generations." A smile beamed to my face, bubbling through my stomach. I had always wanted to make it clear to my beloved that for me it was always truly an honour to be in her presence.

"I don't know anyone who can say that..."

"It's all forgotten now." Temperance lifted her head from burrowing into my chest. "Written in the annals of yesteryear." She swiped away a tear and cleared her throat. "Our daughters only have stories of their mother." Temperance looked up the steps when she heard Georgiana say "*You're it!*".

"They've seen their father perform unbelievable feats. But imagine if they had seen me when I was in St. Bride's." Temperance sniffled and I handed her a tissue. "They would look at me differently." She dabbed her nostril. "As they have looked at you today and many other moments preceding..." Temperance looked away. "As others once did with me..." She looked back in my direction. "To our daughters, I am the one who leads their lessons, teaches them how to fold their washing, and do interesting tricks to entertain them."

It was a concern of mine that followed me for a while now, I knew Temperance over the span of many years would grow tired of being a homemaker. The woman has such passion and a desire to explore new things and stimulate her mind. Her intelligence is far greater than mine and her brain had to constantly be fed. Nevertheless, I wanted to reassure her that she was extraordinary even if she felt she had become otherwise.

"Temp, my love, they've seen you do things that no one can do..." I stroked her cheek. "Anything I have ever done pales in comparison."

"Whereas, it's all confined within these very walls, never breaching the edge of our back garden." Temperance crossed her arms and pensively stared at her own reflection in the glare of the television screen.

"I thought you wanted that?"

"I am not sure what I desire, any more..."

X.

A sense of urgency overcame Georgiana. Her blue eyes stared up at the ceiling as her lungs rose and fell rapidly, each breath creasing and flattening her shiny leotard. Her hand pressed to her hip just over the belt, two knuckles against the heliotrope leather briefs. She snapped her fingers and the Georgia Bulldog jersey she was wearing covered her, though she could have easily picked it up off the floor and put it back on. She ran off the front room, her strawberry blonde hair flaring behind her as she ran off.

My beloved held our twin daughters, Elizabeth and Henrietta against her breasts and stroked the back of their heads as she pressed her cheek against the domes of her heads. Both girls' mahogany hair scattered across the silky and creamy complexion of Temperance's bust and the shiny lilac leotard she had tucked into her heliotrope leather leggings. She too had a matching belt to Georgiana's; boding a pink T buckle which coincided with Georgiana's pink G buckle. They had just finished horsing around but my beloved was so consumed by our daughters' that she held them close to her and shut her eyes, glowing with a joy and affection that could not be concealed, escaping in the form of a simple smile.

"Mummy!" Georgiana ran into the room, a stuffed animal in hand that I could not distinguish from the speed our baby girl appeared. "Look at what I have!"

Temperance opened her eyes and glanced down at a stuffed toy elephant that rested in Georgiana's arms. A look of alarm swept across her face, wiping away her previous solace. I too was haunted by what I saw, it was an artefact that was imperceptibly in Georgiana's possession.

"Is that Mister Ruffles?" I clutched her hand.

Temperance leered at me from the corner of her eyes and nodded softly. A silence descended upon the room until she snapped her fingers. Temperance had returned to the striped gown she was wearing before the instantaneous wardrobe change. My beloved knelt down to Georgie's eye level and left her hand just over the toy. It was as if she wanted to touch it but was afraid to do so.

"Where did you find this, Georgeanne?"

The question was topical. How could she have gotten her hands on such a thing? It would be impossible unless...

Two sets of knocks clanged against the front door prompting the hairs on my neck to rise. Temperance drew closer to me, her hands latched in me as I held her tightly. Georgiana dropped Mr. Ruffles on the couch and burrowed under my arm.

Another knock prompted Elizabeth and Henrietta to draw close, they were demure and elegant in cadence, nevertheless strong with intent.

"That must be her." Georgiana smiled at the door. I held my arm tightly around Georgiana's chest and her little fingers pressed over my wrists. Elizabeth, Henrietta, and Temperance's eyes were also fixed on the same object: the door. Their matching blue eyes all enlarged and dilated as their breaths filled the air. Then came another knock.

I lifted my arm over Georgiana and moved my arm from around Temperance.

"Girls, stay with your mom, please." I made my way to the door; Georgiana ran toward the window and waved with a smile. In a moment, she covered her face with her hands and scampered off.

"Who is it, Georgiana?" Henrietta whispered.

"Is it Nana?" Elizabeth followed up with an intonation of excitement in her voice.

I reached for the door handle and opened it. Before me, outside stood a woman with whitish, blonde hair, and piercing blue eyes. Her eyes dilated when I opened the door, they had an eerie resemblance to my beloved; with the same intrigue; assertiveness; and inquisitiveness. She wore a yellow lycra tank top tucked into a long red skirt. Her hair was tucked behind a pink headband doffed with carnations and chrysanthemums. The woman had a red scarf around her neck and held a box in her hand.

"Hello, Maam. Can I help you?"

Temperance peered out from the kitchen with all three of our daughters standing beside her. Hetta and Bet eyed the visitor who smiled pleasantly at them.

"Is this the Lee residence?" She glanced down at the box. "House Name Sycamore Grove, Slade Lane, Goostrey, yes?" She smiled at me. "I have a parcel for you."

I looked beyond the gate to the lane and the green field that stood beyond it. There was no red Royal Mail van parked on the side, as it normally was.

"Thank you, Madame, it's just that Sally normally..."

Before I could finish my statement about our usual postwoman leaving parcels on the other side of the gate, the woman interrupted my remarks with a playful gest.

"You are not from around Cheshire, are you?" She chuckled. "I know who you are...."

"I am sorry?"

Temperance and the woman made eye contact for the first time, it seemed to prompt her to step forward instead of retreating.

"You are that writer from New York, you did a reading on The Moor, last summer…" She extended the parcel toward me. "…I was in attendance and recall your work in particular. It spoke to me…"

"I appreciate that very much, that's extremely kind of you." I opened my hand to receive the box. "I apologise for being short, madame but you don't look like someone that works for the Royal Mail…"

"Do I not?"

"Forgive me if I am forward but the next house is about half a mile that way." I pointed. "And I feel compelled to ask you, where is your van?"

"Do you reckon I look the way I do by motoring everywhere?" The woman winked.

"Good afternoon." Temperance hooked my arm and greeted with a nod.

"Just the lass, I was looking for." She smiled. "Missus Lee?"

Temperance looked down at the box. "…And you are?"

"A courier with a parcel for you." She smirked. "Though your husband doesn't take me for one that works for the post office.

"I can't recall placing an order by post." Temperance squinted. "Are you sure it's not for my husband as it is his birthday today…"

"Happy birthday." She smiled politely and glanced down at the envelope. "No, it's marked for you." She moved her chin up. "Temperance, right?"

My beloved turned her head to me, subtle in how she refused to identify herself whilst hoping I would provide answers but I was as confused as her. "Did you send me a parcel…?" She whispered. I glanced back at the mailwoman who was studying Temperance's every move. "No." I placed my hand around her back. "Don't worry though, I will take care of this…" I spoke lowly.

We both looked at Henrietta and Elizabeth who both had a hand on Georgiana's shoulder. Hetta's blue eyes were imbued with concern whilst Bet's blue eyes were ripe with intrigue.

"Sweetings..." Temperance peered back into the house. "Do any of you know anything about this?"

When I looked back at them, all three shook their heads in unison afraid of what the ramifications may be if they had admitted to such a thing although they genuinely looked as surprised as my beloved.

"You didn't click any buttons on the computer in error?"

They responded just as they had to the previous question.

"Perhaps it's an old friend or distant relative?" The woman's voice spoke over our muffled chatter. My beloved turned back and politely smiled at the woman, an effort to gloss over any sense of being startled or surprised. "If I may comment, Temperance is certainly a nostalgic given name. I always fancied my mother's name." The woman smiled casually. "...she is called Abbie..." My beloved tensed as she locked eyes with the woman. "...as in Abigail..."

The two kept their stare locked on one another until Temperance broke the silence "...I am sorry, have we met before?"

"Mummy!" Georgie called out to her. Temperance looked inside. "Give us a moment, treacle."

"I feel as though I know so much about you already..." She stared at Temperance. "...I have heard so many things about you...." She raised her hand and turned her attention toward me "...I was telling your husband that I was at his reading last summer." A smile broke from her face. "...he spoke so affectionately of you..."

"Perchance, we saw each other there." Temperance glared at the stranger.

"Perhaps...." The woman looked out toward the road. "or there may be a punter's chance that we have a mutual friend in the area..."

"I doubt that to be the case..." My beloved bit her lip.

"It's not as big of a world as you fancy it to be, Missus Lee." The woman volleyed.

"I feel as I have seen you elsewhere...." Temperance's eyes locked in on her.

"I don't suppose you hang around graveyards, do you?" The woman shrugged her shoulders, Temperance bowed her eyebrows. "...I heard it can be a bit dead there..."

The comment prompted me to shoot a steely gaze on this strange woman. Before I could do any further arithmetic as to what was going on, she fixed her smile on Temperance with a clear desire to bring the conversation back to a pleasant space with an awkward and rather flimsy joke.

"So, he wrote the novel about you, did he?"

I placed my arm around her waist.

"I just wanted to say that it is incredible to see the woman that inspired such art in the flesh ..." She stressed the word incredible but Temperance did not react to it. It seemed to go over her head while I detected a deeper meaning to the delivery. However, I could have very well been hypervigilant since minutes ago Georgiana was describing someone who knew of my beloved's previous exploits.

The woman attempted to hand the parcel to Temperance who placed one hand on the edge of the box with reluctance. "What's in here?"

"I don't wish to undermine the quality of that question but that is the first silly thing you have said this afternoon..." She chuckled. "It would be prohibited under Royal Mail protocol for me to open that parcel and examine its contents. However, I can assure you that it passed all of our safety checks."

Temperance appeared haunted by the presence of the parcel as if whatever was in the box had uncovered what she was trying to keep within.

"...You will have to forgive me, miss." Temperance sighed. "...I was caught out by how you resemble my late mother; she was called Abigail as well."

The woman kept her gaze on Temperance unmoved by her remarks. An awkward silence and tension started to build again.

"I don't wish to be a skilamalink..." Temperance feigned a smile with a nervous laugh; the mention of the term prompted an immediate response from this mysterious postwoman.

"Now there is a word that hasn't been said since Queen Victoria's reign." Her tone of voice once again had an intonation of menace. "But I do not wish to suggestionise that you or I would know about such a time."

Temperance and her locked eyes again. Any agitation that had left my wife soon returned in a hurry. The tact of the wording and the nature of her inquiries certainly seemed deliberate and intentional.

"I reckon if you and I got to know each other a bit more, you'd think I'd be fit for a character from a Jane Austen novel..." The woman giggled and rolled her eyes. "...both literally and metaphorically speaking..."

"I wouldn't rush to any conclusions since I am not thoroughly acquainted with you."

"That can change." The woman smiled. "After all, I feel as if I learned so much about you, Miss Lee."

"Missus Lee..." Temperance corrected her with a stern tone of voice.

"Apologies." The woman put her hand behind her back.

"And what are you called?"

"I am called Triphy..." She grinned. "...it's short for Tryphena..."

"Tryphena, you say?" My beloved took the box. "That's jolly Elizabethan..." My beloved responded with a smugness, sending a signal to this unknown visitor that her presence had become irksome and that her domain had been impinged upon. I stood by my wife's side, following her lead but ready to intervene at any moment should the conversation turn into a confrontation. There was, after all, a weird tension in the air between Triphy and Tempie that seemed as if it had been building for centuries though they had just met. Though they never encountered each other, it seemed as if they were bound by some sort of weird happenstance. In many ways, Triphy looked like Temperance and even sounded like her. Her build was nearly identical, as was her complexion, and even her mannerisms; it was as if they were long-lost sisters, it was startling, to put it mildly.

I glanced down at Triphy's wrists and noticed they were soaked. It reminded me of Henrietta when she was younger and learning about her abilities to control water. However, Triphy had been walking and it was quite a muggy day....

"...Poppets, can one of you take this in?" My beloved looked back inside with the box under her arm.

"Yes, Mummy." Henrietta came forward to take the package, her cream-coloured blouse glowed in the sunlight until she withdrew to the shadowy front room.

"Poppet." She simpered as batted her eyebrows.

"Thank you, my dear." Temperance shot a brief smile at Henrietta as she took my hand.

"Mummy!" Georgiana's voice charged through the hall as she scurried toward the door.

"I'll be right there, Giggle." Temperance blocked the door and leaned her hand against the frame. "Elizabeth, can you grab her please?"

Georgiana had nearly made it to the opening and made eye contact with Triphy. Before she could say anything, Elizabeth came behind her and got her arms around her.

"Georgie-Anne." Bet gently pulled her back two steps. "Come with me, darling." Elizabeth peered over at Triphy and smiled at my beloved. "You know how this one is..." She peered again at Triphy before smirking at Temp. "Mischievous like our mother..." Elizabeth pinched Temp's rear playfully, clearly done to make her mother laugh.

"You little brat." Temperance broke a smile and smacked Elizabeth's butt as she walked away with Georgiana's hand in hers. Bet let out a yelp, embellishing as she held her glute with a look of shock on her face as she laughed.

"I'm going to get you later..." Elizabeth threw her hair back over her white blouse.

"You can give it your best go..." Temperance chuckled and stuck out her tongue, appearing more relaxed as she turned her attention back to our visitor. "Triphy, I apologise if I was cross with you, I was just aghast by this abrupt surprise."

"No injury given." She put both her hands behind her back.

"Thank you for calling, it's a pleasure to have met you."

"You are quite welcome, Lady Lee." Triphy nodded. "I hope to see you and your girls again, soon."

"Thanks again." I took a step to follow my wife in.

"Three girls, aye?"

"That's right." I turned back to see Triphy with her hand on her hip.

"I reckon you two are shaggin' like rabbits..."

"What?" I raised my eyebrows at Triphy who shook her head.

"Never mind me, I think out loud at times."

"Be careful with that..." I grabbed the door handle as a queue to transition to the end of the conversation. "It may piss off the wrong person...."

"But not you though?" She raised her eyebrows.

"Normally no, but please be mindful of what you say around my wife and my daughters."

"Very well." She shrugged her shoulders. "Has anyone told you before that your missus and daughters look like sisters?" Triphy smiled and I didn't respond, she grew timid and worrisome. "...to that end, both of you have aged well..."

"Thanks..." I jostled the door to start closing it, hoping it would once again prompt Triphy to move along.

"And what are they called?"

"Henrietta and Elizabeth are the twins. Georgiana is the baby."

"Elizabeth..." Triphy looked down and glanced upward as if she was looking inside to see Temperance again "...I am rather fond of it as that's my mother's middle name..."

The name Abigail Elizabeth Lee crossed my mind in that instant; Temperance's mother's name in full. I found it ironic considering we were just talking about her before this unplanned call from Triphy transpired.

"Albeit, I've always adored my surname most of all." Triphy laughed and made her way toward the gate. She undid her scarf, exposing the nape of her neck along with the folds in her back and shoulder muscles. Triphy turned and smiled at me as she ran her scarf down toward her bust. "It's Taylor, in case you were interested..." She yanked on her dress to expose more of what appeared to be a bodysuit until she tugged the skirt upward and stepped outside of the gate. "...but my maiden name is..." Triphy froze in place as she looked back to see Temperance's fingers lock in mine.

"Are you still out here, my love?"

My eyes darted into the cerulean blue of my beloved. She had a bright smile that concealed the concern that bulged through her irises. "Having a chin-wag with our new mate?" Temperance glared across at Triphy who shut the gate with a smile. She waved at

Temperance who waved back at her before she continued further down the lane into the secluded plains of Cheshire.

"What a peculiar woman."

"She was trying it on with you..." Temperance raised her eyebrows and glared down the road.

"I doubt that..." I shook my head and put my arm around her waist. "She knew we were married."

"She was blatant." Temperance's response was icy. "Flicking her daddles all over the show. "

"I don't know why she would even bother since she has no chance anyway." I kissed Temperance's head. "I am devoted to my queen." I wrapped my arms around my beloved and pressed my lips to hers.

"Regardless, I don't want to ever see her here again." Temperance stared at Triphy's figure vanished out of sight into the Cheshire countryside.

XI.

P rior to my retelling of that night terror, I hadn't written for yonks but it proved cathartic and thus I felt inclined to capture my feelings and reactions toward this mysterious parcel which consumed me with preoccupation. I descended the stairs and held the gleaming brass candleholder in my hand, its light casting flickering shadows on the walls. The house was quiet except for the occasional faint tapping of keys in the kitchen where my beloved was working on his computer. I plucked the parcel from the piano and examined it thoroughly: there was no return address on the back of the envelope.

I looked around the house for a brief moment to check no one else was stirring, then I stepped into the dining room. A window was open with a cold draught blowing in, briefly flickering the candles. I set the envelope on the table and the candleholder beside it on the table before making my way to the window. I peered out into the black night; no light was visible. The only sound was the whisper of leaves in the intermittent breeze.

I shut the window and ambled back to the table to take hold of the envelope. I opened it and reached inside to pull out a flimsy piece of laminated plastic containing a sepia-faded article dated to 16th of September, 1884. (My beloved's birthday) by the Illustrated Police News. Vertigo washed over me as I contemplated the passage of time. Reflecting on the date, the realisation struck me: my dearest wasn't even a thought then, he was still 103 years away from entering this world in a place across an ocean; our daughters wouldn't be born for *nearly 135 years later. Almost 150 years had gone by in a flash and I still remembered everything vividly.*

I looked over my shoulder in the direction of the kitchen beyond the slightly ajar door, did he send this? I glanced down to see a picture inserted of someone I recognised: Me. Below the black and white image of me in my leotard was the caption: The Incredible Temperance posing for spectators in Covent Garden after lifting record-breaking challenge bell. My eyes scanned upward to the title written on the clipping: Incredible Temperance Dazzles Audiences and Apprehends Child-mugger. Memories flooded back as I began to read:

"In a dashing display of athletic prowess and ethereal strength, the Incredible Temperance appeared before a mid-sized crowd on James Street outside the entrances of the marketplace. Clad in her signature lilac leotard, paired with a silver belt with a Pink T buckle, I.T. stood out amidst the sea of drab, everyday attire. Her outfit, a practical yet eye-catching ensemble, hugged her powerful frame, showcasing her toned muscles. She wore a long-flowing pink silk cape along with matching sturdy leather boots and fingerless gloves, her long auburn hair tied back to keep it out of her face. The costume, though visually striking, was designed for her feats of strength and heroism.

The crowd murmured in anticipation as she approached the bell, her demeanour calm and confident as she rubbed her defined arms and chiselled thighs with oil. With a determined look, Temperance threw off her cape, took a deep breath, bent her knees, and wrapped her hands around the handle of the bell.

Muscles straining, teeth gritted, and costume stretching, she slowly began to lift the enormous 70 kg weight. Her biceps bulged, and her legs tensed as she powered the bell upward. The crowd gasped in awe as she hoisted the bell above her head, holding it steady for a moment whilst posing with a smile before gently placing it back down. A thunderous applause erupted, cheers echoing through the square.

Temperance winked at child onlookers who were awe-struck by her uncanny exhibition of power."

A smile broke on my face and I looked back out into the front room, it must have been my Butterscotch who sent this after all, going through the trouble to surprise me and play it down to sweetly remind me of my previous triumphs all the while on a day we dedicated to him. I would expect nothing less of him to do something so thoughtful yet modest.

"As Incredible Temperance further acknowledged the applause with a gracious bow, her keen eyes caught sight of a commotion at the edge of the crowd. A young woman was struggling with a man who was trying to snatch her baby from her arms. Without hesitation, she sprang into action."

I was taken back to that day, remembering the scent of autumn lingering in the breeze amidst the warm and humid evening.

"Stop right there!" I commanded; my voice cut through the chatter of the bustling marketplace. A man halted in his tracks as I approached him, a slim menace in a hulking grey overcoat and flat-brimmed hat with navy trousers which were torn at the end of the pant legs. His hesitation enabled me to close the distance but he kept his grip tight around the baby wrapped in white linens.

I chased him through the crowd and though he was quick, I was faster. I sprung and leapt to intercept him, grabbing his arm and twisting it, forcing him to release the child.

"AAH!" the man yelped, dropping the baby safely into my waiting arms. I smoothly transferred the infant into my own protective embrace. My arms cradled the baby securely, as I quickly handed the baby back to its terrified mother. "Your baby is safe now," I assured with her a comforting smile. "Stay here, whilst I handle this."

The young mother, tears streaming down her rosy-cheeked face, nodded gratefully, clutching her child to her chest. One of her brown locks descended in between two of the baby's little fingers.

Turning my attention back to the would-be kidnapper, I saw the fear in his eyes. He tried to run until he was met by a wall of bobbies on the beat. He was cornered and drew a chain garrotte, moving toward me with the weapon to hand, but when he raised the chain (to perhaps use it as a whip to strike me instead of its primary method: strangulation) he was met with a swift, well-placed kick to his chest, which knocked him off the ground, sending the instrument free from his grasp as he crashed. Once sprawled out, he turned over and reached for the weapon which lay just beyond him, I acted quickly and pinned him down with a knee into his back, my strength making any resistance from him futile.

"You're not going anywhere," I applied an iron-clad grip around his collar with my knee still pressed into his back. He strained for the black steel chain but could not reach it. I plucked it from the cobbles and it jangled it in my grasp. The assailant threw his arms out, sighing in defeat.

Moments later, police officers arrived, having been alerted by the commotion.

"Up you go, mate." I lifted my knee and brought the offender to his feet. "Lads, this man tried to abduct that woman's baby." I handed him over to one of the officers who kept his sap to hand and pointed in the direction of the woman who shivered with her child in her arms.

One of the officers looked over at the mother; his black handlebar moustache twitched to acknowledge her.

"He was also carrying this on his person." I handed him the weapon. "Make sure he faces justice for his actions."

"A garrotter and a kidnapper, I see." His colleague applied the handcuffs. "We'll take it from here." The officer nodded at me and gripped the brim of his blue hat, his silver star was dull and scuffed with black markings. "Many thanks for your help, madame. We appreciate it as always."

"A privilege and a pleasure." I smiled and nodded once.

"Good show today too." He shot me a smile as he and the other officer led the criminal away.

"Cheers." I modestly nodded once more.

The young mother paced toward me with tears of gratitude descending from her blue eyes. "Thank you so much," she said, her voice trembling. "You saved my baby."

"Happy to be of service to you." I placed a hand on her shoulder. "Look after yourself and your little one."

All who bore witness erupted in applause. I nodded with a slight smile before I tried to slip away into the crowd. Emerging from the crowd was a smiling face that I recognised.

"You've saved the day again!" A young pre-adolescent boy ran toward me with his arms open. His teeth matched the colour of his long-sleeved undershirt. His brown eyes which matched his suspenders and corduroys glowed with admiration. He ran into my arms, my cheek resting over his wool cap. His head leaned into my sweaty bosom as his arms wrapped tight around my stomach and back.

"Anthony, I am so glad you are here." I held him tight until he moved his head back.

"Not to mention the impressive bell lifting." He clutched my pink cape in one of his hands. "How many times have you done that now? Three, four?" Anthony smiled at me with a playful glint in his eye.

"Oh, it's just another day at the office." I chuckled as I brushed a lock of hair away from my face. "Thank you for always cheering me on Ant, it means a lot."

"You make it look effortless." He looked at me up and down with an admiration that radiated from his eyes.

I grinned and puffed out her chest. "Well, what can I say?" I raised my eyebrows and replied casually. "It's all in the muscles," I quipped as I flexed for him playfully. Anthony gave my biceps a squeeze. "Right?" I raised my eyebrows and gave him a gentle nudge with my elbow and watched a smile unravel across his face as he put his arm around me, his hands pressing against my waist.

It was then that I felt all the stares of pedestrians who had never taken their eyes off me. I looked up to the windows above the storefronts, several opened with residents of all ages and sexes watching from above.

"Gosh, I didn't realise how much I don't like having all this attention on me." I leaned into Anthony and whispered to him.

"This may help you blend in then." Anthony threw my cape around me. "I picked this up off the ground after you leapt off the stage to stop that mugger." His hands made a bow with the front of the cloak. "Fit for a superheroine." He tied the bow and smiled at me, tapping my cheeks twice gently yet playfully.

"Huh" I gasped, opened my mouth, and bulged my eyes to appear shocked and surprised. "You are not supposed to hit a girl."

"I wasn't" He replied defensively, full of remorse. "I would never...."

"I am just winding you up..." My lips pressed against his cheek. "You have always been quite the gentleman." A smile returned to his face. "Fancy a meat pie?" I stroked the top of his head.

He nodded enthusiastically.

"Lovely." I put my hand around his back. "Missus Rutherford just opened a bakery on Long Acre, they are luscious."

Anthony placed his arm around my waist and kept close to me, his hands cleaving to my oblique as I kept my hand around his back, pressed to his shoulder. We continued through the busy

London street with the central market of Covent Garden and all the noise that came with it fading as we passed by rows of people who watched us walk on.

"You are not going to wear your costume in the bakery, are you?" Anthony bantered.

"What's wrong with my costume?" I exclaimed with mock offence and feigned a face of disappointment. "I think I look rather presentable." I gave him a slight playful tap on the shoulder, and he giggled.

"Missus Rutherford may say it's unsuitable dress for service."

"Well..." I stopped and rested my hands upon Anthony's bony shoulders before I bent down to eye level. "...fortunately, I can sort that with the snap of a finger!" I snapped my fingers and elicited another giggle from him. "Can't I?" I ran my fingers under his chin and he tee-heed, drawing close to me and pressing his head against my chest, his arms wrapping around me as his soft lips pressed against my warm flesh as I embraced him; the cape enveloped the both of us.

"You are all sweaty..." He teased as he wiped sweat from his lips, scrunching his nose.

"Oh, hush." I teased back. "I had a few things on the go, didn't I?"

He nodded with vehemence. "But you smell really nice." His eyes twinkled. "Like roses, actually..."

"I am delighted to hear so." I chuckled as his eyes also sparkled with amusement. When I turned my attention from Anthony toward the foot traffic of the street, my eyes stopped upon a woman who was about my height, standing in the midst of the crowd formed several rows back closer to the storefronts on the pavement. Her long dark auburn hair draped from beneath a black velvet bonnet with a white bow that wrapped around it. She was dressed in a matching gown that clung to her svelte and shapely figure. Her milky skin shined from the humidity; when she lifted her head, her eyes shined like beryl sapphire. Did my eyes deceive me? Was it Mother? I stood idle in the street, hypnotised by the sight. The woman made eye contact briefly and cracked a smile for a moment. My mouth opened but the words couldn't escape fast enough to say "Mummy!", caught in my throat from being overwhelmed at the sight. Two fingers tapped against my abdominals which jerked my eyes down to the source for an instant.

"Is everything alright, Tempie?" Anthony's inquisitive eyes looked up at me, his hands under my cape latched at my belt with his knuckles gently pressing into my side, as he waited for my response. When I looked back to where she stood, no one was there. I put my thumb below the corner of my lip and pressed my ring finger to my cheek, pondering how to address what I had seen and Anthony's question.

"I'm fine, Ant." I shook my head and smiled. "I thought I saw someone that I knew." I flicked out my cape and chuckled softly. "Goodness me, I am famished, shall we carry on?"

I wrapped my arm around him, and Anthony nodded with a smile, keeping his hand tight on my hip as we resumed walking. Glancing over my shoulder once more to where the woman had been, I hoped to see her again in the bustling crowd of James Street, but she had disappeared.

"Honey Bee?" My beloved's voice interrupted the flashback. I looked back at the door and didn't respond, looking back down at the article firm in my grip.

"Is everything alright?" His voice entered the room.

I shook myself from the reverie, still holding the article. "You can stop the pantomime and admit that you posted an impromptu gift to surprise me." A smile formed across my face. "It was awfully kind and sweet of you to make your birthday about me, as well."

"*I wish I sent it...*" His puzzled voice came closer. "*...but I would like to believe I would be a bit more creative about it.*" He chuckled with a hope I would do the same but I was unphased. I was consumed by the article, re-reading the headline and examining the font of the typed text.

"*I opened the parcel and there was an old newspaper clipping from my time in London...*"

A silence filled the room, it was ominous and ripe with confusion.

"*...from your date of birth oddly enough, when I performed a feat of strength.*" I looked out the window beyond the reflection of the candlelight into the dark night. "*It appears as if it has been preserved for nearly 150 years.*"

"*I have tried to find stuff like that about you before and it is very difficult to come across.*" He said.

I put the article back in the envelope. "*But who could do such a thing?*" The candles dimmed down momentarily as the image of my mother from that day long ago flashed before me. "*And why?*"

XII.

"Can you tell me when you are writing your next top-seller?" A voice called out to me. When I looked right, a hand extended toward me from an old friend I had not seen in a while.

"I thought that was you, mate, you've hardly changed a bit."

"Andy!" I reached my arms around his dark blue hooded sweatshirt. In one hand was a green ASDA bag and he reciprocated the embrace with his free hand. "Of course, I'd find you in a bookstore..."

His short brown hair descended over his forehead which wrinkled when he was engaged in something.

"How is the writing business treating you?"

"It goes well." He placed the bag down on the floor, beside his fresh white Adidas trainers which were partially covered by his grey denim jeans which clung to his husky frame. "My Amanda and I are on our twenty-first collection of poetry..."

"Wow..." I nodded in recognition.

"And yourself?"

I looked back at Temperance who was browsing the shelves, all three girls had hooked their arms, reminding me of the beauty found in the pastel brushstrokes in a Renoir painting. Temperance was clad in a pink day dress with a white sunhat, Henrietta in a sky-blue day dress and her hair down, Elizabeth in a white and red polka-dot blouse with a black skirt that hugged her figure, and Georgiana in a bright marigold dress with strawberry hair down over the back. In her many attempts to emulate her mother, she wore a white sunhat, as well.

"I have my muses." I smiled and turned back to him.

Andy looked over my shoulder in the direction of the girls, his eyebrows raising at the sight of my beloved. "Ah, so Temperance is with you?" He chuckled. "I should have known as you two have always been attached at the hip." Andy squinted in the direction of our daughters, unsure if they were with us.

Temperance smiled warmly as she walked over with Henrietta and Elizabeth flanking her on both sides and Georgiana trailing behind her. "Hello, Andy, you all right?" She let a slight curtsy. "It's lovely to see you again..."

"What is it that you two eat?" He appeared gobsmacked. "You look the same as the day you came around and told us you were married."

"My wife is a great cook so it's her food combined with good genes, I guess..."

"You are too kind, darling..." Temperance blushed as she kissed my cheek.

I placed my arm around her. "Always so modest." I gave her a quick peck on the lips and she smiled some more.

Before I could look back, Hetta had nestled up under my arm on my right side. Elizabeth joined her mother on her vacant side and Georgiana looked up at Andy and waved at him. He looked visibly perplexed at what he witnessed.

"Apologies, Andy." I rubbed Henrietta's back. "These are my daughters."

"Your daughters?" Andy scratched his head.

I nodded.

"All three of them?"

They all nodded in their own way, Georgiana being the most expressive of the bunch.

"Last time, I checked." I let out an untimely joke. "Bet?"

"Papa!" Bet scowled at me playfully and Georgie looked up and shook her head, not amused by my joke.

"Bad joke..." I smiled at each of them and glanced back at Andy. "These are my babies..."

"My goodness, I thought that these two were Temperance's sisters."

Henrietta and Elizabeth laughed at Andy's remark.

"As far as I am aware, I am an only child." Temperance chuckled; the gaze soon shifted upon her from our daughters whilst I laughed knowing she was building off my previous gaff. "Good joke?"

"Oh, my goodness." Bet rolled her eyes and put her hands on her hips. "That made Papa's joke actually funny." She shook her head at Temperance, the two always enjoyed joking around with each other.

"To be fair, we could pass for it..." Henrietta leaned into Temperance. "Mummy can be like our big sister at times to be fair." She smirked back at Elizabeth and batted her eyebrows to acknowledge her commentary.

"They are my sisters." Georgiana interjected enthusiastically and took hold of Hetta and Bet's fingers.

"My loves..." I looked left and right. "...this is my old friend Andy that I used to do a lot of writing with before I met Mommy."

They all nodded politely with a smile, including Georgiana.

"Please allow me to introduce you to our girls." I bent my hand toward Hetta. "This is Henrietta."

Hettie extended her hand to Andy. "Hetta, for short. It is a pleasure to meet you."

He took her hand and forced a smile to break up his bewilderment. "I've heard so much about you."

"All good things, I hope?" She smiled skittishly. Despite there being a room full of people, it was as if we were in our own bubble; or perhaps on some lonely country road with Andy stumbling across some antiquarian landmark that hadn't been seen for years. All the chatter in the room had gone silent around us.

"Your dad speaks so highly of your talents and gifts." Andy smiled. "He has always been quite complimentary of all three of you."

The girls all smiled at me.

"Hetta..." Andy raised his eyebrows and nodded. "That reminds me of a book, I read once..." He pressed his hands against his chin. "...but Hetta was the villain."

"Bubble?" A smile broke from Elizabeth. "Nah, she is as sweet as lemon curd, her." She waved her hands. "Villainy is more my department."

Hetta smiled at Bet.

"You can also call her Harriet, by the way..." Elizabeth winked over at Henrietta and stuck her tongue out. Henrietta's smile turned into a scowl.

"The one with the jokes is Elizabeth..."

"Bet..." She was far more composed in her response. "...It's wonderful to meet you."

"Elizabeth is a bit of a pistol..."

Everyone laughed.

"I take after my mother..." Elizabeth spoke at length. "...many thanks..."

"That much is true." I placed my hands upon Georgie's shoulders and she drew them closer around her neck, looking up at Andy with a wide smile. "And this is our youngest, Georgiana..."

"Hello, sir..."

"Well hello there, young lady..." Andy was taken back by Georgiana's cuteness. She had an innocence and purity about her that could never be undermined or overlooked even when she got up to mischief. "...she looks like a younger version of you, Temperance..."

Temperance gleamed at the notion and glanced down at our baby girl.

Despite the tension that was often alleviated with proper introductions, Andy appeared beleaguered and confused. It was as if he wasn't sure what he was seeing.

"So, there you have it..." I shot him a look that I hoped would offer some form of reassurance that what he was seeing was not an illusion or hallucination.

"Correct me if I am wrong, but they aren't much different in age, are they?" Andy pinched his lower lip with his thumb. "When I last spoke to you, they were so little..."

"You know how it goes man; they grow quick..." I rubbed Georgie's shoulder. "Gee will be like them before you know it..."

Andy didn't respond; his slacked jaw provided direct insight into what he was perceiving and thinking.

"It's been a while since we last spoke and the twins hit a rather unusually large growth spurt since then..."

Temperance, Henrietta, and Elizabeth all shared quick glances at each other; they were speaking their own surreptitious language, alerting each other to the inquisitiveness and interrogative nature of their new acquaintance. I could sense it from a mile away.

"And they inherited their beauty and grace from their mother..." I winked at all three of the girls who burst into smiles. "They certainly didn't get it from me."

"You are so self-deprecating, Papa." Hetta pressed her hand against my chest.

"Yea, Daddy!" Georgiana chirped. "Too self-depressing."

I laughed at Georgie's forwardness. "Depreciating, Jelly Bean!"

"Whoops!" She covered her mouth with both her hands. "Sorry!"

"So, let me understand this..." Andy's boot grazed against his shopping bag. "Temperance and you look unchanged whilst Henrietta and Elizabeth..."

"Please call me, Bet." She interjected.

"...Bet." Andy corrected himself "...look like they are approaching womanhood but are still children?"

Temperance looked at me and I back at her. Should we try to make a quick exit or attempt to resolve this inquiry? Since she didn't move her eyes toward the door, I chose the latter course.

"I've seen kids their age hit puberty early and they look adults." I threw my hand out. "They are going to adolescence, so that seems to be the case here."

"But the little one is only a few years younger and looks her age..." Andy clutched the handle of his bag harder.

"However, if you got to know Georgie some more, you would come to find that she is very mature for her age."

"Thank you, Daddy." Georgiana looked up at me and leaned back into me.

"You are welcome, sweetheart." I smiled back at her as I gazed downward toward her.

"I'd chalk it up to us sisters knowing how to doll ourselves up." Elizabeth giggled. "Cheers for that, Mumma..."

"We also have Mummy's agency." Hetta added.

"And her superpowers!" Georgie squealed.

Henrietta and Elizabeth's eyes gorged at the mention of it.

"Giggle has quite the keen imagination..." Henrietta smiled and made a face at Georgiana. Her little sister quickly gave a defensive look back, the words "I'm Sorry" written in her green eyes.

"Cheers, poppets. That's terribly kind of you." Temperance always had a way to keep things measured and classy, no matter what the situation.

"Could have fooled me, the three of you look like Irish triplets..." Andy leaned back for a moment and tilted his head to the side.

"Though I have no Irish in me, I assure you." Bet raised her hands.

Everyone laughed.

"I am surprised they haven't thought them two were your sisters-in-law?" Andy joked

"I've heard the whole brother-in-law thing before..." I stroked the back of Georgiana's head and ran it down her hair.

"He's not our brother, he's our Papa..." Georgiana smiled. "He takes care of us and he's always there to protect us and tells us he loves us."

Henrietta and Elizabeth glowed as they nodded in agreement.

"Daddy is too nice to be a brother..."

"Brother in Law, Giggle..."

"Same thing, Bubble..." Georgiana looked over her shoulder at Henrietta. "If he were a brother, we'd have to stop him from beating us up..." Gee flexed her arm "...which I would do..."

I gently coaxed Georgiana's arm downward.

"Papa would fight a dragon for us." Elizabeth smiled.

"Of course, I would, baby girl..." I smiled at her.

"Pity the dragon as that is when you see The Mongrel in the flesh..." Elizabeth rolled her eyes and everyone soon laughed thereafter, as she was referencing the performance work I was doing earlier in the store, which all of them came to join me and lend support. I looked around the bookstore at the various patrons browsing the shelves, delving into whatever world they wished to explore pondering what they were looking for and what they were hoping to escape. There is something about passing by strangers in a bookstore that always preoccupied me. A person you never met that has their own world, their own life, and their own problems, but like you looking for the answers in text from someone who may have lived over 100 years ago. There was something truly visceral and real about the experience.

"You've seen The Mongrel..." Henrietta feigned an accent and threw a playful jab of her own.

"Who is this you speak of?" Temperance leaned back at squinted at Hetta.

"Oh, come now, Mother..." Hetta smirked. "You are a part of the skit and Papa's split-personality balderdash won't take me for my sixpence..."

"I wasn't aware you had sixpence on you Bubble. Can you get us a drink then?" Temperance bantered.

"Aye." Bet leaned across as she chimed in. "I'll have a Sprite, ta."

"I do love their spirit..." Andy had a brief chuckle.

"They also get that from their Mom..." I glanced over at Temperance who subtly motioned her head towards the exit. "Anyways, we best get going. We've got a special day planned for the girls." I looked around at all three of them and moved my hands up from Georgiana's shoulders. "Andy, it's great to run into you, dude. I extended my hand to shake his hand again. "Send our best to Amanda, please..."

"I will do..." He took it. "It's lovely to meet your daughters, finally..."

"I am honoured that you met them." I stepped to the side.

"Let us not forget to bid our olive oil then." Temperance drew towards my side to let the girls go ahead toward the door.

"It was a pleasure to meet you." Henrietta smiled as she went past with a polite nod. Elizabeth flanked her and followed taking her hand. "In a bit."

"Salutations, sir..." Georgie skipped by as she took Elizabeth's hand.

"Good afternoon, Andy." Temperance bowed her head slightly as I cuffed her arm. We walked behind the three girls as we made our way toward the staircase down to the exit. As I glanced back over my shoulder, I saw Andy watching our every step. He was stunned and still unsure of what he saw. I could only imagine what would transpire if some more time had gone by and he came across us again, what would he start to think?

I waved goodbye one more time as I took hold of my wife's hand, remaining one step ahead of her as I descended the steps. Georgiana held my other hand and walked beside me, Henrietta and Elizabeth stepped down arm-in-arm behind them, I looked up at them to watch their steps downward as I reached for the door for them. I held the door open as my wife followed by Henrietta and Elizabeth stepped out into the bustle of South Manchester.

"Thank you, Papa." Henrietta took Elizabeth's hand whilst she smiled at me to acknowledge my holding the door for her. I followed them out with Georgiana's hand in mine as we re-joined Temperance. Henrietta and Elizabeth walked behind us as I walked closest to the street. Georgiana's hands now in both Temperance and mine.

As we traversed the pavement en route to our car, a grocers', café, and estate agents slugged by. Each premises carved out in the red-bricked Victorian buildings dated with a capstone carved from 1896.

"Younger than Mummy!" Georgiana pointed upward.

Henrietta and Elizabeth both laughed behind us. Temperance looked over her shoulder and shot them both a glare of contempt.

"Younger than our house though?" Elizabeth smirked.

"I think there was an error in the date, I was certain it was 19 next to the 96." Henrietta patted Temperance's shoulder and she reached her hand over Hetta's to press it against her. The car became visible parked down on our left. Georgiana pointed at it and winked at Temperance.

"Giggle..." She looked down at her sternly. Georgiana smiled and let go of my hand as she tugged Temperance's hand when she started to skip on the pavement. Temperance found amusement in our daughter's antics and thus went ahead toward the car.

"Gee!"

She stopped and looked back at me; her blue eyes paused on what I said next.

"Don't let go of my hand on a busy road, sweetheart."

"I am sorry, Papa." Her eyes were filled with remorse. "I was playing with Mummy..."

"That's fine, just remember to let go of either of our hands on a busy road..."

"But Papa, you know what I can do..."

"And as amazing as you are, it makes no difference to me." I raised my eyebrows. "Stay close to your Mother, okay?"

She nodded in agreement.

"That's my girl." I smiled at her and she smiled back.

We continued down the road toward the car, passing by a pub/restaurant which had a few punters standing outside enjoying the radiant day; cigarettes and beers in hand; laughs were a plenty. Footsteps followed by a racing shadow were the prelude to a mass latching to my back. Two legs wrapped around my ribs and an arm around my chest, followed by a giggle that belonged to Henrietta.

Instinctively, my hand reached back to make sure she didn't fall off of me. My daughter however was unaware of her own strength much like her mother on many occasions. Her arm wrapped around my neck and her bicep clamped against my chest with a pressure that reflected her might. Though she was a fully grown girl, she was acting as if she were four or five again.

"Goodness Hen, you are certainly not a little girl anymore."

"I just wanted a piggy-back ride for old times." She kissed my cheek and laughed. I smiled at the mention and once again assured she was secure. Elizabeth came up behind her and adjusted her dress to make sure it didn't ride up her.

"Thank you, Squeak."

"No worries, big sister." Bet tapped Hetta's backside playfully forcing a squeal from her. Elizabeth laughed briefly. "Can I have one next, Papa?"

"Of course, Bet." I laughed. "Hen, you got a hold of me?"

"Yes, Papa."

She intensified her grip.

"You are strong as an ox, Hetta."

"Well stop feeding me those biscuits with the gravy, then." She stuck out her tongue and spat some mist into my face. I started running with her and her giggling and laughing grew louder. It reminded me of when she was younger and I used to hold her on my shoulders to watch the trains go by at Acton Bridge railway station.

Temperance looked back when she saw that we weren't behind her and Georgiana. With Georgiana's hand in hers, she walked back in a straight line with a look of displeasure.

"Henrietta Anne Lee."

I stopped with Henrietta still on my back, both of us frozen at the authoritative disposition of Temperance who squinted her eyes.

"You are in public, Poppet..."

"And?" Henrietta strained to speak as she kept hold of me.

"Should you be jumping on your father's back when you are nearly a lady?"

"But I do when we are in the back garden."

"That is entirely different, sweet." Temperance shook her head and spoke in a softer tone.

"I wrestle with Papa all the time, Mumma." Georgiana looked up at her.

"You are still little, cherub..." She smiled at Georgie.

"What about you, Mumma?" Bet interjected. "You all over Papa in public, you never hold back..."

Temperance had lost her tongue for a moment, a brief smile flashed across her face. I looked over at Elizabeth and smiled at her, appreciating the quick wit in her response. Her pout broke into a smile when she caught me giving a slight nod.

"We're just having a bit of fun, darling." I spoke to break the silence and emerge as a voice of reason. I reached back and tickled Henrietta's rib to force a giggle from her. "Hey!" She started to tickle my neck in retaliation.

Temperance was about to say something but her attention diverted over to the restaurant where many of the punters had their attention upon us. Alarm filled her face.

"Bubble, get down please..."

Suddenly, I heard a "wheyyyy" from across the street, coming from a group of four men smoking outside a restaurant. I looked unsure of what was going on. Henrietta's dress had ridden up and her backside was out. Temperance and I plucked the dress and pulled it down.

"Awwww. Boooo"

The noises came from the restaurant from four men stood looking on across the street; I established eye contact with them and wouldn't take my eyes off of them. Quite frankly, I wanted to punch all four of them but was trying to maintain control of my temper in front of my wife and my daughters.

"This is what I was concerned about, my dear." Temperance brushed her dress and fixed her hair. "You don't want to be acting unruly out in public..." She ran her hand up and down Hetta's back.

"...it's ill-mannered; it lacks etiquette; and these sorts of things have a tendency to occur, as result."

Henrietta looked embarrassed as she looked down to the ground. Temperance's tone shifted when she saw Hetta's reaction. "Now they are completely out of order, over there..." Temperance stood in between the line of sight of Henrietta and whoever was across the street at the restaurant.

"Yes, they are..." I placed my arm around Henrietta; she said nothing but her face went red.

"It's okay, sweetheart." I kissed her forehead. "Bet..." I looked back at the four men across the street.

"Yes, Papa?

I placed the keys to the car in her hand. "Take your mother and your sisters to the car, please."

"Father?" Bet grabbed my wrist. "What are you going to do?"

"I'm just going to speak to them quick about their behaviour."

"Papa, it's fine..." Henrietta spoke to quell the tension. "Maybe they weren't even laughing at us."

"I know what they were doing, sweetheart."

"You don't need to do anything, Papa." Georgiana grabbed my hand.

"Let's carry on, Butterscotch." Temperance put her arms around Henrietta and Elizabeth. "I am equally unhappy but we are having a nice day together, let's carry on..." She extended her hand towards me. "It will worry the girls and they look up to you."

"That's why I need to do this, then." I looked at Henrietta then Elizabeth and down at Georgiana. "Every man should treat you with respect." I extended my hand against Henrietta's cheek and held the bottom of her chin. "And if they won't, I will remind them." I smiled at all three of them. "Georgie, go you with your mom and your sisters, okay?" I stroked the dome of her head.

Georgiana shook her head and clutched my hand harder; it wasn't an act of disobedience; it was a show of concern and affection.

"Papa, please don't." Henrietta grabbed my shirt. "It's not worth the bother."

"You are to me, sweetheart." I rubbed her cheek then I tapped Bet's nose. "All of you are so precious to me."

All three girls smiled. "Now go ahead to the car with Mom." I kissed them all on the head. "There won't be any trouble." I started across the street and glanced back at them once, they watched my every move with overwhelming scrutiny.

"MUMMA, WHAT DO WE DO?" Hetta looked up at me with concern in her eyes. I watched him go over the road and toward the steps. I didn't want him to get involved but he's always been so protective of me and the daughters, to deny him would be to not appreciate who he was.

"Bubble, don't worry." Elizabeth's voice interrupted. "Should it come to it, we have some tricks up our sleeve." Her free hand started to smoke as her eyes flashed red. A smile broke from Henrietta's face; Georgiana looked up at her older sister with a childish grin.

"Let's be sensible." I looked at all three of our daughters. "The last thing your father would want is us getting into mischief whilst he is present..."

"Does he know about the..." Henrietta raised her eyebrows to invoke what has been pressing on our minds for a while.

I shook my head. "Not yet..." My eyes scanned from Harriet to Ellie and back to Georgeanne. "There is an appropriate occasion for that."

"YO!" I PACED OVER TO the four men. One was bald with a big beer belly, wearing a blue collared shirt, the other was a younger guy wearing a white polo shirt and black pants, he was clean-shaven and had short black wavy hair. One left to go inside, the last was a red-haired middle-aged man with a black hooded sweatshirt, jeans, and work boots. He flicked his cigarette to the floor.

"You alright?" The bald one addressed me.

"Look I know you are all having a good time." My hand swept across the air. "...but do not catcall my daughter."

"Your daughter?" His glassy eyes narrowed; his lips softened as confusion replaced his bravado.

"Yes, my daughter!" I looked back over my shoulder and saw that my beloved and the girls took a few steps closer to the car but they were standing in a huddle observing the confrontation.

"I thought the little one was your daughter..."

"She is..."

"And the one on your back, I thought was your sister." The wavy-haired man took his pint glass to hand.

"It doesn't matter."

His yellow eyes dilated.

"That's no way to treat any woman."

"Look mate, I didn't come here for a lecture." The third man with the red hair, broader in build put a cigarette between his lips.

"And I am not here to give you one." I pointed at him. "...just don't do it." I raised my hand and swiped it across the air. The three of them all stared a hole in me, I knew a fight might be underway but I wasn't afraid of them, and they knew I was ready. "Alright then..." I turned my back and started to walk away. I let out a deep breath and descended the steps. As I looked both ways to cross the street, the voice of the bald man called out to me.

"Hey, mate, which one is your missus?" He looked over at his two companions before they all glanced at me.

"That's irrelevant."

"Honestly, I am a bit confused because they all look similar." He itched black rubble on the side of his cheek. "How old are they?"

The lad in the sweatshirt crossed his arms, the other two squinted over and took a sip of ales sweating in their mugs. The red-haired man snorted after taking a sip.

"Not old enough to be doing that." I pointed at the mugs, and each of their faces dropped. They were unsure of how to move forward from a mix of confusion, shame, and bewilderment. As I turned my back to once again cross, another comment was sent in my direction.

"So, what's it like living with all the Oestrogen?" The bald fellow spoke with a sardonic tone. "You don't want a son?"

The three laughed.

"That's a stupid question to ask." My eyes locked onto him. "...I wouldn't trade my daughters for anything in the world. It's not like I am going to miss out on going to the pub and getting drunk with them to cat-call an adolescent girl." Their laughs and smiles were gone; They were looking to provoke me but they failed miserably, each of them looked naked and ashamed.

Before this could go any further, I left them frozen, perplexed as to what they heard and saw.

Henrietta, Elizabeth, and Georgiana smiled warmly, waiting to greet me as I crossed the street. Temperance chuckled and shook her head.

"You see girls, I told you it'd be fine." I put my arms around Henrietta and Elizabeth's waists and they both leaned their heads into my shoulders. I kissed them both on their heads and then smiled at Temperance who gleamed at me. I winked back at Georgiana who winked at me first.

"No threats?" Hetta giggled.

"There was no need." I started walking towards the car. "They got the point." Temperance led the way with Georgiana on her hand.

Elizabeth looked over at me and arched your eyebrows until we had arrived at the car. I opened the door and extended my hand to help Henrietta into the car.

"Thank you, Daddy..." Henrietta kissed my cheek as she stepped in.

"Anything for you, my dear." I smiled at her and placed my hand around her back as she filed into the far window seat. Elizabeth leaned against me with her arms crossed.

"They didn't say anything I wouldn't approve of to you, did they?"

"No, Carrot. All is good, darling." I extended my hand to Georgiana.

"Because if they had the bloody cheek..." Her first curled until I placed one hand around her back.

"I appreciate it sweetheart, but we are good." I rubbed her back once and raised my eyebrow.

Georgiana threw her hand on her hip. "...and I was ready to throw on my cape and costume to help you..."

I laughed and picked up Georgiana. "It would have definitely made them think twice." I tapped her nose and she giggled. "...but everything is okay, baby girl. Thank you." I extended my hand to Bet.

"You haven't seen me in action yet, I would have suited up like Giggle and created a spectacle..."

"I never thought otherwise." I smirked. "You always have a way of directing traffic..."

"Cheeky git." She shoved me and got in the car laughing. "Weirdo, you are..."

"Thanks, Bet, I love you too." I shut the door behind her and made my way around to open the door for Temperance but she had already gone in and shut the door. I looked once over my shoulder at the three men who were then joined by their fourth companion. All stood vigil with pint glasses in hand, conversing no doubt about the affairs of the afternoon but glued to where they were standing. I opened the door and jumped into the car, fastening my seat belt and locking all the doors before we drove off.

XIII.

Watching Temperance rest her eyes filled my soul with joy and always etched a smile on my face no matter how tired, frustrated, or even sad I may become; it was peaceful. Her soft eyelashes fluttered with her gentle brown eyebrows furrowed upward, her lips shut as her hair fell behind her, her hand resting on my chest as her head fit perfectly across me. Under my arm, she appeared content and enjoying her reprieve. There were times I would watch her and she wasn't aware; there were times when I was around her and I couldn't breathe.

She appeared near-lifeless as she rested but then she would stir and she would slowly raise it, letting a subtle yawn before her eyes would open flooding with me a glimpse of skies and ocean, her irises shimmering like the sea.

"So much for painting today." Temperance put her hand in front of her mouth.

"It's nice just to have some time together." I stroked her arm. "We can put the star light on and look up at the ceiling and talk..."

Her eyes illuminated.

"It'll be like when we courting again."

She raised her head. "We don't have to collect them until five." Temperance pressed her lips gently against mine. "We can do that instead."

"Why paint, when I can kiss you all day?" I smiled at her and drew lips close to hers, and once again they locked together like a jigsaw. We enjoyed the kiss for a brief moment until I heard a knock in the kitchen and turned my head for a moment

"What was that?"

"Just a branch at the window, I reckon…" Her head turned and my eyes fixed on the blue butterfly hair clip inserted into her plait which reminded me of a wagon wheel.

I didn't think much of it and embraced Temperance, shutting my eyes for a moment and enjoying the tender moment with her. A smile filled my face holding her close to me and then I heard another rustle. Temperance moved her head this time as she clearly acknowledged the sound, as well.

I heard footsteps for a moment. Temperance raised her head, raising her finger over her lips. I saw a pink blur cross the steps and ascend to the landing until a small canister hit the carpet. I pointed at the kitchen and then the steps to my beloved, she nodded in agreement with my plan to foil whatever plot was unfolding. I slowly crept into the kitchen through it and back down the corridor, halting at the base of the steps. When I looked up there was no sign of anything, but I waited patiently, reaching down onto the floor to pluck a white lip gloss container. I made my way up the steps and heard feet patter down the corridor.

"You can come out, there is no use" I spoke at length and waited. Soon thereafter, Georgiana emerged clad in a variation of her "Super Georgiana" costume that she loved to wear. A pink sleeveless bodysuit with shiny spandex lilac briefs worn over them along with a belt like her Mum's and her hair down. A lilac silk cape flowed behind her long strawberry-blonde hair. Her green eyes dilated at the sight of me like she had been caught stealing or found out.

"What is it, my love?"

"Georgiana…" I looked over at Temperance for a moment and then turned to my youngest. "What are you doing sweetheart? You are supposed to be with your sisters." Concern filled me. "Where are they?"

"Bets told me to get her lip balm..." She swallowed and stroked her hair. "She forgot it..."

"Are they still at Jodrell Bank?"

She nodded slowly.

"Why didn't you call if you needed something?"

"You weren't painting..." Gee jabbered.

"No further questions are required, my dear." Temperance joined me clothed in white combinations tucked into purple bloomers. "It appears someone was sneaking around and eavesdropping..." She crossed her arms. "Georgiana Rose Lee, get down here this instant!"

She levitated and landed behind me, she was intimidated by her mother and saw me as a safe haven to hide behind. Georgie knew I wouldn't yell at her, she never wanted to anger Temperance but it appeared she did so in the instant.

"How did you get back here?" Temperance interrogated.

"I flew..."

"Flew?" I knelt down.

"Yes, Papa..." She swallowed. "That's why I am wearing this, so when I came back none would notice I had left...."

"You flew here from Jodrell Bank all on your own?" Temperance put her hand on her hip. "...because Elizabeth asked you to grab her lip salve?" She raised her eyebrows. "Do you suppose I was born yesterday?"

"No, Mumma, you were born in 1855..." A smile broke from her face.

"Georgie..." I looked down at her and she stopped smiling because she knew I was becoming upset with her too. "Don't talk back to your mother."

"Sorry, Papa." She flicked out her cape.

"Explain to us why your sisters are not with you and what you are doing mousing about, young lady..." Temperance spoke at length. "Did they really let you fly here on your own or are you telling stories?"

"No, they told me to fly." She nodded again. "So, I did..."

I smiled at her and she smiled back at me as she took my hand. Georgiana's eyes always seemed to twinkle brighter when she was in trouble or when she had our attention; both applied here.

"Don't encourage her." She directed her attention to me.

"What's wrong if Papa is encouraging me?" Georgiana's smile grew wider.

"What was that?" Temperance stepped towards Georgiana with a wider frown on her face. Georgie grabbed my arms and hid behind me.

"For what it's worth..." I extended my hand. "She was the Rose Queen of the fete last week and now she's flying from Jodrell Bank." I stayed between the two of them. "I am proud of my little girl, what can I say." I shrugged my shoulders. "She is strong, she's beautiful, she's clever, and she can do all these amazing things."

"You endorse this?"

"No, I don't..." I looked down at Georgiana and picked her up. "Now Georgiana, tell us the truth or you are going to be in big trouble."

"She already is...." Temperance glared at her.

Georgie gulped and wrapped her arms tighter around me. I held her but matched my wife's seriousness. "Tell us what happened...."

"I told you..." Her lips quivered. "...Bet asked me to grab her Chappy, she forgot it..."

"Then why didn't she take your sister and come back here with you?" Temperance crossed her arms. "...we left you in their care and it's just over Bomish Lane there."

"Your mother is right, Georgie." I looked back at Temperance. "...I know what happened..." I placed Georgie down. "...Elizabeth happened..." I shook my head. "...she put her up to this."

"How do you know it wasn't the both of them?" Temperance shot me a look.

"We're talking about Elizabeth." I put my hands out. "That girl is always up to something." I laughed for a brief moment but Temperance was only bemused.

"I'll call them now and find out..." I looked back at Georgiana and she had her hands on her hips, glancing at the ground. I reached into my pocket and removed my mobile.

"So here is the deal, sweetheart, I am going to call Henrietta and if her story doesn't match up with yours..." I knelt down. "You are grounded." I looked up at Temperance who sat there tapping her toe. "And whatever else your mother decides is appropriate..." I joined her and put my arm around her, presenting the united front which brought a brief smile to wife's face for the first time since we detected Georgiana's incursion.

"Can you promise to keep a secret?" Georgiana looked up at us.

"Start talking..." Temperance instructed.

"But I don't want Henna and Bets to be mad at me..." She threw her hands out.

"So, it was the both of them?" Temperance continued to interrogate.

Georgiana looked up and then down again.

"Answer me, young lady!"

"Yes..." She blurted it out.

"Okay, then..." I took the phone out. "I am ringing them up..."

"Papa!" She ran forward and clutched my arm. "Wait..." I looked down at her. "...I flew here because...." I could see the gears in motion; behind her face and piercing blue eyes was an active mind trying to craft a tale to either protect her sisters or work her way out of the pickle. Georgiana had a confidence and prowess about her that was imposing, even if she was only seven years of age. Though Georgie was stronger, more powerful, and supremely intelligent compared to any of her age, at that moment, she seemed like any child trying to get out of trouble.

"Because what, Jelly Bean?"

Tears filled her eyes. "Right, they let me fly so I can practice..." She sniffled. "...but they had a bet..."

"A bet, you say?" Temperance interjected.

Georgiana nodded.

"Elizabeth said you weren't painting but Henrietta said you were." The truth was revealed from her little pink lips. "So, they made a bet as to who was right." She looked up at the both of us. "...the only way they could find out was by sending me to collect the Chappy that Bet forgot and..."

"Spy on us whilst you were at it?" Temperance timed her witty rebuff perfectly, as she had a talent to do.

"That didn't really work out too well, did it?" I broke a smile.

"I suppose not, my love." Temperance smirked and placed her hand on her hip.

"They said they trusted me to fly here and back because they knew I could do it." Gee replied with an intonation of urgency in her voice. "...they said they would buy me a Bakewell Tart, as well, but they had to know who won the bet..."

"Well they have both lost when we deal with the two of them, that I can assure you"

Georgiana's eyes darted between us, searching for a lifeline. She fidgeted with her cape, her small hands twisting the fabric nervously.

'We trusted your sisters to take you up the road to see some exhibits, and they couldn't even manage that responsibly,' I said, my tone softening as I glanced at Temperance.

'But then they'll know, I....' Georgiana's voice trembled slightly, her eyes wide with worry.

'They won't know anything, Honey,' I assured her, kneeling to her level and gently placing a hand on her shoulder. Temperance's stern expression softened ever so slightly, her eyes locking with mine in a moment of understanding.

"I was supposed to be stealth..." Georgiana looked down.

"Stealth?"

"That's the word Bets used." She looked up quickly.

"A word to the wise." I grabbed her cape. "Bet should have advised you that wearing electric pink is a bad start, darling..."

"I thought you like my costume though?" She looked up at me with puppy eyes, fishing for another compliment to steer the anger away.

"I do but that's not the point..."

"And I also wear lilac, thank you..." Georgiana pouted.

"Don't you dare get chatty..." Temperance pointed at Georgiana who now crossed her arms and looked away with a crankiness spread across her flawless complexion. "Now go put your dress on..."

"Must I?" She scowled. "I look cool like this..."

"Do you want Papa to take you to see the fire engine on Friday or do you want to be in your room for the next two weeks?" Temperance looked at me from the side of her eye, assuring me that she was in command of the situation.

"But you wear yours, all the time...." Georgiana stamped her feet. "It's always underneath your clothes, it isn't fair..."

I glanced over at Temperance who looked disarmed for a moment at her response before shifting back to a stern and steely glare. "Get a move on, young lady!" She pointed to the kitchen.

"Papa, can you help me?" Georgiana fretted; this was yet another strategic ploy, however. Every time Temperance attempted to discipline her, she would then act distressed so I would step in and protect her or so the punishment was less severe. In doing so, Georgiana would cause a rift between my beloved and me as we would argue over what measures to take. Considering the girl could snap her fingers and change back into her dress. She didn't need any help; it was a way for her to divide and conquer. This was the same girl after all that put on a long flowing pink dress with sparkly silver shoulder straps and did her long hair in a sea of strawberry blonde waves the week before when at the Gooseberry Fete without any help.

"You put on what you are wearing now without our help..." Temperance scolded Georgiana some more. "Butterscotch, ring them..."

I hit the send button and drew the phone to my ear. "...I can't wait to see what Elizabeth has to say about this one..."

"'Papa, do you still love me?' Georgiana's voice was small, her eyes glistening with unshed tears.

I placed my hand over the speaker, my heart aching at the question. My eyes softened as I looked at her. 'I am hurt that you would even ask that, sweetheart...'

Her eyes met mine, full of an innocent hope that pierced through my resolve.

'Of course, I love you,' I said, my voice thick with emotion. 'That will never change, no matter what.'

As the words left my lips, her face lit up with a relieved smile, a warmth spreading through me at the sight. It was impossible not to smile back, the connection between us reaffirming itself in that tender moment.

My wife far more intelligent than I and adept to the stunts and tricks of our youngest daughter was more resolved. She didn't flinch and only shot me a look to reinforce me. Georgiana could break me easier than her, my beloved was tougher than I when it came to our daughters and maintained a firm disposition.

"We both love you, even when you are being a naughty girl..." Temperance's finger erected in the direction of the kitchen door.

And just like that, my beloved showcased flawlessly how to be loving but firm, at the same time; she had a talent for it. There was a reason why I've always said my wife runs the house because *everyone* listens to her. Make no mistake, she is no tyrant either. She is very affectionate; supportive; protective; comforting; and the best role model for a young girl. However, she tolerated no nonsense or 'nanty narking' as she calls it.

Georgiana walked toward the kitchen slowly with her head down. Temperance leaned back against the white moulding, monitoring Gee's every move as she listened on when the phone continued to ring.

"Hi, Papa." Elizabeth answered on the other end, cordial in her tone of voice.

"Hey, Bet." I looked over at Temperance. "I was just calling to see how everything is going over there. Are you guys having fun?"

"We are, thank you. How is the painting going?"

"We're fine, thank you..." I put the call on speaker. "Do you need anything?"

"No, we were just about to check out this exhibit on the Great Red Storm of Jupiter. Cheers for asking..."

"Okay, you will have to tell me more about it when you get back..."

"I will do, Papa..."

"How is your baby sister liking it? Did you and Hen do anything special with her since it's the three of you together?"

"You know what she's like, always scurrying about..." She replied cordially, still acutely unaware that she was caught or even that we were on to her.

"...can I speak to Hen?"

"She's gone with Georgie to the loo..." Elizabeth's response was succinct and brief. It was evident that given her pace and intonation, she wanted the chat to come to an end.

"Well, I'll call back then..." I shook my finger with a brief smirk in the direction of my beloved. "...I want to make sure she is alright with Georgiana..."

My wife smiled back with a nod of approval.

"...That's not necessary Papa, the three of us are always together, to be fair..." Her tone was more dismissive, she was trying to deflect and get off the phone as quick as she could.

"That much is true but this is the first time in a public place without your mother or I there to keep an eye on things. You may get overwhelmed, you might forget something, or maybe you are worried about getting in some form of trouble, just because..."

The phone went quiet, excepting Bet's breaths which were faintly audible on the other side. "Speaking of which..." I paused for a moment to see if Elizabeth would come clean about anything. If it was Henrietta she would have, as Hetta struggles with being deceptive, especially with me in particular. However, Elizabeth wasn't going to show her cards here, so I prodded a bit more.

"...Did you forget your lip balm? I noticed it just now and know that this time of year, you like to have it on you..."

Temperance put her hand over her mouth.

"Would you like me to drop it off for you?"

"Actually, Henrietta had some on her, so I am all right. Thank you though."

"It's no problem, I can be there in five minutes and meet you in the front..."

"That's really kind of you, Papa but..."

"And I'll also be sure to drop off Gee too..."

The phone went silent again.

"I tried to give you a chance to come forward but we caught Georgie sneaking around upstairs..."

"...but Georgie..." Bet protested, urgency emanating from the speaker of the phone.

"Now, do not feed us any dogs Elizabeth, you hear?" Temperance interrupted with fury. "We asked you and Henrietta to look after your sister and instead it seems she has gone off a reconnaissance mission..."

Elizabeth didn't respond.

"...one apparently of your design..."

"That's not entirely true...." Bet retorted.

"...Go on then, tell us what happened. And dare not craft any wild tales either, do I make myself clear?" Temperance's voice was stern but Elizabeth went silent. She was crafty and clever in how she worded things and as such we would be going around in circles for who knows how long. Instead, we could take a quicker and more expedient approach...

"Bet, put your sister on the phone..." I covered the speaker. "She'll talk." I whispered to Temperance who nodded back at me in agreement.

"Papa?" Hen's voice broke through the momentary silence.

"Henrietta, I need you tell to me what on Earth you two are up to."

"I am really sorry Papa; it was completely out of order by the both of us. It started with Bet and I getting into silly debate as to whether you were sending us off with Giggle for the day because you were going to have some romantic afternoon out and we wanted to know if we were right."

"Why do you need to know? Besides, I was giving you two an opportunity to spend time with your little sister without us having to monitor you."

"You are right, Papa." Henrietta spoke with genuine remorse in her voice. "And we've let you down. I am truly sorry and I speak for Elizabeth, as well, when we say we wholeheartedly apologise and we regret taking your trust for granted. Will you forgive us and grant us one more chance to make this right?"

"Do you realise what you could have caused by letting Georgiana fly off on her own as you did?"

"We do but we also know that Giggle was keen to use her abilities. I understand we were careless and reckless but we wanted to encourage our baby sister in an innovative way..."

Innovative way? I said it silently to Temperance who smiled briefly, breaking from her strict disciplinarian character at the audacity of our oldest daughter.

Henrietta not hearing me respond immediately, continued to rant. "...but we could have handled it with more tact and discretion. Please don't blame Georgiana, it's our fault, blame us and we are sorry." The tension in her voice continued to build. "Please forgive us, Daddy." She sounded ready to weep. "Please."

Her pleads pierced my heart. I put my hand over the speaker and looked at Temperance, my eyes begging for clemency on behalf of them. Temperance showed initial reluctance but affirmed it with the wave of a hand.

"Right..." I sighed. "We'll be there in five minutes to pick you up." I shook my head. "At the back entrance."

"Very well."

"And Hen..."

"Yes, Papa?"

"You and your sister cannot do this again. Your mother and I are letting you off because you told us the truth and took responsibility."

"Thank you, Papa."

"You are welcome but remember what I said."

"I will..."

"Okay, I love you."

"Love you too."

The phone call ended and I sighed again, looking over at Temperance who now had Georgiana's hand in hers. "What are we going to do with these kids?"

XIV.

"Who would like to say grace?" I looked around the large dining table draped in ivory linen, my beloved sat at the other end flanked by Henrietta and Elizabeth. My beloved sat in a white chemise with her long hair descending upon her shoulders, her fair skin and high cheekbones glistened under the fading sunlight shimmering through the green valance in the top window. Elizabeth sat to her right, her hair down over a cerulean ruffled blouse. Henrietta wore a chemise that matched her mother's, her hair was also down. A big red bow sat in the centre of her mane which conjoined the various strands of her hair dancing down her back and neck. The three of them looked alike, even in the subtlest of ways. Their hands each held a fork and knife with their wrist pressed against the lip of the table. There was only a slice of pizza on their plate.

Georgiana raised her hand as she sat next to me. She chewed on a piece of pepperoni as her hand flew up. Her long strawberry blonde hair descended down over a pink sundress. Some sauce had already formed around her lips as she had bitten into a slice of the pizza. Her fingers were still coated in garlic powder.

"You are supposed to say it before you eat, darling..." I smiled at her and tapped her nose.

"Sorry, I was peckish, Papa..." She broke a smile and everyone let out a laugh.

"Go ahead, sweetheart..." I closed my hands and pressed my hands together.

"Dear Lord, thank you for this pizza and for Mumma, Papa, Bets, Henna, and I being able to enjoy it together. Thank you for blessing our home with love and for all that you have done for our family. We love you..." She paused. "...Amen."

"Amen." I responded with enthusiasm and opened my eyes. My wife and our daughters let their hands down and picked up their silverware. Each of them made their first cuts into their slices of pizza. I looked down and folded up my pizza like a paper airplane and then bit into it. When I looked over at Georgiana out of the corner of my eye, she was holding her pizza where it flopped in her hands and chomped into the top of it, the triangle barely fit in her little mouth. I swallowed my first bite and wiped my mouth.

"Be careful honey, you'll dirty your dress."

She continued to nibble but her sparkly green eyes grew a bit bigger to acknowledge my caution.

"Are you taking in any shouts, Lieutenant?" My beloved forked a piece of pizza and placed a small bite of it into her mouth.

I reached for the pitcher of water and poured some into my glass. "There probably won't be much going on though, it goes quiet when the weather is frigid like this..."

"Well let's hope it stays that way..." Temperance cut another piece. "...perhaps we can watch a movie and have some hot chocolate."

"There is supposed to be a meteor shower tonight." Henrietta placed a blue cup to her lips. "If you are up for it, we can view it from the back garden..."

"Did you learn about that at Jodrell Bank when your sister was skulking around?" Temperance placed another piece of pizza in her mouth with the fork.

A smirk formed on Elizabeth's face, fading into a sheepish grin as she sipped her Vimto, trying to hide her amusement in a red plastic cup. Temperance chewed and glared at Elizabeth who looked over at her from the corner of her eye and placed the cup down with a submissive expression.

"I am sorry, Mumma." Henrietta sat up. "...It was careless and thoughtless of us; I understand why you are still niggled about it." Henrietta's face flushed slightly, her eyes darting toward me for support. "...It won't happen again."

"It best not, I was absolutely fuming." Temperance nodded but Elizabeth didn't say anything, she just pressed a napkin to her mouth to conceal her laugh. She cleared her throat trying to cover up.

"Do you have something to say, Squeak?" Temperance dabbed her lips.

"Harriet would fold under questioning..." Elizabeth chuckled.

"Funnily enough, I am the only one that ever talks..." Henrietta replied.

"Oh aye, sometimes too much..." Elizabeth smirked. "Grass..." She spoke under her breath.

"Bubble's honesty is what spared you three from a severe punishment." Temperance spoke firmly. "Your father and I showed you clemency with the hope that you won't ever pull a stunt like that again.' Her gaze lingered on each girl, conveying both love and the weight of responsibility.

"Well, at least we can trust El Giggle, right?" She looked down at Georgiana who looked up at her with a smile and nod. Bet shot a playful look at Temperance who peered back at her with a peeved look.

"Papa, can you pass the pepper please?" Elizabeth glanced across at me.

I extended my arm over the two red boxes of pizza with the pepper jar in hand. Elizabeth took it and sprinkled it over her slice. "Thank you, Papa."

I bit into my slice and glanced over at Georgiana who was copying me still. I dabbed her face with my napkin to clear off the sauce, she smiled back at me and I returned the smile to her. I clenched down into the hot cheese and sauce as my eyes wandered across the table to where the two girls were both cutting into their slices some more and placing some more bites in between their pink lips. Temperance did the same and I marvelled in the spectacle of it all.

As I looked around the table, a wave of gratitude washed over me. The joy and laughter, the simple togetherness—it was all I had ever wanted. My voice trembled slightly as I spoke, 'I love the four of you so very much.' The tears welled up unbidden, a testament to the depth of my feelings."

Smiles broke from each of their faces; a warm countenance of affection received and reciprocated in full.

"...you guys are everything to me..." I ran my fingers through my eyes to swipe away the tears. Georgiana scooted out from her seat and jumped onto my lap to press her head against me and her arms around me. Elizabeth and Henrietta each took my hand and drew closer to me. Temperance smiled warmly across at me and I blew her a kiss before kissing each of my girls on the domes of their head.

IN THE SPIRIT OF BREAKING the habit of not composing memoirs, I have crafted another composition to mirror my previously narrated anecdotes. The last occasion I composed previous to the parcel and dream with the wave was well before we married when Harriet, Ellie, or Georgeanne weren't even a glint in my eye. This evening's events however were so challenging to everything that comprised my reality, compelling me to confide in these very pages.

Only hours ago, were the five of us sat in the kitchen enjoying pizza as a family, him pouring out his affection for us in an eye-watering display of love. We lay together until his pager chirped and vibrated violently followed by a shouting of vernacular and language that activated him to rush out of bed. The charred flavour of smoke filled our noses as soon as we awoke; a merciless blaze raged onward without relent, sending glowing plumes of white smoke towering into the frosty air. The flames were in his irises; he knew what was ahead and gave me a powerful kiss before he stormed off; the moistness of his lips still wet on mine; his eyes fixed on me as the words I love you chased him out the door when he reluctantly let go of my hand.

I stood alone in the darkness, surrounded by silence; my hair thrown about over a periwinkle dressing down as I glanced out our large bay window at white plumes of smoke rising above the horizon line into the clear starry sky. I could imagine the scene; the smoke; the haze; the many vehicles parked in no particular arrangement with their lights oscillating and blinking across the landscape. He was there and all I could do was sit in the quiet and contemplate what he was facing. I could not be there with him, though I desired to be. A fear overcame me, what if the fire or the smoke could overtake him? But how? Everything had changed, it had done for so long now but this inferno was different...

The best confirmation would be him returning home to the girls and me safely. Should I clutch his shoulders and embrace him again, a joy would surge upward from my stomach and pulsate through every corner of my body. I longed for him and wanted to rest peacefully in his arms, safe and snug under the duvet and quilt.

Must he persist in this trade? Why did I support him in his ascension to Lieutenant? My reward for being a steadfast wife and encouraging lover resulted in my being consumed by a terror that filled every inch of my being. Though there was no reason to believe he would not return to me, I nonetheless prayed a chorus of petitions for it to be so.

My desire for adventure swooned within me, I too used to march into conflagrations; I too saved children from certain peril; I overpowered men twice my size and made it look effortless; I could leap through the air and perform acrobatics - it was second nature to me. Now, I was a mother, a governess to my poppets, and a housewife. And though I had clamoured for this lifestyle, I yearned for where I could use my talents as I had once done before I had the girls. I have done for years now.

Perchance, I could be incredible again for me. He had the success as a writer; he was able to perform on stage around the country and abroad; he served the fire brigade; and he enjoyed all the accolades, distinctions, and gratuities that came with these various enterprises. He was modest and eager to share them with me, citing time and time again that it was as much mine as it was his; that it wouldn't be tenable without my standing behind him. As sweet as these sentiments were, I wanted something for my own; I wanted what was always my own: my abdominals oiled as I slipped on my lilac leotard which wrapped perfectly around my body, and tucked into those fashionable heliotrope leather leggings. The sensation of tying the pink front lacing on my leggings, fixing the matching bow around my throat, and snapping my belt buckle into place. The feeling of sliding on my boots and my gloves before I step out into the night...

The knowledge that I wasn't wearing them just for a romp, fancy dress, or a bit of play but for something more. I could be strong; I could be brave; I could be a marvel; and I could be the mother that my little ones often emulated in the merriment. I could no longer be the heroine they imagined but the incarnate of this character in the flesh: one chronicled and now re-emerged. I could reach far beyond that of Ludgate Circus, St. Bride's, Angel Meadow, Marple, or Manchester in previous iterations. Maybe, the girls and I could do this together; we were all uniquely gifted. Imagine...

A scenario where he wouldn't be nervous; where he wouldn't obsessed with safeguarding me but rather trust in my talents. Perhaps, he wouldn't have a strop but instead, he'd be proud...

The lights turned on and I saw the reflection of Henrietta in the window. Her long reddish-brown hair fell over her pink flannel pyjamas as she turned on the small black scanner which she placed on our coffee table.

"Central, 422 is signal 17, Lieutenant – M2" My Butterscotch's voice called out over the radio.

"422." The radio buzzed back.

"That was Papa, Mumma." Henrietta drew to my side and clutched my bicep with both her arms. "Would you like to sit?" I placed my hand over hers and we plopped down on the cream-coloured cushions of the couch.

Henrietta rested her head against my chest and put her arm around me. Tears filled my eyes as I stroked her scalp. The stairs creaked.

"Are you two alright?" Elizabeth leaned over the handrail, her long plait descending as it suspended in the air above.

"Papa has gone to the fire." Henrietta raised her head.

"I can smell the smoke..." Ellie descended the steps in a white tank top and pink spandex bike shorts. "It sounds like it's a proper shout..." She crossed in front of us before sitting on my other side. "Surely, Papa will be alright..." Elizabeth's hands caressed my shoulders. "He is like you, is he not?"

Henrietta's head raised from my breast as she looked up at me for answers; both daughters were waiting for the reply that hung my lips. I cupped my hand under Henrietta's jaw and stroked her cheek to comfort her. I recall when these two were two little girls and though they had grown substantially, when I saw them then and there, I was reminded of the small lasses that used to frolic in the meadows across the lane.

"422, Central..." The dispatcher called out over the airwaves.

"422." The sirens blared in the background as I heard my dearest's voice respond.

"It's Papa again." Henrietta stared at the scanner, followed by Elizabeth.

"Multiple notifications of fire and smoke showing in all exposures."

"Central, 4203 is signal 17." Another voice materialised on the radio.

"4203, 422." My beloved called out to his colleague.

"Go ahead, Yorkie..."

"Chief, I have a visual of a fully alighted structural fire, it's not the dairy farm, it's the adjacent grain silo, approximately three storeys, contents unknown at this time. Recommending you transmit the two."

"Code Two." Henrietta interjected as the Chief Manager affirmed the message and transmitted the Code Two which meant it was an active incident. A heat filled me and I untied my dressing gown which only had a pink sports bra and spandex briefs beneath it.

"Don't be scared, Mumma." Elizabeth pressed her lips against my cheek and pressed her cold hands against the flesh of my stomach.

"Central, Code Two as per the recommendation of 422B." The manager's voice came over the radio. *"Please refer to our aid scheme from adjacent brigades. I have a visual of fire through the roof with rapid acceleration down the face of the structure on all sides. Upgrade this to a three, please."*

"Oh, my goodness..." Henrietta's eyes glassed up as she burrowed her head into my bosom, her hand coming to rest over her sister's. A tear escaped as I rubbed both my girls' backs. *"It's an awful fire, children..."* I sniffled, holding them both against me. I could feel Henrietta's eyelashes fluttering against my skin. My hand reached to the side of her face to stroke her cheek.

"4203, 422..."

"Go on Yorkie, what do you have?" The chatter filled the background.

A brief smile crossed my face at the mention of his nickname. The girls chuckled as well, a brief respite from the tension that consumed us. Elizabeth sat up with a large smile on her face. "Shall I make us all a cuppa then?"

"If you don't mind, sweet..." I looked up at Elizabeth whose face was far more animated than mine from outward appearance.

"Yeah, Chief. We had to go hydrant to fire, Firefighter Bellamy is at our source. We're down a guy, as a result..." Static filled the radio until the manager responded. "Central, 4203 is 18."

"Lieutenant, I hope your missus and the lasses aren't waiting up for you, this looks like a ...." The scanner broke up briefly "...drown..."

Temperance clutched Henrietta's hand. "What was on he about, concerning us?"

"Affirmative, Chief. Temp and the girls will be..." The radio squelched and broke up in a cloud of static.

"Awww." Henrietta blushed. "...Mummy, he's thinking about us at the fire."

Elizabeth entered with a tray of mugs; boiling water smoked from the top.

"That was fast..." I watched as she placed the tray down on the coffee table. "...I need to use my powers for something useful, aye?" She handed me a mug. "Ta, Squeak..."

She handed another to Henrietta who sat up.

"Thank you, sister...."

"Yorkie, you can open it up." The chatter of the radio cleared up and filled the room.

"Can anyone confirm the origins of that nickname for Papa?" Elizabeth sat down beside us with a yellow Cadbury mug in her hand, blowing on the lip.

"Michael [Firefighter Bellamy] told me it was because Papa put out a fire whilst he ate a Yorkie bar." Henrietta looked up.

"And you actually believe that, Bubble?" Bet took a sip.

"No, because he doesn't like Yorkie bars." Henrietta reached for a spoon to stir her tea.

"His favourite sweet are bons bons; I always remember to grab him some whenever I visit the confectioners." I looked at our wedding picture briefly.

"His favourite sweet, next to you, of course, Mummy."

"Mind your sauce-box." I rolled my eyes. For a young child still, she was quite suggestive.

"It's because he's from New York, originally." Elizabeth laughed. "It's his accent, they are poking fun at."

"That claim is preposterous. Are you sure it's not due to him possessing the temperament of a Yorkshire Terrier?"

"You know full well, it's due to his accent." Ellie shook her head with a smirk. "That display of political correctness is utter poppycock, Mother."

"I thought I'd give it a go." I giggled for the first time since he had run off into the night. The anxiety had started to quell, perhaps he would be back to us soon enough. These accounts of him filled me with a joyful presence as if he was there with us. I was met by a resurgent feeling of hope that he would be back.

"Funny, how none of us speak remotely close to him." Henrietta broke her silence and sat back sipping on her tea.

"And Papa says us four sound charming when we chat..." Bet took another sip of tea.

"Central, 4203..." The manager shouted.

"Command..." The despatcher responded over the radio.

"...we are going to have to step this up. Send assistance provided from Knutsford and Northwich, two apparatus, to the scene..."

"23, 4203...we'll re-route them..."

A silence filled the room as our eyes all meandered out the window toward several ashen columns of smoke rising into the night sky. The fire was even more severe than we could fathom, the sheer scale of response revealed this.

"...I have two more from Wilmslow and Chelford standing by..."

"23, Central. Divert Wilmslow and Chelford to the scene, as well..."

"I should put the bloody thing out myself." I clenched my fist, my heart rate started to rise as some flashes of light filled the plumes of smoke above the tree line outside our window. This fire was bad and I had to do something, but had we drawn our curtains and kept our heads down, we would have never known.

The immediate vicinity of our house had a silence that could unveil the faintest of breezes. Yet, just a short distance a field, a chaotic scene contrary to all that surrounded the Cheshire countryside was unfolding and I didn't know truly where my darling stood amidst it.

"We can all go..." Harriet wrapped her arms around me and massaged my hand. "I can control water."

I looked down at Henrietta. "Your father wouldn't be happy with that and I am not keen on it either..." I placed my hand over hers and ran my thumb against her knuckle....

"The suits you gave us then, are they only for show?"

"Bubble raises a point." Elizabeth's fingers pressed against my arm. "...there is no point in us having them if we can't ever use them..."

"Mhmm..." Henrietta stroked my arm. "and Baby Sister practically lives in her costume..."

"Giggle does look cute in her cape, doesn't she?" Elizabeth aimed to distract us with a joke, it was her go-to tactic whenever times got difficult.

The three of us shared a brief smile at the thought of the youngest lass in our household.

"...We could hatch a solution far easier with all of us, as opposed to you going solo, Mumma." Elizabeth's eyes flickered for a moment.

"Your father would have a fit." I shook my head as was expected to be the sensible response. However, the more I pondered the possibility, the more it intrigued me; it had always intrigued me. If there was no progress in the short term, I couldn't suppress it any longer regarding this occasion.

"Central, 4203." The radio squelched again.

"Central...."

"Status of our relief units?" The manager replied with haste in his voice.

"Knutsford three minutes ETA, Northwich five minutes ETA, Wilmslow and Chelford presently in route." The dispatcher's response was muffled and broken up.

"23, Central. Have the Knutsford unit come in and secure a secondary water source on Twemlow Lane..."

"Twemlow Lane..." Henrietta tapped my thigh. "...that's not far from here, at all..."

"If this goes sideways, I am not going to leave your father..." I sipped on my mug.

"And what's your plan, Mumma?" Elizabeth peered at me.

"I will go there and remove him; I cannot bear the thought of him not returning..."

"That's a flawed plan." Elizabeth stroked a strand of my hair. "...do you realise how hot it will be in there?"

"The fires can't destroy her or us, Bets..." Henrietta lurched forward.

"So, you are just going to turn up in your jammies and pull him from the fire?" Elizabeth set her mug down with a soft clink.

"I will dress accordingly."

"*That won't be a distraction....*" Elizabeth crossed her arms, her mahogany hair falling down her back into the cream cushion. "*...prancing around in that skimpy costume of yours...*"

"*Skimpy?*" I glared at her. "*It suits its purpose, no pun intended...*"

Elizabeth snorted as she looked at me out of the corner of her eyes, evident she was ready to laugh. "*If you say so....*"

"*What's wrong with it?*"

She shrugged her shoulders. "*It's skin tight, why do you need a belt?*"

"*The belt allows me to look professional and it's a bang up to elephant accessory.*" I raised my chin. "*...I haven't seen any of you three complain about your belts...*"

"*But do you really require yours Mumma? since the front of it laces up over your crotch?*"

"*Lace-up is the style from my time...*" I looked at Elizabeth. "*...it also matches my boots and my belt buckle...*"

Henrietta drew close to me. "*...I like it personally...*"

"*And why wear a leotard tucked into the leggings?*" Elizabeth raised her eyebrows.

"*I am a gymnast and nimble on my feet, it allows me to move, stay cool, and breathe.*"

"*...all true but it makes your bum look massive....*" Elizabeth chuckled.

"*Elizabeth!*"

"*I mean that in a good way, Mumma....*" She smirked as she raised her hands in defence. "*You have an amazing tush and the leotard into the leggings enhances that...*"

"*Squeak's right, Mummy.*" Henrietta placed her arm around me and smiled warmly. "*...you have an enviable set of thighs too...*" She glanced down and pressed her fingers to my quadricep.

I smiled back at her; Harriet's intonation and disposition exuded her innocence. Unlike Elizabeth whose impetus was to invoke and evoke, Henrietta's compliments were sincere and bereft of any mischief. She genuinely meant what she said and did so to be kind. Elizabeth to be fair operated under similar intent but enjoyed having a laugh as she did so, often through the incorporation of perverse and vulgar discourse.

"Has Papa gone to a fire?" Georgiana's voice squeaked from the top of the steps. She rubbed her eyes with a white quilt in hand.

I nodded. "I'm afraid so, my love...."

Tears filled Georgiana's eyes as she ran down the steps.

"Don't cry, little sister...." Henrietta spoke softly as opened her arms to Georgiana who exploded into her embrace.

"...Papa will be okay, right?" Georgiana sniffled as she curled up between Henrietta and me.

"I reckon so, Giggle." Elizabeth reached over and rubbed the back of Georgiana's head. Comparatively, she was the steadiest of us, confident in her father and his ability to navigate the circumstances.

"Central, 4023. Urgent, copy? Have Northwich and Knutsford report to 422B who presently has a high-volume delivery line in operation."

"23, Central...."

"Papa is in the fire?" Henrietta's lips quivered.

"422, 4203..."

We all looked at the radio awaiting, for his voice to correspond back to the manager. Minutes went by and no reply.

"422, 4203..."

Georgiana looked up at me, tears started to trickle down her cheek, followed by mine. She threw her arms around me, pressing her head against my bosom. Her head shook violently as snot and tears filled into my cleavage. I rubbed the back of Georgiana's head and Henrietta soon started to cry, as well. The four of us huddled together waiting for any further developments. Seconds went by in hours; the silence was no longer a comforter but now a most brutal adversary.

"422...." Static filled the radio until it was apparent that all forms of transmission were dead. I snapped my fingers and the power was off, it was no use if we could no longer hear what was going on. We sobbed and held each other until we realised that we were left with two choices: wait it out or intervene.

"Mumma, it may only be exterior." Elizabeth placed her arm around Georgiana and nuzzled under my chin.

"I wish it so, my dear..."

Georgiana's sobs became more obvious as she shook. "Daddy!" She screamed and sobbed. Henrietta caressed her and sniffled as she comforted her baby sister. Elizabeth kissed the back of Georgiana's head.

"Oh, how I want him to burst through the door, so we can be in each other's arms, again." I held my daughters close to me as I wept.

"You are just going to have to beat us to him when he's back." Henrietta rubbed my cheeks hoping it would prompt a smile from me.

"You girls hold your father as much as you desire." I sniffled "...as long as I get to do the same..."

We consoled each other and found solace in each other's arms, feeling helpless and out of control with respect to all of the variables in play. But then I realised, it didn't perhaps need to be that way. A thought crossed my head; a suggestion implied by our Henrietta which I finally had given into, the times were desperate and such recourse had to be undertaken.

"Squeak..." I gazed out the windows as the white plumes of smoke had now mushroomed over and descended back toward the treeline.

"Yes, Mumma..."

My eyes never moved from the image of the wafting billows of soot, ash, and cinder that fell back toward the Earth. "...I need you to take care of your little sister for me..."

Water, perhaps they needed more water on the fire. Perhaps then that would put this tempest into check. I glanced over at Henrietta, "...Care to join us, Bubble?"

XV.

The silo glowed a brilliant orange in the night, the smoke was accented by the luminescent glow of the fire against the silver metallic glaze of the building. The panelling on the side of the building scolded and flailed off from the roof shedding smaller particles which flurried into the air. The smell of burning tickled my nose as I reached into my turnout coat pocket and removed a small metallic ornament. I opened the accessory and held it up to the light of the burning fire, inside were two photographs on either panel, with a lock of red hair that could be removed from the glassy encase. Behind the strand of hair, a black and white photograph inserted that displayed my wife's beautiful face; her dazzling blue eyes stared back at me with an effervescent hope. Veiled behind her mysterious visage, a palpable sadness that she could not disguise.

A black bow tied around her throat descending over a white satin blouse that hugged her figure, exposing the top of her bosom. Her long cinnamon-auburn har trickled from below a white sunhat with a carnation fixed to the centre. When I looked at her, she was all around me. There was no fire in front of me nor smoke wafting through her hair; instead, the fragrance of her body oil which smelled like Parma Violets and the safe presence that encapsulated me in a warm embrace.

The other picture was one of my three precious daughters, taken recently at my friend Scott's wedding reception. Elizabeth stood to the left with a bright smile etched across her face, her poinsettia hair dangling down her back in a plait as she had one arm around Henrietta's waist and the other over Georgiana. She wore a pink dress which cascaded from two straps set to her shoulders down to her knees, a yellow bow fixed over her chest. Georgiana in the centre with her jovial, playful, and vivacious smile, a daisy tucked into her long strawberry blonde hair dangling down to her marigold lace dress with her hands wrapped over the arms of her big sisters. Elizabeth and Henrietta's faces pressed against her on either side, both radiating the warmth, joy, and affection that ceaselessly flowed from them. Their smiles reflected the true sisterly love they had for each other. Henrietta's gentle smile was more subtle and dignified, and though it was far less expressive than Elizabeth and Georgiana's, it still could not conceal her kindness. Her hair fell down her back and sides, pooling over her shoulders, accenting a white lace blouse that clung to her svelte physique and tucked into a long navy skirt that was anchored by a black belt with a small gold buckle. Her arm was around her sister Elizabeth's waist, her other reaching across to hold Georgiana who held her arm against her. I reminisced of the day we took these photographs along with a family portrait of the five of us which rests on the mantle above our fireplace. It was a pleasant autumn day when we enjoyed a garden party to mark the occasion. Scott told me how long we both had come from that day in the flat in Audenshaw when we were talking about suicide. I was there with them again, basking in the peace and joy, longing to be in the moment with my precious wife and daughters.

I rubbed the pictures and kissed them both, along with the locks of hair from each of them before placing them back in my turnout coat. I kissed my Cross and made another with my hands as I looked up at the blaze.

"LT..." A black sphere rushed toward me which became a figure cloaked in a black turnout coat, black turnout pants, and a black helmet which was littered with sand and dust on the dome as it approached. It was Elijah's [one of the firemen in my company] voice but his dark features could only be made out under his helmet as he neared the lights of the engine.

"The radios are dead..." Smoke rushed from his breath.

I stood up off the front of the bumper and placed my arm around his back. "Where's Xavo and Z?"

"Aziz is on the nozzle and Xavier is backing him up."

"...Should we make a push?"

"Not yet..." I walked in the dark field which was decorated with a cornucopia of fire hoses. As we approached the line, I looked out and saw two more blacked-huddled masses. Xavier held the shiny nozzle in his hand as he knelt on the ground, Aziz closely behind him.

"I hope you are comfortable, Xavo..." I chuckled. "We may not be going anywhere for a while..."

"I thought you were going to lead us in, LT..." His white teeth escaped from behind his dark complexion.

"Maybe I'll send you in Xavo because I don't like you." I teased him and patted his back. "You not much better, Z..."

Aziz's brown eyes looked up as he smirked. They soon rose to their feet and watched the flames rip into the sky. The heat generated was a spectacle in itself, though it was a frigid eve the fire made the air around us warm.

As we stood idle, I removed my mobile phone from my pocket after I took it off the rig when things started to slow down. I saw a multitude of messages from my beloved, followed by one from Elizabeth which read "Daddy, are you alright? I know you will sort this out but Mumma, Hen, and Georgie are inconsolable..."

I started to text back my response: *Hi Carrot, I am fine, it's going to be a long night because we have to surround and drown it.* [Elizabeth knew the firematic terminology as I took on all the trucks and showed her so much as she always had an interest].

Please tell your mother and sisters I will be home in a few hours and I love them. I love you so much, Bet. Love, Papa.

My plan was to send the text message first and then give my beloved a ring. I paused to consider all that I had written to Bet. In doing so, I looked into the field and saw a stream of water fly from the black abyss, illuminated by the glow of the fire.

"What is that?" Xavier looked over in awe.

A purple spark flickered beside it.

"LT, you don't think another line is in operation over there, right?" Aziz interjected as the water darkened down the flames which sent a fresh plume of black smoke upwards.

"I'll go check it out." I pressed send and jogged as fast I could through the field while calling Chief's mobile phone. I heard it ring through twice before I could hear him breathing on the other end.

"Yes, Yorkie?"

"Chief, did you call for water on the south side of the field?" I hurried through the brush until I saw two figures ahead of me. Their silhouettes weren't bulky like that of a fireman, nor did they have any helmets on their head; their figures were curvy and feminine.

"No, but communications are all muffled with the radio signal being dodgy... "He replied. "It's possible someone opened up because they thought we gave them the go-ahead. You can tell them to shut it down."

"23, Chief, I'll check it out and relay your message."

"Cheers, Yorkie..."

As I hung up the phone and got closer, the stream of water tapered off. The two figures seemed to turn and freeze in place I closed in. I halted in my travel and looked ahead. The two silhouettes observed me and there was a timidity that was detectable within them. When I approached them from afar, they were more fluid but once I had gotten within close proximity, their movements stiffened. As I took one step forward, they took another back. Only the silhouettes of two women were perceptible. I had an overwhelming suspicion as to who the two figures in front of me were, but they couldn't be here, could they?

"Mama?" I called out but there was no response.

"Hen, is that you?"

One of the figures rushed toward me until two purple and pink sprites flashed in front of me and extended toward the sky. Once the light had vanished, so too did the two silhouettes...

I walked to where the shadowy figures once stood and glanced around, all I could see was the outline of a puddle of water on the grass below me and a faint scent of hyacinth which lingered in the air. I took out my phone and selected *My Queen* on the menu and called her. The phone never rang once and went to an automated message stating that a voice mailbox had not been set up. The one brief ring also signified it was off.

I ended the call and sent "Chief" a text stating the water line was no longer in operation and the personnel had abandoned the scene for respite. His text was prompt in response, stating that I should go back to the apparatus and cool down, so I did.

When I arrived back at our engine, the boys were all standing by the rear step with cups of tea and coffee in hand. They had removed all their helmets, dropped down their tan hoods, and had their black turnout coats unbuttoned. Mike had joined us from the hydrant, his white t-shirt soaked and covered in black; his dark skin covered in sweat as his broad shoulders remained hunched.

"Boys..."

"LT..." Xavier replied, his faded haircut seemed unscathed from helmet hair. His brown skin glistened with sweat as he plucked a packet of cigarettes from his coat pocket. Mike opened it and offered me one.

"Thanks, brother." I patted Xavier's back. "I'm good..." I removed my phone, scrolling down the menu until my most recent conversation with Elizabeth filled the screen. *Carrot, are your mother and sister there?* I sent the message to Bet and then sent another to Temperance: *Hello my love, all is well. I'll be home soon enough. I love you loads xx.* I put the phone back in my pocket.

"There is a cup of tea there with your name on it, Yorkie..." Aziz's black curls were scattered about as his black irises focused on me.

"You got any neck oil?" I smirked as I placed my boot on the rear bumper.

Aziz and Mike laughed, as Jonathan "Johnny G" Gerrard emerged from the side of the rig with a massive smile. He was a fair-skinned and pudgy middle-aged man with a strong Welsh drawl. "Sorry, lads I had that all to me-self when I was feeding you the water..." Johnny G's face illuminated as he chuckled, his boyish blue eyes matched his short flip of grey hair at the top of his ovular head. "From the sight of it, LT...you don't need it..." His large fingers gripped the silver handle above the amber directional light.

"Shall we all have a tipple when we are dismissed?" He looked around at the three of us. "Non-alcoholic for Zee and Yorkie..." John's (or Taffy as he was affectionately known) eyes zoomed in on Mike before he smacked his back affectionately. "Full pint for you though, boy..."

"Job opportunity, Xavo..." I took hold of a white disposal cup filled with hot black tea. "I texted my wife to let her know what's going on." I took a sip of tea. "I suggest you all do the same..." I had another swig. "Man, I wish this was coffee." I licked my lips. "Where's Eli?"

Xavier's fingers pointed ahead. "...Speaking of your wife..." He took a puff of his cigarette. "Is that her there?" He looked at me and then waved back in the direction of Elijah. I looked over toward Eli who was still in his helmet and turnout coat, pointing towards us. Temperance stood there with her hand over her chest, clad in a large wool purple shawl which covered her completely; besides her was Henrietta who was in a large black puffy coat which draped over leggings. My beloved's hair was up whilst Henrietta's was down. They held each other's hands as they gazed upon me with a mix of fear and relief on both their faces. John and Aziz looked back at my wife and daughter, and each acknowledged them in their own way with a raise of a hand or a polite smile.

"Excuse me, guys..." I placed the tea on the back step and took off my turnout coat as I jogged towards them. Elijah tipped his helmet to both my wife and daughter before he started his walk back to the rig.

"You're doing overhaul, right LT?" Eli laughed and tapped my shoulder as he walked past.

"Thanks, Eli..." I patted his back as I went onto Temp and Hen.

"You alright, Yorkie." He spoke over his shoulder as we moved away from each other.

Temperance took Henrietta by the hand and started jogging towards me while holding up her skirt with the other hand. I threw my helmet on the ground and dropped the suspenders of my bunker pants. I was in my grey t-shirt which was otherwise clean had it not been consumed by the odour of sweat. None of that would have mattered to my beloved whose eyes were imbued with a frantic energy that would not be extinguished until she was able to touch me.

Temperance threw herself into my arms and pressed her lips against mine forcefully, a volley of smaller and emphatic pecks and kisses followed.

"I am sorry, I was worried you had gone missing when you went off the radio..." She threw her arms around me and rested her head on my shoulder. The scent of hyacinth tickled my nose again which prompted my eyes to open; it was identical to what I had smelled minutes before in the field. But I didn't say anything then and there...

"I sent Bet a text to tell you I was alright and that we were delayed..." I moved my head back and pulled Henrietta into my arms to join her mother and me. "...I sent you a message as well and tried ringing you..." I smiled at them both and held them tight against me.

"We didn't have the mobile on us..." Henrietta's words were warm and soft against my neck compared to the overbearing heat the fire produced during its peak. Both did not speak again after Hen's brief reply, they both broke down into tears. Temperance's weeping was more pronounced compared to Henrietta who shook vigorously, their hands both dug into my back as I held them both against me.

"Everything is okay now, loves." I kissed their heads, cheeks, and foreheads repeatedly with the hope it would settle them. After a few minutes, their crying calmed but their grip intensified. I glanced back at the silo which was now cascaded in black smoke, it had collapsed to the ground and the support units blanketed the debris with steady streams of water.

"The fire is down." I kissed Temperance on the lips, followed by Henrietta. Temperance's arms felt like a boa constrictor around me. Henrietta burrowed deeper against me. I pressed my chin on the domes of their heads. "...once we get this cleaned up, I'll be home in an hour or two." My hands ran up and down their backs.

"Papa, we were scared that you weren't coming back..."

I moved my head down and looked Henrietta in her eyes, I dabbed her tear. "Of course, I'd come back..." I smiled at her. "I have to take you for that sheet music you want tomorrow ..." I gazed at Temperance. "...And how wish I was cuddled up with you, my queen..."

A smile broke from my beloved's face which made me happy, her hands clung to my wrists tight. "I love you both so much...." I pulled them in for another embrace.

"No more shouts?" Temperance looked up at me.

I shook my head.

"Promise?" Henrietta sniffled.

"I promise."

"I'll wait up for you to return..." She glowed with relief and excitement as she released hold of me.

Hetta's zipper had come down a bit and it looked like she was wearing a blue swimsuit under the coat. I reached for the zipper to pull it back up for her and make sure she was warm, but she sharply grabbed my hand and two took steps back.

"Thank you, Papa." She smiled with palpable nervousness. "I've got it."

I saw a faint outline of a belt and pink buckle briefly visible under her coat until she pulled the zipper up fully and covered herself completely.

"I just want to make sure you are staying warm..." I drew close and rubbed Henrietta's back to ease her tension. "...I reckon Elizabeth and Georgiana are as nervous about you as they are me, now..."

"They were desperate to come with us..." Temperance took Henrietta's hand. "Shall we go then, Bubble?" Henrietta stroked a stand of her hair and nodded.

"I will see you soon." I kissed them both once more. "I love you both so much."

I watched them leave hand-in-hand after they took a few steps, what occurred in the field just before flooded my thoughts like the water that submerged the grass. I had to know.

"Mama..." I called to her and she swung around immediately in response; she didn't say anything but only raised her eyebrows to demonstrate I had her undivided attention. I glanced down at Henrietta's fingertips which were saturated in water. She ran them up to her eye to dab some of the remaining tears which pooled under her eyebrow and flick them to the ground.

I peered over at the fog of white smoke which drifted into the night sky which became visible as the soot and dust had cleared.

"Were you?" I pointed at the scene of the now collapsed silo. Temperance's eyes rested on the location for a few moments, as if she were reflecting back to an instance where she was present or perhaps imagining what it must have been like to witness such an incident; I could not determine which of the two it was but I was under the notion that it was the former and not the latter.

My beloved would offer no clues as she blew a kiss at me before turning her back and continuing her walk toward the car which was parked just ahead in a lay-by on the lane. Henrietta's eyes were glued to Temperance as they carried on until she looked over her shoulder at me once more and nodded gently with a slight smile. Hen turned her head back and matched her mother's steps back onto the lane. When I looked at Temperance's boots, hers were shiny and clear of any debris. Henrietta's matching pink boots were dashed with mud around the heel.

The mobile vibrated in my hand, I looked down and saw Bet had corresponded: *I am glad you are alright; I knew you would be ; -0. Please come back, we miss you!* There was however no response to my additional correspondence.

When I arrived home an hour and twenty minutes later, I was mauled by all three daughters. Bet and Gee had also stayed up to greet me when I came home and when I stepped through the door, they all leapt from the couch to tackle me with affection. After settling in, having a quick shower, and a change of clothes, all three of them followed me to bed and cuddled up against me, so they could finally settle as well. Georgiana and Henrietta also both asked me to not go to any more fire calls because it scared them. Temperance did not say such a thing but she needn't reiterate herself as she was clearly rattled by the evening.

There wasn't much rest that night but when we finally did so, we were a family sharing one bed; it was a recreation of the Victorian era though we were well into the twenty-first century. I guess fires can create such events, as well. Nevertheless, I didn't want my daughters to ever be frightened like that again nor did I ever want to see Temperance look so spooked. They always come first and with this being the case always. The very next day I put in forms for resignation from the fire service for personal reasons.

XVI.

It had been days now since the silo fire. And though the conclusion to that harrowing course of events ended in a peaceful conclusion, there was nonetheless an uneasiness that permeated throughout the house. My Butterscotch had filed for a resignation from the fire brigade and despite his constant efforts to reassure us all, the girls followed him everywhere he went with the hope they would stop him at the door from going to any alarm shouts. He had the paperwork to hand but nonetheless, the echoes of that evening rang through their heads like the sirens of the trucks rushing to the location. Admittedly, I too drew close to him, feeling a need to keep him near after the scare.

The one thing that remained undaunted was the love between us, it grows stronger with every day we are together. It is reinforced by moments like these. Indeed, we have bickered but we do not splinter; we have faced challenges but we do not fracture. Our devotion to each other is paramount.

Nevertheless, as a family, we had to move past the scare and realise that is what it all in fact was in the final analysis: a dreadful fright and nothing more. Henceforth, we could either acquiesce that such scenarios are part of parcel of his role as a newly commissioned Lieutenant in the fire brigade and wrestle with the human concerns that come with being at his side or we leisure in his resignation, an action borne out of a selfless devotion to us. Supernatural attributes cast aside regardless of the paths we chose as the Lee family, we had to get back to normal; this Saturday morning was set to be like many others that preceded them and return us to a more familiar place.

On some Saturday mornings, I often took our littlest one to gymnastics at the local recreation centre. More often than not, our little spitfire would need to run off the excess energy after and as such I would take Georgiana to the play area in Cranage. It was a refreshing change of scenery and a chance to have some quality mother-daughter time with Georgeanne. As much as I loved my home and everyone in it, that hour spent watching Georgiana tumble, cartwheel, flip, and do her splits felt like a mini-holiday. I could delight in my little girl's amusement whilst gaining respite from the monotony and arduous routine of overseeing so many tasks, errands, and chores at home. I could have a brew, take a seat, and watch Georgiana move with grace and elegance as she practised; it was soothing and calming. Perchance, this was the one diversion from the norm that l required.

As we left Cranage, I remained deep in my thoughts. I pondered and reflected on so many different subjects in between the occasional jostles of a pothole as I drove us back towards home. The endless green fields and hedgerows passed to our left and right as I navigated the meandering country lanes that swerved through small villages. In this constellation of thoroughfares, we found ourselves amongst one of many modest tributaries of asphalt that led us back to Sycamore Grove.

The sign for Goostrey and Twemlow greeted us ahead as I pressed my heel against the brake pedal; the arrows pointed left with a two next to Twemlow and three next to Goostrey. I came to the A-road and looked to my left, then my right. A silver work van streamed by, its metallic paint glowed under the sunlight; fresh, clean, and without any visible blemishes. I glanced left and then right: just desolate pavement with dotted white lines in its centre and yellow lines hugging the periphery with no cars visible. I began to turn left but saw a garage situated about half a mile down the road on the right. My eyes peered at the fuel levels which were approaching a quarter of a tank. My beloved told me he would take the car for petrol when I *came back with Georgiana. However, perhaps, I could extend my stay out for another ten minutes and visit a place I hadn't been previously. After all, in all the time we had lived here, I had never visited let alone noticed the garage because I hadn't been up this way or when I had done, my dearest was driving and I was more immersed in discussion or focused on one of the poppets. Perhaps, there would be an interesting story to read about in the newspaper or another mother passing through with a child of her own that I could converse with.*

"Treacle?" I placed my hand on the indicator to activate it and signal that I was turning right.

"Yes, Mummy?" Her eyes twinkled as she looked up at me.

"How about a strawberry milk?"

She nodded vehemently with a huge smile. I smiled back at her and stroked her cheek briefly before turning right to head toward the garage. Moments later, I arrived and added some fuel to the car. I took Georgiana by the hand and crossed the forecourt. On our way to the entrance, I passed by the pumps and saw a lad who reminded me of my dearest. He had the same buzzcut, facial hair hugging his jawline and extended up to his sideburn; he had a loose-fitting black sweatshirt draped over a pair of blue jeans. He inserted his gas cap into an older maroon Honda which looked a lot like Cordelia (our old Honda which we retained for sentimental value). The lad opened his car door and sat in, turning the key in the ignition. I stopped for a moment and removed my mobile from my satchel, I scrolled down to the Messages menu and typed I LOVE YOU XOXO into the screen before I sent it to my dearest; I am most keen on unscripted acts of romance, their unrehearsed nature demonstrates the most care and thought, despite their spontaneity. I placed the phone back in the satchel, as we stepped into the shoppe. Georgiana's little fingers gripped in mine as a bell sound chimed to signify our entry.

A familiar song greeted us as we stepped in: She's Electric. The tune brought me back to the first day my beloved and I had met so many years ago in Marple. In my reverie, I re-traced all the history that had elapsed between that day to this one, culminating in me glancing down at our youngest daughter who scurried towards the illuminated refrigerators eager for her treat. The time that had gone by had been quicker than the velocity at which she ran. A smile filled my face; we were once two strangers who encountered each other inexplicably and now so long since, were as madly in love as ever and raised three lovely young women. I looked ahead to an older woman waiting behind the counter who looked back at me with an amiable countenance as she awaited my approach. Her white hair was curled against her wrinkly skin which was smooth around her hearty rosy cheeks.

"Good morning." I smiled and nodded at her. Her beryl eyes amplified at my greeting.

"Good morning, my dear..." She smiled. "May I compliment you on your choice of dress?" Her name tag came to the foreground as she inched forward. The name Florence was inscribed in black on her white name badge.

"Thank you, Madame."

"That is quite a charming skirt and that top fits you marvellously." Her eyes traced upward from my long and flowing marigold-flowered skirt and navy blouse which cut off at my arms. The collar was traced in a faint white and red line.

"You are too kind, Florence..." I glanced over at Georgiana who shut one of the refrigerator cases, a bottle of pink strawberry milk in her other hand matching her leotard she wore tucked into black leggings. "Florence is quite a charming name..." Georgie brushed her hair back and ran over, placing the drink on the counter. "That was a name we had shortlisted for her..."

Florence gripped the scan gun. "And what did you call her..." The bottle scanned in at £1.99 with a loud chirp.

"Georgiana."

"Hello!" My little one placed her hands on the counter and smiled at Florence. Who couldn't help but smile back at her.

I adjusted the strap of my white satchel crossed over my chest. "I am called Temperance..." I reached in and removed a shiny two-quid coin.

"Temperance...." Florence nodded with approval. "...that's delightful and one you never hear anymore."

"My husband tells me that all the time..." I ran my hand through Georgiana's long strawberry-blonde hair. "Ready to go see, Papa?"

As I placed the coinage into Florence's hand, the door opened and the bell sounded. I felt Florence clutch the coin with an intense grip; her pulse throbbed through her fingers. Georgiana and I looked back at the sight of a youngster in a black hooded sweatshirt with pudgy cheeks and mop brown hair with an older lad who hid his eyes under a baseball cap. The lad wore a grin over his veiny skinny cheeks, he was thin and frail cloaked under a baggy black tracksuit. With him, a woman in her late teens wearing leggings and a black Adidas sport coat. Her black hair was up in a bobble and her blue eyes were cold and measured. Her thin frame was cloaked in a loose-fitting grey sweatshirt that had London embroidered on the chest along with black leggings similar to what my daughter was wearing. An adolescent lad followed them in who was not much younger than her entered with a garrulous laugh. His brown beady eyes twitched as he plucked a bag of Haribo Starmix from the shelving display and placed it into his navy sports jacket. He had a cotton shirt on beneath tucked into matching corduroys.

The youngster snagged a packet of gummy worms off the display and laughed as he did so. Georgiana shot daggers at them, angry at the display of hubris by this lot. The lad and his missus encouraged such behaviour as they filled their pockets and threw a two-finger salute at Florence.

"There is nothing that old wretch can do..." The adolescent lad laughed as he ridiculed her.

"They'll be off shortly, I do apologise..." Florence looked down, helpless in the face of what seemed to be a regular occurrence. I wasn't going to stand for this ridicule and bullying.

"Allow me to have a quiet word with them..." I raised my eyebrows.

Florence's head lifted and she looked both surprised by my coming to her defence. When I turned back to take my first steps toward them, Georgiana had already blocked the door. She stood with her hands on her hips in her shiny pink spandex unitard with lilac briefs over them, brought together by a silver belt with a pink G. Her long lilac silk cape flailing behind her. Her skin glistened in oil, shimmering like her heliotrope leather gloves and boots. For a young lass, she had quite the impressive physique as six lines were visible around her navel and her thighs were a resemblance of mine. Georgie's arms were bulky for a seven-year-old yet smooth, feminine, and girly.

"Put the sweets back as you found them..." Georgiana's eyes twinkled with a confident smile.

"And who are you?" The younger boy chuckled.

"I'm..."

I raised my hand at Georgiana to halt her words.

"My daughter is quite imaginative and spirited." I chuckled as the four of them looked at me. "...can you kindly put the sweets back as it is distressing our Florence..."

The older lad removed his hat to reveal his bulging yellow eyes before placing it back over his brow. "No..."

The four of them all laughed.

"Do you know who we are with?" The lad chuckled.

"No one of consequence I am sure."

His face dropped as she appeared shocked by my response; his ego was clearly wounded by my lack of intimidation toward him.

"Nonetheless, if this is a matter of affording those confectionaries, I am happy to pay for you this once but please be kinder towards Florence, she is a timid soul..."

Georgiana crossed her arms and stood by the door, offering a glare of disapproval.

"Whatever you say, Mary Poppins." The lad responded in a condescending tone. "...daft bint..." The four broke out in a burst of laughter. "Let's go, she is not even worth the bother..."

"Don't you insult, my mum!" Georgiana's voice raised and the laughter of the four ruffians came to a screeching halt.

"And what are you going to do about it, pip-squeak?" The adolescent teased Georgiana.

"You don't want to find out..." Georgiana made a face and threw her hands at her hips.

My little girl was a bold filly and she was never shy from facing down a bully. I had hoped to reconcile this conflict but it was evident that Georgie wanted to be Super Georgiana and save the day. Georgiana looked at me for reassurance that I wasn't going to let her go this alone, my expression to her clear that she wouldn't do. An urge and temptation had long filled me to feed the itch, but I wasn't expecting it to occur this way.

"Get her, Dec..." The adolescent patted the younger lad on the back who curled his fist. As he charged forward, Georgiana flew up and ice formed at her fingertips before it streamed on the tiles in front of the boy and he lost his footing. Georgiana chuckled. "Is that it?"

I snapped my fingers and I was in costume, it felt good to finally dust it off and put it to good use. The rest of the trio charged at Georgiana but I got their attention with a whistle.

"All that vitriol but no lemon to squeeze..." I put my fists up to divert them toward me. The lad and his missus pivoted and ran towards me whilst the adolescent carried on toward my daughter.

Georgiana levitated with arms crossed and got into a fighting stance. She flicked back her cape and beckoned him forward to say "bring it".

The lass swung first at me but I dodged her punch and threw her to the side. She slid across the floor. The lad was more tactical in his approach he threw a jab at me which, I moved to the left and came back with a right hook toward my ribs which I blocked with my bicep. I gritted my teeth as I absorbed the impact before extending my hand forward into his chest and sending him onto his back.

The ruffian rushed to his feet and swung wildly but I caught his punch and quickly twisted his arm in a reverse technique, pinning his head on the counter. He cried out in pain.

"He says he is sorry." I pushed my knuckle into his head and gave him a quick noogie until his missus tried to sneak up behind me. I extended my leg toward her and caught her in the waist with a firm kick, sending her into a display case which had potato crisps on offer. She picked up a few packets and flung them at me, one of which smacked against my face, the other against my side which irritated me. I yanked the lad backwards and let out a ferocious grunt as I launched him towards her.

Georgiana deftly avoided her attackers, her movements fluid and precise. She ducked under a punch and countered with a swift kick, using her agility to keep one of her adversaries off balance, flying through the air with her cape flowing beautifully behind her. Her jabs were quick, her kicks were surgical, and it culminated with her landing a bridge suplex on the adolescent. She smiled at me and rubbed her hands together; sparks flew from her fingertips and I smiled back as they filled mine. I glanced down at my adversaries and looked back at Georgiana who launched into the air back toward the young lad, as she did so the entrance opened and two more yobs entered into the fray, clad in black hoodies, jeans, and boots from head to toe. One of the two tugged on her cape and plucked it from around her causing her to lose control of her flight and tumble to the ground.

Georgie braced herself for the worst of it but nevertheless became a pink ball of shiny spandex and sweat-drenched skin rolling across the hard floor, groaning and grunting with each bump she took until her bum smacked into the glass. "Oww!" She cried out as the glass spider-webbed behind her, Georgiana winced from the impact as she lay on her stomach. I froze at the sight of her crash and instinct took over to run to her aid, taking my eyes off of those as I despatched.

I rushed toward her, but then, 'Crack!' followed with a stifled "Hngh!" from my lips. A sharp pain shot through my spine as I was struck. I grimaced, feeling the ache spread down my spine and spread to my shoulders, causing me to arch my back. I turned to face my attacker with a steely resolve, appearing unfazed, and ready to retaliate.

There before me stood the woman who looked down at a splintered broom across the floor with a small stub of wood in her hand, terrified that her attack had failed and her weapon had taken the worst of the exchange.

I let out a sigh and released the pain. "...You'll have to do better than that, love." I taunted her; she threw the stub at me which I swatted away and then attempted to slap me but I caught her hand and pushed downward as the pain from the blow of the broken broom threshed through my back. I got her to her knees with relative ease before I swept her feet out from under her. My peripheral version once again focused on Georgiana who was gritting her teeth as she crawled on her fours holding her lower back.

"That's no way to treat a lady." Georgiana gaffed as she tried to get back on fours but one yob stomped her back. "Ah!" She cried out; another yob kicked one of her glutes when she tried again. "Ouch!" She grunted. "So much for her being a sidekick..." The first yob clenched down on her briefs when she was lying on her stomach and yanked her up, essentially giving her a wedgie. Georgiana yelped until he shifted his control to her head; she held her glutes as her fingers dug into her *pink tights and she flailed her slender body about, kicking out her legs. The other yob laughed mockingly as the other two started to come to. Use your electricity powers and shock them! My thoughts screamed aloud. I felt the loud smack of his hand against her chest followed by an "OHH!" fleeing from her lips. Georgiana crossed her arms over her chest; the yob then curled his fist and threw an uppercut into her stomach "OOF!" She grunted loudly as her body recoiled with the punch before she slumped over; The yob laughed aloud and threw her down to the floor landing on her knees. Georgiana held her stomach as she flapped her legs in pain. The other yob threw her cape to the ground. I had seen enough and took two steps forward with urgency and plucked at my hat pins in my hair, releasing the woman.*

"What a lightweight!" One of the yobs advanced on Giggle cracking his knuckles as she remained doubled over on her knees. I flung the first hat pin went between him and Georgiana, startling him in place. I threw the second hat pin and it precisely hit on the second yob's shoulder and sent him to the ground. The distraction bought Georgiana time to recover and roll out from danger; her eyes turned blue and she formed ice at her fingers and punched one across the face, dropping him to his knees. She zapped a beam of ice to freeze the second until he passed out. "Big mistake!" Georgiana lunged to her feet and threw her pigtails back as she grabbed her cape off the ground.

The lad attempted to take advantage of the momentary distraction but I heard his footsteps and breaths as he approached, I cartwheeled away from him and got him into a fighting stance. He feigned a punch which I went to block but followed with a stinging kick to my thigh. "Ehhh." I breathfully grunted with a wince, the blow was sharp and crisp to my thigh. The lad more confident stepped forward and threw a punch at my face, I moved my head back at the last minute to avert the blow as the tip of his knuckle grazed the tip of my nose. His left hand came back with a straight jab at my stomach, I flexed my abdominals and shifted my hips to guide it toward my obliques, allowing the blow to roll off me. "Uhh" I breathfully exhaled as I felt a slight twinge and sting. The fabric of the leotard certainly allowed me to feel the slightest of contact and thus I felt it fully. I had never dropped my hands and thus took the opening to jab him with my right hand and cock his head backwards. His missus came back for a second go, cocking her fist back and telegraphing her punch; I blocked the first attack toward my face and then the second before she aimed lower to my body. I assumed she would go there and thus I side-stepped her attack, trapping her fist against my ribs as I locked it against me. I clenched one arm down around her fist to keep it trapped against my side and grabbed her hoodie, nearly tearing her hoodie off as the sheer force pinned her place. I gave the woman a quick jolt of electricity which paralysed her momentarily as I extended my other leg forward into the stomach of the lad as he was starting to shake off the effects of my jab, the force of the kick sent him stumbling backwards. I then threw the woman upwards in the direction of the lad who had placed his hand on one of the tiles to regain his composure.

The woman took the brunt of the collision between the two as both flew backwards into the popcorn machine and tumbled into another display of nibbles. I nimbly backflipped away. The woman now lay supine on the ground with the lad over her, a pile of packets of biltong, cheese balls, and cashews scattered over them along with golden kernels of popcorn swept across the floor. I lunged forward and threw some bolts of electricity from my palms toward the shelving display to give my foes a zap from the metal around them; it was enough to subdue them and assert my dominance without harming them. I ran my fingers up and down my leotard checking for any damage, which there was none.

"Hiya!" Georgiana spun kick the little lad to the floor. "You shouldn't underestimate my powers..." She taunted as she pulled the boy up by his shirt. Georgiana tied her cape around her neck, undid

her plaits to let her hair down, and winked. In a stunning act of defiance, the lad kicked Georgiana in the midsection.

"OOH!" She gasped and scrunched her face, wrapping her arms around her stomach. Her cape clung to her back and wrapped itself around her, her doubled-over physique outlined in the lilac silk cape clad to her; she waited too long to subdue him and loved to show off, despite my teaching her to always keep her eyes on her opponents; now she paid for it. "That hurt." She winced and clutched her belly tight with flayed fingers.

The boy hit her with a hard punch, making her head snap to the right with a spray of sweat exploding from around her. Her cape flew behind her as she felt the impact on her cheek.

"Oww!" Georgiana grunted, her hand quickly touched her face, feeling some blood on her lip before she held her cheek. I felt reassured that I wouldn't need to intervene though as she looked at the boy with a glare of determination and waved her finger at him to show the blow had no lasting effects. She was strong, she always teased how she had eight stomach muscles to my six and never had any reservations about proving her point.

He went for another strike but he never got the chance as she ran a beam of electricity into his chest. Georgiana followed up with a handstand into a cartwheel and landed her legs over the back of his neck to finish him off. All three assailants looked on in awe and halted in their tracks.

"Do you want some too?" She dusted off her cape and stood firm exuding her confidence and pride.

Two ran for the door and Georgiana darted in their direction, the adolescent pivoted on his foot and fled in my direction with my daughter soon flying after him in pursuit. As he watched her fly after him whilst still running in my direction, he collided with my shoulder and bounced to the floor.

"Going somewhere?" I looked down at him with a smile as he rolled over onto his stomach. Georgiana landed behind him to cut off any escape.

"Up and at them, now, chap..." I pulled him by his hood.

"Mummy, look out!" Georgiana screamed.

I saw a glint of metal as he flailed his arms, lunging toward my stomach. I dodged the instrument but felt the wind of it as it nearly penetrated my midsection. I let go of him and he had another go, grunting as he swiped at my stomach, I extended my arms forward and bent over to evade the sweeping slice. His next attempt was more methodical as he aimed for my bicep, I jerked it away at the last minute to avoid a direct hit, but still felt the blade nick my upper arm.

"UGH!" I reacted as blood trickled from the side of my bicep. I pressed my hand firmly against the wound and took a deep breath cognisant that could have been a lot worse but it still had a bitter and stinging bite. He reached for my hair to gain control of me but I swatted his hand away, jarring his movements for a moment. Before I could parry his next attack, Georgiana flew through the air and her foot crossed his face sending him to the floor.

"Don't touch my Mum!" She screamed in defiance. Georgiana clapped her hands and froze the knife in his hand. He tried to tap the ice formed around the knife against the floor to free it but it was rock solid. He rushed to his feet with a sense of urgency as I straightened up. I surged forward and form-tackled him, pinning him to the floor with the mass of my chest and bust pressing against his face. At that moment, he didn't seem too bothered. I pressed my left hand against the sheath of ice around the knife and his grasp. Purple and pink sprites melted the ice and seized his hand as I took the knife from him. His head started to move around in my cleavage, gasping for air but I soon wrapped my arms around him to wrench him in place. "I'm sorry!" His words muffled against my chest.

"What was that?"

I gave him a moment to catch his breath.

"Let me go." He gasped.

Georgiana jumped down next to him. Her cape flicked up behind her as she drew her arms back to form electricity on the fingertips of her left hand and ice on her right.

I noticed the blood had reached my elbow from the cut. "You nicked my arm, why should I?" I clenched down harder on his ribs but let his head move free, he grovelled in pain.

"Please, I'll never set foot in this garage again..." He squealed.

"Did you hear that Florence?" I looked up at her and smiled. "Let us know if he doesn't keep his word." I intensified my grasp around him. "...you won't be naughty if I release you, will you"

"No!" He cried out.

"Very well." I let go of him and he curled up in a ball on the floor, gathering his breath and his constitution. I took another deep breath and quickly got to my feet. Sweat had formed and coated all the areas of my exposed skin. I glanced down at my arm as the blood had slowed noticeably.

The bloke got back to his feet and put his hand on the lad I had just subdued. "You two best get your skates on before we have you detained."

The older lad and the adolescent who previously both taunted, jeered, and ridiculed both Georgiana and I had done a complete reversal. Now, they were timid, meek, and docile. Both raised their hands to signal their complaisance as they backed away to the door before fleeing like those that did before them. The woman had already vanished in the midst of the chaos.

"Are you alright, darling?" I knelt down and cupped Georgie's face. "You took some nasty hits there..." Her cheeks were red and some blood formed in the corner of her mouth. Some swelling formed under her left eye.

"I am okay, just a bit sore..." Her wince turned to a smile.

"You did great, I knew you would..." I beamed at her with pride as I caressed her cheek and dabbed her lip.

"Are you okay, Mummy?" Georgiana pointed at the wound; her voice tinged with worries and her eyes were filled with concern.

"Merely a scratch, Giggle." I embraced her; her little arms wrapped around my waist as my hands ran up and down the back of her cape. *"Besides, your Mummy is tough!"* I overaccentuated my accent to excite her, playfully tapping her nose before she giggled and kissed my cheek, as we embraced again.

"We did it." She breathed heavy with her arms, abdomen, and thighs soaked in sweat.

"Ladies..." Flo called out to us with the bottle of strawberry milk still in hand, the two-quid coin resting on the corner untouched. *"...This one is my treat..."*

I rose to my feet and took Georgiana by the hand over to the counter.

"What do you say, darling?" I glanced down at her.

"Thank you!" She beamed with enthusiasm as Flo extended the bottle forward to her and the two-quid coin toward me.

"Those Widows have been a problem for weeks; I am glad you put things right."

"Widows?"

"Oh, aye." Her eyes dilated on the door, the spider-webbed glass where Georgiana banged her bum when she crashed. *"A group of roughnecks based in Blackpool that have recently been coming round this way to grace us with their presence."*

"Quite a hike to be sent back home with your tail between your legs." I batted my eyebrows with a smile. *"I reckon you won't be seeing them again."* I pushed the coin back toward her. *"Call that a gratuity for exceptional service."*

Flo nodded at me to express her gratitude; her eyes focused on my arm. *"That must have stung."* I looked down at my arm at noticed *the bleeding had stopped and most of the flesh repaired from when my hand was over it. Fortunately, it appeared that Florence didn't notice this.*

"He barely nicked me..." I put my hand over my arm where I was cut.

Florence reached under the counter to grab a roll of gauze.

"My mummy is tough!" Georgiana smacked her hands. "...No one can stop her."

Florence looked down at Georgiana with a smile and extended the roll toward me, her eyes enlarged at my arm as I took hold of the gauze. Before she could inspect my arm and determine how much more it had healed, I turned my back to Florence, casually glancing over at the shelving display which remained toppled on the floor with snacks cast everywhere.

"I apologise for any mess we have caused..." I rolled out some gauze around the wound and bit off a piece. "We'll tidy before we go, as we didn't intend to..." I wrapped a bandage around my arm and turned back to her.

"I'll sort it." Florence raised her hand gently and looked over at Georgiana. "Good job your bruise is clearing up there too, sweet."

The swelling was rapidly clearing from around Georgeanne's eye. Florence's eyebrows wrinkled as she looked at my arm, then Georgiana's eye again, and up at the ceiling; before she could form any more lines of inquiry, I had to make a hasty exit.

"Can I ask a favour of you?" I placed the gauze back on the counter. "Will you keep this incident today between the three of us?".

Florence wrapped her wrinkled fingers around the roll and looked up at me. "I cannot explain what happened since there is no CCTV footage of the occurrence."

"Cheers." I took Georgiana's hand. "Good day." I bowed my head subtly and led Georgiana out toward the car. As we left, we were still in costume, sweaty and hot; exhilarated and proud but still mindful

not to look back or stop and have a chin-wag with any we cross. A police car passed on the A50, creeping as if it were meant to turn in but instead carried on. A black Citroen turned in from the opposite end of the road, a darker figure tinted behind the windscreen with shiny sunglasses which were only perceptible. I unlocked the car doors as he pulled into a stall in front of the entrance, making sure not to form any eye contact.

Once inside the car, I raised my hand for Georgiana to high-five me. "We make a good team, treacle."

She pressed her little palm against mine.

"That was your first bout and I was fearful I had lost it as I was a tad rusty..." I snapped her seat belt into place and then followed with mine. "Well done." Our ribs both rose up and down, mine noticeable in the leotard, hers plainly visible in her singlet.

"Wait until daddy hears..." Her voice was ripe with excitement.

"No, no, no..." I raised my finger and pointed at her sternly. Georgiana looked up at me with confusion, despaired as to why it seemed like she was being scolded. "...You cannot say a word to your father, he will have a conniption if he finds out." I turned over the ignition. "This has to be our secret for now..."

"But wouldn't he get mad if he found out otherwise?" Georgiana stared at the dashboard.

I plucked off my bandage which was tinged red in the centre from trace forms of bleeding before the wound had finally sealed. "We'll tell him." I blew over my skin which appeared that it had never been touched by a knife. "We just have to time it right..." I looked down at Georgiana and swiped dry blood away from her lip.

"Can we do this again?" She broke a smile.

I smiled back at her. "We'll have to train a bit more as those were only amateurs today." I stroked her hair. "We made quick work of them but some won't be as easy..."

"Do you think Bubble and Squeak would want to help?"

"The four of us together would be unstoppable." I checked her eye once more as it was nearly cleared. "...but we have to make sure we are all on the top of our game..." I placed my hands around the steering wheel. "...let's go home..." I reversed out of the stall and turned out of the garage car park and just like that the climax was anti-climactic; the adventure had ended as quickly as it had begun. The two of us cooled off in our suits as we made our way back to Sycamore Grove. When we were just down the road, we both snapped our fingers to revert back to what we had worn out that day before the proceedings that followed were not once a consideration. When we arrived home, my Butterscotch and our elder daughters remained blissfully unaware of the confrontation.

Part II

XVII.

"So, the girls told me a funny story today..."

"Did they?" Temperance turned on the vacuum cleaner and passed it along the rug, I moved the table out of the way for her until the loud motor turned off.

"Apparently, the three of them can combine their powers to disintegrate toys they don't want any more."

Temperance giggled. "Now there is pause for thought, I don't know why I hadn't imagined such collaboration."

"Collaboration?"

"Indeed..." She fluffed two large black pillows on our couch. "...we would make a great team, the four of us..."

"Did you miss the part about them destroying their toys?" I grabbed a spray bottle of antibacterial cleaner and the rag on the coffee table.

"They simply attempting to master their skills."

"So, when I came home from the grocery store the other day, were you helping them to master their combat skills?" I ran the cloth across the surface to bring back its shine. "Some of those strikes looked full on."

"We were just messing about." Temperance tied the cord around the vacuum until it was fixed in place. "...but is it a problem if they learn a bit of self-defence?" She rolled the grey vacuum cleaner into the corner of the room. "They may find it useful..." She threw her hands on her hips, I could see it through the shine of the wood on the table.

"Such as when you and Georgiana got into a fight at the gas station?"

Temperance paced toward the mantle and adjusted a vase; her back turned to me. "Did Harriet tell you that?" She looked over her shoulder. "I love her to pieces but that child is under your thumb, I tell you..."

"No..." I rose to my feet and took hold of the rag and bottle. "Actually, one of the guys at the fire station said he had a friend whose mother-in-law works at the garage near Cranage. He told me that a woman and a young girl helped her on Saturday morning..."

"...What does that have to do with us?" She plucked a leaf from the Carnation plant in the vase.

"You were out with Georgiana on Saturday morning."

"...And?" She examined the leaf; her shoulders were hunched.

"...well according to this woman, some idiots gave her some trouble until this mother and daughter duo who she wouldn't name, apparently defeated them..." I glanced at the window and a bottle of window cleaner resting on the windowsill. "...the daughter was dressed in pink tights with a long lilac cape and was around Georgie's age." I shrugged her shoulders. "I need not go any further."

Temperance kept her back turned to me as she continued to inspect the plant.

"...but to go further, one of the kids tugged on her cape as she flew and she nearly crashed through the glass of the door. Somehow, this young girl managed to beat up three kids who were twice her age, even after they were stomping her, one apparently punched her in the stomach, and she was tossed onto the ground..." My hands started to twitch, the liquid in the bottle started to jostle in the container. "...and the mother overpowered three adults. She got sliced on the arm with a knife and didn't need stitches or even a bandage. Apparently, she was trying to hide it..."

My beloved's head rose at the mention of the details.

"...all this woman had to do was put her hand over where she was cut and it seems she healed quickly..."

I paused to gauge Temperance's reaction to see if she made any additional furtive movements or sudden reactions, I already had her but she could at least cut the act, at this point.

"...this woman with such extraordinary abilities was wearing a costume that just sounded like what you typically wear. It was described as a shiny lilac sleeveless one-piece tucked into darker purple leather leggings with pink bows and laces." I put the bottle down on the table. "Now to anyone else, that could be anyone but unless you and Jelly Bean have identical twins that we don't know about, it is pretty obvious. Of course, I acted like I had no idea what was going on, even though I was ready to black out wanting to find out who these jackasses were and execute every last one of them for touching my baby girl and my wife...." I squeezed the rag to release the aggression building within me.

"Sod it, Florence." She spoke under her breath.

"So, you are finally admitting that it that it was you two?"

Temperance looked to the side, holding her tongue.

"It was merely a formality when I asked her, but Georgiana already told me."

She turned her head to me and her eyes were filled with remorse perhaps from accusing our eldest daughter of giving her up. "I am surprised Georgeanne would do that."

"Why?" I picked up the bottle. "She wouldn't lie to me after she got caught out in that Jodrell Bank incident, a couple of weeks ago." I looked upstairs. "We both stressed the importance of honesty to her." I looked back at Temperance. "It was Henrietta's honesty that you so eloquently championed which got them off the hook." I shook my head. "But before we get into that, where can I find these clowns?"

"I honestly don't know." Temperance said, with no emotion or intonation.

"Why didn't you tell me?" My tone by contrast was far more interrogative.

"You are a sharp lad." She snickered. "you already know the answer to that one..."

I took a deep breath and paced toward the kitchen attempting to keep my anger in check as I breathed in and out, focusing on my breaths to divert from the rage burning within me. Was I most mad that Temperance kept it from me? Not by a long shot, I was more infuriated at whoever tried to harm her and Gee. Angered that I wasn't there to intervene.

"Were supposed to stand there and do nowt?" She spoke at length as she followed me into the kitchen.

I remained mute as I opened a cupboard door and placed the bottle under the sink. "Those no-good muppets were taking the Albert Edward out of that poor old woman!"

"I've always admired your desire to help others, Honey Bee, you know that!" I shut the door with some energy and walked back into the front room. "That's not the issue!"

"She was in a blighted state and bloody terrified, we had to do something!" She stepped in front of me. "What would you have done if you were knocking about and someone's car was alight?" Temperance leaned toward me. "Be that as it may, you scarpered off from tea many times to put out a rubbish fire." Temperance threw her hand at her hip. "...running off into the middle of the night in the bitter cold for hours upon end whilst we sat there wondering what is going on?!"

"So, this is about the silo fire?"

Our eyes locked for a moment.

"What am I trying to say is, we do what we must even if it affects the other in a way we don't wish to."

"So, I am being punished for going off and doing my job because it upset you?" I nodded for a moment. "Have you forgotten that I handed in my leave for the very reason that I don't want to ever give you or the girls a scare anymore?"

"Are you throwing it back in our face, then?" Her eyes rose with her voice.

"No, I don't want to do anything that's going to upset you guys, just like this whole thing upset me..."

"It would be selfish of us to keep you from firefighting if it is something you love..." She glanced into the fireplace. "Regardless of whether it can frighten us ill, or not."

"But I don't want to frighten you ill to begin with!" I approached her and drew close. "That's why I removed myself from the fire service because I understand it can be scary and worrying for the loved ones of the firefighter." I sighed and took her hands. "Look, Temperance, you are a magical woman..." My hands shook with hers in mine "...supernatural not just for the obvious but because of who you are..." I glanced down at the freshly cleaned ivory carpet. "...I love you more than life itself and I would never want to keep you all for myself or deprive you of using your talents to bless others." I rubbed her hands. "However, I am not going to remain idle while you put yourself in precarious situations with our daughters no less..."

"Would I put our girls in any form of peril, if I thought it so?" She looked deep into my eyes. "They cannot be harmed; they are like me..."

"Regardless, I don't want to ever hear of anyone hitting and/or trying to hurt you or them!" My tone of voice rose and my shoulders hunched. "The idea of it makes me sick."

"For what it's worth, the lad barely nicked me." She let go of my hands and responded with an air of confidence. "It wasn't much more than a paper cut..." Temperance chuckled smugly. "...if that..."

"What about Georgiana? Because let me tell you something, if anyone ever touched her in front of me, I'd fucking end them and I'd have no remorse either..." I nearly let out a laugh from the anger brewing inside me.

"Sure, you would. You are not that sort of bloke." She shot me a look at saw right through me, diving into my soul.

"I imagine your reaction would be even worse..." I let out a deep breath and a snort. "You are her mother..."

"I didn't stand and watch let me assure you..." Temperance reached into her hair and plucked a hat pin from behind a yellow butterfly hair clip. "...I acted swiftly and hit one of them with these." She held the pin up to the light and placed it back in her hair, glancing over at the small oaken looking glass also on the mantle. "...Equally though, I found solace in knowing Georgiana can handle herself well and she is far stronger than any can fathom."

"I know how strong she is, I don't know any kid that has her physique or strength..." I stroked my chin to quell the rebellion within me. "But that doesn't make any difference to me..."

"This is something she's always wanted to do; you've seen her running about on her little adventures." She glanced at her wedding ring and squeezed her hands gently. "...and it's something I've always wanted to do again..."

"She said to me that it was her first taste of action and you were getting out some rust..."

"And we did well, considering...." She paced over toward the window and took hold of the kitchen towel. "...with a bit of training and sparring, the four of us would be superb." She grabbed the window cleaner and sprayed it against the window pane, swiping all the white bubbles forming on the panes. "That being said, you can rescind your leave..."

"But even though I share some of the abilities that this family has, you were nonetheless worried that I wasn't coming back from that fire, correct?" I threw my hands out. "You were afraid of anything happening to me, right?"

She about-faced, her cheeks were red.

"I am the same way with you and that's why I am not going back." I put my hands together in a slow and gentle manner. "Please, if it's the last thing you do..." Tears could have filled my eyes as I felt them grow heavy. "No more..."

Temperance looked at me, she could detect my distress but she shook off any brief sentimentality with a firmness and resolve. "Is this all there is me for, then?" She threw her hand back to her hip. "Cleaning, cooking, picking up after the lasses, and managing all the finer details of your career whilst you go out to perform, sign your books, and do your lectures?!" Her tone of voice rose rapidly from the beginning to the end of her response.

"No, but I thought this is what you wanted?"

"Things have changed" Her reply was steadier and more resolute.

"Do you remember when you were pregnant with the twins? You asked what comes next and I said we'll figure it out but you insisted on me publishing my work and exploring my creativity."

She nodded her head and pouted her lips. "And are you unhappy with the outcome?"

"I just want to be a good dad and husband, that's all that I care about..." I couldn't control the words that escaped my lips. "I've always said that if you wanted to be a nurse again or do whatever your heart desires, I'd step back and support you." I ran my fingers against my cheek and down my scruff. "I will always be behind you and stand beside you..."

"I know that." She kept her steely gaze on me, but her tone of voice was contrary to her stoicism, it was ripe with kindness.

"And I'll also always stand in front of you." I threw my hands at my sides. "I'd consider it an honour to suffer for you if it would spare you the slightest discomfort." I smiled at her, the love I had for her was welling up within me and filled me with great joy despite the intensity of the moment. I just wanted to hug her. "Just please stop."

Temperance looked down, remorse in her eyes as she placed the crumbled-up kitchen roll on the windowsill pensive in thought. "But what if this is what I want?

I didn't know how to answer.

"What if the girls want this too?"

"You told me all you wanted was a life of peace with a bunch of little girls running around our house on a Sunday morning." I paused briefly. "...We have that now and I feel as if you are inviting problems to an otherwise peaceful existence. Lord knows that's all I ever wanted..." I swiped a tear from my eye. "...peace." I rubbed my chin. "Have you considered what could come of all of this?"

Temperance took my hand. "The four of us have been granted some extraordinary abilities, why should we waste them?" Her thumb ran along my knuckles. "...just as we would never want you to waste yours. They are just a few of the many things we admire about you..." She spoke softly, clearly trying to reason with me. "I've told you before that our daughters should see their father at his best..."

"I know where you are going with this but I am sorry but I can't agree to it..." I looked down, feeling a deep sense of sympathy because I never wanted to disappoint my beloved but I have principles. My duty is to always protect my wife and daughters and do whatever I had to do to ensure they were in safety, had a good place to live; for all their dreams to come true; and to know that there is one man in their life that would never hurt them and truly loved them with every ounce of his soul.

"They are as much my daughters, as they are yours..."

I sat on the couch and shut my eyes for a moment, trying to make sense of what I was hearing and what I was trying to prevent.

"And yet, Henrietta idolises you; Elizabeth adores you; and Georgiana wants to do everything with you." She sat beside me. "I am glad it is so, but I want to be a woman that they can truly look up to." Temperance drew close. "I don't want to be their Mother that only cooks them tea, teaches them sing songs, and does their laundry." She clutched my bicep. "They always want to see me use my powers and now we can do much more than mere exhibitions...

"So, you want our daughters to respect you more?" I leaned my head over hers. "Temperance, they already look up to you." I grazed my nose against hers. "They've learned so much from you and everyone that works their salt around here knows you are the head of this house."

"It doesn't feel that way." She contested. "Do you think I made them those costumes so they can emulate me and pretend to be my sidekicks?". Temperance moved my head along my shoulder. "Or can we finally get the chance to do this together?"

"But why now? Why didn't you want to do this when we were together in the beginning?"

Temperance looked up at the brocade ceilings and around the crown mouldings of the front room. "I wanted a life of seclusion because no one could know." Her eyes focused back on me. "Then you came and I was able to unload this enormous burden that had been plaguing me for over a century. When the girls were younger and they caught wind of my abilities, they always fancy dressed and pretended to be me. They were so eager to learn about all of the things I could do and it was never more than anything round the house in a bit of rough and tumble." Her eyes moved upward to the picture of her mother in an oak frame, standing next to our wedding photograph. "I had been thinking about this for years but it all changed at the garage..." Temperance smiled subtly. "I knew I still had it and I could be me again; I have never seen Georgiana look at me as she did after we had helped Florence." Her smile widened. "It reminded me of the many instances the girls glowed over you when you were promoted to Lieutenant or when you received that literary award in Knutsford for the novel whilst we were all there to share it with you." She placed her hands on her lap and sat on the lip of the couch. "This is something that we can share."

I didn't know what to say. I was at an impasse. I could either go along with it and live every day worried sick and knowing I am not doing everything I can to keep my most precious blessings safe or I could be the villain that suppresses the woman that I love and keeps her from being who she truly is or who she wanted to be; this was who she was before I met her. There was no right answer in this situation, there were only two wrong answers.

"I have trained the three of them extensively. We can give it a go for a little bit and if it becomes too much we can step aside." She spoke at length to quell any further questions from me. "At least then we can say we had an honest effort and to that end, you were kind enough to support us in doing so.

"I can't..." I sat back, throwing my elbows on my knees, reverting to a pensive posture. "I'm sorry."

I wanted to ask whether she and Henrietta were at the Silo Fire but the bigger question was had I left the pager off that night, would we have avoided this reality altogether? It wouldn't make a difference because I wouldn't be able to get a word in edge-wise, Temperance had a response for everything.

"How about me, then?" Temperance raised her eyebrows at me and I looked up at her. I didn't know how to respond to it because it was something that was a part of her long before she and I were ever a couple. She did this longer than I was alive.

"I don't want you to." I placed my hands over my mouth and started to breathe in and out with my nostrils pressed together. "But I know I cannot tell you what to do..."

"I need you to be with me." There was an added strain in her voice. "I can't have you against me."

"I am never against you, Mama." I pressed my hands to hers. "You are the first thing I think about in the morning and the last thing I think about at the end of the day."

"And I the same, Butterscotch." Temperance smiled warmly. "That is why I must have your support."

It was never a question of support, she had that without condition. She knew what I was truly worried about but this had always been a flash point for us previously. My wanting her to never be harmed in the slightest is construed as an obsessive overprotection.

"On the plus side, you will get to see me in my tights more often." She smirked. "...and it looks different when I am in Incredible Temperance mode, I'll be all hot, wet, and sweaty..." Her tone turned seductive as she got close to me. "As soon as we..." She cleared her throat. "...Sorry, I, come back, you can take it off me." She spoke in whispers while blowing on my earlobe. Blood started to rush through me. "...I'll need you to give me a nice rub down as I may return home a little beat up on some days..."

The adrenaline surging through my veins at the notion of her looking so sensual and alluring had just vanished; it was replaced by anxiety, anger, and reluctance. I wouldn't let anything happen to her; I couldn't bear the thought. Before I could respond, Temperance interjected as she had already deciphered what I was thinking.

"Not often though..." She raised her hands. "...if ever..." Her hands fell down upon mine. "I wish I had told you on Saturday though as I was a tad sore after..." She winked. "It was a bit of work out as I hadn't been in any form of combat in nearly 80 years..."

I wasn't amused.

"...who knows perhaps it may grow stale after a week. It may not be as stimulating as imagined and that will put it all to rest..."

"Is that what the problem is?" I turned my head to look her in the eyes. "...you're bored?"

"Flippin heck." She scowled. "The better question is what would have happened if I never sent your poems out to all those publishers and organisations that curate readings?" Temperance shook her head before her smile returned, a maternal and sisterly energy behind it. "...would you be satisfied knowing you spent your entire life hiding your gifts from the world?"

"All I care about is you, Henrietta, Elizabeth, and Georgiana..." I threw my hands out. "...I'd walk away from it tomorrow for the four of you; you are always the top priority. I mean I've driven eight hours round trip in a day just to make sure I was home with you at night and to be able to tuck the girls into bed..."

"And we appreciate it, greatly." Temperance's eyes turned white as she pressed her hands to the wick of a crimson candle in the middle of our coffee table. "More than words can ever describe." The fragrance of candy apple filled the room as the flame started to glow. "We've always cheered you on." She flicked out a pink sprite of electricity. "Won't you do that for us?"

"When you have sung or Henrietta had a recital, I've never missed it. When Georgiana was Rose Queen and Elizabeth had painting class, the same holds true."

Temperance raised her hand slowly. "I am not challenging your devotion." She smiled back at me. "What I am asking you here and now is will you support me in this endeavour?" Purple electricity formed in the palms of her hands, cascading light against her periwinkle cotton gown. Her white linen stockings tucked into her leather boots nearly laced up as they pressed firmly into the carpet.

I glanced over at the stairs and saw our three daughters leaning over the bannister. Henrietta's blue eyes enlarged with intrigue; Elizabeth raised her eyebrows with admiration; and Georgiana's eyes sparkled with excitement and jubilance. All three of our daughters smiled, their eyes sparkling from the light of the electricity in my beloved's hands; they all looked at her with reverence. No matter how the conversation made me feel, I was touched at the sight of all of our girls admiring their mother. She deserved that as much as anyone. Perhaps now she could be more of the woman that they looked up to. I didn't want her to be in danger but I wanted my daughters to admire every aspect of their mother.

I didn't want her to do it but I didn't want to hold her back. A personal turmoil and a fear engulfed me but I was willing to endure it if it somehow made Temperance happy to resume what she did which helped so many people in so many places. I was sick at the thought of her getting hit, hurt, bound, or in any form of danger. I longed to protect her at every turn and would be overjoyed to endure suffering that would prevent anything that I feared coming to her. Love drives this madness. I would do anything for her and truly cannot put into context the love that I have for her.

XVIII.

It was a clear and starry eve as I looked out upon the mirror-like stillness of the boating lake in Redesmere; the moon reflected off the water which was without a ripple. My thoughts wandered to my family.

Henrietta had taken Georgiana around the cabin across the lake to show her all the old photos of when the facility was a train station. Elizabeth was looking at all the paintings; Temperance had gone to the bathroom.

Many had gathered to hear words from a variety of authors, myself included. I had to step out once I had completed my reading because public spaces often became too much for me. I took my phone out and looked for any messages from them, only the image of the four of them on the lock screen but nothing else.

"Hi Honey, where are you and Gee?" I typed into my phone. "I am going to collect you and Bet once your Mum is back from the toilet..." I sent the text and placed the phone back in my pocket. When I looked over the right, I saw Temperance standing in her costume with electricity forming at her fingertips in a fighting posture.

"Mama, what are you doing?"

Temperance looked at me with a determined look on her face. Her skin glistened in the moonlight from a combination of oil and sweat. Darker shades of lilac on her leotard further indicated her sweat. The leotard was neat and tidy, shimmering from its spandex composition and carefully tucked into her heliotrope leather leggings which also shimmered. Her belt buckle was centred with the pink T and her pink front-laced crotch tied in a bow which was also centred.

"I gave him a quiet talking to..." Her breasts heaved from the cleavage of her leotard as her toned abs rose and fell; each contour noticeable in the leotard.

"Everything is fine, Honey Bee..." I made contact with her arm, sweat dabbed my fingertips.

"...Nevertheless, I felt inclined to warn that maestro in the event he should say anything offensive about you..." Her navel could be made out in the fabric as I looked down into her leotard.

"Not even a remote possibility." I ran my hands along her ribs. "Plus, you'll get yourself in trouble when there is no reason for it..."

"Well, what if he said something about me?" Temperance raised her eyebrows as she continued to breathe heavily. "You would pull him, would you not?"

"It'd get handled."

So, you can defend my honour but I cannot defend yours?" She crossed her arms. "That is a bit of a double standard, is it not?"

"I am not arguing with you..." I embraced her and yielded in submission to her. "I learned a long time ago that is a poor choice." I stroked a strand of her hair. "But what if I said to you that there is no need to escalate the scenario and it's better to walk away..."

Her muscles tensed, her bosom rose and fell with each breath she took as she smiled back. "Have I not been in such a scenario with you previously?"

"I did listen to you though and respect your wishes..."

Temperance smirked. "...Reluctantly..."

"Not that I would ever complain about it, but you had to full-on suit up to do that?" I chuckled whilst she remained stoic.

"There were some mischief-makers in the cloakroom..." Temperance glanced over at the building and ran her hand over her midsection to ensure the garment was still firm and tight to her abdomen. My eyes wandered downward in a lustful fire of passion, as I pulled her into for an embrace.

"They were seen to..." She embraced me. "Before you ask, I'm fine." Temperance pressed her lips against my cheek.

"You just realised you were fine, now?" I winked at her and she smiled back at me mischievously. "And the only one who should be seen too around here, is you..." I ran my hand around her waist and squeezed her buttocks. "By me..."

"Mmmm, that'd be delightful..." Temperance moaned.

"All sweaty and wet, as you are..."

"I am sweaty and wet in other places too..." She took hold of my tie.

"Are you?"

"Mhmm". She batted her eyebrows flirtatiously. "I could ride you sideways right now..." She spoke under her breath.

"What did you say?" I raised her eyebrows at her.

"I said pride could drive you sideways anyhow..." She smiled as she adjusted my tie. "Sage words of advice..."

"I thought you said something else..." I pulled her in again and she nestled her head against my chest. "Because if you did..." I stroked her hair and pressed my lips to the side of your head "I want to break you in half." I whispered faintly.

"Pardon?"

"I said I long to make you laugh...."

Temperance moved her head back. "...that's not what you said..." She pressed her lips to mine. Our kisses grew deeper until my hands ran up and down her stomach and breasts, she gasped and squirmed until she clinched me and rested her head on my shoulder. Her hand took hold of my free hand and guided it over her midsection toward her belt buckle.

"Rub me there." She whispered into my ear and bit my earlobe. "That feels so good." She gripped the back of my head and engaged me in a deeper kissing pattern, my hands running up her body toward her cleavage as she moaned in my ear. Our affections were interrupted by a rustling of the leaves, which caused us to settle with the physicality and retreat into a tight hug.

"Thank you for being supportive..." Temperance rested her head against my chest. "I know it must be difficult for you as I know you would greet danger merrily to ensure I was safe..."

"It is incredibly difficult..." I leaned my cheek over the dome of her head. "But I understand that this whole Incredible Temperance thing is a part of you and was there before you I met you..." I looked away. "...Still, I don't want anyone to hurt you..."

"Well, you would have liked how I did in the cloakroom then..." She giggled. "...I was barely touched, at all...."

"What do you mean?"

"It means I was dominant." She pressed her lips against mine for a long passionate kiss before she collapsed in my arms. "I love you..."

"I love you too..." I kissed the dome of her head and held her tight; our arms were wrapped tight around each other as Temperance's head remained snug in my chest. She felt safe in my embrace, she was resting quietly with contentment in her exhalations. I stroked my hands up and down her back until I worked my hands around her thigh and squeezed them "I do love these leggings..." I giggled in her ear and moved my hands up over her laced crotch. "Mmmm..." Temperance's fingers meandered toward the zipper of my pants, as my fingers found their way through the webbing of the crotch. She gasped as I ran my finger upward into her, her nails pressing into my shoulder as she stroked me with her other hand. Temperance tensed some more as I reached for her belt and continued to pleasure her.

"Do you want to go in the woods for a moment?" I whispered in her ear, she squeezed my hand and led me, her other hand waving behind her to follow. We walked toward a clearing between elm trees and a chilled breeze crossed us. Temperance shivered and I pulled her into my arms to keep her warm. The tenseness from the chilled air soon left her as she turned and relaxed in my arms. I shook off my coat and wrapped it around her shoulders, Temperance pressed her lips to my chest.

I held her tight and felt a smile etch into my chest as she relaxed in my arms. We held each other and listened to the breeze intermittently blow by, Temperance pressed harder into my embrace as she snuggled against me. Shortly thereafter, I felt a little hand push into my and Temperance's stomach, moving us apart. My eyes opened and I looked down: it was Georgiana who wanted to join the hug.

"Well, well..." I raised my eyebrows playfully. "Do you want to tell our daughter what happens when someone interrupts a Mummy and Daddy hug?" I looked over at Temperance.

"We have a Georgiana sandwich?" Temperance shrugged her shoulders to play along.

"Correct, my love..." I picked up Georgiana and she squealed throwing her hands around me. "I have this little piggy right here." I put her pinkie in my mouth and growled. Georgiana laughed as Temperance took her ring finger. "Yummy..." Temperance licked Georgiana's finger and made a slurping sound as she rubbed her stomach. Gee giggled and threw her arms around each of our necks, culminating in the three of us embracing each other snugly.

"Did you miss having me as your sidekick?" Georgiana laughed with a hint of mischief in her voice.

"It was certainly more of a challenge without you." Temperance stroked the bottom of her chin. "But I am glad you were safe with Papa..."

Georgiana's eyes widened with concern. "Mummy, did anyone hit you in the cloakroom?" Her voice was filled with genuine worry. "Are you hurt anywhere?"

Temperance's expression softened as she knelt down to meet Georgiana's gaze. "Oh, my sweet girl, there were a few unexpected visitors, but it's nothing I couldn't handle."

However, there was a slight tension in Temperance's voice, and her eyes briefly darted towards the cloakroom as if she was recalling the encounter.

"Mummy is fine, I promise." She ran her fingers against the side of Georgie's jaw to reassure her. Georgiana, still concerned, reached out to gently touch her mother's cheek. "Let me check, just to be sure."

Temperance offered a small nod, allowing Georgiana to inspect her for any signs of harm. As Georgiana carefully examined her mother's arms and face, I watched with a mix of relief and concern. I didn't want to acknowledge the potential danger Temperance faced as I reluctantly yielded to what she wanted. It was like being flanked on both sides by a depressive episode and OCD joining together. Intrusive and disturbing thoughts, images, and ideas that could not be controlled to form gruesome and haunting episodes which seemed real to the touch though imaginary in their very constitution.

Georgiana's hands worked around my beloved's waist until fingers brushed over a faint discolouration on the fabric of Temperance's leotard, just beneath the bottom of her breast. Georgiana's brows furrowed as she noticed the mark. "Mummy, what's this?"

Temperance smiled down at our daughter, appreciating her genuine concern. "Don't worry, my love. I'm just a little sweaty from all the action." She continued to breath heavy, drenched in sweat.

Georgiana, unconvinced, wrinkled her nose and continued to inspect Temperance for any signs of harm, her fingers inadvertently brushed near the part of Temperance's stomach where she placed my hand just before. It appeared to be tender as Temperance flinched and tensed up momentarily when Georgiana's fingers palpated the area. Concern filled me and I started to assume the worst.

Georgiana's brows furrowed again as she felt the area, her concern deepening. "Mummy, is everything okay?"

Temperance took a deep breath, her smile remaining steady despite the discomfort. "I promise, I'm perfectly fine."

I noticed Temperance's subtle tension and stepped closer, placing my hand on her shoulder. "Are you sure you're alright, Temp?" I could hear the blood in my veins start to throb as Temperance nodded.

Georgiana looked up a bit puzzled as her mother spoke to me with a reassuring voice. "Yes, darling. It's just a certain little peach tickled me!" Her face turned and her eyes bulged as she roared, kneeling down and tickling Georgiana's sides as our daughter giggled and squirmed with laughter. Temperance hugged Georgiana tightly and our daughter leaned into her embrace.

A smile returned to my face and a deep exhalation left my lungs. Perhaps, my anxiety had gotten the best of me.

THE TYRES OF THE CAR whispered against the pavement as we made our way along the M55. The illuminated Blackpool Tower emerged above the flat dark plains that surrounded the motorway.

My eyes glanced upward as we passed under the sign for Blackpool North and Central. I flicked on the indicator as the car guided into the right lane of a road that was otherwise empty. Night had fallen, it was off-season, and it was a Monday; all three combined to give us a quick journey to the seaside without any impediment.

"Are we having a doughnut before we clean up the Promenade?" I looked to my left at Elizabeth who was curled up against the window in a purple hooded sweatshirt that bore the insignia of my darling's fire brigade company. Her hair was up in a white bobble, she appeared lethargic and disinterested, her hand resting under her chin. A faint glimmer of purple glistened on her legs under a passing lamppost.

There was no response from anyone.

"Or shall we work up an appetite and have a treat after?" I looked back into the rear-view mirror at Henrietta who looked back at me with her hoodie unzipped, a shimmer of blue reflected back at me when she exhaled.

"I vote before." Georgiana's voice squealed and I smiled as we exited the motorway and halted at a red traffic light.

"Henrietta, can you do my hair please?"

"Sure, Giggle." Hetta patted Georgiana's shoulder and took hold her of long hair which was down her back.

As the light turned green and we travelled onward, an exhilaration and excitement filled me that I hadn't felt in years. The lights of the waterfront glowed in the distance against the night sky. I carried on following the signs which led us toward the centre of town. In a matter of minutes, the detached new builds with red brick and brown plasticine framing transitioned into older terraced houses with chipped white and oaken windows which had some form of deterioration. The streets became narrower as the signs of various car parks emerged on the thoroughfare. The car came to a halt at another red light, small clusters of revellers and holidaymakers meandered along the footpaths adjacent to the road heading in the direction of the

Blackpool Tower which became the prominent structure ahead of us, pink and blue lights shooting up the cast-iron base toward its pinnacle. The Winter Gardens and the white lighting which traced the frame of the building, also emerged above the cityscape to the rear of the tower.

"So, when are you going to tell Papa?" Henrietta's voice broke the silence, I looked down for a moment at my heliotrope leather leggings and ran my hand into the crotch to make sure every pink lace was tied.

"Don't hold your breath, Bubble. It will be stopping at her lips for the foreseeable."

I ran my finger against my pink leather glove. "That's not true, Squeak."

"Why haven't you told him about our girls' nights, then?"

"He only knows about me..." I pressed my foot to the gas as the light turned green. "...along with Giggle's involvement..."

"In the petrol station." Elizabeth interjected. "You've said nowt about anything else since then..."

"You should tell him, Mumma..." I looked in the rear-view mirror at Georgiana who sat in the back with her arms folded, clad in her shiny pink lycra singlet, her breaths were perceptible as the singlet wrinkled and relaxed with her respirations. Georgiana's arms and legs shined under the light that passed into the car. Georgiana's hair was in a plait and yet her cape was off, but her determined look said it all that was required.

"You look even stronger, Giggle." Henrietta ran her finger against Georgiana's arm, she then flexed in Henrietta's hand. "Your arms are massive..."

Georgiana's eyes lit up as she smiled back at Henrietta, encouraged and roused by the compliment.

"I want to go solo tonight, Mumma..." Georgiana nodded with confidence.

"I am not sure if that is a good idea, poppet." I turned down a residential road beyond Blackpool North railway station, passing by

a series of pubs that reverberated with bass from techno and dance music. "You've done well staying close to me." I looked back again to her and she shot a glare of disapproval. "Perhaps, you'd fancy accompanying one of your sisters..."

"We'd make a good team, wouldn't we?" Henrietta put her hand out, her lilac briefs and silver belt back visible for a moment and she stretched her legs, revealing the lycra unitard she wore beneath them.

Georgiana gave her sister a high-five. Henrietta chuckled and pulled her black puffy coat over her costume. "I love you Henna, but I am Super Georgiana." She crossed her arms again. "We can cover more ground quicker if I smash some of them yobs." Georgeanne crunched her knuckles.

I pulled the car over and parked in an open area along the road. I moved and glanced back at the both of them.

"I think she would do well." Henrietta ran her hand against Georgiana's sides and defined midsection. "Solid as a rock, her." Georgiana gave the thumbs up to Henrietta with a smile.

"Right..." I turned the car off. "...Here is the plan..."

"So, when are you going to tell Papa?" Elizabeth's eyes leered across at me, the glimmer of her irises reflected the twinkling lampposts up and down the street.

I paused for a moment.

"We shouldn't delay any more, Mumma ..." Henrietta's voice spoke over her rustling coat sleeve. "You have any of that oil, Giggle?" She pulled out her sleeve until she was in her sleeveless unitard. The blue straps snug to her shoulder.

Georgiana shook her head.

Elizabeth opened a glove box. "Of course, you are eager to tell him..." She removed a glass vial and tossed it in the back toward Henrietta. "You are his little pet, aren't you?" Ellie chuckled.

"For goodness sake, Bets." Henrietta scowled in a defensive tone.

"You are the first one to tell Papa anything." She continued to tease Henrietta. "What's the weather like?"

"20 and chilly with a spot of rain in the afternoon, says Henrietta the Weatherwoman."

"Elizabeth..." I placed my hand on her wrist.

"You should tell Papa the truth, Mumma." Georgiana interjected, her face growing serious when she otherwise always had some form of a smile or mischievous smirk on. "He is always honest with us, so we should be honest with him."

"You are right, Georgiana." I glanced over at Henrietta and Elizabeth. "I require you all to keep it quiet until I tell him..." I spoke firmly. "When Giggle told your father about what happened with her and I in the petrol station, it put me in an awkward position."

Henrietta sat back and crossed her arms. "Well it wouldn't have done, if you told him in the first place."

"Henrietta, I need you to keep this secret until we are ready."

"I don't want to lie to Papa, Mummy." Bubble pleaded. "What if he asks me?"

"For fuck sake, Bubble..." Elizabeth slapped her hand against her thigh. "Just keep your lips sealed!"

"Language, miss." I spoke at length to Bet. "We are asking you to keep it between us until I have the conversation with your father about the three of you being involved in this business..."

"Papa will get mad and what if he tells us to stop?" Georgiana looked out the window and sat up, tying a long silk lilac cape around her neck.

"I thought you just said we should tell him the truth, little sister?" Elizabeth sat against the car door.

"We should, but he will get upset." She looked at Henrietta who gave her the thumbs up. "Especially since, he gave up the fire service for us."

"To be fair, I did tell him to rescind his leave..."

"But he was willing to make the sacrifice because he loves us and didn't want us to be scared." Georgiana spoke with moxie.

"So where are you going with this, Giggle?" I retorted.

"You should let me talk to him..."

My eldest daughters and I shared a smile at each other and each raised our eyebrows at our little spitfire.

"And what would you say, Georgie Pie?" Bet roused Georgiana further.

"That we are a team and that he shouldn't worry because Mumma is a great leader." Georgiana's response was cool and confident. "...I can persuade Papa, trust me..."

"Good word, Giggle."

"Thanks, big sister!" Georgiana looked up at Henrietta. "...I'd do a really good job, especially if I went on a solo mission and kicked butt like I am supposed to..." She smirked at me like a child ready to ask for extra candy or a toy she had her eye on at the store.

A silence filled the car again, none of us how to respond to Georgiana's attempt to leverage her position.

"I do fear you overestimate your influence on your father, Georgiana. He had to ease into accepting my sole excursions with reluctance but he acknowledged the fact that I did all this racket before he and I were a thing..." I sighed. "...I think he would lose the plot with the three of you..."

"I am Papa's number one" Georgiana countered with a wry smile. "I can get him to go along with it better than anyone." Georgie's eyes softened as she glanced at both Henrietta and Elizabeth "No disrespect."

Elizabeth snorted as she held back a laugh. We all looked over at her but she put her hands in the air. "Mother, I think you should lead and we all present beside you. He's not going to take it well but at least we're all there together." She looked in the mirror to check her cheeks.

"Undoubtedly, he will say that you are being careless and reckless with us and object to you going Incredible Temperance altogether."

"Squeak's right." Henrietta chimed in.

Elizabeth glanced at Henrietta. "But if someone were to grass us up, he'll feel betrayed we were keeping it from him." Her eyes flickered red. "...Someone may do that to be a good little girl and make her Daddy happy..."

Henrietta cringed. "...You can knock those innuendos on the head, you..."

Elizabeth smiled. "I wasn't referring to you, Henrietta." She raised her eyebrow. "Although a guilty conscience can cause one to flee without pursuit..."

"Alright, Squeak." I spoke at length.

"Proverbs." Elizabeth batted her eyebrows.

"The last time I checked, Papa was your father too, Elizabeth." Henrietta shook her head.

"Yeah, but you know what he's like." Elizabeth threw off her sweatshirt to reveal her purple leather sleeveless top which cut off at her midriff and had pink lacing like mine over her bust.

"Let's put a lid on it!" I raised my voice over the both of them and raised my hand. "It's time to focus."

Elizabeth stopped and looked at me, she said nothing and checked that the pink E buckle was fastened over her silver belt which hugged her waist and held her matching leather leggings in place. Both Henrietta and Elizabeth had matured well ahead of their age, appearing as older teenagers though being only early adolescents. On some days depending on what they wore, they looked like my sisters more than my daughters.

"Here is the plan. I will take the back streets and make my way toward the North Pier. A majority of these scrotes will be skulking about in there." I looked over at Henrietta whose eyes were fixed on Georgie as she did a ponytail.

"Henrietta you take the Promenade."

"Won't you need my help though?" Henrietta looked up at me.

I shook my head. "Start from the Central Pier and make your way toward the Tower. We can meet just before the North Pier."

Elizabeth nodded.

"With you on the Promenade and Squeak on the waterside, you'll have each other nearby and I don't suspect there will be as much action as I will encounter..."

"It appears Mother will be taking the lion's share again."

"I will be fine." I arched my back and applied the oil to my chest, pulling down a strap of my leotard to work the oil into my abdomen and ribs. "I may have a few more bumps but I would have it no other way." The oil started to cool my breasts and stomach.

"You do eat those body shots, don't you?" Elizabeth's eyes made their way down toward my midsection. "With abs like that, I can see why..." Her irises grew larger as her eyes dilated at my shiny spandex leotard contouring to my abdominal muscles, navel, and obliques.

"Better it be I than you." I checked the strap of the undergarment and made sure I could move my arms keeping my breasts in place. "If they can even land one, of course." I stroked a strand of hair back. "I should hope not as a jab or a swift kick to the gut are the worst as they almost always catch me off guard." I winced at the thought of a knuckle or the toe of a shoe digging into my abdomen and the queasy feeling that could accompany it, even after I tighten my core to absorb any more blows. I found relief in my superior strength and ability to recover and withstand the punishment. "Fortunately, I haven't had too much of either since I've finally cleared the rust off..."

"I don't like it when you get hit, Mummy." Georgiana sulked.

I smiled at the innocence of her comments, reflecting back on her reactions after our win at the garage and when she celebrated me defeating some ruffians in a cloakroom without sustaining damage.

"Can I go solo?"

I turned my head and saw Georgiana awaiting my instructions eagerly. "Perhaps, we can swap ginnels and meet at the end of the back streets leading to the Tower."

Georgiana's smile widened.

"It's a bit of a first solo mission, wouldn't you agree?" I had hoped that this would appease her and buy me some time to tell my husband about our adventures. Fortunately, the bribe seemed to work as her eyes sparkled with exuberance as she looked at me.

"Since you can fly, if you get into any trouble, you come right to me." I raised my finger. "Do I make myself clear?"

She nodded.

"If you can't, I want you to shoot a bolt of lightning into the sky and I will come find you."

"Yes, Mumma." Georgiana mimicked my flexing just a minute ago to ensure her singlet was snug. "But I am really strong, I do have abs like you..." Her shiny pink singlet contoured to her chiselled core.

"I think Giggle has an eight-pack." Henrietta tapped Georgiana's stomach playfully and tousled her hair. "Do you know much about this lot?" She glanced out the window. "These Widows as they are called...."

"I know that they cannot withstand us."

"I did a bit of research into them and from what I read in my deep dive of various local chat forums; their leader is called Albie."

"Albie?" I looked back at Henrietta.

"Or AL B., none can say for certain." Hetta appeared puzzled momentarily. "some suggest it may be a shortened name or even an acronym but it's hard to determine as none have ever seen him..."

"The end will be the same as every other that preceded him or will follow. Should he dare reveal himself, he will be apprehended." I flexed a muscle and extended my hand between the front and back seats.

"Hands in, my darlings." I smiled as my daughters joined their hands with mine. United, we split to our respective assignments and smashed the Widows impeccably. We made quick work of the miscreants with little to no resistance and I captured the highlights in a collection of memoirs only I could access.

In this anecdote, it was sheer and utter domination by the four of us. Our opposition was demoralised and downtrodden; they ran in shame as we ran through them. Their fleeting threats of reprisals were a listless attempt at self-preservation, failing miserably as they fled, defeated and scared.

It was the beginning of our emergence, leading to a rapid rise in notoriety. Our distinct successes wove together into a tapestry that bolstered our reputation. Those who dared cause mischief and crossed our path were swiftly defeated, leaving a memorable impression on both the assailed and would-be assailants. Perchance, I could pen narratives of each and every occasion to form a grand novel which spoke of our achievements, comparable to my beloved's works; who hitherto hadn't the slightest knowledge of our collective efforts.

XIX.

"Jelly Bean!" I called upstairs.

"Yes, Daddy!" Her voice much higher pitched and bubbly, screeched back to me.

"The wrestling is starting, Button..." I grabbed a handful of popcorn from the wooden bowl beside me as the introduction music started to play.

Georgiana scuttled down the steps, her two ponytails bouncing with each step. When she reached the bottom of the steps, I saw she was wearing a Wyatt Family t-shirt as a nightgown, solid black with the picture of a sheep face in white and the words *Run* written above it. I smiled at the sight of it, finding something typically cryptic and menacing to be so endearing on her. Georgiana climbed on the couch and then onto my lap, my hands gripping the sides of the shirt to make sure she didn't fall. Georgiana however rolled about, hastily taking a handful of popcorn and shovelling it into her mouth as she kicked out her legs, getting settled upon me. Her hair was still wet with the scent of the bubble-gum shampoo she loved to use.

"Papa, can you comb my hair?" She looked over her shoulder at me.

"Sure, sweetheart." I plucked at each pink bobble in her hair and let her hair down, water forming at my fingertips as I did so. Georgiana lunged forward and removed a hair comb from the coffee table, it was the same one Temperance used and has kept for over a century. As she placed it in my hand, I was met with nostalgia, envisioning Temperance's mother combing her hair with the same brush that I had combed her hair with, as well, when we were unsure if this was even a possibility.

I ran the comb through Georgiana's rich strawberry-blonde hair and dropped it over her shoulder. It descended down to her lower back with a deep volume. Under the light, it had a similar tinge to my beloved's. Georgiana had the same broad shoulders and relentless energy.

With the background chatter of the commentary, I thought about how cyclical life could be and how this all unfolded, albeit over the course of three centuries. Despite all that went into it, another generation had materialised even if there were copious variables in play that had to make it happen. There wasn't a thought of such things in our little girl's mind, the glint in her eye was solely a light from her anticipation of the forthcoming television programme. She took more popcorn from the bowl and watched the television as if my combing her hair were a part of the routine. I found it comical, it isn't much different with Henrietta and Elizabeth.

The entrance theme for Rhea Ripley started to play, and Georgiana nearly leapt from my grasp. I got up off the couch quickly after her. She clapped with excitement at the sight of her favourite wrestler, then paused to sweep her arms out and bend down to the ground. Pumping her leg, she did Ripley's signature stomp. I joined in, which made her laugh.

"Doesn't she remind you of Mumma?!" Georgiana pointed at the television.

"I can see some similarities, Jelly Bean." I chuckled and put my hands under Georgiana's armpits and lifted her. As I did so, Georgiana reached under her t-shirt and removed her belt with the pink G buckle, doing a sparkling rendition of raising the belt in the same manner Ripley did, mimicking the same menacing grin nearly identically. Georgiana was quite the thespian and her imitation was flawless.

I took Georgiana back to the couch and she sat back on my lap. Georgiana started to bang her hair to the music, I put my hands around Georgiana's ribs and gently bounced her up and down, banging my head slowly in rhythm with her; both acting like kids.

My beloved passed by on her way to the steps, peeking in and rolling her eyes as she swung her hand around the bannister to make her way upstairs. I shot a guilty look at Temperance for getting carried away with my daughter but Georgiana didn't notice and kept going.

"We just did your hair, silly." I shook my head.

"Sorry, Papa." Georgiana giggled, throwing her wild hair back. She became more animated, standing up on my lap in her exuberance. Then she threw off her t-shirt, spiking it on the ground. She was now wearing a shiny pink lycra singlet that clung to her little body. She snapped her hands, and her poinsettia hair was back in two ponytails. Her hands and feet were clad in heliotrope leather gloves, matching Temperance's leggings.

"I am going to be the next world champion." She flexed her arm muscle and smirked. Her leg muscles became more defined, her singlet contouring to her abdominal muscles. "In addition to being a superhero like Mummy and my big sisters, of course." She crossed her arms and nodded with confidence.

"Of course..." I chuckled.

"The only thing I am missing is my cape." She put a finger under her chin and looked up for a moment. "I cannot wear that in a wrestling ring, can I?"

I shrugged my shoulders. "You tell me..." I pressed my hand over my mouth to hold back my laughter at my youngest daughter's antics.

"It still looks nice though, right?"

I gave her the thumbs up. "You always look beautiful, darling." I reclined on the sofa. "I have to warn you though that you are missing the programme..."

"Discussion to be continued..." Georgiana responded with sass and turned back to look at the television, clearly mimicking her mother as she did so. I got a kick out of her antics and watched her for a moment, her eyes engrossed in what she was watching as the light carved around the silhouette of her as put her hands on her hips; the racerback straps of the singlet appeared darker against her fair skin until she turned around and climbed back onto my lap with haste. Georgiana put one of her arms around my neck and nuzzled her head against mine, her other hand digging into the bowl of popcorn with less caution as she sloppily placed the white kernels into her mouth. Crystals of salt formed around her pink lips. I handed her a napkin and she wiped her mouth. Our eyes fixed to the television as the match concluded with a pin-fall. Georgiana threw up one finger, followed by two, and then three as she won. Georgiana clasped her hands together, she turned back. "As I was saying..." A smile crossed her face as she growled and flexed her arm. I placed my arm around her bicep, it was large for a girl of her age. "That's very impressive, Gee."

I looked up at the steps as I heard a creek, Henrietta peered down from the railing into the living room and reversed when she saw Georgiana on my lap.

"Hey!" Georgiana's little hands clasped against my cheeks to divert my attention to her. "And I can do this too..." Georgiana stood up on my thigh did a handstand backwards and flipped off the couch. I sat up abruptly prepared to catch her but she had other ideas, she was floating in the air with electricity forming at her fingertips until she gently pressed her toes against the top of the coffee table, showcasing a dexterity and balance that perhaps even the nimblest of athletes could pull off. "How did I go?" One of her feet touched on the remote control as she was busy striking a pose and she lost her footing and slipped, tumbling into me. As she came forward, I opened my arms and cupped her gently. She burrowed her head into my chest for a moment before peering up at me with curiosity, a smile replacing a fleeting bashfulness.

"I think you can't be tripping over remote controls if you are busy saving the day." I tapped her nose. "It may complicate things." She retaliated with a loud laugh and tried to dig her fingers under my chin to tickle me and playfully smacked my chest. I embellished to encourage her as she then jumped onto me to attack me, all in full but nevertheless, she loved to wrestle around with me. As the dad, I could expect to this happen frequently and Georgiana was the most rambunctious out of the three of them. I covered myself up and she smacked and struck me playfully, taunting me as she had the upper hand.

"Give up?" She giggled as she pushed my chest, exerting her strength upon me.

"Not quite..." I tickled her stomach, she flinched and play-slapped me. I poked her in the gut.

"Ooof!" She pressed her hand to her core and acted dramatically as if she were actually hurt, even if we were play fighting. I poked her in the rib. "Oooh!" She grimaced and scrunched her face as if she were winded. However, it was a part of her antics as I was always extremely gentle with her whilst she was ruthless with me in her merriment. But that comes with being the dad, you are always the prime target and for what it's worth Georgiana despite her long hair, flowery dresses, and love of pink and bright colours was the tomboy of the crew. I encouraged her always but at the end of the day she was my little girl and she knew it too.

"Such a drama queen." I teased her. She growled and giggled as she smacked my shoulder and flexed her abdominal muscles.

Now, my pokes had no effect on her as they were tapping against a rock, her midsection chiselled in eight areas, easily discernible in the fabric as she flexed. Georgiana lunged at me and tried to pin my arms down on the couch laughing as she forced me backward, she poked my armpit and I laughed. I playfully tapped her thigh in retaliation.

"Oww!" She embellished and looked down at her thigh which gave me another chance to land another one. I then tapped her shoulder. "Hey!" She furrowed her eyebrows and made a nasty look at me, it was soon disarmed when I scooped her up in my arms and flipped her upside down, making sound effects as if I slammed her but in reality, I gently put her down on my lap. All the while she giggled and guffawed from the tomfoolery until Georgiana sprang to her feet and swatted my hand away before she dove on me. I covered up and screamed help! as she started hitting my arms and legs. The more I sold it, the more she laughed.

"Alright, Giggle, that's enough." Temperance's voice entered into the chaos of spilt popcorn across the couch, my t-shirt all scrunched up, and Georgiana panting and covered in sweat.

"You win."

"We're going to have to give you a bath before bed." Temperance instructed.

"You are no match for me, Papa." She kissed my cheek before getting back to her feet. As she strutted off, I gave her bum a tap with my foot softly to tease her.

"Ow!" She yelled aloud and held her bum, her face turning to a smile of both surprise and mischief.

"Got ya!" I laughed.

Temperance shot me a look for instigating her.

"That hurt!" She embellished again.

"Come on..." I waved my hand at her. "I barely tapped you..."

I was always extremely careful with her because I could never live with myself if we had an accident during rough play. Everything I did I made sure was gentle, cushioned, and safe. I had been yelled at previously for having an inclination that she should live in bubble wrap. As such, I knew full well she was being dramatic because it was a part of her act and she loved to start a ruckus, it incited her to raise the stakes.

She pouted for a moment and bought herself some time. And then on cue, soon thereafter, she charged back at me, diving onto me again and filling the room with an uproar of commotion and laughter. The scent of her sweat filled my nose as she tried to overpower me, laughing hysterically as she did so, some of the sweat from her arms and legs dampening my t-shirt and shorts.

"No cheap shots!" Her hot breath blew against my face as she slammed her little hands against the top of my head.

"Okay, okay." I covered up and smiled. "You win..." Georgiana desisted and I embraced her. In the snap of a finger, Georgiana threw her arms around me and hugged me as tight, as I hugged her. "You nearly had me..." She giggled and laughed.

"I never stood a chance." I stroked the dome of her head and kissed her forehead. "I know better at this point." She nipped my wrist once and laughed before pressing her lips to it, still full of energy and excitement before she caught her breath relaxing against me.

"I reckon we shouldn't have her watching this before bed..." Temperance put her hand on her hips. "It will only make it more difficult for her to settle in and you winding her up, won't help matters..."

"We are just messing around, Honey Bee."

Temperance briefly glanced at the television. "It's time to get her down..."

"But there are two more matches, Mumma." Georgiana put her hand into the bowl of popcorn.

"Can she watch the end? We are having a good time." I looked across at Temperance. "She's already burnt herself out anyhow..." I glanced at Georgiana. "You'll be good, right?"

She nodded and smiled.

"Right?" I tickled her rib and she giggled before I picked her up and put her gently down on the couch, pressing my lips against her belly button discernible in the pink spandex and gave her raspberry which made her laugh out loud hysterically. I picked Georgie back up and placed her on my lap and stroked her hair once.

Temperance shook her head. "I dare say, she could commit murder and you would be her co-conspirator."

"Co-conspirator?" I looked up at Temperance with a raised eyebrow. "I'd do the bid for her." I stroked Georgiana's chin. "Right, sweetheart?" She smiled and pressed her head against mine, placing her littler hand under my chin.

"And how would that play out with respect to all the variables?" Temperance responded sardonically.

"No one will take you away from me, Daddy..." Georgiana's voice squeaked as she kept her head pressed to mine.

"She's only young once..." I stroked back a strand of loose hair from Georgiana's head; she reclined against me and reached her arm back to touch the side of my face, relaxing as she watched the television. "Someone has to watch wrestling with them and play video games..."

"I reckon you enjoy it more than they do..." Temperance shut her eyes and made a face.

I put one arm around her stomach and bent down to pick up her t-shirt, returning it to my lap and sitting back with her. "Let's put your t-shirt back on, superstar."

Georgiana obliged and raised her arms. I draped the t-shirt over her and pulled it down, bringing her hair down over the back of the t-shirt. "There you go, Jelly Bean..." I gave it a flick and stroke before she leaned back into me and sucked on a piece of popcorn. Temperance's eyes leered at the television out of the corner of her eyes, it was hard to determine whether she was amused or appalled at what she was watching. A brief smile filled her face before she went stoic again.

"Daddy, when is my football team playing again?" She snapped her fingers and now reverted to a red Home Georgia jersey.

"Saturday, darling..." I pulled her hair down gently over her back. "...nice jersey..."

Georgiana smirked back at me.

"First Henrietta and now Georgiana..." Temperance bantered. "Enticing them with such an uninviting subject..."

"Uninviting, Mumma?" Georgiana scowled and wrinkled her eyebrows. "Submit to the fact that they are unparalleled."

"Wow." I looked at Gee with amazement. "Where did you learn those words from?"

"Mummy." She giggled after she shot a look at Temperance which in turn lit up my beloved who was amused and impressed by our eldest daughter.

"Join us, my love..." I pat the open area of the couch next to us.

"I will have to give it a miss as I am tending to Elizabeth with her studies..." She stretched "...I bet my buttons that she might need my assistance when it concerns asymptotes or quadratic algebra."

"What happened to her reading Smith?"

"She finished it already."

My eyes bulged. "But she only started last night..."

"You know how Squeak is when she puts her mind to something..." Temperance took a small book off the side table, the writing imperceptible with the lights turned low. "To be fair, I don't find a smidge of appeal in Cold Stone Steve Austin..."

"Stone Cold, Honey Bee..." I chuckled. "...Stone Cold...."

The discussion was briefly interrupted by Henrietta descending the steps in pink and grey plaid pyjama pants and a matching button-up top. Her reddish auburn hair was down across her back.

"Or that Wyatt fellow...." Temperance shook her head with a smirk. "...I'd say I married him but you are far worse..."

"Definitely worse..." Hetta made her way to sit beside me on the couch, she did all she could to subtly look at Georgiana and then skittishly back toward the match before she plopped down next to me and reached over me to steal a handful of popcorn. "Papa is scarier."

"On that note, I will leave you to all this suplex and body slam business." Temperance waved her hand as she turned toward the stairs.

Georgiana looked over inquisitively and squinted her eyes with confusion. "But you body slam people, Mumma..."

Temperance turned around and wrinkled her eyebrows at Georgiana, shooting a stern look. "And I will body slam you in a minute..."

"I'd like to see you try." Georgiana spat her tongue and made a weird blubbering noise, a mist of spit and spray soon showered upon my wrists.

"Alright, Gee..." I intensified my grip around her stomach and gave her a pat. I chuckled intermittently and Temperance placed the book down.

"And you too..." She crossed her arms.

"Me?" I looked over at her.

She gave me one firm nod.

"Well, I hope you do..." I shot her a flirtatious look. "Unlike Miss Georgiana, I have no qualms about that..."

A smile broke from Temperance's face then to a scowl. "Children" My beloved said quietly.

I raised my hand briefly with a "sorry" said in a similar fashion. Temperance subtly batted her eyebrows and gave me a wink.

"If Squeak were here, she'd have a lot to say." Henrietta teased.

"Speaking of which..." Temperance glanced at both of them. "Poppets, may I ask a favour?"

Both our daughters looked at their mother with attention. "Can you fetch Bet and grab my slippers in your travels..." Temperance very subtly raised her eyebrows to cue them to move along.

Henrietta responded first and nodded. "Right." She got up. "Papa, can you pause it please?"

"Sure, honey." I reached for the remote.

"Come on, Giggle." Henrietta took Georgiana's hand and she soon scurried off the couch.

"Thank you, Bubble." Temperance remained standing as the girls went around her. "You are an absolute star..."

Henrietta and Georgiana were immersed in conversation, Hetta gently gazing over the bannister to see what Temperance was doing until they both were upstairs.

"Do you mind?" Temperance plopped her bum down over my groin and I flinched from the force. "My, my, someone is jumpy..." Her hands gripped my thigh stronger until she started to massage them, her lips drawing close to mine as I could feel the breath kissing my lips.

"Did Georgiana have a chat with you?" She spoke softly.

"Regarding?" I looked to the side and then back at Temperance. My beloved looked a bit puzzled as if something had not gone according to plan. My beloved glanced up at the steps and wiggled her hands.

"Is everything alright?"

"It's fine." She smiled briefly. "Never mind it then..." She drew closer. "...I guess she left it to me..."

"Left what to you?"

Temperance shook her head once and raised her eyebrows, tilting it towards the steps before she pressed her lips to me. She moaned and kissed my lips again, I responded with a kiss to hers but she pulled back and giggled, before engaging deeper with me, our tongues swimming in each other's mouths as I wrapped my arms around her and she started to slowly grind on me, until I turned her over and rolled her up on the couch. My beloved giggled and started jabbing me as she started to horse around but very quickly it escalated to another kiss. The kisses became deeper and fuller, and before long my hand was riding up her midsection toward her breast and we were grinding on the couch, as we engaged some more.

Then we heard running down the steps and shot up from our position, when Henrietta returned with her little sister, she had a set of purple fuzzy slippers in her hand but didn't seem too bothered. Temperance and I both looked like deer in headlights, pulled away from each other quickly with the hope of not giving anything away.

"Well played." Henrietta held the slippers up. Temperance took the slippers from Henrietta's hand with crimson cheeks as Hetta sat beside me. I hit the play button on the TV and we resumed watching. Temperance cuddled up against me and Henrietta soon did the same. Georgiana stood in front of the television, unsure of what to do or where to go.

"Come on, Giggle." Temperance waved our daughter to join us and she nestled up between the both of us on the couch, getting comfortable against my chest and under her mother's arm.

Temperance pulled the quilt off of the top of the couch, spreading its black and orange checkerboard patchwork across us.

I took it and tucked it over Henrietta, then Temperance, and Georgiana who was nestled against her mother.

"Bet!" I called out.

There was no response from her.

"Where is my phone..." I looked around but didn't want to shuffle around with the mass of bodies lying across me. "Can you one of you text her, please?" The heat started to build around my legs and hips from the quilt. "Tell her to come join us..."

"Well isn't this, cute?" Bet entered the room.

"And there she is..." I hit the power button on the remote to turn on the electric fireplace. "...shut the door, please, honey..."

"Wrestling, Papa?" She raised her eyebrows and snickered. "Seriously?"

"We can change it if you'd like..."

"No, please!" Georgiana whimpered.

"If it will oblige, my little sister..." Elizabeth made her way to the couch. "Scoot over..." She leaned into Temperance with a chuckle, Temperance smiled back at her and playfully tapped her. "Would you like some quilt, daughter?"

Elizabeth nodded with a coy smile and watched the television along with the rest of us. "...so, I reckon the lot of you weren't able to have that conversation then..."

"Pack it in, Elizabeth." Temperance admonished her.

"Wasn't this your ploy, Mumma?"

"What is this big mystery..." I looked around the room. "Talk about what?"

"There is nothing to speak about..." Temperance quickly dismissed any notion of any subject. Gee and Hen looked at each other for a moment, as if they were trying to subliminally speak to one another before glancing back at Elizabeth.

"Elizabeth loves to provoke." Temperance glared at Elizabeth in an authoritative manner, a scolding "knock it off" look that was unmistakable.

Bet waved her hand and yielded, seeming inclined to continue on with whatever was on her mind but she seemed disinterested. There was merit in the fact that Bet was the one in our family who liked to get a rise out of others. However, she never did it for no reason. More often than not, there was something that was unsaid because it was either left unconfronted, disguised, or avoided and Bet was always one for taking things head-on. It was often attested that she inherited such a demeanour from being my daughter. Though she exhibited all the propriety and agency of a lady which she undoubtedly gained from Temperance's influence, Elizabeth was direct and not one for dancing around matters. She was more matter-of-fact and straight-on.

Why though was everyone being so defensive about her utterings? Usually, they ignored her knowing full well that if they reacted it was fuel for her. This time, however, Elizabeth did not follow up with quips which would suggest that there was some verity in what she was speaking about. She didn't seem to be looking for a reaction but instead answers, perhaps she had a better idea of how to handle a certain matter that these four had been keeping amongst themselves and was merely trying to prove that she was right. I had my suspicions as to what this entailed but remained in denial, I didn't want to imagine the possibilities as they filled with me an anxiety that I couldn't even attempt to articulate if I wanted to. I didn't want to know if she was communicating something covertly in her messaging; instead, I enjoyed the company of my wife and daughters and left tomorrow's worries for the next sunrise.

XX.

Suspicion continued to grow, and conspiracies reared their ugly heads—or at least, that's how it felt in my mind. Temperance and the girls would go off together for what they called "girl days out" and come back late. Sometimes, they would go out for a meal, returning later and later. There was no hard evidence to suggest that she had incorporated them into her own enterprise, but my gut feeling told me she was hiding something under my nose.

One time, they all came back, and though they looked as they left, I noticed Henrietta's torn white blouse and a big splotch of red descending from her chest toward her ribs; it looked like dried blood. Instinctively, I ran to check if she was alright, but she insisted she had dropped a plate of medium-rare steak all over herself. I was perplexed, as she usually preferred her steak medium-well. However, she abruptly responded that she liked trying new things.

Denial overruled my instincts. I wanted to believe her because I didn't want to imagine anything worse—like Temperance taking them out to fight Lord knows who, and something happening to my beloved daughters.

I entered the bedroom, fresh out of the shower, my clothes already resting on the bed. I put on a pair of boxers and threw the towel into the white laundry basket at the base of one of our dressers. I pulled on a white tee and a pair of black and grey basketball shorts. As I reached for a ball of white cotton socks in the dresser, my eyes wandered over to the closet. I peeped my head out the door into the hall: no sign of anyone. I stepped back into the bedroom and locked the door behind me.

The memory box! It may have the answers I was looking for! Temperance kept it in the second-from-bottom drawer of her dresser at the opposite end of the bedroom. A small lime antique chair dated to 1835 sat in front of a small mahogany table next to the dresser, with a matching mahogany dressing table mirror atop it. I recalled many nights watching Temperance sit on the edge of the cushion, the red cushioned back coinciding with her overskirt impeccably though she didn't plan it so, as she did her eyelashes, rouged her cheeks, or styled her hair. Even in those simple moments, she took my breath away. Even now, I was bewitched by the image of such a scene in my recollections.

I knelt down and pulled at the brass handle of the drawer, which creaked open. The box was missing, but two leaves of paper remained. I plucked one and examined its contents. It was an excerpt from when Henrietta and Temperance were standing in the field, glancing up at the inferno, the night I rushed off to the silo fire. The second leaf was the first page of a re-telling of Temperance and Georgiana's petrol station incident.

The piano started to play, making me flinch. I quickly put the documents back and put on my socks, leaving the bedroom to avoid suspicion. I unlocked the door and slowly shut it before creeping down the steps. Henrietta sat on the stool, her hair cascading down her back as she stared intently at the keys. She launched into Chopin's *Wrong Keys* etude. I sat on the step for a moment and listened, marvelling at her work. "My little girl is a genius," I thought to myself and walked in. Hetta looked up at me and stopped playing, the vibrations of the keys fading into silence.

"Sorry, I was just having a go..." Henrietta responded with a tremor in her voice as she put the key cover down. "The others are outside." She ran her hand over the top of the key cover, a subtle display of affection for the instrument. "I know I am supposed to be lending a hand in the garden but this helps clear my mind."

"I was listening to you," I smiled at her. "Breath-taking stuff, Hen." I held the wooden ball terminus at the end of the bannister. "You are very talented."

"Many thanks." She blushed and looked at me with heavy eyes, feigning a smile.

"Is everything alright though?" I came closer to her and leaned over the piano.

Henrietta nodded but didn't say anything.

I rubbed her cheek once, and she smiled a bit wider. "I should go back outside..."

"Hold on." I put my hand on Henrietta's shoulder. She turned her head to look up at me, her disposition cold, an avoidant energy permeating from behind her doleful visage. It looked as if she was dying to tell me something, prompting me to delve deeper. I wanted to ask her about the entry from the silo fire, but it might spoil any chance of finding out what I really wanted to know. It might alert Temperance that I was on her tail, looking for clues. I was grateful no queries left my lips and instead thought of something we could do to take our minds off whatever was troubling us.

"Do you want to play that Allman Brothers song together?"

Hetta nodded with more enthusiasm, her smile filled with eagerness and excitement.

"Let's do it." I rubbed the back of her head as I went to collect my guitar and amp from the closet in the corridor. Henrietta removed the key cover and stretched out her hands as I plugged the amp into the outlet beside the piano and sat on top of it. I plugged my cherry red guitar into the amp and hit the red power switch. "Ready?" I smiled at her and she nodded watching for my hands to start moving.

I played the opening chords to *Jessica*, Hetta soon glided her hands over the keys to throw in the few piano notes that bounced off the guitar and then together we played the chorus, Hetta providing a bassline with the piano keys. I shut my eyes and ran my fingers up the fretboard as Hetta tapped the side of the piano to give me percussion until she on cue started to play the piano notes and we bounced the melody back and forth off each other. When I opened my eyes, Georgiana had materialised, dancing her heart out. We both shared a look at Georgiana twirling her pink skirt and pirouetting around the front room, smiling at her jubilance. Hetta and I continued to play together, I fed the rhythm so Henrietta could do the piano solo, her hair splashing behind her as she struck the chords and jostled her head occasionally, throwing her fingers down with passion, she started to work her away across the piano in the transition to the guitar solo but before she completed it, she ignited the room with a powerful glissando. I broke out into the guitar solo and Henrietta gave me some rhythm and bass with the piano, our eyes meeting and sharing smiles as I did so, the ivory white of Hetta's teeth with an occasional flick of the tongue the most memorable feature.

Finally, we shifted back into the final chorus and then slowed it down to the coda. I strung a few notes, and Henrietta gracefully glided her fingers over the piano, belting out a few harmonies that she sung and hummed to add another layer. We did it again, and then after a couple of volleys, we nodded at each other and entered the coda, I wailed on the guitar and the whammy bar, and Henrietta stood up and pushed down on the piano with vigour. Soon thereafter the only noise in the room was the sound of little hands clapping as Georgiana stood there applauding us, her long strawberry-blonde hair up and down her back, her pink lips widely smiling to match the flower decal on her white tank top and her long pink ruffled skirt.

I put the guitar down and took Henrietta's hand and we both bowed. I pulled her in for a hug and kissed the top of her head. "That was amazing."

"Next time, Papa should rap and Henna should sing." Georgiana exclaimed.

"We'll do that, baby girl." I smiled at Georgie and she scurried off down the hall humming the song we were just playing, eagerly running toward the kitchen and back door. Henrietta watched her go and tensed, seemingly lost in her thoughts. She looked up at me briefly, as if there was something that she was clamouring to tell me but seemingly did not possess the courage to do so.

"Are you sure there is nothing want to tell me, Hen?" I pulled the piano stool out from behind Hetta and she leered at me. Her forehead wrinkled and her irises narrowed in on me. She bit her lip once and reverted to the expressionless pout that she inherited from her mother. Hetta and I shared a bond that when we played together, we would know what the other was thinking and communicated solely by giving each other a look. That ability transcended music, the music was just another way that we drew close to each other, and as such we could know when the other has something weighing heavy on their mind for better or for worse. I knew she had something to say and I was inviting her to do so in confidence. However, she didn't respond and reacted only moments later when she came out of her gaze to place the key cover down. "I was just reflecting on how well we harmonise. Our chemistry is fabulous."

"You were carrying it." I smiled at Henrietta and put my arm around her back. "We should get outside and help." She nodded, and together we made our way to the back garden.

As we emerged, Temperance was tending to the flowers with a green watering can in hand, matching her long dress. Her cinnamon-auburn hair cascaded down her back, reminiscent of

Georgiana's style. Gee darted about the grass, energetically scattering seeds under Elizabeth's nurturing guidance, carefully choreographing her little sister's enthusiastic exertions. I picked up a wooden rake lying beside a freshly groomed patch of rich, black soil. Gripping the handle, I began to stroke through the earth I had turned over an hour ago. The air outside was now warmer and more humid compared to the cool interior of the house we had just left. Sunlight cascaded over the soil until Henrietta's shadow stretched across it into the lush green grass.

"Papa?" Henrietta stood at the back door with her hand still on the white ivory door knob.

I looked up at her with the rake in hand.

"Can I talk to you?"

"Sure, sweetheart." I put the rake down. Hetta looked out nervously at Temperance and Elizabeth who seemed to be monitoring her closely.

"Alone?" Henrietta spoke lowly from the corner of her mouth.

While I wanted my daughter to confide in me and be of any help I could to her in all things, I had a premonition that this discussion would illuminate what I was searching for in the shadows; the answers I was seeking in the memory box that had suddenly vanished.

I glanced back at Temperance, her piercing blue eyes watched our every move. Her porcelain complexion was expressionless. Elizabeth turned briefly to oversee Georgiana who was kneeling down to press some seeds into the grass and equally shot a hawk-like stare at us. Her white blouse ruffled in the wind along with her maroon cloth skirt. She wore a leather belt to bring the two together. Her cabernet hair was down her back in a series of plaits.

Henrietta faked a sneeze. "Don't make it obvious." She pinched her nostril.

"I have to go to the front yard in five minutes." I picked up the rake and started going at it again. "Will you help me with washing the car?" I raised my right eyebrow at Henrietta who nodded at me discretely. Elizabeth continued to clock Henrietta's movements but soon went back to throwing seeds on the soil, leaning into Temperance. When the three of them were pre-occupied, I placed the rake down and went back through the house to meet Henrietta on the swing tethered to the big willow tree in our front yard.

"We used to have a lot of fun on these when you were younger." I pushed her back.

"I used to love it when you gave me an underdog."

"I can still do it." I pushed her back. "I don't know if it will work well on these compared to the ones at the park."

She swung more.

"What did you want to talk about, honey?" I asked as Henrietta extended her legs and kicked out.

"I don't know how to describe it to you."

"Take your time." I watched her swing up and down until she let go and landed in the front yard ahead of me. She crouched down in the grass. Her thighs were clad in shiny blue spandex, accentuating the contours of her quadriceps and calves. As she rose, her arms were bare, hands on her hips. She wore lilac trunks over a unitard with a silver belt and a pink 'H' matching the one on her briefs. Her hair flowed freely, adorned with heliotrope gloves and boots.

My heart sank as fear and dread washed over me. My anxieties were becoming a reality. I forced a smile to mask the effect this anticipated revelation had on me.

"That's an amazing costume. Did your mother and Georgiana make it for you?" I spoke lightly, keeping my smile to retain the security of this conversation. "That's nice of them to include you."

"This isn't any form of a dress rehearsal, Papa." Henrietta took a step forward, anxiety and sadness in her eyes. I was deeply disturbed. "Mumma doesn't go it alone. All three of us help her. We're not just a team in theory," she glanced over her shoulder, checking if anyone was watching from the window, "we are a team, literally."

I looked up at the bedroom window and shook my head. "I always had a feeling."

Henrietta grabbed my arm. "Please don't be angered."

I put my arm around her back and stroked her hip. "I am not mad at you, sweetheart." I rubbed her back and plopped down on the swing; my every thought consumed by a thousand scenarios.

"How long has this been going on for?"

Henrietta looked back at the window and snapped her fingers; she was back in her normal dress. "Do you recall when Mumma and Giggle bollocked those lads in the garage?"

"How could I forget?" I recalled just reading one of the pages of that tale minutes ago and reliving the event all over again.

"Truth be told, she was preparing us for such an adventure priorly but when Georgie incited that scuffle, it pre-empted her to bring things forward."

"That's why she moved the memory box." I sighed. "She was planning this all along..."

"Wait..." Henrietta gripped one of the tethers of the swing. "...did you see what was in the memory box?!" Alarm filled her voice.

"No, Skittle." I reassured her, stroking her back. "But I had a feeling if I did, I would have been confronted by what I always feared to be true..." I sighed and looked down at the ground. "...by what you have told me." I glanced up again at the house. "It all makes sense though...the suggestive nature of her questions, the sneaking around, the tact she employed when she has brought this stuff up." I looked at Henrietta whose eyes were filled with remorse.

"Your mother is a clever woman but she knows full well how this would affect me."

"She's been talking of going back to Blackpool." Henrietta looked behind her at the gate, the lane, and the meadow behind. "For Albie...." She muttered the words under her breath and looked down at the grass dancing in the breeze.

"Who?"

"I am sorry, Papa." Henrietta put her hand on my shoulder. "I shouldn't have said anything but I felt you needed to know.'" She sat on my lap.

"I appreciate it, Hen." I patted her thigh. "You have always been honest with me."

Henrietta smiled at me; her eyes matched the colour of the sky as little red dots formed under her eyelashes. "You've always trusted me and I will always be loyal to you Papa...."

My eyes swelled up with tears at these proclamations, I took her hand and held it tenderly.

Her eyes started to water. "...Alas, I couldn't hold this secret anymore."

As I was about to embrace her, our moment was interrupted by a snarky comment.

"No surprise there." A voice spoke out to us as our heads turned toward Temperance standing in the front of the yard, flanked by Elizabeth and Georgiana on either side, their skin glowing as the late afternoon sun bounced off them. All three were giving Henrietta all sorts of looks of disdain. Elizabeth in particular sported a murderous glare.

"It's alright, darling." I kept a steady hand in front of Henrietta.

"Big sister, how could you?" Georgiana ran off into the house,

"This was long overdue." Temperance leaned back and crossed her arms. "Though it was unnecessary for Bubble to reveal this prematurely, we were going to tell you in the coming days."

Temperance glanced out at the sun. "Will you both step inside, please?"

I got up from the swing and looked over at Henrietta who wouldn't leave my side, she stayed off to my left, gripping my arm with both her hands. I kept my arm around her as I passed Temperance on my right. My beloved's glower at Henrietta echoed the sentiments of her siblings whilst she appeared exposed every chance her and I made eye contact. Words weren't said as we made our way to the dining table and though no one spoke, my thoughts were screaming everywhere, desperate to know the truth.

I reclined in the oaken dining chair stiff in my posture, the white cushion sliding out from behind me but I didn't even notice. Henrietta sat behind me in another dining chair pitched against the wall. Elizabeth and Georgiana stood at the other end of the table watching onward.

I fluttered my fingers against the oaken armrest, twiddling an empty cup that had dried tea markings in it from being used earlier that day. My eyes briefly shot toward a glass cask of whisky locked in a liquor cabinet on the far side of the dining room, the cherrywood tarnished in dust.

"I don't know what you expect me to say, Honey Bee..." I twirled the cup once and tilted it on its recess, I couldn't even look up at Temperance, only listen to her breaths and smell her perfume which tickled my nose. "I am not going to get behind this."

"Our daughters have been gifted special powers and they wish to use them." She paused for a moment. "...and like I, they don't wish to live in your shadow but set their own mark." Temperance knelt over the table.

"I never understand that comment." I rubbed my cheek briefly. "About living in my shadow." I shrugged my shoulders. "I've always encouraged you. I thought we are in everything together." I emphasised the word together to demonstrate my displeasure with her unilateral decision-making amongst everything else.

"We are." Temperance stepped closer. "And we will always will be." Her hands gripped the headrest of the dining chair closest to me. "But am I supposed to be curtailed to the domestic realms, forever?"

My eyes peered up at hers, her blue eyes bulging with determination and urgency. "You weren't supposed to be, to begin with." I gazed across at Bet and Gee. "...but this isn't about you..." My finger flung from the white tablecloth in their direction. "It's about them..." I sat up and clasped my hands together. "And though it doesn't change the fact that you are playing a treacherous game, you are now adding them to it." I unfolded my hands. "You reminded me that they are your daughters too but equally, they are my children and my responsibility, and now I have to step in..."

"To be fair, you wouldn't know if someone..." Temperance glowered at Henrietta. "...didn't gabble."

"Don't blame, Hetta. You said you were going to tell me, anyways." I sat back in the chair. "And I would have found out eventually, even if you didn't." I closed my mouth and swirled my tongue through it. "Where did you put the memory box?"

She crossed her arms and gazed down at me with a look of displeasure.

"You should see us, Papa." Bet's voice entered the discussion. "...we are quite an extraordinary squad." She stood in the shadowy recess of the room with her hands upon Georgiana's shoulder.

Temperance raised her eyebrows, offering a brief look of approval from Bet's commentary.

"When someone doesn't freelance." Bet jeered as she loured at Henrietta.

"We are not half bad." Hetta nodded in agreement with her twin sister's statement. Her taut expression and mannerisms suggested that she was desperate to get back into her mother's and sisters' good graces.

"We work well together!" Georgiana smiled and nodded enthusiastically.

"Indeed, we do." Temperance chuckled, a warm smile filled both Elizabeth and Henrietta's faces.

"I would never think otherwise, but what you are doing is far different. I can only visualise what sort of Neanderthals you run into, people I'd like to kill if I could get away with it."

"Charming." Temperance retorted.

"That's not what I mean." The anger was misguided and misdirected, it was only natural that I'd want to destroy anyone or anything that posed any threat to my wife and my little girls. "It's not like fighting a fire where it's a straightforward process and even the lowest of dregs cheer for you." I threw my hands out again. "These people, who knows what they are capable of." I cupped my hands against my mouth and blew into them before I shot to my feet, "This needs to stop."

Temperance and the girls all looked at me with alarm.

"Papa, we know that you have nothing but good intentions for us." Elizabeth spoke softly to me. Georgiana nodded in agreement; I looked back at Henrietta and she smiled at me, gently putting her finger against my hand.

"Elizabeth Grace, this discussion isn't open for any further conversation..."

All four of them conveyed their own look of disappointment at me. I wasn't a stupid man; my approval was only a gratuity or luxury to them, it would be nice to have but they would be perfectly fine without it, especially with my counterpart leading the charge and fostering such an adventure. Even if I was avidly against it for their own good, I was outnumbered four-to-one, as I was not just in gender distribution but in the collective consciousness of this household. Normally, I was one to appease and accommodate because their happiness superseded my own, but at this intersection, I couldn't yield.

"What if someone harbours a grudge and then they try to make this personal?" My fist curled and I leaned forward on my knuckles. "What if they resort to things that you fear happening to you, even to this day?"

"Such as?" Temperance gave me a steely gaze.

"The reasons why you are still afraid to be in close proximity of any cathedral?

Temperance glunched.

"Even after three people had the same dream which argued the opposite." I scratched my forehead for a brief second. "As you recall."

"It was a dream and it was years ago."

"It seemed real to me and I am certain that we don't have anything to fear as The Lord after all is our father."

"If I concede to that, then may I ask what worries you?" Temperance looked back up at me and sealed her lips firmly.

"You already know what I am preoccupied about." I leaned back in the chair and rested my arm on the armrest.

"No one has harmed us and we have never come back hurt, have we?"

"Not that I know about." I looked up at her with my eyebrows scrunching. "But you know better than I."

"And no one anything about us, other than our costumes."

"That could change, you've had close calls in the past personally." I put my finger on the table. "What perplexes me is your avoidance of London. You haven't been there in 100 years as you are terrified of being discovered amongst millions of people, but you want to overtly draw attention to yourself in a place where everyone is watching now?"

Temperance leaned back for a moment pondering my commentary until she spoke. "Let us go tonight..." She sat in the chair beside me pressing her hand to mine. "...we are going to just to check that they are not there, anymore."

"Does this have anything to do with a fellow called Albie?" I watched for a reaction but Temperance kept a straight face, she was clearly playing her cards close to her chest.

"From what I understand you defeated them?" I prodded with a hope to unearth answers. "Why bother going at all?"

"We'll be gone, a couple of hours, tops." Temperance ran her hand up to my wrist. "We'll pop down, see if anyone is about which they won't be and then we'll come on back in time to have a board game night."

"Where are you going?"

"To see a man about a dog." Her response was measured and firm.

"Don't be cute." I snickered.

Temperance and I stared at each other, she shed a brief smug smile at me before she composed herself, her tone growing colder in her reply. "For all I know, we could turn up in Handforth having a brew by the by-pass."

"If that's the case, why don't I come?" I looked over at Elizabeth and Georgiana whose expressions grew meek. "Or are you going to Blackpool?"

Temperance didn't answer initially but her eyes flaring gave me a hint. She glared at Henrietta for a moment, a forewarning not to speak which Hetta looked away, feeling every eye upon her. I glanced back at Henrietta to see if she could subtly give me an answer. She remained mute, all she could do was look at me with remorse, sorry that she could not tell me the answer.

"I'll figure it out."

"Are you planning to chase us around every corner of the country?" She gaffed. "You might be off out on a long drive heading in the wrong direction whilst we're already back." She turned her gaze upon me, it was authoritative and assertive. I rubbed my mouth and itched my scruff for a moment to gather my thoughts.

"Is that it, after this?"

"For now..." Temperance's determination emanated from her eyes. "You are best just going along with it."

"Or what?" I glared at her. "What if I don't?"

"Poppets." Temperance stared down at me. "Give us a moment, will you?"

"Wait a minute, girls." I sat up and Temperance gently coaxed me back into my chair.

"They'll just be outside."

Elizabeth and Georgiana made their way to the door, looking onward as Henrietta got up from the chair, I took her hand and she froze in place. In that moment, Hetta appeared lost in a crossfire between her devotion to me and her fear of being out of her sister's good graces.

"Harriet."

"Yes, Mother?" She couldn't even establish eye contact with Temperance.

"I wish to have a word with you."

I clutched Henrietta's hand hard, my eyes begging her not to go. Pity was in her eyes when she looked at me whilst fear was written across her face when she looked at her mother.

"But for now, you may go."

I got to my feet and tried to pull Henrietta back but met Temperance's hand against my chest. "Shut the door on your way out." She gave Hetta a look as she walked toward the door and then closed it. Temperance walked over to ensure it was completely shut. "Now, where were we?"

"You are trying to convince me to be alright with this..." I frowned. "But there is no way that I will budge."

"I am sure there will be a way for me to enable you to see things in a new light." She tugged at the pink bow in her crotch and sauntered slowly toward me.

I couldn't help but salivate over how her legs and ass looked in those tight form-fitting leathers, I bit the back of my thumb but tried to keep it to myself. However, Temperance already knew she had leverage.

"If you cooperate, I'm all yours when I return." She spoke in a sultry tone and snapped her fingers. She was now wearing black silk vest top with an open chest that showed her cleavage and bore her midriff along with black lycra leggings. "We both have been wanting to have a go on each other for a while but we haven't done..."

"Do you think I was born yesterday, Honey Bee?"

She thrusted her hips against my crotch once. "Compared to me, you may as well have been." She plucked a vial of oil from her bosom and untied the bow around her top as I felt the warmth of the flask rest in my palms. "Put the oil on me." She drew close and straddled my lap.

I looked at the flask again, she put her hands over mine and grinded her hips against me, putting a kiss on my lips. "Don't resist it, you know you want to." Temperance threw her top on the floor and pressed her bare chest against me. "You do trust me, right?"

"More than anyone."

"Well then trust me with this, too, please."

Her gaze always had a strong effect on me. When I looked into the blue of her eyes, I was hypnotised and thus I looked out the window for a moment to free myself from its effect.

"Now, please put the oil on my back."

Temperance threw her arms around me and I put some of the oil in my hands and ran it through her shoulder blades and down her spinal cord.

"Keep going." Temperance breathed into my eye and started with a serenade of soft kisses against the side of my neck. As my hands reached to the top of her butt, she backed away.

"Cheers, Butterscotch." She placed her hands over her head and thrusted her hip once more against my crotch, I was at this point near ready to ejaculate into my pants. "Now do my front, please."

I poured more of the oil into my hands and started my working my way down from her neck, when I reached her breasts, she sighed with pleasure. "If I thought there was a thing to fuss about, I wouldn't entertain the possibility of the lasses accompanying me. But you must be assured that the girls are very capable and quite strong. You shouldn't underestimate their capacity by any means, we mangled those malevolent goons and had time for a proper catch-up after."

"I have a bad feeling about it." My hands worked down toward her abdominals, traversing each curve and bend in her musculature.

"You usually do about most things."

"What?" I looked up at her and paused for a moment.

"Teasing, darling." She exhaled. "Keep going." My hands meandered down her toward her belt when it was met by her hand. "How can I reassure you?"

A buzzing sound filled the room as we locked eyes on each other, I put the oil on the ground and leapt for her, our lips colliding as we volleyed kisses which resulted in Temperance lying on her back on the table, the white tablecloth shifting as the large maroon candle jostled across the table.

"You know I could make love to you on this table right now."
My lips and tongue swam down her neck toward her breasts.

"And I want you all to myself...." Temperance snapped her
fingers back and she was back in costume. "When we return, you
will be rewarded for your cooperation." She gently guided me back
and rose to her feet off the table. "I dare say that you will be
remunerated in a way that you never have done previously." She
checked the front laces again and adjusted her belt. "You don't have
to say yes, in fact, you can say nothing and that will suffice..." She
licked her lips and drew her finger down towards her cleavage.

I shut my eyes, heaving as I was caught in a passion; my
hormones flowing through me as I stroked myself to try to calm
myself down. My boxers were already wet from the explosion of
bodily fluids that escaped me; she had that sort of power over me.
Lethargy and euphoria overtook me like I was drunk. I slumped
over in my chair and relaxed for a moment until I heard the door
close and saw I was alone in the room. The house was silent and
in the midst of the coloured spots flash in my eyes from the blood
flowing back to my head and the buzzing sound returning to my
ears, it had dawned upon me that they were leaving. An
anxiousness filled me, my mind screaming at me: *what are you
doing?!*

"Shit!" I leapt out of my seat and stormed out of the dining
room, my socks causing me to slide on the area rug as I made
my way toward the foyer and front door. "Wait!" I screamed as I
opened the front door and was met with a crisp blast of Cheshire
country air.

The car had started to head down the lane and I ran after
it, sprinting toward the open gate. As I emerged onto the lane, I
looked to my immediate left and saw the blue hatchback drifting
away. I waved my hands and I saw Georgiana's little head look
back at me with a brief smile, as the car made its way further away.

She thought I was waving goodbye when I was trying to get her attention.

"Jelly bean! Tell Mommy to answer the phone!" I made a phone symbol with my fingers. "Fuck!" I slipped my hands into my jean pockets and violently gripped the phone, my feet pressing down on the jagged rocks of the lane, causing my feet to twinge from the discomfort caused. I removed my phone and nearly dropped it, before gaining control of it. I dialled my beloved and listened on intently, indifferent to the chirps of blackbirds in the meadow beside me or any potential car coming down the road that may descend upon me. The phone rang once and went to voicemail.

"Fuck!" I hung up the phone and immediately tried again, but the same situation occurred. She must have turned the phone off. "Darling, it's me, please call me back as soon as you get this, I just want you to turn the car around. Please, there is no need for this. Thank you, love you!" I hung up and exhaled violently, I glanced out at our house tucked away behind the hedges and the large willow tree in our front garden, poking its head out as it played a game of hide and go seek with the occasional traveller coming down our lane.

An idea entered my mind: Hetta. I scrolled down to the phone and dialled our spare mobile number, the one the girls took when they went out. This time the phone rang and continued to do so until it went to voicemail. Immediately, I hung up and tried again, placing a hand over my eyes as I glared down the lane hoping I would see their car returning back. This time it went to voicemail again. "Skittle, it's Dad. Please call me back as soon as you get this, I want to speak to Mommy. You guys need to come back. Thank you, sweetheart, I love you." I hung up the phone and sprinted back toward the house.

I wasn't thinking, I had to get my keys and go after them. They were going to Blackpool and only had a brief head start. I ran into the house and dialled Hetta as I grabbed my car keys from the kitchen. The phone started to ring again and as I sprinted back towards the steps to grab my shoes, I heard the ringing of the phone. An eerie chime that repeated over and over again, was the only accompaniment in the empty and quiet manor house. They didn't take the phone. Why?! I threw on my shoes and tied them in record time before shutting the door and sprinting down to the drive. I hopped in my pick-up truck, put the key into the ignition, and put the pedal to the floor, a cloud of dust kicked up behind me as I veered sharply onto the lane, not thinking of who or what may have been coming the other way. Fortunately, the road was empty and the pick-up roared down the lane, speeding at the national speed limit though few actually drive at such velocity on an English lane. I veered onto another lane, this one leading toward the road that led to Goostrey and then onward to the A50.

"Call Mama." I shouted at the radio and the Bluetooth responded by calling her. The same cadence of tones filled the car as I glanced out the window, the sun now getting ready to dart below the treeline nestled behind the pastures of sheep on my left. In the distance, the telescope dish of Jodrell Bank was supine as it stared up at the evening sky which was filled with a gradient of gold into sky blue into amethyst. The outline of the dish's shimmering into a white as the car roared onward. Just as before, the phone went to voicemail and it was evident it was powered off.

"Honey bee, I tried ringing before and the phone was off. Please call me back as soon as you get this, I hope you turn this on soon. Please, just call me back, I beg you. Thank you." My voice strained as I finished my message. I swiped some sweat from the brow of my forehead and exhaled, my heartbeat was thundering and smashing out of my chest. I kept on driving and in a matter of minutes through my aggressive motoring, I got to the A50 without incident. I looked left then right and without hesitation, sped out onto the road hanging a right and following the sign for Knutsford and the blue M6 icon. If they were going to Blackpool, they would have to take the motorway!

Knutsford had a tendency to get crowded on weekend nights and it could sometimes slow down the road, as it was notorious for the police to set up speed traps on it, as you entered the town. Moreover, with the foot traffic flooding the village, it was a bottleneck waiting to happen.

I couldn't take any chances, a sign emerged for a road that led to Byley and Tabley, another lane I could tear up and bypass the village to find myself right at the junction of the M6 outside Knutsford. There is a chance that Temperance could have been slowed down by the Knutsford traffic but she was clever and observant. She knew the short-cut like I did and chances are if I was thinking about it, she already thought of it.

The car jerked as it went over the dips of the road, screeching as it cut through bends. Hedgerows framed both sides of the lane, whizzing by in a blur, the road narrowed and as I came around another turn, a silver BMW sauntered onward. I was forced to slow down and creep by them to the side to give them a wide enough berth to pass. An elderly couple sat in the car donned in khaki cardigans and white sweaters, likely out for a leisurely evening cruise.

Perhaps, Temperance and I would be there one day, but then again, Temperance would never be elderly even if she were older than the two occupants of the vehicle combined. I picked up speed and careened down the lane, oaken fences now lined both sides of the road, farmlands pitched behind them with an occasional ash or sycamore tree greeting motorists as the Cheshire countryside got more rural. I had made good progress until a mile down the road, I came up behind another car that was travelling at a more moderate pace. A small black Mini Cooper with a white roof, the road once again narrowed and every time I tried to overtake on the right, another car would appear over the brow of the hill travelling in the opposite direction.

"Move!" I revved the engine and finally went by with haste. The owner of the Mini, a young woman with her hair up and a discontent look glared back at me as if my behaviour was out of line. Perhaps, it was. A sign passed which indicated that I had entered Tabley, a sign that also welcomed safe drivers. I reckon I wasn't welcome on this occasion. As the area became more populated with red brick new build houses lining the road, a roundabout greeted me and a right turn was required to go to the M6. I looked right and saw no traffic but as soon as I got onto the lane into a more rural enclave, I was halted by a pack of cyclists. An army of geese, blocking a towpath as one looked to walk past. Should you get too close, like the geese who hiss, the cyclists could also present a peril to all parties. I had to be sensible and kept a safe distance behind the crew of 10 maybe 20 road users all clad in blue or red lycra tops with black-hemmed short sleeves. Their white, black, yellow, and gold helmets shone from the faint sun which now hid behind the trees. After a couple of minutes of biding time to pass them, the opportunity presented itself and I was off again, the M6 now visible in the distance as the road rang alongside it. Nearly there, only one impediment left: the railroad crossing but as it would be: when I finally approached it, a queue was there behind a gate which was down. The red lights flickered as if the sign was taunting me and sticking out its tongue.

"Come on!" I put the car in park and punched the steering wheel. "Fucking shit!" The wait gave me time to think. Maybe they got my message and went back home. Maybe they were waiting for me and I was out here like a maniac driving aimlessly. But she would have called, she wouldn't just disappear and turn up like that unless she never intended to go to begin with. I rehearsed scenarios; I was assuming the worst. I was filled with the image of something horrific happening up there that I could not stop. I couldn't save them from some form of danger that didn't have a face but had the capacity to harm them and destroy them. But why think this? For all we know, they could have gone somewhere else altogether. A diversion could easily have manifested.

Or maybe, they would go there and like Temperance said, it would be quick and they would come straight back. Perhaps, I was overthinking all of this and needed to trust her. After all, it's not like Temperance was a disreputable and feckless woman. She was adaptive, pragmatic, and measured. Out of the two of us, she was the one who always had a sounder head and clearer mind, she knew what she was doing and seldom ever caught out completely. Temperance was the voice of reason, perhaps I was being unreasonable. I started to tell myself: just turn back around and go home, it will be alright.

That's what I thought for a moment as the initial scourge of panic left and adrenaline wore off, my eyes becoming heavier by the second. But when the gates went up, I found a second wind and kept driving, uttering prayers that they were safe, praying that she would call, praying that this would be over soon. As I carried on down the road, I came upon a convenience store and pulled over into the car park. All I could do was recline back in my car seat and weep as the ending of Poison the Well's *Apathy is a Cold Body* finally started to ring out in the speakers behind me as I checked my phone for any missed calls or messages, though I would have undoubtedly heard them come through. I was clinging to the hope that somehow, I didn't hear the call by error and that this had already come to an end; that it was all some misunderstanding that was never what I imagined it to be.

I stepped out of the car and tried to ring Temperance again, stretching my back and yawning as I did so to give myself a moment of relief from all the tension within me. Just as before, the phone went straight to voicemail. My heart started to race and my pulse began throbbing.

"Honey bee, I tried you again as I am sitting here getting wound up more by the moment. Please let me know that you are okay, please let me know that you are safe and I will come to you." I glanced up at the white signage with red lettering Barton's Quick Stop General Store. As I hung up the phone, a man emerged from the triple-paned window red wooden door, puffing on a vape as he held a six-pack of Stella Artois in his head, pressing the box against his navy tank top. His skin was tanned from the sun, his eyes hidden under the shadow of his white baseball hat as he sandals scratched against the asphalt walking away from the store. In that moment, a thought; a temptation entered my mind. Two that had not confronted me in nearly a decade. I glanced at the door with the advertisements all pasted on the panes of the window. A multi-coloured tapestry that invited me into the cool oasis to find nourishment from the desert of uncertainty and trepidation outside.

It was like being back on the aqueduct, the day that I met her. I was moving in a direction but not sure of where I was going whilst imagining a thousand more possibilities and standing still unsure of what to do. I returned to the car and I was frozen in the seat as *She Bangs the Drums* played on the radio. I was taken back to our wedding night, another song that Temp and I danced around to like a bunch of goofballs; the joy that we had found each other, the elation in the adventure we were embarking on together. The tears welled up in my eyes and I started to weep, degrading to a full-blown episode of sobbing and hysterics. It all came back to me, the day I walked to Marple; the late Autumn afternoons we walked on the canal together; the hope intermingled with the suffering; a wistful nostalgia of the infancy of our romance when we both didn't know what we were doing but knew we wanted to be with each other. For so long, I pined for the day and then she came, and now it felt as if she was gone again.

XXI.

T he only discernible sound I could hear in our journey to the seaside was the reverberations of the tyres against the road. There was no chatter or music playing in the background, just the four of us together on our way to determine if we had put our boots down once and for all. I will be honest; I was truly unsure if what I told my dearest was the whole truth. There were too many questions to provide accurate answers. Most notably, this Albie or AL B., or whatever they call themselves. If this character was in fact real and not a work of fiction, how would they respond knowing that a woman and three girls who albeit were extraordinarily gifted decimated a whole assortment of their heels, goons, and louts rather effortlessly. It either would be as we suspect to be the case where they are demoralised to a point that they disband and disappear into the unwritten history of the Fylde or they are waiting for retribution.

Tonight, was the night that The Widows was first established, from further research it seems that they have been about since the nineteenth century. If there was a night that we would learn their fate, it would be this one. Because tonight would be the night that they would be most visible if they were still in operation. If there was a night that we could anticipate confrontation, it would be this one. If there was an opportunity to finish off whatever was left of them, this was the eve, as well.

I circled around the Promenade in Blackpool and there were no signs of trouble. In fact, the Golden Mile was acutely quiet...perhaps too quiet for my liking but it was still technically off-season. The pier *appeared abandoned; no signs of activity other than a light on at the far end of the pier where the carousel stood.*

I looked out the window at the open iron gate that led to the North Pier, swinging open as the car came to a halt at a red light. My eyes diverted from the open entrance to Henrietta who sat up front with me, her body squeezed up against the door as far away as she could be from me, watching a passing tram on the line beside us. Elizabeth sat behind her glancing at me before fixing her glare on Harriet. Georgiana's head was slumped over, her chin burrowing into her chest as she had drifted off for a brief kip.

"We'll pull off by the Wedding Chapel and have a quick look." I pressed my foot down onto the gas pedal and carried on as the light flashed amber.

"There is no one there." A muffled voice tugged at my left ear.

I looked left at Henrietta who remained sat in the position she was before shooting a glance backwards to Elizabeth whose eyes scrunched up.

"What was that?"

Henrietta fidgeted in her seat, a bright light escaped briefly, illuminating the shiny blue of her bodysuit before it disappeared again as she moved.

"What did you say?" I raised my voice louder.

. "Is that your mobile, turncoat?" Elizabeth tapped the back of the seat with her boot. "Are you sending Papa messages?"

I put the car in park and fixed my gaze upon Henrietta who looked at both Elizabeth and me, unsure of what to do next. I pointed at her hands. "It's powered off."

Georgiana sighed as she woke up, letting out a yawn as I heard her shift in the back seat.

"Place the phone below the handbrake." I ordered and Henrietta leaned toward me with nervousness as she deposited the device where I asked.

"*You are to remain in the car whilst Squeak, Giggle, and I have a quick peek.*" *I pointed at Henrietta and continued on driving toward the parks near the chapel, only feet away.*

"*With all due respect, Mumma. It could be a trap.*"

I continued driving onward, showing little reaction to her prompt, turning on my indicator as I pulled into the space.

"*What if they were hoping we came back tonight, knowing it is their anniversary?*" *Hetta spoke at a faster pace.* "*Wouldn't that throw this entire plan into the sink?*"

"*The only one who is undermining our plans is you, Harriet.*" *I slammed the car into park and glared at her.*

"*Hear, Hear.*" *Bet kept her eyes fixed on her sister. Henrietta moved her head around the car looking for an ally, glancing for someone who would come to her aid in this moment of interrogation. My dearest wasn't here to protect her and now she had to deal with the ramifications of her choices.*

I powered on the mobile for a moment and as it loaded, the screen became barraged with voicemail notifications and text messages from one culprit.

"*This lad is so bloody clingy with his twenty-odd messages begging to determine our whereabouts.*" *I turned the phone back off and took hold of the other mobile.* "*Blinking hysteric, him!*"

"*Papa is worried about us and cares for us.*"

"*Naturally you would say that wouldn't you?*" *I snickered at Hetta who looked back at me with a deep set of betrayal in her eyes.* "*Squeak, take these will you?*"

"*Sound.*" *Bet took hold of the devices.*

"*We'll have them with us, as we go.*"

"*I don't mean to pry.*" *Georgiana's voice squeaked for the first time, cutting through the tension in the car. All three of our heads pivoted toward her.* "*But four are better than three and Henna is still our sister.*"

A smile broke from Henrietta's face for a glimmer.

"I for one don't care to see her at the moment." Elizabeth crossed her arms. "Her attendance would be a distraction."

Harriet's expression returned to a frown.

"Henrietta, you will do your bit and do as you're told." I turned off the ignition. "You may step out of the car if you wish, but you do not move unless instructed otherwise."

"But Mummy, Bubble is super strong." Georgiana interrupted. "And she controls water, both can really help us!"

"It shalln't take long, Georgiana." I looked back at her. "We won't be five minutes."

"Don't be down on yourself now, big sister." Bet reached for the door handle. "You were happy as Larry to give us up when it mattered most.". She opened the door hoping to leave with the parting word but Harriet wouldn't let her have it. Henrietta stormed out of the car.

"You accuse me of kissing up to Papa, but I see you've carved out a nice little niche for yourself as Mummy's right hand."

"The only right hand that you will be seeing is mine, if you don't mind that beak of yours!" Elizabeth curled her fist.

"Bets, don't say that to her!" Georgiana emerged from the car and stepped in between them, her lilac cape billowing behind her as she freed herself from the vehicle with haste. I stepped out with matching vigour and made my way over toward the confrontation. I took hold of Georgiana's cape and gently tugged her behind me. "Let's go you two." I placed my hand around Elizabeth's chest, my forearm cupping against her bust and pressing into the violet leather before my hand made its way down to her midsection and gripped her flesh, tugging her back with a gentle squeeze of her abs. "Elizabeth." I stroked a strand of her hair behind her ear as the sea breeze started to roar behind us, a lone spectator to the scene. "Go stand with your sister, please."

Bet retreated and strutted toward Georgiana, her purple leggings and crop top glistening under the moonlight, as did Georgiana's pink singlet with her cape dancing wildly behind her. I stared down at Henrietta, her back pressed against the cold metal of the car, her wide eyes tracking my every move as if waiting for a strike that never came. Her breath quickened, shallow and fast, like a bird trapped in a cage.

I drew close to her and her hand drew to my stomach, not to strike me but to keep distance. My abdominal muscles flexed and I took in a deep breath as I felt the sensation of her hand push into my torso. My chest rose and fell as I looked down at her hand gripping at two of the six contours in the leotard, clinging to my abdominal muscles as if they were a way back to me.

I stood stoic and showed no reaction. Henrietta's face fell even more, understanding that my anger had not yet subsided. Her hand slipped down toward my belt buckle as she looked towards the ground. My fingers met hers as I calmly took her hand off of me.

I looked over my outfit for a moment, checking that every lace was tied and there were no creases in my leather leggings or the leotard tucked into the leggings. Bubble glanced up at me with remorse in her eyes. As the wind started to blow, she put her hands to her arms as a shiver sent down her spine. I snapped my fingers and my pink shawl-like cape wrapped around my neck, flicking in the wind behind me. I undid the shawl and wrapped it around Henrietta. I didn't smile at her, still vexed with her conduct without any desire to show otherwise. However, I didn't want her to be cold.

"Stay here." I rubbed her sides for a couple of seconds as my hands warmed from the electrolytic capabilities I possessed. Henrietta looked up at me, tugging on the cloak with big glassy eyes, she looked desperate to reconcile with me; remorseful for her actions and far less angered compared to her interactions with Elizabeth. I ran my hands through her hair to ensure it didn't tangle down her back from the wind blowing it about and turned away from her.

"Let's go." I marched forward; Elizabeth and Georgiana flanked me on my left and right, both looking back at Harriet for a brief moment as I kept my sights fixed on the dark pier whose silhouette stood in front of us, drowning out the roar of the sea breeze or the sounds of the waves breaking at the shore on the beach beside us.

Our heels and boots clattered against the pavement as we moved through the shadows en route to the entrance to the pier. A faint light glimmered from out on the pier which grabbed all our attention whilst everything else close to us was desolate. As we came upon the gate, an ice cream concession was shut to our left. The metal grades down over the stall window, all the lights off. I glanced up at the sign above the overhang, 1 Scoop £4, 2 Scoops £5. That used to pay for an entire weekend here at one point, now it only provides a temporary amusement and novelty for a sweet snack consumed in minutes.

The gate creaked as it swung open, the wind the likely culprit but it was nonetheless eerie. I glanced down the wooden planks which disappeared around the bend, spanning the full diameter of the amusement hall beside us. I took two steps onto the gangway, my steps the loudest sound in another wise silent soundscape.

"We should go, Mumma." I looked back at the silhouette of Georgiana's little frame standing in the gangway. The shadow of her cape and hair, a black blur next to a larger figure of her older sister. "There is no one here." She whispered.

"Let's make sure." I spoke soft in tone but loud enough for both to hear me. Elizabeth's figure came forward to join me whilst Georgiana lingered at the edge of the ramp, her small frame silhouetted against the dim light. Her feet shuffled, hesitant, as her eyes flicked between me and the yawning darkness of the pier. She bit her lip, the gesture more about holding back her own fear than anything else. Bet and I carried on, assured that it would prompt Georgie to follow us.

"Wait!" Georgiana cried out. Elizabeth and I turned around to see Georgiana's figure toddling down the ramp. "Don't go, Mummy."

Georgiana pressed her head against my stomach and threw her hands around my waist, squeezing my back and glutes as if she were trying to inhibit me from moving any further.

"Giggle, we've already had enough theatrics from another one of your sisters tonight..." I placed my hand down over her head and swam my fingers through her hair before plucking gently at her pigtails.

"I am not trying to defy you, Mummy." She whinged. "I am trying to help."

"I'll tell you what?" I knelt down to make eye level with her, her glimmering green eyes visible in the beam of moonlight. "Go have a fly around and take a look." I turned my head toward the exit onto the outer deck of the pier. "And we'll meet you, there." I pointed at the location. "If you don't see anyone, we'll get off."

Georgiana nodded and started to levitate, her cape flicking behind her as she ascended upward and darted forward. As she left, Bet and I looked at each other and didn't say anything but carried on walking side by side. When we emerged onto the outer deck of the pier, the lights at the end of the pier turned off. The night sky was now fully clear: every star and constellation fully visible as the cosmos cascaded around the full moon hung high in the sky. Another gust of wind followed, rattling the deck and filling the area around us with creaking and clanking sounds. After the wind broke, the only sounds that remained were the dissonances of Bet and my exhalations along with the crashing of waves from the sea below, forming a symphony that was rhythmic though the two contributors operated independently of each other.

Elizabeth and I ambled further, passing by a bench with a glass overhang and the silhouette of the first roundel until we were now in the middle of the pier. Behind us, lampposts twinkled on the promenade with the main lighting coming from the Blackpool Tower, bands of pink then purple then blue shooting up the bracing of the main structure until it reached the top platform. The lighting then recessed to red but seemed to have paused on that hue. When we looked down to the opposite end of the pier, nothing but darkness was ahead; the faint outlines of the buildings were faintly perceptible.

A spark of lilac light bubbled above us, followed by two boots thumping against the deck. "Hup!" Georgiana grunted as she landed, her cape rustled behind her as another breeze blew. Her shoes sparkled pink and purple in the heels when they made contact with the ground.

"It's empty, Mummy." Georgiana drew close to us, her hot breath tickling the hairs on my wrist.

I put my arm around her back and rubbed the back of her cape, its leathery/silk material compressing in my hands. I looked up at the Tower lighting which had shifted to white while we took our attention off of it. I glanced over in Elizabeth's direction; the side of her face now accented by the illumination from the Tower. My head pivoted once more to the end of the pier. Another light waved across ahead of us, followed by a laugh. I gazed at Elizabeth and down to Georgiana to detect any reaction, to see if they saw or heard anything but both looked to be awaiting my go-ahead to depart. I looked back once more and saw the moonlight for a white beam of light off a large wave that was making its way to shore, the rush of the tide sounded like a breathy giggle against the low howl of wind coming in with it.

I ran my hand under Georgiana's cape and pressed it to the back of her, the smooth spandex of her singlet was wet from sweat. "Let's carry on."

Elizabeth placed her arm on Georgiana's shoulder and we took two steps forward, the brightness of the Blackpool Tower's white lighting had recessed back to red. Static filled the speakers as we passed them and then the overhead lighting on the pier turned on.

The ending of Peggy Lee's "Is That All There Is?" started to play through the speakers. Georgiana froze in place, her eyes peering up at the speakers until a smile filled her face. Bet however looked more startled, her eyes bulging with surprise as her lips descended to the

floor. I too was taken by surprise, I confess. After all, the music playing
was performed by an artist who had the same surname as us. Some
coincidences some times are not so coincidental.

Before we could determine what caused this incident, we heard a
pop and then the sound of broken glass. Another popping sound; as
we turned around on the pier there was the dark blur of two figures
standing at the end of the pier. The popping sounds volleyed again and
it was followed by the sound of Georgiana grunting as she dodged and
then flipped to the side until she jolted in place, and all went silent.
Was she hit?

"That was close." Georgiana giggled as she held out her cape which
had a small hole through the back of it. Her giggles turned to a loud
moan after the popping sound resumed. "OOF!" She doubled over and
held her midsection, gritting her teeth. Elizabeth reached down to
tend to her and she soon shrieked.

"UGH!" She cried out as she was hit by a projectile on her
shoulder as she lunged forward, gritting her teeth against the searing
pain in her arm, as she pulled Georgiana behind the cover of a nearby
roundel. I jumped in front of them to shield them; a clink of another
projectile hitting the bench beside me echoed through the night,
sending a jolt of adrenaline surging through my veins.

My eyes darted toward the source of the popping sounds,
narrowing as I spotted two masked figures about 100 yards away.

"Air rifle pellets." Elizabeth winced. "Gosh, they hurt." Bet seethed
as she kept her arms tight around Georgiana, her shoulder showed a
bit of blood but was bruised primarily. Georgiana held her stomach,
a bit of blood formed beneath her pink singlet where she was hit: the
sight of which made my blood boil.

Fury surged through me, I gained clarity and understood the
pent-up angst, aggression, and worry that consumed my beloved when
it came to our daughters. Verily, they would heal and be fit as a flea

but that didn't provide me with any consolation. Those masked hoods had to recompense for what they had done.

"You two, stay here!" I shouted as I leapt onto the roundel, dodging more pellets as I somersaulted and flipped onto the deck, backflipping twice more across the pier. Their shots were delayed, targeting where I had been rather than where I was going.

Once, I landed in front of them, they realised their mistake and threw their rifles, fleeing towards the carousel. But my rage fuelled me and my pace was far faster than theirs. I leapt into the air and tackled the first one, slamming him to the ground after passing two more roundels.

His accomplice charged at me when I was on the ground but I nimbly rolled out of the way. As he passed me, I swept his feet and sent him tumbling onto this compatriot. I brought my hands together and I summoned a purple storm of electricity from my fingertips upon both of them. The lads screamed in agony as they convulsed against the wood panels.

"Get up!" I kicked one of them in the ribs and he rolled across the pier. The other staggered as he got to his feet. "I'll try to make this fair."

When the other goblin got to his feet, I jabbed him once and his head recoiled backwards; I followed up again and he nearly lost his balance, I pivoted my foot and spun around kicking him in the chest and he flew through a closet door for a storage shed which stood behind him. I then cartwheeled to get back into a natural posture and standing position. As I did so, the other rodent was back on his feet and threw a kick to my midsection which I caught and then twisted his leg to send him flipping onto the pier.

"Take this!" I raised my leg and dropped it over the back of his neck, his hands clenched into the wood as he was lying on his stomach, woozy and gasping for air as if an anvil had fallen on his back.

I tugged him by the back of his hood and raised him up in the air. "Another Widow, have we?"

"Ahh!" He screamed as I clenched down on him and pinned him against one of the roundels.

"You wound my daughters and reckon you will get away with that?!" I gripped his sweatshirt hard and pressed him against the wall. "Now there is no use in fighting me." My hands started to glow purple. "Are there any more of you here?"

He strained and squirmed but didn't say anything.

"You will answer me!" I clenched down on his shoulders and threw him down onto the pier, several feet onward back in the direction I came. The yob rushed to his feet and when he turned to sprint off from me yet again, a sheath of ice appeared before him and he fell to the ground.

"Hiya!" A blur whooshed across his face and he was knocked out. Seconds later, Georgiana landed in front of me and placed her hands on her hips, dried blood over where she was hit by the air pellet but in high spirits otherwise. You would have never guessed what would have happened minutes ago.

"Payback is best served cold." She quipped, her voice carrying a playful edge.

"It's revenge, darling." I knelt down beside her and corrected her, a smile tugged at my lips.

"I am not for semantics." She batted her eyebrows and I couldn't help but laugh until her little green eyes embossed with alarm.

"Mummy!" Georgiana pointed and the doors from the roundels ahead of us flew open. Emerging from them were a total of six more combatants, all clad in black hoodies and jeans masked with matching yellow frown faces; a couple of which were equipped with pipes and knives. Behind them, another commotion was stirring as a mass of bodies were converging on another. Grunts and groans filled the air and moments later, Henrietta emerged from the shadowy recess of the entrance lying on the pier. The sight filled Elizabeth with alarm.

"Rough her up!" A voice yelled out and Elizabeth soon turned in the direction of Henrietta.

"She never listens!" Bet ran to her sister's aid.

"Help your sister, Giggle!"

She saluted me and sprung into the air, shooting two blasts of electricity and a beam of ice in the direction of the six combatants who stood between us and Elizabeth as she went airborne. The bolts hit a bench behind two of them and directly connected with another two dropping them instantaneously. One of the remaining two was hit by the ice beam and bounced off the railing of the pier before the ice formed a barrier between the remaining three opponents who were on their feet and myself.

Behind them, a battle ensued as Georgiana was pursued by two more of these mongs as she darted and flew about. Elizabeth was holding her own until numbers added up and she received a punch to the stomach which doubled her over and a punishing uppercut which cocked her head back before she was deposited over the side of the pier. Georgiana taking notice of this flew off and darted under the pier. Henrietta remained lost in the kerfuffle.

"I don't have time for this." I reached into my hair and removed two hat pins, I threw one at the first one that charged me and hit him in the shoulder, I leapt into the air and my foot crashed down upon his nose, knocking him out in an instant. One of the final two combatants slipped over the ice whilst the other got through nimbly. I chucked the second hat pin at the one that got through and it grazed his arm piercing into the wood of the roundel behind him. He and I both glanced at the shiny hat pin lodged in the wood and he looked down at the ground to find a glass milk bottle lying on the deck below the seats which lined the exterior of the pier. Pink and purple electricity started to form at my fingertips and as I released it at him, he dove out of the way, but it hit three of his colleagues behind him. The ruffian grabbed the bottle and ran toward me. I jumped onto the seating of the pier

and he swung the bottle at my legs, I hopped over it and when he came to swing it back in my direction after hitting open air the first time, I kicked him in his jaw and sent him stumbling backwards. Despite the blow, he did not drop the bottle.

I assumed a fighting stance and when he lunged at me with the bottle, I blocked the attack, jabbed him in the face, and twisted his arm to force him to drop the weapon. He groaned in agony and tried to punch me with his other hand but I swatted it away and brought both his arms down. Now in control of both of his wrists, I wrenched them in the opposite direction, finally making him drop the bottle.

"Let go of me, you freak!" The yob in desperation flung his knee into my side.

"OOH!" I let out a gasp as my body recoiled from the sharp pain, some of my strength waning from the biting blow. I gritted my teeth as the bruising sensation spread across my torso. My body leaned to the left as the burning and throbbing radiated up and down my sides. Emboldened by his success, he followed with a swift toe kick to my gut near to my navel.

"OOFF!" I grunted and bent forward, heaving from the blow as I clenched my teeth trying to get my breath back. My mouth opened with widened eyes, showing my shock and discomfort. I felt a throb in my belly as if I had been punched hard. Though he was meagre, the kick hurt like the dickens and knocked the wind out of me. Before I could fully recover, a sudden, sharp knee drove into my stomach, just above the belt buckle. The impact muffled against the spandex of my leotard, the pain was sharp and immediate.

"OHH!" I gasped as my muscles tightened reflexively. My breath hitched, and for a moment, everything else faded but the burning ache spreading from my core. My breaths coming in short, painful gasps. I held myself, wincing with every breath as I tried to regain my composure and maintain my balance.

He chuckled as I was doubled over clutching my stomach with both hands. "Not so tough now, are you?" At that moment, I heard footsteps from behind me as one of his downed compatriots emerged and attempted to put me in a full nelson but I ducked under his attempt and flipped him onto the pier. His back thudded against the wood as he cried out in pain, disabled for the moment. The hooligan that landed his hits on me threw another punch at me but I dodged it and applied a reverse chokehold to him, taking him down to the ground quickly.

"And you never were!"

He struggled and grunted, his face turning red as he tried to resist but it was futile. I maintained my grip, fighting through the throbbing pain in my abdomen as my muscles tensed with determination. I applied just enough pressure to keep him subdued, but not enough to cause serious harm yet. He started to fade from the lack of oxygen, soon passing out. The other brave soul who I flipped just before, rolled over and attempted to get back up but he couldn't as I hit him with another load of electricity to knock him back.

I got back to my feet and I flipped into the air, landing with grace. Two swift cartwheels took me across the pier, momentum building. As I reached him, my leg arced in a perfect roundhouse kick, striking his throat with precision.

"Cheerio." I waved at his unconscious body and brushed myself off, wicking all the sweat off my chest and shoulders along with any dust and dirt that coated my skin from grappling on the ground. I glanced around at the downed thugs and drew some more voltage to my fingers. I cast the electricity across the pier to ensure they were sprawled out and incapacitated.

"Good sport." I taunted the lot of them as I surveyed the scene to make sure they were all defeated. My attention turned to the scuffle ensuing at the end of the pier between my daughters and the remaining adversaries. I sprinted toward the post where the hat pin *was lodged in place and removed it from the wood, placing it back in my hair.*

The scent of saltwater and old wood filled my nostrils. I heard another pop, followed by another. When I turned in the direction of where they came from, another pop followed by a large smack into my bust.

"OWW!" I cried out and clutched my bosom, as blood trickled into my cleavage. I looked across at two more hoodlums cloaked in all black with obscure white hockey masks, who emerged from one of the roundels. They must have been hiding in there and fancied having a go at trying their luck. "That's it!" I growled, my patience snapping as I surged forward. Flipping into the air, I landed just in front of them, ready to end this. I was met with another pop, followed by a sudden, hot pain that lanced into my thigh where the pellet had struck. "Aah!" I grunted, clenching my teeth to stifle a cry. I glanced down, noticing that no blood was seeping through my leggings, though I could feel the sting of the projectile breaking the skin. It was wet and painful, but not enough to bleed through the fabric of my bottoms. I quickly assessed the wound on my breast before looking back up at the culprits, my breath heavy. Their masked faces betrayed their confusion, their initial bravado crumbling under my defiant glare.

"Give me that!" I demanded, extending my hand toward them. The two of them exchanged nervous glances before raising their hands in surrender, the fight draining from their posture. The tension in the air was suddenly punctuated by the eerie strains of a calliope. The carousel behind me had come to life, playing Scott Joplin's "The Entertainer," a haunting melody befitting of the surroundings.

I turned toward the carousel as the lights flickered ominously, casting long shadows across the pier. For a brief moment, the music transported me elsewhere. I longed to see my dearest; Hoping and wishing in the midst of this chaos, my Butterscotch was there to rescue me.

My heart skipped as a figure emerged from the darkness, dressed in an orchid tailcoat that seemed to glow under the moonlight. He took a step forward where the carousel lighting could illuminate his features, his black shirt formed a chasm that his silver cravat hovered within. His trousers were a silverfish grey which descended into black loafers. He smiled and nodded once at me, before doffing his top hat to reveal his blonde hair. His smile reminiscent of a smile I hadn't seen since the last time I saw my mother. I blinked my eyes once to ensure what I was seeing was in fact true; his face had transformed and his almond-shaped eyes had turned into beady red eyes, his smile replaced by fangs. Tremors filled my body, and a feeling of horror descended down my spine. My breath caught, the world narrowing to just him. No, it couldn't be... I didn't want to even say his name... "

"Good evening, Temperance." A voice greeted me and before I could detect the source of it, a boot crossed my jaw which sent me spinning sideways. I struggled to regain my balance but placed a hand down to prevent me from falling, my cheek and chin ached from the impact. When I got back to my feet, a woman stood in front of me with flaming orange hair, she was dressed in an all-white muslin bodysuit and had menacing yellow eyes.

"I'm ALB." She smiled at me and from beneath her sleeve, I saw it, the muzzle of a hand pistol. I flicked some electricity at her hands and the gun was knocked away. "Ah!" She grunted and waved out her hand.

I threw another bolt at her and she dodged it, much to my chagrin and surprise. Albie leapt forward and her boot crossed my chest, sending me flying backwards into a lamppost centred in the middle of the pier.

"Ugh!" I reached behind to where the bruising was flaring up in the small of my back.

"*This engagement is too intimate for guns.*" *Albie flicked out her hand and came forward with intent, her boots clanking against the planks of the pier.* "*It's not like they work on you, anyhow...*"

I rolled forward and performed a cartwheel to get back to my feet before I threw a punch and she dodged to the left, I threw another and she dodged to the right, laughing as she evaded. I feigned another punch and swung over her hitting open air as she ducked again. The next thing I felt was her little fist burrow into my stomach.

"*Ooomph!*" *I bent forward and gasped, the first jab disrupting my breathing, followed by an uppercut to my lower abdomen.* "*Ooff!*" *A sharp grunt escaped my lips as the air left my lungs from the forceful and sudden impact, as my abs absorbed the brunt of the blow. I clutched my stomach one hand froze in place, bending over further as I tried to regain my breath. Albie threw her elbow into my lips which recoiled my head backward.* "*Argh!*" *I grunted as I saw spots for a moment, blood started to form around my lips. She threw another punch but I smacked it downward and disoriented her, I countered with a spin kick to her stomach.*

"*Ow!*" *She doubled over, the kick effectively slowed her down, enabling me to plant my leg and throw another spin kick at her face which caught her directly on the chin, sending her to the ground.* "*Is that it, flower?*" *I stood over her as she was lying on her side, trying to catch her breath.* "*It's going to take more than that.*" *I pulled her up by her hair.*

"*I know!*" *Her voice squeaked with joy, letting out a wide smile before a large black pen knife jabbed into my bum.*

"*Ack!*" *I cried out and my knee nearly buckled from the pain shooting down my leg, releasing Albie from my grasp.*

Enough tricks! Purple and pink lightning formed at my fingertips. I threw some electricity toward her but she removed a metal medallion from her person and deflected the energy back toward me, I was paralysed for a moment as my body seized and shook, the voltage for the first time ever running through me, as opposed to my target. I was in shock both physically and mentally

"You don't know who I am, do you?" Her boot flew up into my groin smacking against the front lacing of my crotch. The impact sent a shockwave of pain through my lower abdomen. "OHH!" I let out an involuntary loud grunt as my body recoiled; my knees nearly buckled as I bent over and clutched the targeted area, my face contorted as I clutched the affected area with both hands, I found myself doubled over, the pain rampaging through my core.

"I was hoping you would as you created me, after all." She smacked my chest on the bare skin, cracking loudly through the air as she continued to wind me from top to bottom.

"AHH!" I shrieked as I held my chest struggling to stand. I was fully bent over trying to suppress the feelings of nausea; it hurt just to breathe as pain seared throughout my body but I had to stop her.

"I am not actually called Albie, you idiot." She baited me and I threw a punch at her which was markedly slower. Albie weaved her head away from the first strike and swatted the next aimed toward her body. When I threw a low kick aimed at her legs, she blocked it with her shins and her fingers swept across, her nails tore through the flesh above my ribs.

"AHHUHHH!" I screamed as I clutched my side, four tears were found in my leotard, blood coated my fingers in a tomato red. "I am so full of pride." She snickered as she licked her nails clean of my blood. I could barely move as the pain from my ribs was excruciating, I had one hand virtually fastened to the wound as I could feel the spandex torn away with only my gashed skin remaining as it profusely bled. "...But you need pride for moments like these!" Her hands clenched around my throat and I strained for air.

"You used to work for a fellow called Coleman, did you not?"

My eyes could barely stay open but they for a brief instant jerked toward Albie.

"*A mutual friend of ours was in business with his family until the governess inserted her nose into the affairs and ruined everything...*" She punched my rib and I felt fresh shockwaves of pain flow through my body, I winced but couldn't let out a whimper. "*She vanished for a while, but we knew you'd turn up eventually.*" She chuckled. "*Long ago, I used to watch you parade around on this very pier in fancy dress, singing and jigging with rhythm and vigour, waiting for this moment.*" Her grip intensified and I jerked in her grasp, sudden movements intensifying the agony of the rib slash, I received. "*For a moment I was despaired, you managed to disappear for over a century.*" She started to lift me off the ground as I gagged and contorted. "*But one day, I stumbled upon a book written about a woman called Temperance who sounded just like you!*" Her hands started to burn as if her hands were a hob.

"*And I went to one of your husband's readings in Northwich.*"

I started to convulse as her chokehold grew even tighter to where no air was entering my throat. "*I had a look around and funnily enough you were sat right there at a table not far from the stage...*" She snorted holding back a laugh. "*I could have attacked you then but despite previous experiences indicating otherwise, I knew I had to be patient and wait for the opportune chance.*" She threw me to the ground, I tumbled across the deck, my back bouncing against the wooden planks feeling as if I were being punched and kicked up and down my body. The knife still lodged in my backside bounced deeper into me which was agonising in its own right.

"*Some of our lads were down Cheshire way and as fate would have it, they encountered a woman fitting your description at a garage who utterly bollocked them...*" I groaned as I attempted to get back to my feet but I could only get one hand down. "*We had a nosy around trying to find you but kismet was kind to us.*" Albie skipped over towards me. "*You stepped into our own back garden to gloat in your success..."* An umbrella formed in her hand. *"And now I have you where I want you!"* The fiend whacked me over the shoulders.

"AGH!" I fell onto fours; as my hands pressed against the deck, it seemed as though she had transformed. The ghoul was wearing thick steel-toed black boots with orchid trousers, comparable to the demon I saw earlier at the end of the pier. *"Fool!"* The boots gnashed down on my hands and sent a flurry of pain through me, crushing several of my fingers and splintering the muscles that held them in place.

"Owww!" I cried out in sheer agony.

"Oops!"

I couldn't move my hands they felt broken into bits and pieces, filled with an excruciating pain that was debilitating. For her to wear me down like this, I had never experienced previously and I confess it was quite humiliating; and yet, she was far from done too.

"You can't use your hat pins or throw your electricity if you have no fingers!" The voice shifted to that of a man from the Victorian times, a voice I hadn't heard since I was a little girl in Evington when Mummy saved me.

"And you can't move if you can't breathe!" The tip of the boot smacked into my ribs, a knife finding a purchase between the bones and tearing into the area she eviscerated minutes ago. The force of the kick felt as if it was delivered by a hulking Olympian or perhaps even a gorilla.

"Eugh!" I cried out from the pain.

I clenched my hands, trying to fight through the pain to get some electricity flowing into my hands but it was debilitating. The swelling proved hard to channel the currents to my fingertips. My stomach and ribs felt as if they had been torn to pieces by a pack of wild dogs.

"Do you remember what you did to my father, nearly two centuries ago?!" Her natural voice returned as she smacked the shaft of the umbrella over my head and blood started to pour from the side of

my head filling my hair. "OUCH!" I screamed out again and held my
head lying on my unharmed side on the floor.

"It's why we were established!" ALB snapped the umbrella in half
over her knee and threw the pieces on the ground in a furious rage.
"He brought me marshmallows and then you took him from me!" She
kicked my injured ribs again.

"OWWUHH!" I cried out and brought my arms down to protect
the tender area. Though I was fatigued and beaten, it was what she
said that left me dizzied. Who was her father? What happened so long
ago? I reckon there were many little girls that could have fathers that
brought them sweets and then had the unfortunate fate of running
into me, should they be up to dastardly tricks. However, one particular
occasion came to mind from long ago, his face was interrupted when
she flicked the tip of her boot into my stomach

"Uh!" I grunted and tried to curl up into a ball, but she
nonetheless threw a harder kick into my gut.

"Ooo!" I moaned louder as was forced to lie on my back, shielding
my ribs from any further damage whilst holding my stomach to protect
myself from any additional punishment. I looked up for a moment
but the sweat and tears had clouded my vision, all I could see was the
red eyes glowing through the haze, a glimmering set of fangs, and a
faint semblance of a black top hat. I held my stomach and swiped my
eyes clear but kept them shut, not wanting to look at the horrifying
monster.

"I am Ada-Louise Broadhurst!"

The daughter of that fiend and the niece of the witch: the ones who
knew my secret and threatened to vanquish if me I didn't cooperate
with their schemes. How could this be though? How was the daughter
of that racket-master still alive? There was only one explanation, she
was supernatural like I. But how?

I felt a tug on one of the straps of my leotard as I was yanked off
my feet. "ALB is a twee little pneumonic device..." She chuckled as her

soft hands briefly massaged my stomach and abdominals, moaning faintly with a woman's voice. "Mmmm, Auntie Del was right, you have a lovely physique." ALB's hands worked into my cleavage, as she squeezed my breasts. "So curvy..." Her hands wandered down to my abdominals. "and so hard..." She purred as I was quite woozy and exhausted.

"I didn't kill your father, Ada." I quavered with any remaining energy I had to expend. "He fell from the pier when I dodged his attempt to tackle me over the side."

The guilt and remorse of that day that I had carried with me for centuries returned with a vengeance like Ada-Louise did.

"Lies!" She clenched down on my leotard strap, nearly tearing my body out of it and exposing half my breast. The force jostled my ribs and caused me to cry out in pain and put my hand on the wound. "My auntie told me what you did!" The sinister cackle soon filled the air. "You threw him onto the rocks!"

"She's wrong."

Ada threw a punch into my ribs and I screamed in agony, unhappy with what she was hearing. Despite the harsh brutality, I had to clear the air about everything, as much for her as me. I had longed for this audience for so long though I was being battered mercilessly.

"I tried to reason with your father..." I strained as I clenched my teeth, trying to suppress the pain. "...to walk away and give you the best life he could."

She gripped the bare skin of my chest and pulled her other hand away to close her fist, but this time she didn't strike me. Her eyes went green, signalling perhaps that she was actually giving me a chance to speak.

"I didn't seek any conflict, your father continued to attack me and it led to his demise." I gasped. "I left you money in an account so you weren't without, I have always thought of you..."

Her grasp on me lightened, perhaps she was coming to her senses after hearing the truth and discovering that her eons of what she felt was justified anger was baseless. I could empathise with Ada, I too could have been consumed by rage and the misgivings bestowed upon me and turned into what she became, but it wasn't too late for her. She was like me, a scared girl looking for answers, resolved to take matters into her own hands to get them.

"...I am like you, an orphan who has always wanted to make the world right." I exhaled. "...for both of us..."

"How touching!" She snickered as her fist crossed my nose and everything went white for a moment. "Too bad, you can't fix this!" She kneed me in the groin.

"OHH!" My body folded in half, the throbbing and aching sensations spread across my beaten torso.

"Wouldn't it be a shame if your daughters didn't have their father?!"

I couldn't answer as I couldn't breathe and everything was blurry. My abdomen was cramped, filled with an overwhelming stabbing feeling that made moving hard work. My ribs were still gushing blood; I was completely disoriented and never had a foe beat me down as Ada had.

When my sight had started to clear, it was then I had noticed the metal spikes that had formed on her nails again. "Now, it's my turn to take you!" Ada yanked me forward and jabbed the nails into my sternum toward my heart, piercing through the spandex of my leotard, and penetrating me deeply, as if my flesh were meat for a kebab.

"Awugh!" I lost my breath again as her nails twisted into my insides, blood flooding everywhere within me and outward. "To think your mother gave up so much of herself, for so little...." She patted my head as I moaned and screamed. "I anticipated more from you, Incredible Temperance!" She pulled her nails out and two spikes remained lodged in me, two larger lances protruding from my

stomach that could have impaled any other. The villain smiled as I fell to my knees holding my stomach, staked and defeated.

"Petty tramp..." She spoke mockingly as her boot smacked upward into my face and sent me flying onto my back.

I held my jaw for a moment, soothing the crushing feeling radiating down my neck. "Nngh." I plucked at one of the spikes and heard the sound of footsteps thundering from the opposite end of the pier where we entered.

"It's time for you to go to Hell, Tempie." Ada jeered; when I looked up at her she had a bottle in her hand gazing at her reflection. She turned the face of the bottle around so I can view what was written on it: Holy Water.

"It's time for you to shut up!"

Both our eyes directed to the far railing of the pier and the sight of Elizabeth climbing over the side railing. Squeak waved her hands and a tornado of fire swept across the deck into Ada. She screamed, seemingly engulfed by the flames and disappearing in the orange, yellow, and white wall that Elizabeth inserted between my adversary and me. Elizabeth took a deep breath and two streams of fire extended forward from her fingertips, mirroring my electricity powers and she launched it forward at the goons rushing towards us. A wall of fire emerged feet in front of them, towering upward into the sky forming a mushroom that dissipated into crackling embers in the night sky.

Elizabeth let out a sigh of relief as I managed to pluck one of the spikes from my abs. The other one that remained in me was larger and wedged deeper. "Oomph!" I let out a deep breath and pressed my hand to the wound as I placed my other hand to the deck, glancing at the spike covered in skin and blood resting in my glove. Elizabeth's boots clanked across the deck until I heard a large smack. When I looked up, she was on the floor holding her face.

"You should have learned from your mother!" Ada put her bicep around Elizabeth's throat and lifted her from behind. A rage filled me; an adrenaline burst into me to rush to my feet.

She fired a punch in between her shoulder blades.

"Ahh!" Elizabeth grunted.

Another to her lower back. I gritted my teeth as the other spike still dug into me, but I had no time to have a go at it. I groaned as the electricity started to form at my fingers, though they were still severely injured they were noticeably less painful compared to minutes ago.

"OHH!" Elizabeth cried out as she arched her back with a painful grimace.

I finally got back to a vertical position to continue fighting though blood still poured from the wounds in my stomach and slowly trickled now from my ribs. Ada landed one more jab to Elizabeth's kidneys to elicit another moan from her, as she torqued on her back. *"You remind me of your Nan."* Her nails drew to Elizabeth's back but she didn't lance her, instead she pressed the tip of the spike to her back with the menacing threat of attack. *"Feckless and maddening."* I sprinted forward but Georgiana flew in front of me. *"Leave my sister alone!"*

Her boot crossed Ada's side, a pink and purple sparkle which actually jarred her and caused her to release Elizabeth. Her body recoiled, the kick leaving a last mark as she winced holding her side *"That's cute."*

I ran to check on Elizabeth who lie on her stomach, groaning and wrenching her back.

"I am just getting started!" Giggle flew forward but she was being governed by her emotions. Georgiana could have thrown some ice or electricity at her but wanted to punish the villain for attacking Elizabeth and me.

"Hiya!" Georgiana landed another kick to Ada's midsection, bending her over. *"How about this?!"* Giggle kicked upward hitting her in the face when she was slumped over, cocking her head back.

Her small but powerful frame exuded confidence as she landed the blows but despite Georgiana's strength and agility, Ada remained calm and calculated, catching her foot mid-kick on her next attempt. Georgiana's eyes bulged when she saw her foot was caught.

I tried to draw some energy to my fingers, but still the swelling was too much to overcome. Perhaps, I could use my feet instead. Ada threw another spike at me as I charged forward, I was forced to leap backward and do a bridge, the wind of the spike passing just over my abdomen. My head was nearly touching the planks, my breasts ready to fall out of the leotard as they descended downward, my thighs flexing to keep me up. When I got back to a vertical position, Ada smirked as she spun Georgiana around. "I am going light on you, little one," she taunted. "You are punching above your weight!"

"Not a chance!" My little girl would not be deterred, she flew forward to land another strike on Ada, but she was caught in her tracks as Ada delivered a precise, light jab to Georgiana's solar plexus, just below the sternum.

"OOF!" Georgiana grunted, doubling over slightly from the pain. Her eyes widened in surprise as the air was momentarily forced from her lungs. Her momentum halted, and she instinctively clutched her midsection. It seemed that the jab wasn't thrown to cause serious injury but hem Georgiana in and keep her at bay. Before she could recover Ada threw another jab to Georgiana's solar plexus, this time with more force.

"OOHH!" Georgiana gasped again, the second jab making her fold further keeping her winded and off-balance. Her eyes watered as she clutched her midsection tighter, her breath coming in short and shallow bursts; the snug fabric of her singlet pressed against her skin, amplifying the sensation of the blows. With Georgiana holding her stomach in mid-air as she descended slowly toward the ground, Ada seized the opportunity to grab Georgiana's cape and yank her towards her in order to subdue her.

Finally, I was able to form electricity at my fingertips without pure unadulterated suffering. But Albie was a step ahead; she swiftly spun and threw Georgiana toward me. As I extended my hands forward to unleash the energy, Georgiana collided into my midsection, her small head driving into my stomach with significant force. The impact jostled the spike still lodged in my abdomen and took the wind out of me.

"OOF!" I dropped to a knee, clutching my stomach as fresh pangs of pain radiated from my injuries and spread across every corner of my torso. The combined effects of the spike and the collision sent sharp, burning sensations through my core.

Though I was stunned for a moment, Georgiana managed to land gracefully. She tumbled, rolled, and leapt back to her feet, her shoes sparkling with pink and purple in all her movements. Ignoring any effects of the offense she received, she keeled back with streaks of ice blue along with magenta electricity and launched it towards Ada, who stood there waving her hand to taunt us.

I groaned and seethed, holding one hand to my body to heal my injuries whilst I gritted my teeth and screamed as I sent a strand of purple and pink electrical charges in the direction of the antagonist, joining Georgiana's. In that same moment, Elizabeth mustered up every ounce of strength she had to lock Ada's legs with her feet. The hues of the colours descended upon Albie, flooding our sight with magenta, ice blue, pink, and purple. All we could see is Elizabeth pull her legs away as the waves of contrasting colours hit our target. When the ice and electricity had cleared, she was finally gone....

"We got her..." I collapsed on the pier and closed my eyes, still holding the spiked region of my abdomen which was still bleeding. I felt faint until I heard Elizabeth's boots clanking across the wood panels, followed by Georgiana's little shoes land beside me prompting me to open my heavy eyes.

"Mumma!" Tears filled her eyes. *"You're hurt bad!"* Georgiana threw off her cape and rushed forward her sweat-soaked skin glistening in the moonlight along with her pink singlet. Elizabeth reached under my armpit and lifted to my feet.

"We need to heal you!" Georgiana pressed her hands against my ribs, the bleeding started to slow as Ellie put her hands on my wounds over my midsection, only left with dried bloodstains. The pain in both areas started to subside until I felt a fresh pang sharply twist out from my stomach.

"OOF!" I doubled over as Georgiana stood there with the spike covered in my blood. *"Sorry, Mummy!"* Georgiana tossed it away and rushed forward, pressing her hand over mine to heal the wound. *"That mean lady hurt your tummy...."* She moved her head and pressed her lips gently over my abdomen, soothing the tender area with her desire to comfort. I could feel the warmth flow into my core followed by a small smack of her little lips.

"Your kisses always make me feel better, they work a treat..." I shot her a reassuring smile.

Georgiana looked up at me shocked and terrified, urgently trying to fix me with a laser-sharp focus. I ran my hand through her hair to ease her but in that moment, another biting pain shot down my leg. When I looked behind me, I glared at Elizabeth who removed the knife that was protruding from my bum.

"That knife was lodged in that massive tush of yours." Elizabeth bantered as she melted the instrument in her hands.

"I didn't will you three into existence to hurt me more."

"I didn't will you three into existence to hurt me more..." She imitated me and gave me a playful slap on the butt.

"Oww." I looked at Elizabeth with contempt. *"Did you forget I was knifed there?"* Bet was bashful, quick to forget the present situation due to her desire to lark about. She placed her warm hands against my bum, it was warm, hot, and numbed the ache as she kissed

my cheek. "Giggle, Mumma has some bruising back here, climb up on her and work your magic."

"Okay!" Georgiana climbed onto my back and pressed her thighs against my ribs, she placed one hand over my stomach wound and I felt a series of kisses make their way up and down my back, as she rubbed my shoulder down to my lower back. One hand was icy cold, she pressed it to the bruised areas and to stop the bleeding. She would then pull her cold hand away and press her other hand which she warmed through her ability to control electricity to massage away any ache.

"Who was that woman?" Elizabeth looked around for any trace of our foe.

"The world famous, Albie." I shut my eyes for a moment and enjoyed the euphoria filling me, smelling the salty air as Georgie accelerated my recovery. "We shalln't be seeing the likes of her again."

"Did you know her?"

My girls never knew about what happened that night, I wouldn't let them read it in the novel that my beloved wrote that mentioned it, nor would I ever let them sniff a line of the diary entry directly corresponding with the whole Broadhurst incident and the trust I set up for Ada thereafter when she was a little girl. My daughters only knew of my powers and the imaginary rehearsals where I prevailed against evil that they created. They were blissfully unaware of the collateral damages such a life could cause. I didn't know how to explain all of this to them, the only person I had told about Ada-Louise was their father. For many years, I wondered what came of the account as though I stopped contributing towards it just after I was hired by the Coleman's [1892], it never closed, precociously operated by phantom activities that couldn't be explained. Now, the explanation had finally arrived, almost 140 years thereafter.

My eyes shot open as I heard a series of grunts when a body rolled across the deck. When we all looked in the direction of where the sounds were coming from, there lie Henrietta with steam and grey water vapour rising off of her blue spandex-clad body. There were scuffs and marks down her back with streaks of blood, some of which were speckled across her lilac briefs. The pink H on the back of her briefs was smeared with black soot.

"Harriet!" Elizabeth sprinted over toward her sister, blood still glistening against her shoulder and dried on areas of her bare stomach. Henrietta twisted her body around and a wave of water flew in the direction she came, before she landed on her knees.

"Some more False Widows were planning to sneak up on you!" She gasped.

Drops of dried blood had pooled at the end of Henrietta's nostrils and she had some bruising on her head along with a scratch on her cheek. Her bodysuit however in the front looked more or less untouched compared to mine.

"I saw them coming when I was standing by the car."

"Good shout that you were there, then." Elizabeth put her arm down to Henrietta and helped her up before both they ran forward to me. I opened my arms to both of them, they huddled under me for safety like chicks seeking shelter under a Mother Hen. Georgiana clenched her arms around my chest and smiled at the sight of her sisters.

The jeers, yells, and clanking of many steps faintly filled our ears, growing louder than the ripples of the fire until a hissing sound formed a static that drowned out all the other sounds. The flames soon darkened down and black plumes of smoke filled the skies.

"How many are there, Bubble?!"

"Twenty maybe thirty-odd" She pressed the side of her head against my breast and looked back towards the smoke barely able to keep her eyes open from the fear that was evident on her face.

As the smoke clouds lightened to an ashen grey, we noticed the outlines of what was a vastly larger contingent of adversaries.

"Papa!" Georgiana as the four huddled together.

The pier started to shake.

"Butterscotch!" I cried out as I held the girls against me; I wish he were here. With all our power and might, there was a safety, a security with my beloved, I took for granted. I...we...all felt when no harm could come to us when he was about, even if he didn't have the capabilities and faculties we possessed.

"What do we do?" Henrietta decried.

"There is a ladder at the end of the pier!" Georgiana screamed. All eyes focused on her as I looked behind me and the girls' eyes soon joined. "I saw it when I went to get Bets. You can climb down on the beach and I will meet you at the car."

"Giggle..." I admonished her, reluctant for her to go it alone against these swarm of wasps.

"I'm only going to distract them." She dropped down onto the pier and let out a grunt. "Now where is my cape?" She looked left and right glancing for her trusty friend until Henrietta already had it in her hand.

"Let me help you." Henrietta knelt down and tied the cape around Georgiana's neck and rubbed her cheek. Giggle broke a brief smile before a look of determination returned to her face.

"Who is that man?" Georgiana appeared puzzled as her eyes dilated toward the end of the pier. When Henrietta took her hands away from Giggle, her eyes bulged with horror as she glanced at the end of the pier. "It's him!" She went pale, the red of his eyes could be seen in her eyes. But it couldn't be! Ada was gone, unless it was Him after all, unless there were two of them....

"Poppets..." I raised my hand slowly to draw her attention toward me, so my adversaries did not know I was aware of their presence. The girls subtly shifted their sights upon me and when I knew all three were looking at me, I covertly about-faced with a quick step and saw no such figure standing at the end of the pier. There was a clear path

forward but the menacing laugh of Ada malingered in the wind, it was all around us.

Dread pooled in my stomach; heavier than any blow I'd taken tonight. Memories I'd buried clawed their way to the surface, each one sharper than the last. This wasn't just a fight—it was personal.

"For Mother A!" A voice cried out from beyond the screen of sluggish blackened smoke; the silhouettes took form in more discernible figures with clear shapes all varying in size.

"Run!" Georgiana dug her heels into the pier and a large sphere of pink electricity formed between her hands, she soon started to levitate and go airborne. She flew forward and we watched for a moment as a series of electric bolts descended from her fingers, creating blinding flashes in between the goons and us. We all blew kisses at Georgie and began our run together making our way to the end of the pier with Georgiana flying not too far behind us, desperate to make an escape.

XXII.

My eyes flung open and the first thing I saw was my phone resting in my hand, the screen locked on the text message from Henrietta. "We are alright, Papa. Be back in a tick :-* Love Hen". The text came through when I was sitting in my truck, outside the convenience store. I scrambled to grab the phone but when I attempted to ring back, it went straight to voicemail as it did in every previous attempt to speak with her or her mother. I sent texts that also remained unanswered. Anxiety has a strange talent of making the time pass in a blink but making the blink seem like a millennium. Such could characterise the period of time from the last correspondence from Hetta.

I sat up as I gained my bearings, the stupor of the alcohol making the brief nap feel like a full night's sleep. I took another cold can of Budweiser into my hand, glancing at the few other cans left on the table which were emptied and gulped as soon as I came through the door. I re-traced every step to where I was deliberating for several minutes in the aisle of the convenience store, the internal dialogue in my mind advocating and arguing against the purchase.

Impulse overruled as my fingers slid under the plastic rings of the six pints of Budweiser. "Fuck it!" I said as I marched onward, the cold metal occasionally pressing against my knuckles as I made my way to the counter to make the payment. I wasn't there to browse the shelves for a quick snack or to find some other momentary distraction, I knew why I set foot in there.

Can I get a pack of Reds too?

Reds? The shopkeeper asked me perplexed. A young lady about a decade older than Hetta and Bet; Her brown eyes bulged with confusion as she put her pink iPhone on the counter next to the glass casing for all the lottery tickets. She threw her sandy blonde hair behind her back and stared at the cigarette cabinet, her ponytail dropping down her green tank top into her skinny black jeans.

"Pardon me, Marlboro's"

She shot me a smile and grabbed a box from the case. "Right. I never heard them called that before..."

"I am from America originally, that's what they call them there. I guess old habits die hard when I am not thinking."

"No worries." She rang in the cigarettes and slid them across to me. A shame filled me; I was going to relapse. What was built over a decade collapsed in a few hours of weakness. I recalled stepping out into the car park and looking around. No one was about, no one saw what I did; you could hear a pin drop and yet I as if all eyes were upon me. Soon thereafter I was back in the truck and heading back this way, I passed by a Cross set upon the hill by the local church in Goostrey. A church I had stumbled upon so many years ago when Temperance herself was a fantasy, a thought, that perhaps was only buried in the graves beside the building. The name for a group of women against the abstinence of alcohol, who still met. A new wave of shame filled me as I felt I was disobedient, defiant, and disregarding all of it. The words I am sorry were being screamed from my mind upward to Heaven though my lips kept them locked within me.

I didn't want to drink, I didn't want to smoke but the agony, the fear, the sorrow was unbearable. My hope is that I would be deterred somehow, that Henrietta's words were true and that by the time I got back, they were already home and I could just chuck it all in the bin as Temperance would say and put this all behind me. But they weren't there.

What kind of father and husband was I, to just let them go off? Was I really mesmerized by my wife's looks that much that it could draw me to a standstill and render me mute? Where was my backbone?

I couldn't be there to protect them and I needed something to quell every dark thought and emotion spiralling through me. Every 30 minutes that went by, I stepped out and sucked down a cigarette like it was a lolly, followed by another barrage of calls, praying that I would speak with them or even better catch them coming back in the drive unscathed. If they did, I would throw all the paraphernalia in the garbage and jump for joy. That was the key, I had to drink enough to numb the feelings but never take it to a point where I was belligerent, unruly, overcome, or unable to drive in the event that they needed me. I had to tow the balance, I had to find the perfect formula to keep my rage, my nerves, and my overwhelming gut-tossing fear in check. I was soon besieged by woe; these girls were my life and I failed them. The thought persistently hammered away at me.

I kept the television on as it was a companion for me in the midst of this chaos. Needless to say, I flicked channels but my mind couldn't settle on a programme. Nothing could distract me until the girls were home.

Temperance always had a way with things. But Temperance, sweet Temperance! She knew how to persuade me; she knew how to disarm me, and I never stood any chance to counter her. I didn't want them to go but somehow, she managed to pull it off. But then again, every oddity and secret that Temperance had was never grounds to drive me away like it would anyone else. No, it drove me barrelling towards her. She had me under her control, she could do as she pleased with me, I was forever hers and in her hands.

Surely, she wouldn't let anything happen to them? She couldn't! After all, nothing had happened so far with the four of them. And I didn't even know about the petrol station incident until Georgiana told me about it. It was only her and Temperance then and look at what they were able to do given the circumstances. Furthermore, Henrietta said they were okay so I should believe my little girl's word. Why was I panicking then? Because I had a feeling that pervaded greater than rationality.

All I wanted was for them to be home. I shot to my feet again to look out the window to see if there was any progress; any semblance of the car coming up the drive and just like the times that preceded it, there was no sign of them. As another hour passed, I tried to find solace in little things. Maybe they would call and the more time elapsed, the sooner they would be back. The worst of it was already over when they first departed.

Nevertheless, there I sat on the couch cursing myself because I knew now that they must have been in trouble; I felt it!

I didn't care about her powers; Nor did I care if she could do things that I could not; Temperance is my queen and I would walk in front of a train to make sure it didn't hit her when she crossed the tracks. I wouldn't even let her step over a puddle without offering to carry her or throw my coat down.

Should I call the police? No, because that would only add more turmoil to this tumult. Besides if anyone did anything to them, I was going to deal with them personally. I would inflict misery and agony on them that they could never imagine!

A wave of rage crashed over to me and I could feel the blood rush to my head. The room started to spin and I dropped my head into my hands. Soon after I reclined backward because I didn't have the energy to sit up. And then it happened, I didn't even remember. But I knew I had passed out because I had a moment of respite from the terror that coursed through me. A black blank in between the worries that keep us up and the horrors that greet us when we awake, pinning us under the duvet to escape an encounter with either adversary.

When my eyes shot open again, I was met with a dry throat, a queasy feeling, a nausea. It was getting late now and they still were not here. I didn't awake from the nightmare nor did I awake to them sitting on the couch beside me. Just a dark home with the TV being a nuisance instead of company, it wasn't who I wanted to be with. I ran outside and lit up another smoke, taking another drag and exhaling smoke into the dark air. The moon hung large over the field across the lane, nothing but blackness beyond the edge of the drive. I stomped on the cigarette and stormed back into the house huffing from the coarseness of the tobacco against my now virgin lungs. Let me get another drink in, I reached for a drink and yanked it into my hand, popping the top and chugging the lager until I let out a belch. What was I doing to myself? Poisoning myself to cope with this trauma? I wiped my lips as I felt another panic attack set in. It was only 10 minutes since I awoke but it felt like an hour.

I made my way to the couch and deliberated what to do, I tried ringing both phones and both went straight to voicemail. The phones were off but I left a brief message on each, begging for them to call me back.

I threw the phone on the couch and placed my hand on my hip, delving further into thought. If they don't come back in an hour, I am going up to Blackpool and tearing the place apart until I find them. However, it may be in vain because they could have diverted to somewhere else and I would be on a wild goose chase. That was the dilemma, I didn't know where to go or what to do!

I sat down and put the beer on the carpet beside me, as I tried to focus on my breathing to prevent another panic attack like the one I had before. The feeling, I could only describe as what I used to feel at 3:00 in the morning when I used to live on my own back in Audenshaw. My head throbbed but my breathing stabilised though I could hear my heart beating louder than the television, shouting loudly over the chatter. *The Partridge Family* theme song was playing, telling me to get happy: but I was the furthest from it. Something was wrong! A piercing and pummelling dissonance drowning out the joyful tune. The words repeating in my hand soon bubbled up to my lips: "I will never let this happen again."

The prayers soon ensued from there. Father, please bring them back to me safely. I am sorry for this foul-up, just please forgive me and please look after them. My lips shook as tears filled my eyes, I pressed the lukewarm can of beer against my head for a moment and rubbed its sweat across my forehead, it was soothing and gripped me. "If you bring them back, I'll never drink or smoke again" A barter that seemed relatively minute compared to what I was truly willing to offer to get them back home safely. I'd give my life if necessary. That was my instinct – love is an instinct, I didn't care how but all that mattered was my wife and my daughters being safe, happy, and well at whatever cost.

I couldn't take another sip; I was getting ill at the thought of it and placed the can back on the floor. I placed my elbows on my knees and clutched my head in my hands, rubbing the circumference of my head and focusing on the sound of my fingers brushing through my buzzed hair. Then without announcement or any form of apprise, the door opened. I shot up and nearly kicked over the beer on the carpet in the process. Butterflies fluttered in my stomach; my heart pounded through my ribs. My anxiety was subdued briefly by a momentary reprieve of supreme jubilance.

My beloved led the way, it didn't take me longer than a second to eye her up and down to see the tears and the bloodstains over the midsection of her leotard, her ribs, her cleavage, and her thigh. But I couldn't even react as she surged to in my arms and put her arms tight around me, burrowing into the hug. Thank you, Father, for answering my prayer!

"I'm safe now." She lurched her head forward and pressed her lips against mine, clenching my cheeks with both her hands. "Hold me." Her arms moved down and she rested in my embrace. I shut my eyes and squeezed her like she had been gone forever. Her grasp of me matched in intensity. When she finally let go, my eyes wandered and I also noticed dried blood stains around her buttocks, her leggings were scuffed. "What happened, my love?"

She didn't respond, her demeanour abruptly shifted and now she appeared traumatised and humiliated, ashamed that something had gone terribly unplanned on this occasion. She didn't just look wounded physically but also mentally. Her face was littered with dry blood from her nose, mouth, and cheeks. I couldn't describe what I felt at the sight of it: a combination of blind rage to maim those responsible for it combined with a pervasive desire to comfort her and take it away from her.

Henrietta stood behind her sporting slight tears in her royal blue unitard. All of their hair was out of order, they were soaked in sweat and appeared fatigued. Elizabeth sported similar discolourations, scuffs, and tears in her ensemble. Her bare abs had bruises on them. Her sweaty arms had dried blood spots on them.

"Have you been drinking?" Temperance peered at the cans on the table. "I could smell the cigarette smoke on your clothes when I came in..."

I froze up, not sure of how to answer with the girls present, my eyes darted over toward the table and back to Georgiana, her pink singlet was splashed with dry blood and she like her sisters had tattered hair.

"Jelly bean." I collapsed to my knees.

"Daddy!" She ran over and I scooped her up, she burrowed into my chest as I held her.

"Don't be upset." She spoke into my ear. "We stopped the baddies." Georgiana flexed, trying to invoke a smile from me. "I did really well..." Her eyes leered over towards Temperance, looking for assurance but she appeared empty and vacant.

"Why is she dressed like that and fighting grown men?!" The rage started to build within me.

"What else am I supposed to wear, Papa?" She adjusted the straps. "I thought you said I look pretty..." Her face started to fill with concern.

"You do honey." I rubbed the back of her head, my eyes glanced down at the stain over her stomach, putting my finger through the hole in her cape. A range filled me until I heard Georgiana's voice and felt her touch.

"We're alright." She smiled and hugged me. "Honest..."

I wrapped my arms around her and held her against me. "I thought this was going to be...." I spoke softly to Temperance but was cut off by her before I could finish my question.

"It was supposed to be but our opponents had other ideas." Temperance let out a deep breath as if she were stuck in a moment that she could not get past. "Things escalated quickly..." Her eyes remained lost, darkened by the recent course of events. "...what were they supposed to do, stand there and watch?"

"She can get hurt."

Georgiana grabbed my hands and shook her head.

"She was exceptional today..." Temperance replied firmly never regressing from her sombre state. "Who knows how this would have gone had she not flown in and saved the day."

"I don't want to hear any more stories of her getting punched in the stomach or seeing her with a bloody lip." I raised my voice. "That goes all for three of them!"

"You must stop being so overprotective..."

"Look, Georgie, if you want to dress up in this and pretend you are a superhero." I stroked her sides. "I can act like a bad guy and we can play fight..."

"You always let me win and I have to make believe." She shook her head and hugged me. "I don't want to fight you, Papa, I love you." Georgie put my hand on her stomach and started counting "1,2,3,4,5,6,7,8. I have eight muscles there." She flexed and I could feel the hard tissue emerge in every location she had accounted for. "It would be a shame if I couldn't use these for anything good right?"

"I know she is your little girl but she has a point."

She hugged me again. "it's hard to hurt me even if I have some boo-boos." Her comments were designed to calm me but they achieved the opposite effect, they made me even angrier. Henrietta caught my eye as she stood there, timid and nervous. I waved her toward me.

My head moved back and I looked around at the three of them. I ran my fingers against the pools of blood over Temperance's stomach, and she let out an "Ow". As my fingers rubbed against the wound, it drew a slight wince and low breathy "Ooh" from her.

"You're really hurt, my beloved." I swallowed hard as my lips quivered. "We'll have to get some bandages."

"I am a still bit tender to the touch that's all." Temperance looked down at her abdomen. "It'll be healed shortly."

Her words released from the imminent fears of injuries to focusing on taking vengeance against those who were responsible.

"Where is a gun, when you need one?" I smacked my hand. "I am going to find who did this." I shot to my feet; hot air snorted from my nose.

Temperance was at a loss for words, trembling too as I shook. I glanced at the bloodstains near her cleavage again along with the scuffs in her costume and I was filled with even more disgust.

"Tell me what they look like." A lump formed in my throat before the rage started to course through my veins. "That's all I need."

Her energy started to fade, she grew stiff like a statue, as if she were trapped in the moment and vividly remembering all the pain that she was put through. I glanced down at her stomach again and watched a wince fill her face, a feeble attempt at trying to hide the pain she was still in; this provoked my rage.

"I must tell you something..." She spoke softly.

"You can start with their names."

"Pardon?" She replied with a look of surprise.

"I am going to get Mike and a few others and we are going take a ride up there." I made my way through the living room toward the kitchen. "I am going to find these motherfuckers." I threw my fist against the wall. "AND THEN I AM GOING TO END THEM!"

"You what?" Temperance's voice followed me.

"Papa!" Henrietta's call was not too far behind her.

"I am going to wipe out every last one of those maggot-ass tea-drinking cocksuckers!"

There were pots and pans on the stove; knives on the block; and a baseball bat lying on the floor. All of them seemed like good choices of weaponry. I grabbed the bat and took a step toward the cutlery selection to take the largest blade I could find.

"Put that down, Butterscotch." Temperance ran over and pressed her hand to my wrist.

"Please step back, my love." I stared into the blue of Temperance's eyes but her hand however would not let go of me. I pulled the Chef's Edge free from the block with my other hand and faced the tip of the blade toward the ground. Temperance shook her head at me to dissuade me and it stopped for a moment and have a think. A new wave of fury washed over me when I saw a few drops of Temperance's blood stain the white caustic tiles, seeping into the grooves of the star design and washing the dark green areas into a brownish tinge. "You are still bleeding." I shook my head up and down as I huffed, filled with a yearning for vengeance. "I am going to fucking kill them for this."

All three of my daughters looked at me from the hall with horror, as if they had encountered some banshee or monster they never met.

"Henrietta."

"Yes, Father?" She came sprinting into the kitchen to join us.

"Please look after your sisters and your mother. I need you to patch up Mommy, as I am going to step out for a moment."

Henrietta's lips shook, she looked ready to burst into tears. "Yes, Papa..."

"Don't cry, sweetheart, I will be back..." A smirk unravelled across my face as I saw my reflection looking back at me from the blade. "I'm just going to go handle this situation quickly."

Two shadows bolted down the corridor until the pink figure of Georgiana entered the room. "Daddy, please don't go." The purple figure of Elizabeth came in thereafter. "If it will stop you, we won't go again."

Henrietta wept. "Bet's right. Please spare us the fright."

"What if these scoundrels come around looking for you?" I began to hyperventilate. "What about CCTV?"

"That's a bit pie in the sky, duck, as we have these arrangements to conceal our identity." Temperance shouted.

"I want them to remember who did this to them." I took the whole block of knives off the countertop and placed it under my shoulder. "There won't be anything left of them anyhow." My babies looked shocked to see me in such a state, Georgiana looked ready to burst into tears.

"You'll never have to deal with them again, my loves." I smiled at the three of them and they returned it to me both from a mix of reciprocated love and nervousness, hoping their smiles would stop me. They had also formed a barrier to prevent me from going to the door.

"Girls, please move out of the way."

The three of them didn't give me an inch though they were all shaking. The last thing I wanted to ever do was scare my daughters.

"Dearest." Temperance reached for my hand that gripped the bat. "Please, listen to me."

I didn't understand why she didn't attempt to overpower me. This woman was five feet eight inches, a hundred-and-fifty pounds of muscle, while still having all the curves, softness, and elegancies of a fair maiden. She was strong and fierce, yet for some reason even then she felt like she couldn't control me. Temperance looked frightened of me too, as if I were some villain or entity that she had never encountered previously.

"My love, I would die for you." I looked at our daughters for a brief moment. "And for my princesses, as well." I broke a smile. "It'd be the greatest honour to off on my shield, being yours."

All three daughters smiled back at me, touched by my remarks.

"But now it's time for me to be the sword." I stepped to the left of Henrietta, slid right around Elizabeth who attempted to intercept me, and juked to the side of Georgiana as I made a straight line for the door. "Let's fucking go!" I punched the wall.

"Daddy!" Georgiana wept and pleaded as she pursued me toward the front door. "Don't leave me." She screamed over the commotion.

"Papa, please." Henrietta's voice followed.

"Mother, do, something!" Elizabeth decried.

"We will do this no more..."

The words stopped in my tracks as I reached for the door handle. When I looked over at Temperance, her eyes were soaked and tears trickled down her cheeks. "Your daughters need their father right now." Temperance paced towards me. "...and I need you to stay, sweeting..." My beloved drew close as I fixed my eyes on Georgiana who was crying. "Hark my word, that was the last time." Her hands wrapped around the knife block. "We'll retire the costumes if we must..."

I looked at her but didn't say anything, I didn't put up any resistance letting her take it from me. "Please let go of it..." Temperance wrapped her fingers around mine and slowly released the bat from my grip.

"I am sorry girls that you had to see and hear that." I looked down at the ground, ashamed that I had exposed them to such terror. Temperance walked away with the knife block in hand toward the kitchen, I watched her every step.

"I love you girls more than life itself, so I get very angry if someone is trying to do something bad to you."

Georgiana pressed her head against my stomach and wrapped her arms around my back. I looked over at Henrietta and Elizabeth, opening my arms to both of them. I nimbly stood upright as Georgiana wouldn't let go of me as Henrietta and Elizabeth rushed forward flanking me on both sides, I squeezed them both as they nuzzled into my embrace and held their younger sister against me.

"I want you to have a think about what you were considering." Temperance drew close to my face. "Should you have been successful and the authorities chased this up, you may never see us again for a very long time never mind the other variables that will undoubtedly get tossed into the mix." She stroked my cheek. "You are the man of this house, Butterscotch. We need you here."

I pulled Temperance in behind Elizabeth and held her against me, as I did Henrietta and Georgiana.

"We love you and we don't want anything to happen to you." Hetta kissed my cheek.

"Please don't go, Papa." Elizabeth rubbed my back.

I stroked the back of their heads as I rested them under my chin, slowly pressing my lips to the domes of each of their heads.

"Well, I can't go anywhere now..." I chuckled. "...with the four of you making a sandwich of me."

The girls responded by squeezing me harder. "Good, we'll make a butty of you more often." Georgiana's voice squeaked from below. My head moved so I could kiss the dome of my wife's head.

"So, what is that you had to tell me?"

"Ada-Louise..."

I remembered that name and the unusually warm winter day when Temperance and I talked about the events surrounding her father after I had learned of her powers for the first time. It was the first time I heard the name in over a decade.

"What about her?"

"She is Albie..." A whirlwind of emotions swirled through her eyes. "She is the leader of this whole racket."

"That can't be..."

"She is the one who did this to me." Temperance appeared haunted and filled with fear. It was distinct as it was something I had seldom ever seen previously. "I also saw him..."

"Who?"

The answer already formed on her lips but her gulp showed the horror of letting the word escape. "...Pride."

XXIII.

"What do you mean you saw him?"

"It looked like him but I cannot say." There was a confusion in Temperance's eyes which glossed over the blue, accentuating to a sky colour.

"But I thought he was..." I ran my finger through the air under my throat.

"As did I." Temperance looked at the portrait of her mother. "My research led me to believe he was but I have had concerns that perhaps he had been in lying in wait."

"But I thought that whole thing was with your mom?"

"What about Nana?" Bet interjected, I pointed my finger up to signal that her mother was about to speak.

"I was likely concussed midway through that scrap." She turned her head when I saw the blood crusted over her hair down the side toward her ear. "Perhaps, my eyes deceived me."

"I saw him." A youthful voice spoke and all eyes turned to Georgiana.

"And I." Henrietta crossed her arms.

"He was scary." Georgiana added. "And I saw him again after you all got off the pier but some lady stopped him."

"What?" Temperance glanced down at Georgiana. "Giggle, you didn't tell me that."

"She put a wall of fire between him and us."

Henrietta, Temperance, and Elizabeth all looked at each other with puzzled faces.

"What did she look like?"

Georgiana's eyes wandered toward the portrait of her grandmother and then to a miniature of her mother. "I could only see her figure."

"Do you reckon that the two of them were working together?" Henrietta squeezed her hands and glanced at Temperance and her sister.

"It would explain her supernatural abilities." Temperance said. "I was severely worked over and could have been imagining things but I saw him and heard him in the midst of the fight."

"It wouldn't be terribly surprising for that lot to resort to the occult to try to beat us." Bet looked over the bruising on her shoulder and cringed. "Assuredly, they couldn't do so otherwise."

"To be fair, they were setting an ambush." Henrietta's comments were met with a glower by Elizabeth.

"Hold on."

Both girls looked at me.

"Who's they?" I spoke at length.

"Papa." Georgiana wrenched her arms around my neck and shook her head. I rubbed her back once and gave her a look to reassure her.

"This gang of yobs that we have had run-ins with previously." Henrietta continued. "False widows they are called."

"Like the spider?"

"Aye, and it is right for Elizabeth to say that they would resort to whatever dastardly methods they could to even the odds." Hetta looked over at Temperance skittishly. "And seems that that their leader harbours some form of a grudge against Mother." Henrietta glanced back at me. "This Albie or ALB as she calls herself."

Temperance and I looked at each other, the girls didn't know the history whilst we did. My eyes peered at the baseball bat on the ground. Georgiana pressed her hands on my cheeks to direct my attention toward her, shaking her head at me.

"I am going to put you down for a moment Jelly Bean, okay?" She nodded reluctantly but obliged, strategically positioning herself between the bat and me.

A silence filled the room as nasty looks descended upon Hetta from Elizabeth and then Temperance. Henrietta looked left and right with a defensive gape, cornered not knowing what to do. "Have I done something wrong that you are giving me the daggers?"

"I think you know the issue, Henrietta." Elizabeth crossed her arms.

"You what?"

"I was merely disclosing what..."

Bet raised her hand and shook her head. "We've had enough of your rubbish."

"There is no need for you to be so condescending, Elizabeth."

"You're quick to tell all, aren't you?"

Henrietta extended her arms out with an appeal. "Shall I tell Papa fibs instead, then?"

"Clearly it upsets him, can't you see?" Elizabeth chastised her sister in response.

"Settle down, daughter." Temperance placed her hand on Elizabeth's shoulder. "I know Henrietta has a penchant for tattling but she's still your sister." Temperance looked across at Henrietta. "I like to believe Hetta does this with good intention..."

"Bubble always has to be on Papa's good side." She threw her hand at her hip. "She's ready to smear her nose in brown and quick to give him every bloody detail without considering he is already in a mood."

Georgiana interjected. "But Daddy only cares because he loves us..."

"I never question Papa's motives, everything he does for us is out of love." Bet shot a smile at me briefly before she scowled again and pointed her finger at Henrietta. "It's her; Harriet the flaming jobs worth."

"That's rich considering you would have told him when you saw fit, aye?"

"You do recall the conversation in the car, do you not?" Elizabeth tilted her head and raised her chin. "Giggle was supposed to get the job done, but she couldn't."

Georgiana looked up at her defensively.

"And Mummy was going to attempt to seduce Papa if that failed." Henrietta replied with a raised voice.

"Pardon me, Bubble?" Temperance glared at her and responded in a stern tone.

"That is what you said, is it not?" Hetta spoke at length.

"Seduce?" A brief smile formed on my face. "Your Mother doesn't have to ever attempt to succeed in doing that."

Elizabeth snorted as she held back a laugh and Georgiana shook her head at me with her hands over her ears, as she smiled.

"I just wanted to tell Papa the truth." Henrietta smiled at me.

I smiled back at her.

"Naturally, as you want to make sure you are the golden goose in this house and Papa's number one." Elizabeth yelled back. "You could care less if you cast Mother and my name in the mud."

"This coming from a trend-setting rogue such as yourself." Henrietta replied smugly. "Sitting up in the attic on your own, brooding all afternoon, always needing to be the centre of attention."

"Speak for yourself, Henrietta." Elizabeth rebuked her coldly. "Crack on with your clever remarks, I dare you too."

"And what would happen, if I did?" Henrietta took a step forward and raised her eyebrows.

"Sisters, stop!" Georgiana pleaded with them.

"I am not even going to get started on her." Elizabeth pointed at Georgiana. "Manipulating her to be your acolyte, from all I can gather..."

"Perhaps Squeak, if you weren't stuck in your own little world you would realise that baby sister..."

"Has everyone wrapped around her finger!" Elizabeth interrupted. Georgiana's lips quivered as she appeared ready to cry, deeply wounded by the remarks and Elizabeth glanced over at her, realising that she had gone too far.

"I am sorry, Georgiana." Bet looked down. "Never forget that you are my favourite sister." She glared across at Henrietta. "As for this thing..."

Henrietta's nose flared and she curled her fist. "You rotten minx!"

"Elizabeth..." Temperance took her wrist. "I say, can we not have a tiff here and endeavour to be more diplomatic about matters?"

"I'll show you diplomatic, mother!" She took another furtive step toward Henrietta with her fist curled up. "I have had my share of Henrietta's wayward behaviour..."

"Come on then." Henrietta waved her hand to beckon Elizabeth forward.

At this point, it was getting ready to go to the next level and so I had to intervene. "That's enough." I stepped in the middle and extended my arm outward. "I am not having any of this!" I kept my arm between Henrietta and Elizabeth to deter any form of physicality.

They shared mutual looks of disdain toward one another, two cats having a stare-down with the arches back waiting for the other to make the first move.

"Girls, I want you to listen to me."

Bet and Hetta continued to stare each other down, their hair may as well have been standing upright.

"Carrot."

"Yes, Papa." Elizabeth never took her eyes off Henrietta.

"Take a step back please."

Henrietta smirked.

"That goes for you too, homegirl." I looked at Henrietta.

Her smile evaporated when she knew I meant business.

"Sorry, Father."

Bet laughed as she crossed her arms, amused by my disciplining of Henrietta.

"What did I say?" I discouraged the antagonism.

"I don't know what it is that has you stitches." Hetta snickered at Elizabeth.

"Let's not egg it on any further..." Temperance spoke coolly to restore reason and rationality into the tense confrontation.

"She best not." Elizabeth quipped.

I turned to Bet. "Elizabeth...." I pointed toward Temperance. "Go stand next to your mother, please."

Henrietta taunted her with a mocking face, standing closer to the steps whilst Elizabeth turned her back to walk away.

"On with yourself like a petulant child, Hetta." Elizabeth spoke under her breath as she retreated next to her mother in the corridor leading toward the kitchen.

"Without commentary, young lady." I pointed at Henrietta. "And you shouldn't be making faces either."

"Thus, proving my point entirely, Father." Elizabeth sneered. "It would have never kicked off if Henrietta kept her gob closed!"

"You know what?!" I spoke over the both of them as they started to chirp at each other. "Any more trash talk from either of you and you are both grounded!" My sight focused on Elizabeth whose eyes started to flicker red. "Knock it off with the red eyes,

Bet..." Her hands briefly sparked and I walked over to her. "I don't understand who made you the sheriff here." The comment broke a smile from her face.

"I know I can become rather temperamental father."

"You think?" Hetta chuckled.

I turned back toward her. "Cut it out, Hen."

Hetta pouted and nodded.

"Now I am going to speak and I am not going to be interrupted by any temper tantrums, taunts, or cute little remarks." My eyes shifted between Henrietta and Elizabeth who appeared to be ready to settle the score with each other.

"You are sisters and you are supposed to take care of one another." I shook my head. "Your mother and I raised you to be loving and affectionate towards each other, we raised you to be friends..." I stroked Georgiana's head. "Best friends, at that..."

Henrietta, Elizabeth, and Georgiana all looked at each other. Temperance normally the prevailing voice in most circumstances had gone quiet and watched on as a spectator all throughout this contest.

"Apologise."

"I am sorry, Papa." Henrietta looked down.

"Me too, Father." Bet let out a breath.

"I meant towards each other."

Elizabeth and Henrietta eyed each other up with reluctance spelt across their face, two mirror images gazing at each other as if they were a reflection of the other. After a moment of silence between the sisters, Henrietta extended her hand to Elizabeth, it dangled in the air for a moment before Bet took it with a soft grip and closed her eyes once to acknowledge the truce offering.

"That's a start." I smiled at both of them. "Now, I will get you guys cleaned up and tuck you in."

"Tuck them in?" Temperance answered coyly. "They are getting too old for that." She stood between the girls and me.

"I don't care!" I put my hand out. "They are my little girls and given what happened tonight, I want to make sure they are okay."

Elizabeth looked over at Georgiana and took her hand, waving her thumb towards the stairs. They quickly ascended the steps and Henrietta waited a minute before she came to me once more and kissed my cheek. I smiled at her and smacked her bum playfully; a smile broke from her face as she laughed. Temperance watched the girls head up the stairs. I drew close to her but she didn't pay it any mind as she was focused on making sure there were no skirmishes in the corridor, confirmed by the hallway going quiet. "Perhaps, I should freshen up."

"Before that, let me have a look at you." I reached out to put my hands around her waist to pull her in close but she brushed my hand away.

"Come on, Honey Bee..." I tried again but she took another step back, as if she didn't want my fingers anywhere on her.

. "I've already healed." She walked toward the steps. "You needn't touch me." Temperance maintained her distance and I followed her up the stairs.

"I'll be a minute." Temperance looked over her shoulder as we got to the top of the stairs.

"Can I come with you?"

Temperance turned around and glared at me. "Do you need to inspect me?" She grabbed one of her leotard straps. "Will that content you?"

"No, I..." I took a step forward and she put her hand up in front of me, once again putting up a boundary between us. She dropped her straps and pulled down her leotard to where her chest, bosom, and abs were all bare, still glistening with sweat revealing all of her wounds. There were several spike markings in her stomach, a slice on her ribs, and bruises scattered over her abs and breasts, and dried blood descending into her breasts, the sight of which made me filled with sadness, sick with woe, and drunk with ire.

"You know what?!" I kissed my teeth. "Where is my fucking knife?" My body recoiled in the opposite direction of the steps, determined to find the nearest weapon to cause mayhem. "It's time to ride." I took out my phone and scrolled down the list of who I could take with me who may have the best weapons available.

"Don't you dare take another pace!" Temperance roared.

I raised my hand and put the phone back in my pocket.

"I'll handle it myself." I cracked my knuckles. "If you'll excuse me." I took a few steps toward the staircase and didn't hear any opposition from Temperance, a smile formed on my face as I was going to get downstairs, take whatever instruments I deemed appropriate, and cause as much carnage against these scumbags, as humanly possible. Then, she spoke.

"If you've left when I have come out, don't bother coming back."

I about-faced, raising my arms in surrender. "Please don't be mad at me."

"I am not angered, yet." Temperance adjusted her costume, pulling the straps back over her and crossing her arms. "When I married you, my intention was for this to be an eternal partnership." Temperance's eyes flared. "If you walk out that door, you are putting me to the test."

"I am sorry." I opened my arms to her but she wouldn't come. "I would never want anything to come between us."

"If that be the case, you best be here, when I come out." Temperance spoke at length.

"I'll go check on the girls in the meantime." I obliged.

Temperance nodded, "I'll be a while." She continued walking to the bathroom.

I carried on making my rounds and all three girls were already off to sleep, exhausted from the day. I sat on top of the bed in our bedroom but couldn't even think let alone settle. My brain was in a tunnel and it was as if I had never left. The evening had gone silent, a silence which was ripe with tension.

Temperance returned but she remained distant and barely spoke. No matter how many times I tried to coax words from her or engage in some form of contact, Temperance lay on her side unresponsive. We didn't make love nor did we even have any conversation; in some regards, it was as if she became made of stone. And yet, I knew she was awake cause I could hear her breathe. Finally, when she drifted off, I kissed her head and put my arm around her, even if she was unaware. If she didn't care to know, I was still there regardless.

XXIV.

When we awoke the following morning, not much had changed. Temperance wouldn't say anything but rather would acknowledge any communication she deemed appropriate to respond to with a stoic nod or expressionless shake of the head. Despite this scourge of silent evasive tactics, I somehow managed to convince Temperance to accompany me on some errands.

Before we set off, we heard Henrietta playing piano and the girls seemed to be equally entertained by it, last night's events now seemingly a distant memory or so it seemed. When I asked Temperance if she was ready to go, she remained in situ until I opened the front door and she followed me out.

When I opened the car door for her, she didn't respond, instead, she was bemused by the gesture, sitting mute in the front seat as she put on her seat belt. An awkward silence filled the car, it continued to stalk us from the night before.

"So, how are you?" I must have asked Temperance countless times now but still remained wordless since before we went to the bedroom last night; it was hard to determine what she was exactly feeling, her eyes were filled with a medley of confronting emotions: anger, embarrassment, shame, sorrow, resentment, regret, duress, and remorse. I was still trying to figure out which one she was navigating through at the present moment.

"The girls seemed to be getting on fine before we left." I arrived at the A50. "Bet and Georgie were bopping along listening to Hetta play the piano." Two cars passed by heading in opposite directions. "That's good, at least..." I broke a smile but there was no response from her, as usual, but at this point, I was committed to keep talking until finally, she said something.

"I'll stop by the bank and grab some money and then I thought we'd hit the garden centre and get a coffee somewhere after..." I turned onto the road. "So, did you hear Henrietta playing?" Temperance still showed no emotion, wafting herself with a lilac silk fan as she kept her eyes fixed on the road ahead. "It's amazing, that she can play the Magnetic Rag, and when she sings, my goodness the beauty and the power..." I glanced over at Temperance who hadn't budged. " ...she sounds just like you..."

Temperance glared at me almost in a deep envy that could not be disguised for anything otherwise. The petrol station where the skirmish happened with Temperance and Georgiana rapidly approached on the right and I felt compelled to re-direct her attention toward me to distract her. "I remember the really bad low blood sugar back in the early days and you sang me to sleep." I smiled at her. "You truly have the voice of an angel, Mama."

Temperance turned her head to me and set a vacant gaze upon me. Just as we were about to pass the garage safely, Temperance looked back at it in the last minute and fanned herself once more.

"Are you going to pop by to get some cash out of the machine?"

A smile filled my face, happy to her voice again after breaking a silence that lasted insufferably.

"I think that can wait until Holmes Chapel."

"Why?" Temperance looked at me with a nasty look on her face. "I am going to stay in the car, you needn't worry."

"Well, it's nice to know that you can still talk." I chuckled.

"I don't have much to say." Temperance bickered, not amused by the joke.

I didn't know what to speak about next, I felt as if I was walking on eggshells afraid of what to say; it reminded me of when I was with Rachel. Tip-toeing around each and every word out of fear it will ignite an explosion. My beloved was different, I could always be open with her as opposed to having to dress things up and avoid trouble. However, that was no longer the case here and now.

"Look, Mama, I have been on edge about what to say but I just want to talk about what happened."

"It doesn't matter...." She put her hand to her head.

"It does to me..."

"Why are you nervous, duck?" Temperance simpered. "You should be made up." Her head tilted toward me, removing her hand for a moment to speak with conviction. "You had your fit about us going out and now we won't any more..."

"I am not happy about what occurred, Temperance."

I was never rooting against her. I was just afraid something bad would happen, and I couldn't understand why she didn't see that.

"When I handed in the resignation to the fire station..."

"Right on cue." Her eyes narrowed. "And when I quit the fire brigade, I was sad to do so but I did it for you and the girls because I didn't want to upset you..." She feigned my accent to imitate me and made a nasty face whilst doing so. "Bloody predictable, you" She shifted back into her normal voice.

"Well, you can read minds, right?" I simpered in retaliation, angered at her mockery of me.

Temperance raised her eyebrows and replied smugly. "If only you could read mine too..." "Muppet." She whispered under her breath.

I put the car in park. "If you got something to say to me, just say it." My voice raised by the provocation. "There is no need for some passive-aggressive out both sides of your mouth antics, alright?"

"So says the master manipulator himself!" Temperance crossed her arms.

"When did I manipulate you?"

"You frequently speak of quitting the fire brigade as if you did us some massive favour."

"I never said that I did you a favour." I swallowed sharply. "I am just saying that I did it strictly it because of you and the girls." My voice rose as I defended myself. "...I made a sacrifice because you are more important to me."

"Tara, chap." She smiled and raised her hands. "You couldn't have illustrated my point any clearer." Temperance clasped her hands together. "It's our fault then, yeah?" Temperance raised her eyebrows forcing me to answer. "That you gave it up?" She raised her voice.

I held my tongue for a moment to compose myself. "I never said that."

"Well, you make it sound that way!"

"I feel like you are putting words in my mouth..." I softened my tone hoping it would bring the conversation back to a more amicable discourse.

"And you've become quite the dog in the manger, haven't you?"

"A what in the who?"

"Don't play stupid with me, you know what I mean." Temperance appeared incensed. "You've been able to do as your heart is content but wish to deprive others of doing the same." Her tone lowered but she was far from done. "It wouldn't prove too difficult for you to comprehend this if you thought about someone beside yourself..."

"You got to be kidding me!" I gripped the steering wheel hard. "You and the girls I always think about before me, that's absurd!"

It was clear now that Temperance was jabbing and probing hoping to find a hole or a soft spot to attack but I wasn't going to bite.

I took a deep breath, once again hoping not to fall into the trap or instigate further. "Look, I understand why you are angry when I bring up the quitting the fire department thing. I should be mindful of how I word things and how I say them, though it's not my intention, it can come off as I am using it as some form of bargaining chip to gain the upper hand."

"That was the first intelligible thing you said this afternoon."

"You don't find a comment like that, a bit pompous?"

"And you don't fancy your response, a bit antagonistic?" Her eyes flared.

"All I was trying to do was explain the motivation behind the decision. It's the same motivation for why when I had to travel for whatever I was doing that I made sure I was home at the end of the day because I couldn't spend a night apart from you."

"You didn't want to be away from either, did you?" Temperance snickered.

"No..." I shook my head. "... I don't, and our family has always been my top priority." I looked over at Temperance. "So, tell me the real issue, not in some roundabout Temperance Lee fashion where I have to sit there and guess all day."

"You wouldn't be stabbing in the dark if the lightbulb switched on, would it?"

"Whatever that means." I waved my hand.

"You are a poet, figure it out."

"Are you mad that I want you and the girls to be at home and I'm happy that you are safe?" I looked down the road and put my fingers to my mouth. "That's all I truly care about." I pointed at the windscreen. "I mean look at what has already transpired with these fucking idiots!"

"You needn't remind me nor is there a need to use profanity to describe it." Temperance crossed her arms with her fan erected in front of her face. "I am still trying to work out what I saw..."

"Are you sure it was Broadhurst's daughter?" I lowered my tone again with the hope she would detect I was aiming to be supportive and not argumentative. "It might have been an imposter..."

Temperance looked over at me. "It wasn't..."

I put my hands over hers. "And you are certain that you saw..." I raised my eyebrows.

"It looked like him but there was some distance between us. The sheer sight of him gave Ada the chance to weaken me, as she did."

The car accelerated faster.

"Upon further reflection, I deem it possible that there is some link or perhaps they were one and the same." She reclined in her seat and threw the fan at her feet.

"it doesn't make any sense though, how is that possible?"

"The whole idea baffles me." Temperance turned on the air conditioning. "But, it's over now." She looked at me reassuringly.

"Father, I hope so..." I glanced out Temperance's window. "Because I'll tell you what...." The anger started to coarse through me and though I tried desperately to suppress it, it forced itself out like vomit when one tries to hold it in when they gag.

"Here we go." She laughed to herself.

"Whoever the fuck is up there, if they want to fuck around, I will fucking wipe them off the fucking face of the Earth in a way you've never seen before. I can promise you that." I looked out the window. "I don't care what they think they are, the motherfuckers."

"Alright, I get the point!" Temperance raised her voice and sighed. "Goodness me, are you going to take the whole of the cutlery and have a Ceilidh?"

"Come to think of it." I nodded and reflected on the prospect of such an action. "I'd play fiddle with their fucking face, that bitch included!" I pointed at the steering wheel. "You think I won't snap a woman's neck if she tried to hurt you?"

"Goodness me, I am surprised that long without an outburst!" Temperance clutched her head for a moment, distressed by my comments. "You are absolutely flippant! More explosive than a satchel of fireworks on the Fourth of July!" She admonished me further.

"Well fortunately we don't celebrate that in this country and I don't like that day cause of what happened on it personally, as you know..."

"That's not what I am saying..." Temperance put her hand against her head. "I feel as if I have to handle this with kids gloves because I don't know if and when you are going to blow."

"Ironically, that is how I've felt around you since last night."

"Your penchant for violence is irksome."

"With respect, you are the one getting into fights." I pressed my fingers against my chest. "I don't want you to be anywhere near one."

"We don't provoke them, unlike some blokes who delight in them..." She simpered.

"And you going up to Blackpool knowing what could go down, that wasn't you looking for one?"

Temperance swept her hand across the car. "You crave conflict."

"I do not!" I curled a fist. "Man, I could use a smoke right now" I exhaled rapidly.

"As you are undoubtedly withdrawing after having nearly a full packet to yourself."

"Because I was worried sick and felt completely helpless because I wanted to be there. I think any man that has any love for his wife and daughters would and equally they would take great pleasure in tearing the face off of any piece of crap that dare..."

"Just stop right there, will you?" She raised her hand as she interrupted. "You wish to punish people; this is not even a matter of defending the girls nor I."

"When have you ever seen me get violent in the time that we've been together?"

"Where shall we begin?" She chuckled. "You've been close many times..."

"You are mentioning times I was provoked." I pointed upward to raise the point. "And what was the X-Factor when that was the case?" I gripped the steering wheel tight, the leather rubbing against the skin of my hand. "Who did I think was being encroached upon or in some form of peril?"

"This has nothing to do with your desire to protect us, there are sensible ways to deal with that..." Her eyes amassed. "You have a rage problem..." She crossed her arms again and looked out the window. "It's cathartic for you to visualise pummelling someone to get retribution for some trauma that is still hidden deep within you."

"Sounds like someone that I know." I snickered.

Temperance didn't respond. She sat there intentionally in silence to bait me into prompting her to retort. She played it well as it didn't take me too long to bite as emotions got the best of me.

"Do you know what I think?" I signalled and took a left turn.

"I am sure you will tell me." She yawned, almost mockingly as she waved her hand in front of her lips.

"I don't think you like it that I want to protect you. I think it makes you feel vulnerable and that's not what I am trying to do. I love you, you are my wife, and I am always going to protect you, but I think this whole thing with the girls was you trying to assert control and dominance. Maybe you are the person working through the childhood trauma..."

"Says the man who has a severe case of obsessive-compulsive disorder!" Temperance raised her voice. "Caught out by every slight perturbation!"

I turned on the radio to drown out her yelling, the chorus to Tom Petty's *You Don't Know How It Feels* surrounded us.

"Perfect song."

Temperance glared at me.

"Not to be cliché, but maybe you should listen to the chorus."

I continued to drive but felt her eyes on me, I tried to immerse myself in the chorus, then the guitar solo, and harmonica music, feeling like someone understood me. Every time I looked at her during these three moments, she was in the same posture, her arms crossed, her eyes staring at me like she wanted to batter me.

I extended my hand towards hers when the chorus came back through, directing her attention to the words. A slight smirk filled her face but she didn't move. Once the final guitar solo came in, she snapped her fingers and the radio had powered off.

"Are you implying that I lack sensitivity and empathy for your many tiresome burdens?" She spoke with a crass tone. "For Mercy's sake." Her head cocked towards me before she turned away. "If anything, I've been too much of a mother hen with you." Temperance snickered. "Spending all these years clutching your hand when you took a turn or reminding you of how lovely you are when you are cruel to yourself!" She pumped her first. "I don't know how you feel?! I feel everything that you do as I love you more than anything!"

My heart melted at her words, I looked at her and fell in love with her all over again then and there, I wanted to tell her how much I appreciated her kindness and nurturing gentleness toward me. I was pining to kiss her and reconcile with her. Just as I was about to move forward to her, she armed herself with another barb.

"But I will tell you the real issue with all this tommy-rot!" Her voice intensified. "I reckon you feel like you don't measure up because your better half is stronger and smarter than you!" Temperance growled. "Perhaps, you don't feel like a proper bloke."

I was infuriated at the remark, in the span of a moment she went from the one I could lay at her feet to stomping on me repeatedly. I was short and quick, not thinking of the snide comeback that would follow.

"That's not what you say when we are in the bedroom!" I cringed at what I said as I knew I crossed a boundary. The car went silent and Temperance sat there with a stunned look on her face like she wanted to eat my soul.

"You can sleep on the couch tonight."

"What?" I reached for her hand and she pulled away. "I am sorry for what I said, it was completely wrong of me. I wasn't thinking."

"Well, you can have a long hard think about it tonight when you are curled up on the sofa cuddling a pillow, instead of me!"

"But we've been together for over a decade and this has never happened." I raised my hands with a tremor in my voice. "Please, I'll be panicking all night."

"Fine!" She threw her hand out. "You can sleep in the bed with me." She pointed her finger at me. "But do not touch me!"

I felt shame and remorse, I had never seen her this angry with me in a long time.

"You are only there because I don't want you to have another meltdown, don't think I will be feeling your manhood anytime soon..." She spoke assertively. "You can keep it." She turned her head away from me. "You'll have to make do with gawking at my bum and using your imagination." Temperance gave me the two-finger salute. "Frigger!"

"What does that mean?"

"Look it up in the dictionary." She leaned against the window. "It's another way of calling someone a tosser from my day."

I didn't want to respond or say anything to hurt her ever, but she kept hitting nerves and I felt bullied.

"Nice stuff, Squirt." It blurted out from my lips.

Temperance turned back around and her eyes were fully white. "What did you say?" She leaned forward towards me in a confrontational posture. "Is that another innuendo?" Electricity started to form around the circumference of her eyes.

The phone started to ring and I looked at the radio display.

"It's Georgiana."

Temperance's eyes went back blue.

"She doesn't normally call unless it's something serious."

Temperance sat back with her arms crossed.

I pressed the green phone decal on one of the steering wheel buttons and the phone call went on speaker.

"Hi Honey..." I pressed my foot to the break petal as we approached a roundabout in Holmes Chapel, glancing briefly at the sign for the M6 and Stoke-on-Trent. "How are you?"

"Hi, Papa, can you and Mummy come back?" Georgiana responded with a sense of urgency in her as if she were scared or disturbed.

"What's wrong?" I hit the gas and carried on through the roundabout before stopping at the next one as we entered the town centre for Holmes Chapel, a cobbled road decorated with multi-coloured bunting hanging over the street between the old Victorian terraced houses.

"Henna and Bets got into a fight."

"Seems to be a lot of that going around." I glanced over at Temperance who was frowning. "What happened?"

"You need to come back, Daddy." Her voice peaked with worry.

"Alright, sweetheart." I took the next left at a sign pointing to Jodrell Bank. "Tell me what's going on."

"Bet smashed Henrietta's figurine."

"The china ballerina with the purple dress and black hair, doing a pirouette?"

"Yep." Georgiana's response was slow and measured.

"What?!" Temperance sat up and spoke with alarm. "That was a special gift that cost a fair few. We got that for her after she played her first recital in Swettenham when she was younger."

"I tried to separate them but Elizabeth screamed at me. Henrietta shoved her and Elizabeth retaliated by smashing the figurine. They started wrestling on the ground and I ran to phone you."

I put my foot down on the gas pedal. "Where are they now, honey?"

"I don't know, I am hiding in the closet."

"Open it, and peep your ear out. Tell me if you can hear them."

"Okay..." She whispered. "...it's gone quiet."

"We'll be home in ten minutes; you can come out of the closet."

"Georgeanne..." Temperance spoke to the speaker. "Go and tell the both of them to remain where they are and if they move an inch, the consequences will be even more severe."

"Yes, Mummy..."

"We'll stay on the phone with you." She rested her head in her hand. "Goodness me, what can cause such a tilt?"

Georgiana hadn't hung up on the phone. "It was about Henna telling Daddy about our adventures, Bet called her a tattle-tail and a brown-noser."

Temperance shrugged her shoulders, almost nodding in agreement.

"Bubble called Squeak a bully and then Squeak threatened to fill Bubble in."

"I wonder where they got that idea from." Temperance glared at me. "Sat next to Solomon Grundy, over here."

"Funny, I wasn't the one teaching them savate in the back garden when I was out performing."

Temperance scrunched her eyes and gave me another nasty look.

"Bets then got in Henrietta's face and said she was a little baby, Hetta warned her to step back, Squeak asked her what is she going to do about it, and then Henrietta shoved her."

"Right, go get them, please!" Temperance commanded.

"Just a minute."

As I sped down the road, I passed a sign for Twemlow 1.5 miles before reaching the Twemlow Viaduct. I looked out at the hulking brick arches rising up from the grassy fields beyond with the train tracks set atop it. The imposing gantries which held the electric lines appeared minute in comparison to the monstrous beast of a structure. A lay-by approached on the left.

"Maybe we ought to come back here and stop off to have a chat, we always enjoyed the peace and quiet."

Temperance's expression shifted, her anger had dissipated and instead was replaced with a gentle gape, her eyes traced each car pulled off on the lay-by, passing it in a blur. She looked back, appearing as if she were longing to recapture those moments we shared together.

Screaming and shouting filled the speakers causing us both to cringe at the sound of it, I couldn't hear anything else as I was sickly worried about Henrietta and Elizabeth. This only worsened when we heard Georgie's voice enter the fray followed by the sounds of grunts and gasps.

"Daddy?" Georgiana spoke into the phone.

"Are you alright, Jelly Bean!"

"Yes, I've put Henrietta in a separate room."

I sighed with relief. "How did you do that?"

"Elizabeth's hands were alight and I threw ice on them which distracted her. I then flew in and grabbed Henrietta, picked her up and flew with her into the dining room. She wanted to come out but I formed some electricity in my hands and pressed one of them to the door handle. She's sat in the chair now, looking like she spat her dummy out." Georgiana chuckled heartily.

"Well done, Giggle." Temperance saluted our youngest daughter. "At least someone knows how to properly take charge instead of putting on a Vaudevillian performance as others do."

"That's enough polemics." I snapped back at Temperance. "Put me on speaker, baby girl."

"Done it." Georgiana acknowledged my response.

"Hen, you listen to me." I spoke sternly. "You stay in the room with your sister until we are back."

"As you wish, Papa." She responded without enthusiasm.

"Georgie."

"Yes, Daddy!" She on the contrary replied with intent, as if she were the hero tasked with solving the crime and case.

"Lock the door."

"Okay!"

"Good girl, we're coming down the road now."

The car rumbled over the pavement with white lines dashed across the centre. "We'll see you in a minute." The phone went off as I pressed the red phone button on the centre console angrily.

"What are we going to do with these kids?"

"Perchance, you should investigate the deeper roots of what invoked this reaction today." Temperance looked ahead. "Whilst I would never condone Squeak's act of vandalism, Harriet betrayed all our trust."

"I am grounding the both of them and we'll take names after." I saw the sign for Slade Lane rapidly approaching and flicked on the indicator. "We need to present a united front otherwise they'll try to play one of us against the other." My foot slowly pressed down on the brakes to decelerate.

"That shouldn't be too difficult with you, Hetta knows what strings to pull."

"She's completely out of line but for what it's worth you know what Elizabeth is like. She loves getting a rise out of people." I turned down the lane. "Even with Georgiana who she dotes on, she likes to excite her and get her to act naughty."

"So, we are going to incriminate Squeak and Bubble walks away with impunity." Temperance curled her lip. "That's the standard practice, that."

"Let's call it what it is here, you are still mad that Henrietta gave you up because she knew it was wrong." I turned into the drive. "She knows I worry about you and you were putting them in danger under my nose." I put the car in park. "You need to get over it."

"Do you know what you can get over?" Temperance flung the door open. "Parking your bum on the couch this evening." She slammed the door and walked up to the house. I stepped out of the car and followed but Temperance about-faced and came back for a parting shot.

"And one more thing!" Her finger was raised. "If you dare try to skulk into the bedroom and beg, I will drag you back downstairs and latch you to the couch with my hat pins!" She screamed as her hair started to dangle wildly; her eyes were filled with fury as she huffed. I felt defeated in the moment but followed her through the door into the house and found a potted plant on its side, soil thrown across the carpet and Elizabeth sat on the couch sporting a bloody lip.

"What on Earth?" I ran over to check her face and she pushed my hand away.

"The state of her!" Temperance put her hand against Bet's face to inspect both sides. "What is going on?!" She shouted. "We come home and find you two have marked each other up!". She knelt down and put her finger to Bet's lip.

"It'll heal, soon." Her eyes sunk low as she responded calmly to her mother. "You know that..."

"It didn't bother when you brought them back from Blackpool and Lord knows what happened to them."

Temperance glowered at me from the corner of her eye. "And you are still going on with yourself about that?"

"That aint happening again." I pointed my finger. "Just like this isn't happening again." Temperance didn't say anything, she didn't need to. Her eyes were storm clouds gathering on the far horizon, a warning to go no further. She kept her eyes on me and glanced down at Elizabeth before she about-faced and stormed off, her boots pouncing down the hallway until she ripped open the door to the dining room. "Out!" She ordered. "Now!" Temperance scolded our two daughters in hiding. "The both of you!"

She came back into the front room with the shoulder of Henrietta's dress crumpled in her hand, Hetta sulked as she came into the room with a large red scratch on her wrist and markings on her cheek. Her white socks were raised high and kept neat, despite the indication she had been in a fight.

Georgiana stood behind Temperance and watched as a careful observer, her hair down her back contrasting against her sky-blue day dress which had white fringes on the hem.

"What do you have to say for yourselves?" Temperance's eyes were nearly bloodshot.

Henrietta wouldn't even utter a sentence as she was terrified to test her mother. Bet looked ahead with a pout on her face.

"I asked you a question and demand an answer!" Temperance bellowed. "The gall of you two! This is the second occasion that we have left you to watch your baby sister and there is yet another incident!"

Temperance froze for a moment, filled with indignation. "Who tipped this plant over?" Her eyes scanned the room, probing to find the culprit. "Who did this?!" She yelled louder and pointed at the mess; her eyes primed with an ire that demanded respect.

"Bets." Georgiana's voice emerged abruptly; Bet scowled in Georgiana's direction.

"Shut your mouth, Giggle." Bet spoke in a menacing tone. "You are turning into a pint-sized version of Harriet."

Georgiana snapped her fingers and was in costume. "I am a pint-sized powerhouse, thank you very much!" She clenched her fists.

"Enough!" I spoke over everyone. Georgiana raised her eyebrows like many times she was caught doing something naughty. She quickly snapped her fingers as was back in her dress.

"Bet, what is this whole thing about with you smashing Hen's figurine?"

Bet looked to the left with the same repugnant and snide look on her face.

"It was an antique and it marked a special occasion that your sister worked really hard for and something that we put a lot of effort into getting..."

. A chill ran down my spine as Temperance's glare bore into me. Her bright blue eyes darkened, freezing the words in my throat. My hands trembled at my sides, the unspoken threat clear—one more word, and I'd regret it

"When push comes to shove, little sister can't manage." Henrietta taunted. "So, she goes on a little tantrum instead."

"Quiet, you!" Temperance tugged on Henrietta's dress where it prompted her attention because it stings.

"Says the lass who got manhandled by a seven-year-old!" Bet teased.

"I didn't manhandle her!" Georgiana protested. "I was splitting you up, I didn't want to see you two fight because I love you both." She drew close to Henrietta and squeezed her hand. "I would never hurt Bubble." Georgiana nuzzled Henrietta, rubbing her face against the back of her hand. Henrietta subtly stroked her cheek.

"From the looks of it, it seems you two got into a full-fledged brawl and that breaks my heart. I don't want to come home and see scratches and bruises on you. Whatever the cause is." Henrietta and Elizabeth both looked down, their eyes both filled with remorse. "...and to know that you did that to each other is truly despairing." I looked at both of them. "Why would you guys want to harm one another? You love each other and care for one another so much!" I couldn't even form legible words to express the mix of sorrow, disappointment, and concern effectively.

"Papa, I challenge you to deal with Miss Prim and Proper Loose Lips over there." Elizabeth snickered. "Henrietta Job's Worth, that's what they call her, remember?"

"You prickly prat!" Henrietta curled her fist.

"If you as so much take one step." Temperance squeezed the sleeve of Henrietta's dress and didn't even finish the sentence; the message was clear and Henrietta's eyes grew larger with intimidation for her mother.

"Bet, I don't want to say this to you but if you make one more comment like that and you are out of here."

"Where am I going, Papa?" She laughed. "Are you going to cast me out?"

"Cast you out?" I shook my head with vehemence. "No, over my dead body." I regained my composure. "But you are going to your room and you are not going anywhere until I say otherwise."

"Everyone can bottle it!" Temperance spoke at length as Henrietta's sleeve crumpled in her hand. "I want to know what happened and why I came home to a tip with you two battering each other? If I hear one quip, one snarky remark, or one gripe spoken out of turn, you will be washing the floors until you are my age. Do I make myself clear?" Her finger erected sharply. "And you down there, if you wish to meddle!" She pointed at Georgiana. "You will be joining your big sisters."

Georgie's eyes bulged and she took a step back, nervous and skittish.

"Temp, Gee has nothing to do with it."

Her finger turned towards me. "You do not speak to me unless you are spoken to!"

My jaw tightened, teeth grinding against the urge to snap back. I held my tongue with reluctance, the condescending rhetoric was pushing my buttons. Temperance didn't fear any resistance from me or anyone else, however...

"And as for you two, one of you best start talking!"

"Papa." Henrietta looked over at me, her eyes pleading desperately for help.

"No!" She yanked Henrietta. "There will be more coddling or hiding behind your father. Two week's mopping duties."

"Temp, let her speak..."

"If you interject, I'll make it three!" The vitriol was now spewed at me. "I will not be usurped nor compromised by your desire to shield her, any longer!"

Elizabeth started laughing.

"Is there something funny?" Temperance scolded her. "Your father is guilty of such offences with you, as well. But I tell you here and now you are going to be doing all the linen in the household for a month to work off the cost of your rampage!" Temperance roared. "Or as collateral, I'll go into your room and smash up everything that I see fit."

"Be my guest." Bet smugly replied.

"Don't be cross!" Temperance stepped toward her with her shoulders tensed.

"Please listen to Mummy, Squeak." Georgiana stood in front of her mother, hoping to serve as some form of an intermediary.

"Go hug something, Georgiana." She snickered.

"Let's go, you are done for the day." I reached down to pull her up. "You can tack on two weeks, no dance classes, no television, and I am taking away your paint set."

Bet walked by me with her head down as she made her way to the steps. "You don't speak to your little sister and certainly not to your mother like that." Temperance was busy unzipping her boots. "Up to your room and I'll be there in a second to look at your lip."

"Cheerio then, lovely to see you all." Bet slammed the door to her bedroom which rattled through the walls.

"You are dismissed, as well." Temperance's eyes flared at me. "I don't want to see you." She looked at Henrietta with pure rage. "I'll deal with this miscreant over here.", Temperance took her arm again and Hetta looked helpless. "When I was your age, they may have flogged you for this exhibition." She dragged her towards the kitchen.

"Daddy, please..." Henrietta looked back ready to cry, I couldn't help but feel sorry for her.

"Woah! Hold on a minute!" I pursued Temperance. "You are not going to hit her, right?"

"Hit her?" Temperance cringed and threw a boot at me which I nearly failed to dodge. "Barmy berk! She's my daughter, I would never strike her." She clutched Henrietta's wrist. "This is your fault as you constantly indulge her and this entire scenario is one of your creation!" Temperance threw the other boot at me and I threw my hands up to deflect it from striking me. "If you had just left me on that canal, we wouldn't be here as we are now!"

Temperance equipped one of the small throw pillows off the couch to form a barrier. I put my hands up and reached out to touch her.

"Bloody feeding me hope when there was never any all along!" She threw the pillow and nearly hit Georgiana but she side-stepped it and ran towards Henrietta. "Stay away from me!"

"And if we never fell in love would we have them?!" I pointed back at Henrietta and Georgiana. "We wouldn't have each other and we wouldn't have this" I moved my hand through the air. "You'd still be all alone and I'd be nothing, probably dead!"

Temperance's shoulders were hunched, as she huffed and puffed. Henrietta and Georgiana looked on visibly shaken by Temperance's display of aggression.

"We are in it together until the end." I showed her the marriage band. "Even if you harbour a disdain for me now, I'll never give up on you..."

Temperance's furious gaze locked with mine, but for a moment, her hardened expression faltered, a flicker of something softer—regret, perhaps—crossing her eyes. She said nothing, but the tension between us shifted, her anger tempered by an unspoken sorrow.

"I'll pursue you until the end of time..."

Temperance's gaze softened further, a fleeting shadow of regret crossing her face. Yet, she straightened her posture, chin held high, her jaw set with determination. Not a single tear or tremor betrayed the iron resolve she fought to maintain.

"Mummy?" Georgiana softly shook Temperance's hand.

Temperance looked down.

"Yes, Georgiana." She sighed

"May I be excused, please?"

"You may." Temperance rubbed Georgiana's head and she scampered away quickly to avoid any trouble.

"Come with me, Harriet." Temperance glared at me and took hold of Henrietta's arm; Hetta looked utterly terrified. "I'll clean you up and we'll discuss your punishment." She shot me a nasty look and walked away with her hand wrapped firmly around Henrietta as she guided her into the dining room and shut the door.

XXV.

After we dished out the punishments, there wasn't much talking between my wife and me. In fact, there wasn't said by anyone outside of the apologies from the girls or anything related to them doing what they were asked. Days rolled on and they grew longer; the house became larger and its halls seemingly provisioned residence to strangers who happened to live under the same roof, imposters of the family that once dwelled in its brace.

Temperance removed a purple cotton bath towel from the dryer under the mahogany worktops that lined our kitchen. She had let her hair down, a cascade of auburn-cinnamon locks that descended down her back and stopped just above her lower back. Her pink sleeves were rolled up with a white chemise rolled over the polyester pink sleeve. A white apron tied around her waist, highlighting the separation of the blouse from the red skirt. Her exhalations filled the room with the occasional tick, as she threw the folded the towel into a laundry basket in front of the dryer door.

"How are you feeling today, my love?"

No response from Temperance, only her removing a blue cotton towel from the dryer, folding it, and dropping it into the same basket.

"Look I just wanted to say that I know there has been a lot of tension lately and I am sorry for where I've made it worse. Can we please just talk about everything? I will listen to everything you have to say without judgment or interruption..." I watched as she worked her way onto a blue bath towel, folding it, and throwing it to the basket until her eyes wandered across toward a wall on the room. "How long must this go on for?"

Temperance actually glanced at me.

"...I just want to talk."

"That's odd..." Temperance's heels clattered against the floor as she went toward our grandfather clock which was hung on the wall. The face of the clock was encased in glass, behind it the face featured Roman numerals with the writing: Paternoster Clock Works, Fleet Street, London, 1863. The gold brass pendulum had stopped swinging and the clock had apparently stopped at 7:15. As Temperance's fingers gripped the skeleton key to open the casing, a knock came on the cupboard.

Temperance and I looked back toward the exit of the kitchen and Henrietta stood there with a smile; her dark auburn hair was placed into two pigtails with red bows at the end of each. She wore a white blouse underneath a blue dress that fell to her knee. Her white socks were halfway up her shin, tucked into red shoes.

"If it isn't your shadow..." Temperance placed the key into the lock and glared at me.

"Shadow?" Henrietta squinted. "What do you mean, Mummy?"

"Mommy is messing around, sweetheart." I raised my eyebrows at Temperance hoping she would confirm this, but she didn't. "Is everything alright?"

Hetta swallowed. "I am sorry for intruding." She clutched one of her plaits. "...I wanted to show you something, Papa." She glanced over at Temperance who glared at her with the key still in the housing. "...when you are done, of course."

"No problem, Skittle. I was speaking with Mom about something, when I am done, I'll come take a look, okay?"

Henrietta beamed and nodded her head. She hopped over on the balls of her heels and gave me a hug. A smile broke from me as I wrapped my arms around her and kissed the top of her head. My hand rubbed against her back as she pressed against me. Hetta turned to look at Temperance who had crossed her arms. Henrietta released her hug and opened her arms toward my beloved. A smile escaped from Temperance's lips and she hugged Henrietta before our daughter stepped out. My cheeks swelled, the joy that the girl brought me could no longer be contained.

"Awfully cheery for a child that was recently reprimanded and disciplined." Any joy from Temperance seemed to have gone and it was replaced by a smug and sullen gape that she often wore before she delivered a witty comment or some form an elegantly-worded condescending statement.

"She's a good kid."

And on cue, she dropped her remark.

"It's nice to know my rival for your heart, is an adolescent girl."

My eyes bulged at the ridiculousness of it. "What does that mean? That's our daughter you are talking about, Temp."

"It doesn't change the fact that the girl knows that you dote upon her incessantly."

"And is there a problem, if I did?" I shrugged my shoulder. "Where are we going with this?"

Temperance squinted her eyes and pouted. "I think you favour her in particular."

"That's absurd." I shook my head. "All three of my daughters are my princesses."

"With Henrietta sat closest to the throne, of course."

"Funny because at one point according to you Georgie was my favourite and now it's Hetta." I shrugged my shoulders. "Maybe Elizabeth will be in the rotation in a month's time, huh?"

Temperance shot me daggers and scrunched her nose to show her discontent with my remarks.

"Do you still resent Henrietta for telling me about what was going on?" I looked over at a family photo of us when the girls were younger and Georgiana was only a baby. The English Channel stood behind us, radiating the sunniness of that day that we posed on a coastal cliff in Northern France. Temperance and I both had large smiles as our two daughters beamed in matching pink dresses in the front. Georgiana's little head was covered in a red-checked sunhat and a purple swimming gown.

"I don't know what to think, any more."

"About what?"

"Everything." Temperance sulked. "I question every last thing that I've done, as of recent."

"Darling..." I reached my hand toward Temperance and she shrugged it off with haste.

"To be fair, Harriet's behaviour is quite undermining." Temperance shot an icy look at me. "...but my remarks are based on what I've observed overall."

"So, you are angry with Henrietta because you think she's trying to position herself with me above everyone else?" I bit my lip "...or is it because you are threatened by my relationship with her and you believe I put her on some pedestal?"

"Either will do..." Temperance smiled coyly. "I'll let you choose that one..." She looked up at the ceiling. "If I were to wager, I would place tuppence on the former because you are in denial of the latter."

"I guess you truly forget how insane I can get over Bet and Gee, then." The volume of my voice started to rise as I made my defence. "And speaking of Georgiana. We never speak of her idolisation of you." I pointed out the window. "That's what got this whole thing started that we have been at odds about. However, I always thought it was wonderful that Georgie is so fond of you."

"So, it's my fault now that you can't acknowledge either of the points that I have raised?" Temperance rolled her eyes and directed her attention toward the laundry basket, forgetting about the clock altogether. "If we cannot have a dialogue over this matter, how then are we to sift through all the other issues?"

"We can and we will." I raised my hands to show my desire to meet her halfway and not let things go completely sideways. "But I do think it's unfair that you have a problem with Hetta being close to me and me being always available to her when I have always encouraged that with you and the girls." I could feel the anger stewing inside me. "...even when it leads to a situation where our daughters are actively put at risk!"

"As has been the theme recently, we are no longer engaging in such activities, now are we?!" Temperance shut the dryer door. "And to recapitulate, assuredly, you know why!"

I took a deep breath and put my hands together. "Henrietta is a very smart girl." I lowered my voice to diffuse the tension that was building in that kitchen. What was a vast space had since drawn to a cluttered cross-section of misguided emotions. "She can sense if someone is displeased with her and she is a sensitive girl."

"Wasn't showing them tough love, the plan?" Temperance reached for the laundry basket.

"You are clearly giving off the vibe that this is not about setting her straight for her unacceptable behaviour..."

"And what of the united front?" She gripped the handles hard. "You are already giving way." Temperance snickered. "No surprise there either..."

Another knock came against the cupboard. It was Henrietta again.

Temperance stood upright and threw her hand at her hip; there was a jealous energy about it which filled every corner of the room.

"Pardon me, Mumma." Henrietta's tone was soft and subtle. Her eyes enlarged with worry as she was walking on eggshells in the presence of Temperance.

"Yes, you can excuse yourself out of here, Bubble!" Temperance raised her voice. "Your father and I are having a conversation."

"Mummy, I just wanted to..." She gazed back defensively.

"I do not care for it, Henrietta." Temperance pointed at her. "You will have to wait for your father, you cannot always be the centre of his world."

"Is that necessary?" I put my hand out "...maybe she has something important to tell us."

"Of course, you would say that..." Temperance snickered. "She runs to you to fight all of her battles for her and you run in without question."

Henrietta's eyes glassed up; I couldn't bear the sight of it.

"This is what she does best!" Temperance exclaimed. "She's the dutiful daughter and loyal sister until the opportune time arises for her to mark her territory, by being a pest."

For the first time ever, I was disgusted by my beloved's behaviour. It was a brutal thing to say to anyone, let alone our child. It wasn't her; it was like another person had taken control of her. She was so confident and alluring, she knew she had me but she always found ways to be affectionate and exciting. When it came to our daughters, she was always so attentive and loving toward them, even when she had to be stern. Her comments had found their mark as a tear trickled down Hetta's cheek. "...I just wanted to tell you..."

"...It doesn't matter young lady!" Temperance scowled. "Quit acting a nuisance."

"...that I changed your bedding for you." Henrietta broke down into cries.

Temperance looked down and tears soon filled her own eyes. The shame washed over instantaneously from her untimely remarks. Despite the aggression shown, she realised that she had taken it too far and hurt our daughter deeply.

"It's not like you to be so mean." I looked at her with concern as I made my way to Hetta.

Temperance's eyes softened as the disappointment radiated from my eyes back towards her before I ran over to Henrietta and threw my arms around her.

"Come here, sweetheart." I held Henrietta tight against my chest. "...Mummy is having a bad day." I looked over at Temperance who had put her hand over her eyes, her remorse had consumed her. "...She didn't mean what she was saying."

Henrietta continued to sob. "I'm sorry..." Her cries intensified as I stroked the back of her head, her warm tears blotted onto the top of my shirt.

"You did nothing wrong, my love." I held her tight and tried to comfort her. "You were being a nice girl, like you always are."

Hetta's hands gripped the back of my shirt as she cried. "I am sorry if I was a pest."

"You are not a pest, my dear." I kissed Henrietta's cheek. "You are a field of flowers, sweetheart." I held Hetta and clutched the sides of her head.

"I don't want Mummy to be angry with me." Her words muffled under her sniffles. "I am sorry..."

"...Mummy was speaking in haste; she is going through a lot ..." I looked up at Temperance as I held Henrietta in my arms. "She loves you..." I raised my eyebrows softly to prompt my beloved to respond accordingly.

"...I love you very much, poppet." Temperance looked up at Henrietta. "Never think anything to the contrary." Though her intonation was monotone, her sincerity was evident. She was bereft of emotion because she appeared in a state of disbelief, shocked that she would act in such a way to her own daughter who without question she loved dearly.

"Harriet..." Elizabeth's tone of voice was provocative as she scurried into the kitchen. Her dark hair was up in a bun, she wore my black hooded sweatshirt which was like a dress on her and pink leggings. The two hadn't spoken much since their blow-out and when they did, they often bickered back and forth although they had reconciled. However, Bet seeing her twin sister in distress always invoked a reaction, she couldn't bear the sight of it. The two could go to blows as they had but if any other cause distressed her twin, the pain sent shockwaves through her. An instinct furrowed within her to act.

"...Sister, what's wrong?" Elizabeth's voice shifted to a tender tone as she placed her hand on Henrietta's shoulder. "Don't cry, it's alright." Bet gazed over at Temperance who was looking down at the floor again. Though she had likely figured out what had transpired, I wanted to make sure it didn't go any further. From the look on her face, it could be detected that she knew that the origins of Henrietta's tears stemmed from my beloved.

"Everything is fine, Bet." I placed one arm around Elizabeth as I held Henrietta with the other.

"Henrietta did the sheets in all the bedrooms..." Elizabeth looked across at Temperance "...I haven't been her biggest fan of late but I must say it was awfully kind of her." Bet rested her head on my shoulder as she placed her arm around Henrietta "She said she knew Mummy was stressed and wanted to make it up to her for what occurred between us..."

I looked up at Temperance and shook my head.

"Where is Gee?"

"Practising cartwheels upstairs." Elizabeth looked up at me.

"Can you go get her, please?" Temperance swiped under her eye.

Bet looked around the room and nodded.

"Thank you."

Elizabeth often loud and vivacious, bowed her head slightly and exited. She was still skating on thin ice after breaking the figurine.

"Baby Sister!" Bet called out her to her as she made her way toward the steps.

Temperance came across the kitchen and ran to Henrietta. "My precious daughter." She took her from me and embraced Hetta tight with her hand around her head and her other around her back as Temperance pressed her against her. "I was wrong for how I spoke to you and I am so sorry..." Temperance sniffled. "Will you please forgive me?"

Henrietta formed tears in her eyes again, moved by the show of love by her mother towards her. "I love you so much, Henrietta Anne." Temperance closed her eyes and leaned her cheek over the dome of Henrietta's head. "We've all been under a lot of stress lately and it hasn't helped any of us." She swung back and forth with her. "I should be mindful in what I say."

"Are you still upset that I told Daddy?" She sniffled. "I don't want you to hold it against me."

"Shh..." Temperance stroked her. "It's fine, daughter. I'm long past it." Temperance opened her eyes. "I've been unjust and unfair toward you; I am truly sorry, Bubble."

"It's okay, Mummy." Henrietta sniffled. "Does this mean I am off punishment?"

"Heavens no..." Temperance chuckled briefly at the audacity of the retort. "That's a good try though." She kissed Henrietta on the dome of her head. "Truthfully, I haven't communicated well and that starts with me." Temperance slowly rubbed Henrietta's back. "We didn't function well as a team and that is why we got battered, as we did..."

"It's okay, Mummy." Henrietta sniffled. "I am sorry if I angered you."

Temperance shut her eyes and hushed Hetta. "Just let me hold you for a minute."

The two shared a silent embrace, holding each other tight. It was as if Temperance had returned to being herself and whatever that was moments ago, had left. Observing her embrace our oldest daughter took me to another time and another place. Her eyes opened briefly to glance in the direction of the clock but then they shut again, it was as if Temperance were imagining she were somewhere else altogether with Hetta. A small smile etched on the sides of her cheeks. "It seems that these powers only create more trouble for us than any good."

"We just had a bad night, Mummy." Henrietta held Temperance firm, equally happy to share the moment of affection with someone she perceived to be her adversary. "You still kicked butt like you always do." Her intonation was encouraging and ripe with admiration.

"If it were only that simple..." A fuller smile filled Temperance's face, it reminded me of one who laughed at an upsetting event. However, Temperance's love for our daughter shone through as she moved her head and directed the smile toward Henrietta. "I suppose I wanted us to do this together because it's something we can share as mother and daughter. I wanted you to have a better life than I did, but it seems that you have inherited my fate, as well as my powers."

"What does that mean, Mummy?"

Temperance glanced over at me. "That's the real dilemma." Her eyes moved toward Henrietta and then back to the stuck clock. "In order for us to move forward, we have to put this all behind us and deal with the real issue."

Elizabeth came racing down the stairs with Georgiana's hand in hers. Both were loud and energised until they stepped into the kitchen, halted by the scene. "Did we miss something?" Elizabeth put her hand upon Georgiana's shoulders.

"No, Squeak." Temperance looked out the window for a moment and then back at our daughters. "You all need to hear this." She glanced down, the words forming first in her mind before transferring to her lips as she looked up. "I know that for the longest time, we have been a family that has kept to themselves. And as such, we formed a bit of a bubble around Sycamore Grove." Temperance looked at Henrietta. "No pun intended."

"For once." Elizabeth smirked and batted her eyebrows.

"And we've all grown comfortable with that and we did it to ensure we could live a peaceful and quiet life..." Temperance's eyes wandered from all three of our daughters. "...until recently when we've made a bit of a name for ourselves in what we've done in Blackpool or at the petrol station." Temperance looked at Georgiana who smiled back. "...or when were at your father's performance" She looked over at Elizabeth. "...or when we were at the fire." Her eyes moved to Henrietta.

"And those yobs on the playground." Georgiana gave her signature thumbs up with a smile.

"When we stopped a car thief in Peover Superior." Elizabeth chuckled.

"And when we helped that old lady from being robbed..." Henrietta added.

"Nevertheless, children. I have failed you."

"Failed us?" Henrietta glanced over at Elizabeth who shrugged her shoulders, as perplexed as her sister.

"Poppets you will have these powers forever." Temperance cupped her hands. "And you have choices: you can live in seclusion like your father and I have done with you all or alternatively, you can carry on wearing these lovely costumes to conceal your identities and do what we do." She looked over at me for a moment, peering for my support because I knew what was about to come next.

"Until I met your father, I did the latter to fill my time with helping others and feeling powerful as I did so. But the reality of it is, I was never in control, my circumstances dictated my every movement." Temperance got lost in a reverie as if she was re-living all of the many experiences she had so long ago as if they were yesterday. "The bigger problem with you three is there is a greater possibility..."

"We'd get found out." Elizabeth interjected.

Temperance raised her hands. "I've failed you because I've allowed this to all go off the rails. My own personal longings and insecurities have steered this vessel into a tempest that only resided in my deepest fears..."

"Mumma, I don't understand." Georgiana interjected and looked up at her inquisitively.

"Your father and I perceived this to be a potential outcome and we thought we were prepared." She looked over at me with pity in her eyes. "Sadly, we were not."

All three of our daughters listened on with intent.

"Right after we were married, some miraculous interventions were staged and I became pregnant with Bubble and Squeak at the drop of a hat."

"Heavens, what did you two do to each other?" Elizabeth's eyes bulged as she delivered her gaff.

I covered my mouth to conceal the brief laugh. "Carrot..." I raised my hand. "...Your mother is trying to tell you something important."

"When you two were young we knew you were gifted but we tried to put it out of our minds because not too long thereafter, we were pleasantly surprised by Georgiana's arrival. With this all being said, we knew that at some distant point that seemed like a blurry horizon, we would have to tell you that despite all the merriment and the extraordinary feats that we can perform, that in a hundred years from now perchance..."

"We're still going to be as we are?" Henrietta looked around.

Temperance nodded. "And we did our best to prevent this from escalating any further but I was the one who insisted on putting my tights back on and including you three..." She looked down. "Your father is a wise man; he saw how this could become calamitous and the events of Blackpool served as a cold reminder."

"Now what?" Bet spoke out.

"We need to let all this die down for a while, we need to be careful in who we interact with."

"Is this why Hayley can't come and play?" Georgiana frowned.

Temperance normally would chastise any of the girls for their manners but in this case all she could do was nod again as Georgiana looked up. "It's the only way we can keep this secret safe." Temperance let out a deep breath. "We've already crossed a boundary that could spell disastrous consequences."

"Will I ever get married like you did Mumma?" Henrietta cried out. "Or have children of my own?"

"It's not that simple, Bubble. I'd love nothing more to see you all grow into the fine women you already are and have your own families..." A sense of urgency filled Temperance's voice.

"But we cannot, can we?" Bet frowned.

"I thought the adventures would make this more pleasurable, it did for me before I met your Papa and something I longed to do with your grandmother." The desperation was more evident in Temperance's voice. "She is what inspired me to be Incredible Temperance."

"But you met, Papa." Henrietta countered with an interrogative tone of voice. "And Bets and I can't make you a Nana and Pop Pop."

"To be fair, you are a bit young to be thinking about that, Skittle." I placed my arm around Temperance's waist. This time, she didn't fight me in drawing close to her or demonstrating any physical display of affection. She settled and seemed more relaxed by my presence.

"Big Sister does raise a valid point though, Papa." Elizabeth crossed her arms.

Georgiana stood in front of her sisters and nodded vehemently.

Temperance's heart was breaking in response to the statement. "It's not meant to be this way, Squeak."

"But it is...." Elizabeth's eyes grew dark. "We're trapped." Her eyes turned red and she about faced, heading for the door.

"Elizabeth, wait!" Temperance called out to her.

"Don't talk to me!" Bet ran away. Tears filled Henrietta's eyes as she followed her out. "Squeak..."

"Let me alone, Hetta!" Her voice screeched as a burning smell emanated from the lounge. Temperance and I scampered out behind Henrietta, Georgiana following us unsure of what to do next. When we entered the lounge, Henrietta stood with her fingertips wet as she shook them out. The ball at the base of the bannister railing had been completely charred, its remains were left in a black heap on the ivory carpet at the first step.

"Bet!" I yelled up the steps to her.

"Don't talk to me, Papa!" Her feet kept marching onward. "You are the one who caused all of this!"

I ran up the steps and heard a door slam. As I entered into the hallway, all the doors were shut to the respective bedrooms, ours on the left, Georgiana's behind us, and Henrietta's across from hers. The bathroom door remained open, a shadowy recess emerging from the opening. I looked to the end of the corridor at the stained-glass window and the silhouette of a tree branch hovering through the red, blue, yellow, and green of the panes. Combined with the white crown mouldings and brocade ceilings, it took me back over a century. The hall had an eeriness in its quiet, the hair stood up on the back of my neck as I heard a smash from above me. My eyes leapt to the brass handle of the door for the attic.

"Bet!" I reached for the door handle and it wouldn't budge; it was locked. A heat started to build behind the door. I knocked my fist against it. "Elizabeth, open up!"

No response only screeches and occasional sobs, followed by thrashing sounds.

"Elizabeth Grace, please..."

"I hate you!" She screamed back at me through the door, and the words broke my heart. However, I just wanted to help her. I didn't care what she said, I just wanted to reason with her and comfort Bet, in any way I could. I thought of what I could do to somehow get into the attic, peering around until an idea dawned upon me. I'll break off the towel rack in the bathroom and force the door: I had to get to her!

"Daddy!" Georgiana called out to me as I heard her little feet scamper up the steps. I turned around and she stopped just behind the top step. Her eyes were enlarged with worry and fear, her strawberry blonde hair neatly organised in bangs and two ponytails joining her down her back. Her arms were clad in a white cotton turtleneck which hid beneath a khaki-denim dress. Georgiana's legs were covered in white cotton stockings and blue loafers. She looked innocent and gentle in the midst of all the madness.

"Henna is really sad."

The sound of a muffled grunt followed by a crash filled the air. Georgiana winced at the sound of it.

"I'll be with her in a minute but Elizabeth is having a crisis." I was stuck in thought, deriving ways to take the door. I suppose I could drive all the way to the fire station to get a halogen to take the door off the hinges, but did I have that sort of time? Would that make it any better?

"Bets will calm down eventually, you shouldn't worry." Georgiana spoke into the situation, offering sage words beyond her years as she put her hands behind her back. "It's Henna..."

"Bet is trashing the attic, as we speak..." I came over to her and put my hands on her sides before I knelt down.

"She overreacts and burns herself out, that's how Bets is." Georgiana shook her head. "It's Henna, she has never been so low..." Georgiana's eyes filled with worry. "Mummy is giving her cuddles but it's not working..." I looked ahead at the steps before my eyes went upward to meet Georgiana's. "And how do you feel about all of this, Jelly Bean?"

Georgiana smiled; her eyes twinkled with excitement. "I think it's pretty neat." Her smile grew wider. "I can be like another Incredible Temperance." She batted her eyebrows and nodded briefly. "But I wear pink!"

"Well, that's why you are Super Georgiana, right?"

She nodded with confidence, wearing a sly smile. "I like being stronger than any lad my age."

"You can't be doing all this crazy stuff, it's dangerous." I put my hand on my hip.

Georgiana sulked.

"You do realise that the only reason why I am so overprotective is because you mean so much to me, right?"

She nodded again without responding audibly.

"What do you think about what your sisters are concerned about?"

"Papa, I am only eight." She held her up eight fingers. "...It'd be previous of me to look into any long-term planning, wouldn't you agree?"

"Previous..." I laughed "...Good word." I opened my arms to her. Georgiana put her arms around my back and rested her head on my shoulder. I picked her up and she wrapped her arms around my neck and her legs near my waist. I looked behind me when I heard another crash.

"Elizabeth!" I called out to her.

No response.

"Can you do me a favour, sweetheart?"

She smiled and nodded in agreement.

"Ice on that doorknob, please?"

Georgie extended her hand and a stream of ice smacked into the brass door latch which had faint glows of red. The colour darkened down as the latch dampened. The ice quickly puddled into streaks of water, billowing down the door.

"I hope she isn't burning the place down."

"That's what we have you for, Papa." Georgiana smirked.

"I am not a firefighter, anymore, baby girl."

"Of course, you are, Daddy." She ran her hands against my scruff. "You are always going to be a fireman to me." She eskimo-kissed me.

"Thank you, sweetheart." I kissed her forehead and adjusted her on my hip.

"Go talk to Bubble and by the time you've cheered her up, Squeak will be calm."

I chuckled at Georgiana's candour; it was refreshing to have a voice of reason come from such a young source in the midst of chaos we adults could not handle.

"I thought you don't do long-term planning?"

"This is more of an intermediate plan."

"You are the expert." I smiled at her.

When I arrived downstairs, Henrietta was in a state of disarray. She could hardly move, apoplectic from what she had discovered. She was sniffling and sobbing modestly with her face planted in a cameo plush pillow on our couch. My beloved held one of her hands while running her hand over her back and stroking her long locks of mahogany hair.

I held Georgiana's hands as we made our way down the steps. As I got to the base of the steps, woe overcame Georgie and prompted her to run over to join her mother immediately.

"Henna..." Her voice gently called out to her older sister but Henrietta was trapped in her own thoughts, jostling and shaking on the pillow without any form of response. Temperance looked up at me, clutching our brave daughter's hand.

"She won't speak." My beloved looked up at me with her eyes glassed over. Temperance looked out the window toward the meadow for a brief moment, deep in thought. Her lips appeared heavy from the concerns that weighed down upon her.

"I never wanted this for her." She looked up at me, desperate for answers. Temperance appeared helpless and in distress, seldom has she ever displayed such vulnerability. My beloved was always steadfast and resolved. Minutes ago, she was my adversary and now she wasn't dogged nor confrontational, she looked acquiescent to a course of events that spiralled out of control leaving her helpless. "Truthfully, the weight of this burden is on my shoulders."

"You are a wonderful mother and a wonderful wife." I drew close to her and spoke softly. "I know we haven't been getting along as of late but it doesn't matter to me because you are more important than any of it." I embraced Temperance and rested my lips against her bun of hair. "We have to work together and figure this out." I ran my hands up her arms. "Can we put everything aside and be a couple again?"

Temperance nodded as she held my arm firmly as I kept my arms around her.

"I can't handle all this without you Mama."

A smile broke from her face briefly.

"Can I run or preferably fly to the shop quick and get Henrietta a blueberry lemonade?" Georgiana's voice cut through the faint whimpers and sobs. "Big sister loves those." Gee stroked a stand of Henrietta's hair and kissed her cheek. Henrietta moved for a moment to put her arm around her little sister's back to acknowledge her before Georgiana rested her head on Henrietta's back in a tender display of affection.

"I am going to take her up to bed." I released Temperance and looked down at Georgie who now gazed around the room, unsure of what was coming next. I swooped down and scooped my arms under Henrietta's body and cradled her against me. She put her arms around my neck as I carefully held her and stepped away from the couch. Though Henrietta was a lot bigger compared to when she was younger, it was no different to me. It was as if she was five years old again and fell asleep on my lap watching a movie. However, this wasn't a peaceful slumber. I recognised what this was as it was the hideous malady that she inherited from me. I didn't want to entertain the possibility that she had been stricken with anxiety attacks and depression like I had once been and it was wreaking havoc on her physiologically.

As I made my way up the steps toward her bedroom, I rehearsed all the many things that could be going through her head and a lump formed in my throat. It was a nightmare for me to experience but even more so if my beautiful precious daughter had fallen under its spell, subjected the anguish that can be crippling. I backed into the door into Henrietta's bedroom, hearing the echoes and thrashes of Elizabeth upstairs. Concern filled me as both my daughters were suffering but their troubles manifested in contrasting methods.

"We need to get you under the covers, okay, Skittle?" I spoke tenderly to Hetta.

The intensity of her grip around my neck intensified. "Don't go." She sniffled. "I need to talk."

"I am not going anywhere, sweetheart." I approached her bed and gently placed her down on top of the duvet. "Let's get you comfortable though." I carefully moved two large fluffy pillows behind her head, they were a powdery white and plush, caving in around Henrietta's head. "It's important to rest, if you have a breakdown."

"Is that what this is?"

"I've had plenty and it's okay to have them, darling." I undid the laces of her shoes. "Would you like me to step out for a minute so you can get out of your dress?"

"No, I'm alright." Her eyes lacked any form of energy, they were bleak with a fleeting light at the base of her dark blue irises. I placed her shoes on the floor and cautiously plucked at her white socks to remove them from her feet. Henrietta moved about after I had removed the socks from her feet until I got her under the duvet.

I placed my arm over her and stroked her hair, a smile escaped from her briefly before sadness filled her face.

"Papa, have you ever felt like you didn't want to be here anymore?"

The words eviscerated my soul, I could feel the tears welling up in my heart because it was the worst thing I could ever hear. Henrietta glanced at me as I gathered my thoughts and what to say next; though she didn't say anything remorse was evident in her glance. Her fingers reached to mine as I placed my hand over hers.

"Yes." I nodded, almost rocking my head. "Many times, actually..."

"What did you do?" Her eyes leered toward the white curtains which darkened down the daylight entering the bedroom. "It's not like, we have a way out now..."

I looked up at the ceiling fan, solitary and idle, a spectator to this heart-breaking episode of melancholy. "I used to think the same thing." I gripped her hand harder. "Talking helps." I smiled at her. "Just tell me what you are feeling, Skittle." I stroked her face. "It may bring you relief."

Tears filled up her eyes.

"Your mind will tell you all sorts of lies." I clutched her fingers. "It'll try to steal your hope and make you feel like you don't matter." I stroked her hair. "None of it's true though, despite how real it may seem."

"But does it ever go away?"

"Believe it or not, it does. Despite at one point, I thought it never would..." I glanced over at the telescope by the window, recalling the day I surprised her with it. My daughter had a keen interest in the stars, celestial bodies, and the universe's expanse and now she was convalescent in her bed. A metaphor for how these conditions operate: a ruthless campaign of condensing and constricting its target to the smallest of spaces.

"And I will be there every step of the way to make sure you get there."

"What changed it for you?"

"The Lord." I glanced out into the hall. "Your mother." My head turned back to Henrietta with a glowing smile. "You."

A smile broke from her face for a fleeting moment.

"How long have you felt like this, darling?" I said a silent prayer in that moment to my Father in Heaven: Please do not let it be long. Please, Lord, make this go as fast as it came.

"On occasion, it has flashed before my mind but I thought it was me going through changes." She cleared her throat. I grabbed a tissue from the nightstand beside her and pressed it to her nose so she could blow her it. She sniffled once more. "...but when Mummy told me that I could never experience what you and her have, it descended upon me..."

I nodded in acknowledgement of her feelings. "Mummy never said you couldn't." I dabbed her once more. "She was expressing her concern that it can create a lot of problems."

Henrietta sat up and I placed my hand over her thigh on the duvet to settle her. A woe cascaded over me; I wanted my daughter to succeed in whatever she desired and to be whatever she wanted to be. I earnestly wanted nothing more but somehow the situation became far complicated where all of that got swept up in the current.

"There is nothing that your mother and I would want more than to see you playing piano in any concert hall you desire and for you to walk down the aisle one day in church. To see you become a Mom, yourself." I raised my hand from her hip briefly to emphasize my next point. "You'd be far better than us in all three."

"I am not going to be a better Mum than Mummy." She showed a sign of jubilance which filled me with joy. "And no one is a better Papa, than you."

My eyes watered up at the latter statement because she said it so effortlessly that the sincerity was overwhelmingly evident. I attempted to maintain composure but I struggled admittedly.

"I can't even tell you what that means to me." I stroked her cheek. "Look, Henrietta, you are a very kind and courteous young lady. You are strong, you are beautiful, you are very intelligent, and you are extremely talented. You can do anything."

"Except what we spoke about..."

I didn't want to lie to her, but I didn't want to tell her that it couldn't happen either.

"You may look like you're sixteen or eighteen even, but you are far younger than that and by the time this becomes an issue for real, who knows...."

"But how?" Henrietta queried, eager for some form of reassurance.

"Mummy and I might figure something out."

"Well, why would you marry her, if you knew this could happen?" Henrietta's response was filled with angst and irritation that was misplaced.

"We didn't know what would happen." I stroked her shoulder. "When we factored in all the possibilities, we trusted The Lord and took a vow before Him."

"And has He offered a solution?"

"Is The Lord finished with his work yet, Skittle?"

Henrietta acquiesced and didn't reply, her silence was an acknowledgment of what I just said. "It's an honour to be married to Mummy. And I know we have hit a rough patch lately but I love her more than anything in this world and if we never married then we wouldn't have had you or your sisters. And make no mistake, I wouldn't change that no matter what comes of it. If you asked your mother, she would say the same."

Our tender moment was interrupted by another thud upstairs. I looked up at the ceiling, imagining what kind of mayhem was transpiring in that attic with Elizabeth. My eyes peered at the window as the outside light darkened, and the wind howled in the walls of the house. The branches of the willow tree in our back garden leaned to the right.

"Daddy, a storm is coming!" Georgiana's voice echoed through the halls. "There are black clouds in the distance!"

"Giggle, come stay with me." Henrietta called out to her; Georgiana's thundering footsteps plumed through the corridor until she stood in front of the doorway with Prudence under her arm.

"I need to shut my eyes." Henrietta reclined into the pillow.

"Georgiana, keep your sister company, please." I got up off the edge of the mattress. "I have to check on Bet."

"Yes, Papa."

I felt Henrietta's cold hand clasp against my wrist.

"Daddy..." Her voice reverted back to an intonation that reminded me of when she was younger. I about-faced and gazed at Hetta; her blue eyes were fixed to the ceiling. "I feel scared."

Georgiana's eyes enlarged as she hopped onto the bed.

"Can you stay until I fall asleep?"

"I'll keep you safe, big sister." Gee nuzzled up against Henrietta and kissed the underside of her jaw. Hetta wrapped her arms around her little sister, Georgiana had become a doll herself to her older sister similar to when she would cuddle Prudie when she was frightened.

I was longing to make sure Elizabeth was alright but Henrietta was overwhelmed and expressing ideas that I prayed she would never experience. Henrietta needed me; Bet wanted to be left alone. If only, I could be in two places at once as I wanted to be there for all three of my daughters as I adored all three of them.

"Please..." Her hand gripped my wrist harder.

"You don't have to ask twice, honey." I stroked her head and sat back on the bed. The sheets rustled as my daughters cuddled against either side of me. I placed my arms over them and watched as they shut their eyes, drifting off peacefully. Soon thereafter the room was filled with their faint exhalations and I shut my eyes unaware I had fallen asleep until my eyes flung open at the sound of another thud from the attic. I stared up, the dissonance reverberating across the beams hidden behind the ceiling. The sound of the hallway light switch being turned on caught my attention and when I moved my head to look toward the corridor, my beloved stood in the doorway.

Temperance's eyes pointed toward the attic and I nodded with my finger pressed over my lips. Temperance responded with a thumbs up. I picked up Georgiana who was asleep against my chest with her old friend Prudence in her clutch. In slow, methodical, and covert fashion I put Georgiana next to Henrietta and instinctively Hetta cuddled her without showing any signs of being awoken. I drew the duvet over both of them and kissed both their foreheads before tip-toeing out of the bedroom, slowly shutting the door behind me as I met with my beloved in the corridor.

"She's been up there now for over two hours." Temperance put her hand on her hip. "I've been trying the door and attempting to reason with her but it's no use."

I reached for the door latch which was locked. "Elizabeth!" I shook the latch. "Please unlock the door, I want to make sure you are alright."

"I'm fine!" She screamed back at me.

"I am going to ask her again." I whispered to Temperance. "If she doesn't cooperate, I am taking the door."

Temperance put her hand against my chest. "I'll spare you the bother, I will re-create the Angel Meadow endeavour and kick through the blasted thing."

"Carrot, I am only going to ask once more." I shook the handle and tried to rattle it loose.

"Go away!" Her voice had a menacing poltergeist-like shriek about it. I wasn't intimidated by it though, I just wanted to get to my daughter.

"We are concerned about you." I leaned against the door and fidgeted with the latch. The temperature started to rise. "This is your last chance or we will force the door."

"Dare you try."

"Do you want Mommy to break down the door and come up instead?"

"Listen to your father, Squeak." Temperance leaned up against me, speaking at length towards the door. All went silent excepting a faded footstep, a brief dissonance before returning to quiet. A moment later, we both heard a slight click and then it returned to silence. When I tried the door again, it opened without any trouble.

"As I told you before, you are the one that makes everything go around here." I rubbed her cheek.

A brief flash directed our attention toward the attic before darkness descended from the staircase into the dim corridor, lit solely by a glass ceiling globe lamp. Another flash escaped from the darkness followed by a loud clap of thunder.

Temperance gazed into the darkness, her eyes filled with sorrow, worry, and concern. "I overheard what you said to Bubble when you were comforting her."

My eyes turned towards her for a brief moment, hanging on what she said next.

"I want you to know that I too will always love you more than anything we face together." A smile broke from her face. "Even when you are my opponent."

The words captured my heart and touched my soul, I was speechless and touched. "I am always on your side Honey Bee, even if it doesn't feel that way sometimes." I smiled at her and kissed my beloved's hand. "My loyalty is to you above all else."

Temperance's smile widened. "As I with you..."

A grunt of anger huffed from the attic which directed our attention into the blackness.

"I best get up there." I took a step toward the attic and looked back at Temperance, one more time. "We've done everything we can for them."

Temperance shed a tear that welled up in her eyes.

"Elizabeth will be okay, my love." I sojourned into the cold column of air, greeted by the whistles of the wind meandering through the draughts in the old latticed roof.

XXVI.

The attic was cold and dark. Dolls sat one beside the other, all with smiles on their faces, hauntingly innocent. All stared at me as if they were under the dominion of a puppeteer. Lightning flashed from the window followed by a loud crack of thunder. I contorted my body as I made my way under the eaves, another dollhouse was turned over with all the heads severed. Three girls with pigtails and plaid dresses, disconnected from the torso. The sight chilled me to my bones. Heat rose and the smell of burning filled the air.

Shreds of paper were scattered on the floor and feathers speckled about. In looking on the bed, the duvet was half hanging off with the middle of each pillow torn to pieces.

"Carrot..." I called out but there was no response. I continued to walk around and only heard an occasional gust of wind rattle the beams. Everything appeared destroyed until I opened a wardrobe, in there the contents remained unscathed. In the middle of the wardrobe was an antique looking glass where I could only see my imperceptible shadow in the reflection. I recognised the mirror; it was a gift from Temperance to Elizabeth when she turned 12. I remember the joy my wife exclaimed when she said she couldn't wait to brush Bet's hair in the mirror, as she got ready for a dance recital. Below the looking glass on the shelf, my Lieutenant badge which Elizabeth asked for. She had propped it up and flanked it with a picture of Elizabeth and I, taken on the day we took her to Haworth to see the Bronte Parsonage Museum. In the picture,

410 K. SCOTT FUCHS

Elizabeth's smile was the central feature of the image, it was bright, warm, and full of life; it was identical to her mother's and in many ways, she looked like Temperance there only a tad younger with her hair falling all over the place. In the image, she pressed her head against my chest and nuzzled it under my chin, burrowing under my arms which wrapped around her. To the right of the image, a drawing: Elizabeth had drawn me in my firefighting gear with a pen in my hand: she had quoted some words from one of my poems in a series of flaming streaks that formed into script ink. Elizabeth framed the drawing with a Victorian-style floral border. She wrote "My Father, My Hero" on the top and bottom of the drawing. My hands plucked at the sketch and tears filled my eyes. Behind the drawing, she had a collection of memoranda from various things she and I had done together. She had some memorabilia of my beloved and her sisters, as well, but seemingly it was some sort of a shrine she had built for me. I was humbled by this unexpected homage and tried to swipe away the tears, but couldn't help but weep.

"Father, please look after my little girl." I prayed and looked once more at the drawing, pressing it to my chest. In the midst of my sighs, I heard footsteps pitter-patter across the attic. My head shot around and I looked behind me.

"Bet?"

I gazed into the darkness, two red eyes stared at me, glowing with a tint of orange.

"Please come out, Elizabeth." I stepped into darkness hoping she could see the desperation in my eyes, longing to see her. The chimes of a music box filled the air, the opening notes of *"Bethena"* by Scott Joplin twinkled in the blackness.

"Are you not afraid?" Her voice called out from the darkness.

"Afraid? You are my precious daughter, I love you." I sniffled. "I want to know you are okay, must I beg?"

"Will we truly be like this forever, Father?"

"We can talk about all of this." I extended my hand toward the red eyes. "Just give me a chance and hear me out."

The red eyes came forward from the darkness; the air around my fingertips started to vibrate as Elizabeth's steps pattered against the old wood; The music box echoed across the rafters until warm flesh clutched my hand. The beady red dots had dissipated into the kind and gentle eyes of Elizabeth. Her hair fell down her back and her lips curved down toward the floor.

"Honey, I don't know what to say to all of this, I am..." I held up the drawing but before I could finish what I was saying, Elizabeth burst into my arms and emerged from her shadows. "I am sorry."

"It's alright." I put the drawing down and wrapped my arms around her, holding her against me. "Bet, I was worried sick about you."

"I never hated you, Papa." She pulled back for a moment. "I love you..." Bet sniffled "...I guess Henrietta is not the only one who idolises you here." She squeezed against me and as I ran my hand up and down her back, I felt a rough and tight fabric followed by her smooth skin.

"I am sorry about the dolls. I had a tantrum and cut their heads with my nails." Her words muffled against my chest.

When I glanced down, I noticed Bet was clad in heliotrope lycra leggings along with a heliotrope leather vest that showed off her midriff; both of which were accentuated by pink lacing. Her abs were oiled, glistening under the moonlight. Her costume also shined in the dark. Her silver armbands and pink open-finger gloves also shimmered. She like her siblings and mother had a silver belt with a pink E in the middle of the buckle. Her costume was an amalgamation of Henrietta, Georgiana, and Temperance's.

"At this point, this is what I feel most comfortable in." She sniffled and threw her hands at her side. "It's all I'm ever going to be."

"That's not true, Bet..." I ran my hand up and down her back to soothe her. "...you can be whatever you want..."

"I knew there was a catch." She sobbed as I held her. Elizabeth moved her head back and looked up at me. "Why did you and Mummy do this to us?" Her eyes were engrossed and immured with a sense of betrayal.

"Sweetheart, we were trying to avoid this." I clutched her arms. "Please believe me..."

Elizabeth gulped and nodded.

I smiled at her and caught one of her tears.

"Then why did this happen?" She sniffled again. "And how?"

"Can I tell you a quick story, Carrot?"

She nodded again.

I sat down on a white rocking chair which seemed to move on its own perhaps from the draught coming through the old Victorian roof. When I sat on the rocking chair, Elizabeth sat on my lap. Though she was nearly a full-grown woman for intent and purpose, she placed her arm around my neck and I placed mine around her waist to hold her. At that moment, she was very much still my little girl and terrified looking for answers from the one man that she knew would never hurt her.

"You were playing *Bethena*." I looked into her eyes. "It has special meaning to me because it was written by Mister Joplin who endured a lot of heartache. He lost a woman that he loved and I never wanted to lose your mom." I swallowed. "When I met your mom, she was as she was now. I thought she was in her late twenties but it turns out she was actually..."

"Over 160 years old"

"That's right..." My thumb rubbed against Bet's skin. "But I didn't know of course until one day, she revealed her powers to me."

"And what did you do?"

"I love your mother, what do you think I did?"

Elizabeth's eyes peered around the attic for a moment until another clap of thunder rumbled against the roof.

"Your mom said that all she wanted was to fall in love and have a bunch of beautiful daughters like you and your sisters." I smiled at her. "I wanted the same and I wanted to have it with her. But most importantly, I wanted her to have it because she deserves it." I reminisced of that day for a moment which was all a blur from that point until now. "Now I was and I still am madly in love with your mom and thought marrying her may resolve this matter and you wouldn't inherit the very powers that have been passed onto you, Henrietta, and Georgiana." I looked into the dark for a moment.

"Did you sell your soul?" Elizabeth looked up at me. "Don't lie to me."

I shook my head. "I meant what I said about doing things before The Lord."

"It doesn't make any sense." She leaned back and looked at me. "I would have thought I was demonic..."

"Your mother used to say the same thing."

Bet gazed into the darkness, confused and shaken.

"There is nothing demonic about you, sweetheart." I rubbed her shoulder. "In fact, when your mother said she was pregnant with you, I thanked The Lord for blessing me with two angels from Heaven."

A smile flashed across her face. "And truly it never scared you that Mumma was born on the 15th of July, 1855?"

"I was in love with your Mom from the moment that I first saw her."

"I know." She bantered. "I've read the book." Elizabeth looked down for a moment. "I just wanted to hear it come from your lips..." She smiled more widely with a youthful innocence.

"What was most remarkable was on the day I met her, minutes before I was standing on the aqueduct in Marple contemplating whether or not to jump..." I reminisced; my eyes went blank for a moment until they illuminated at the thought of the moment that I first met her. "But when I first saw your Mother, I saw Henrietta, I saw Georgiana, and I saw you." Tears filled my eyes. "You are the light of our lives, Elizabeth."

She blushed. "And you never wanted sons?"

I shook my head with a smile. "No, but to be fair you and Gee..."

Bet raised her hands and chuckled. "I reckon I am the son of the lot."

"Well some of the jokes you make, you wouldn't even hear in a locker room." I smiled. "But I always wanted a daughter so I can have moments like this." A smirk formed across my face. "Minus the severed doll heads and the red eyes, of course..." I tapped her arm playfully.

"Oh, hush." She smiled and punched my arm softly before she fully embraced me. "I was having a fit..." I held her for a moment and closed my eyes until she moved her back keeping her arms around my neck.

"You don't like my red eyes?" She bantered.

"You have beautiful blue eyes like your mother."

"At least I get a cool outfit out of this commotion, aye?"

"You look amazing and you definitely outdid your mom..." I shot her a look to make her laugh before I placed my finger to my lips. "But don't tell anyone, I said that though..." I winked at her to elicit another smile from her. "...Georgie or your mom may have something to say about that..."

Elizabeth punched my arm playfully again. "You goon..."

"I remember when you were around Georgiana's age before you shot up so quickly. You loved to run around the field trying to catch the butterflies and get into all sorts of mischief." A smile returned to my face. "Your mother was the same when she was little." I nearly became choked up at the image of my wife being young. I wish I had known Temperance was she was just a girl and I just a boy so I could have watched her grow and blossom into what she became.

"We would watch Masha and The Bear and you used to carry around a Snow Maiden plush toy like Georgiana does now with Prudence. Do you still have it?"

Bet nodded. "I am always going to keep it, it's like being there with you again." Her eyes grew glassy and some tears welled up in my eyes too. At the end of the episode, the Snow Maiden melted from jumping over a fire despite her parents doing everything they could to keep her safe and away from trouble. I used to cry because it reminded me of Elizabeth as she used to wear her hair similarly in a long plait down her back and she had a white dress with blue accents. Bet had a smile that matched the doll's and she might as well have looked like one too. Similarly, I have always been preoccupied with making sure nothing ever happened to her. I felt as if I had failed them.

"You always cried at the end of the cartoon because you are so bloody sensitive." Elizabeth smiled back at me for a moment and it was like talking to her when she was seven again, when she was a little girl. "You always hugged me at the end and told me how much you loved me." Elizabeth recalled and then as she did previously in the moments she just described, embraced me again.

I closed my eyes for a moment and I was taken back to a spring day years ago when Bet was standing in the field, dressed and looking as I described; gazing around with an innocent and curious look in her eyes. She waved at everyone she saw and she was eager to make friends with whoever she encountered. Like her sister, she was eager to share and very affectionate. When Henrietta and Elizabeth came, it may as well have been something that Temperance and I dreamed into life.

"Not much has changed." I touched her cheek and looked into her eyes. "No matter what happens, I am always going to be here for you." My hands held her firmer. "...I love you so much and your mother and your sisters adore you." I smiled at her. "You are never going to be on your own, I want you to remember that."

She didn't respond but the softening of her face reflected she was moved by the words. "I love you too, Papa."

The rumbles of thunder had dispensed. There was no longer any noise of raindrops pattering against the roof or faint whistles or howls of wind.

The door creaked open.

"Squeak?" A voice called up to the attic. At the bottom of the steps was Henrietta, her blue eyes gazed up at me with an inquisitiveness. Henrietta had emerged from her bed, her hair down and scattered over her white blouse. Her heels clanked against the hollow wood as she ascended the steps, holding her skirt with one hand as she gripped the railing with the other.

"You alright?" She got to the top of the steps.

Elizabeth smiled at her sister and nodded once. "And you?"

"Not bad, thanks." Hetta nonchalantly sat up on my other knee and like her sister threw her arm around my neck.

"I was just reminiscing about when you the two were a bit younger..." I kept my arms around both of their backs. "I get emotional thinking about that, you know..."

"If that be the case..." Bet pulled her hand from behind my neck and held both in front of Henrietta. "Double Double, Bubble?"

Hetta smiled and snapped her fingers; she was now in her royal blue unitard. Her hair had a blue butterfly hair clip in it. She wore lilac briefs over her unitard and a silver belt with a pink H in the buckle. On the back of her briefs like Elizabeth and Georgiana was a pink H. She wore pink leather gloves and leather boots to complement her look. Bet smirked at Hen, as the gesture was a method for Hetta to demonstrate solidarity with her sister.

"I thought you would never ask." Hetta threw the first two hands to start the clapping game "Double, double, this, that." Bet played along. "Double, double, criss, cross," Both giggled "Back and forth, this and that, "Double, double, criss, cross," they could barely finish "Bubble and Squeak are having a laugh."

The childish game culminated in the two of them embracing each other and pressing their heads against one another.

"I am sorry for before, Bubble." Elizabeth drew her hand to around Henrietta's head. "I cannot bear the thought of being without you, my dear."

"We'll always have each other, Squeak." Henrietta kissed her forehead and the two both leaned into me as I held them both. I stroked the both of them as they held each other and rested against me.

"Come on, you two…" I kept my arms around them and gave them a gentle pat "Let's go downstairs, Mommy's been worried."

Bet and Hen sat up and I rose to my feet thereafter. I walked ahead of them to go down the steps ahead of them. Both took my hands and I led them down the narrow and steep stairs. "Be careful, please. The staircase is nearly as old as Mommy."

"Fortunately, the steps themselves are in good working order." Hetta chirped as I got to the bottom of the stairs and emerged from the shadowy chasm into the dim corridor.

"I had to touch them up, I wasn't going to have you two running around up here unless they were safe to climb."

"We know, Papa." They both spoke in unison and looked back at me with a joyful smile.

The scent of hyacinth filled the air as Temperance ascended the steps from the ground floor. "Squeak." She opened her arms and embraced her daughter, smiling briefly at her before she embraced Henrietta thereafter. Temperance put her lips to each of theirs and pressed her forehead against the sides of their heads. "My little cherubs." They held each other for a moment before the silent embrace was broken.

"Playtime is over." My beloved smacked Bet's bum playfully, a crack from her hand against leather. "Get yourselves tidied up for tea." She shot a wry smile as she grabbed Hetta's butt too as she passed. Both squeaked and squealed in response to the playful gest. "Chop, Chop." She teased them some more.

"We are going!" Bet whined in gest.

"Make like a monkey then and swing."

Both leered back at Temperance with a mischievous look in their eye, clearly more amused by their mother's antics.

Temperance turned and flanked me as she watched them go down the hall toward the bathroom. Like many girl friends had a tendency to do, Bet and Hen often frequented the toilet together.

"I didn't get a chance to say it before either but I am sorry that we've been at each other's throats and if I have been the cause of it." I ran my hand up and down Temperance's side, the red pansy print on her blouse curled in my hand. "I have made some stupid comments and at times I have been antagonistic because I couldn't control my emotions."

Temperance looked at me out of the side of her eye.

"Though I never intended to, I have been overbearing, oppressive, and perhaps even controlling." I looked down for a moment. "...though I never meant to be." I re-established eye contact. "I love you and I trust you, and even when I act like a maniac..."

"I never thought any different, darling..." She interjected with a smile on her face. "I love you too. I admit that I too have been a bit of elbow grease to get on with, as of recent." My beloved sighed. "Allow me to say that I regret giving you an experience that you do not deserve. In some instances, I have completely ignored you and it must have reminded of you the very people I swore I would never be to you. Wrongfully, I took out most of my anger on you and I am deeply sorry for this..." She peered down at her boot. "I have also been domineering, tyrannical, and shamefully obstinate. I hope you will forgive me..."

I smiled at her. "You are strong-willed and resolute." I put my hand around her back. "It's what I admire about you."

"And I appreciate how caring and gallant, you are."

We shared a mutual smile and my eyes glanced down at her wedding ring which she ran her index finger over carefully yet intently.

"We should go out one night, just you and I."

She put her hands together, actively listening to what I had to say.

"We haven't spent time as a couple together other than when the kids are in bed or when we are in bed." I watched the door as I listened to Henrietta and Elizabeth giggling in the bathroom, their laughter perceptible even outside at the far end of the hall.

"They'll be fine with Gee..."

"Third time is the charm?" Temperance swirled her eyes around, less sure by comparison.

"We'll bribe them with pizza..." I chuckled. "Besides, maybe what we need is to be us a little more..."

"Go out on a date and hire a babysitter, you say?" Temperance fluttered her eyes and spoke coyly with a stern accent. "For old time's sake..." She nodded. "I like the sound of it and I know where we should go..." Her eyes moved to the door and then downstairs at the sound of Georgiana singing in the front room.

"Marple?"

"Very good." Temperance's eyes enlarged as I had answered correctly before she continued with her suggestion. "I thought that we could go to the Ring of Bells and have a ramble on the canal before we sit for our meal."

For a brief moment, I was back there on an autumn day hiding in the back pages of my mind, I could still feel the air and smell the winter in the air. "Just like the day, we met...."

"Mhmm." Temperance's eyes softened as mine did when we shared a glance. "We'll park in front of the old house and reflect back to where it all started."

"As you do"

"As you do." She fluttered her eyebrows as she replied coyly.

"Let's make the arrangements."

Temperance smiled with her lips shut, her eyes sparkling at the comment. My head drew close to hers and our foreheads pressed together, our eyes shut as we listened to each other breathe. The door opened from the bathroom and out came Henrietta and Elizabeth hurrying forward, wearing what they wore before everything kicked off.

"We heard you gabbing when we were in the loo." Bet spoke loudly.

"And we are happy to watch The Giggle." Henrietta enthusiastically pointed and pulled her finger. "Just let us know when."

"Then you can do whatever it is, you people do over in Marple." Bet waved her fingers and scrunched her nose, speaking in a playful tone of voice and childish accent as she made her way to the steps with Henrietta close behind her.

"Incidentally..." Henrietta turned back and looked at us. "Pepperoni is definitely a good shout." She flicked her long mahogany hair. "Cheers"

"Extra Cheese!" Bet yelled up the steps. "Ta!"

"You can put them both together, Elizabeth." Henrietta teased.

"Come off it, Hetta. I'll pass on that rancid frisbee meat." Bet bantered as their conversation turned to muffle as they descended the stairs.

"We'll get one of each." I shouted down the steps at them.

"Thank you, Papa!" Both girls spoke at length back to me.

"Wait, I want pizza!" Georgiana protested and it prompted a chuckle from both of us.

"To be fair, most places have a twofer offer on". A spark of light formed at Temperance's fingertip before she waved it out. "Needs must."

We shared a laugh.

"Shall we?" Temperance raised her eyebrows and moved her head in the direction of the stairs.

As she made her way to the stairs, I took her hand and yanked her back to me, she yelped as she fell into my arms and I caught her, holding her close against me. Our eyes and lips were now separated by inches. I stroked a strand of her hair and she rubbed her nose gently against mine, putting her hand against my cheek. Our lips met and locked as I bent her down, holding her tight with one arm whilst I held her face firmly yet gently with the other. Temperance leaned into me and gripped my collar as she kissed me back with matched might and passion. A nostalgic recapitulation of the first time our lips ever met.

"The reward...." I held her close to me. "When can I redeem that?" I raised my eyebrows.

Temperance's eyes lit up with a mischievous and flirtatious grin. "We do need to tidy the attic, right?"

"It is a complete mess up there." I exaggerated a look of concern. "I've never seen it so bad."

Her eyes glanced upward for a moment. "We might need a moment then, won't we?" She turned her head toward the steps. "Bubble!"

"Yes, Mumma."

"Please put the hob on low and keep an eye on everything until your father and I come down."

"Okay!" She called back.

"Come along then." She took my hand and made her way toward the door. I opened the door for her and shut it behind us. Temperance locked it and she jumped onto me, I lifted her off the ground and kissed her passionately as we pressed into the wall. We spent the next hour at the base of the steps making passionate love that undoubtedly shook the entire house to its foundation.

XXVII.

It was a quiet Sunday afternoon. Each of us had spent the day engaged in various activities common to the household. The aroma of roast chicken filled the air as I ascended the stairs with mop in hand. Our youngest daughter was eager to help her mother cook in the kitchen. I passed by Henrietta's room and watched as she and her sister laughed when they pressed a duvet together at the two corners. Hetta and Bet were engaged in their own conversation, imperceptible to a passing ear but their immersive dialogue with each other was evident in their bright eyes and wide smiles fixed upon each other. As I drew close to the far white door on the left to the bathroom, I was halted at the sight of a book resting beside a potted plant on a cherry-wood side table. It was the copy of *Time and Temperance* that I had bound for my beloved as our first wedding anniversary gift to her. The girls' jeers and laughter leapt from Hetta's room and filled the hall, perhaps they were reading it again before they moved on to sorting through their laundry. I opened the door to the bathroom and slid the mop in, before shutting it abruptly.

I ran my hand along the gold-leaf lettering and a chill shot down my spine. I picked it up off the table and skimmed through the pages, an anxiousness and excitement filled me which nearly made me woozy. I recollected writing the pages in a wistful nostalgia as I jumped around the book, freezing for a moment when the echo of Hetta and Bet's laughter joined me at the table. I glanced around at the wall panels that matched the side table and how they glistened in the late afternoon sun that came through the stained-glass window. Their protrusions created a gradient of shading without any need for paint, carving a stark contrast from the periwinkle and white pin-striped wallpaper that reached toward the crown mouldings before hitting the brocade ceiling which matched the wainscoting that separated the two entities.

I opened to the page which recalled the day I met Temperance for the first time. That day was so long ago but it felt like yesterday. As I re-read the words, the sounds, the smells, and the air of the day surrounded me. The sense of panic had recapitulated and my heart started to pump. I saw black spots with each heartbeat and a weakness in my knees.

I was back on the canal and Temperance was emerging from beneath the brick bridge. Her heels clattering against the cobbles as I watched on in awe. My eyes wandered back to the page, my eyelashes reverberating with every line that I read. Before I rose to my feet, I already felt myself falling. A loss of equilibrium from the vertigo but more so, falling in love with her, as if it were happening all over again. The image flashed in front of me, taking a spill before uttering the first words to her. Eyes shut and on the flat of my back, I could see her running toward me until she was leaning over me, her blue eyes fixed on mine as my irises were desperate to emerge from behind the eyelids to behold her; an occupant in a room with curtains drawn longing to indulge in the splendour of spring. A shadow crossed the light of the window, distracting me from my reverie: a silhouette of a butterfly fluttering its wings outside as it flew onward, its colour veiled behind the drawn lace valance.

My eyes peered back to the book and the vertigo, the racing heart, and the joy filled me again as I re-read the words that I chose to describe my beloved. I shut my eyes and closed the book, pressing it against my heart. I stood still and listened to the sounds of the birds chirping outside.

"Daddy!" Georgiana screamed upstairs, her voice sounding more high-pitched and expressive. "Someone is at the door!"

My eyes flung open and I put the book down on the side table. Swinging the crimson ribbon around to mark the page I was on.

"Who is knocking on, on a Sunday?" Elizabeth emerged from Henrietta's bedroom followed by her sister.

"Probably some guy advertising a new takeaway..."

Henrietta and Elizabeth laughed at my remarks.

"They've come all the way out here to promote a banging kebab" Hetta feigned an attempt at my accent.

"Deadass they did." Bet chimed in, staying in her received pronunciation accent but using appropriate New York-associated slang terms.

"Funny..." I laughed at their comic routine. "Can you two goofballs go downstairs and help Mommy with setting the table while I see what this is all about?"

Henrietta and Elizabeth nodded.

I smiled at them and cupped their cheeks for a moment until the knock thundered up to us.

"I got it, Honey Bee." I called to my beloved as I descended the steps.

"Ta, Butterscotch." She replied from the kitchen; I heard her stirring gravy on the hob. The girls followed me down in a conversation of their own. I couldn't make out the words as I was focused on the familiar knock that rang against the door; it was one that echoed from long ago. I had heard it before, but I could not recall as to when precisely; It was elegant in rhythm and demure in cadence, yet strong with confidence to demonstrate that the visitor knew they were at the right house. I sprinted down the steps and gave Georgiana a quick smile. She returned the pleasantry and stood vigil with her doll in her arm, her long strawberry blonde hair down her back and kept in place with a pink bow that matched her undershirt. She wore a white dress with matching linen stockings and her black buckled boots. Very much, she reminded me of Alice from the fabled Lewis Carroll adventure.

When I opened the door, I was met by a familiar face.

"Tryphena, is it?"

She nodded with a smile. "You remembered..."

"How could I not?" I stepped out onto the first step. "My wife and you have the two most exotic names I've ever heard..."

"Do recall though it's Triphy for short..."

"I didn't know that we received mail on Sundays..."

Her smile grew larger this time, her blue eyes were filled with excitement. Triphy wasn't dressed as she was the last time that she delivered the mail; this time she wore a long goldenrod gown and had her blonde hair set back with a large red bow. Her fingers were covered in white linen gloves which matched her stockings. She had on blue-heeled shoes which had a matching red bow over the toe.

"...So, in addition to the uniform for a postwoman, have you also re-invented the work schedule now as well, Triphy?"

"I am afraid not, love..." She looked into the house. "I apologise for the intrusion but can I enquire as to whether Missus Lee ever opened the parcel that we delivered?"

The sound of Temperance stirring the pot with an occasional clang proved to be the only dissonance at that point. I closed the door and leaned against the framing.

"I thought recorded delivery only required a signature when the parcel is received?" I ran my fingers against my chin. "Is this a follow-up visit?"

"I didn't think she would open it..." Tryphena threw her hands on her hip. "That was a cock-up on Mother Dearest's part." She shook her head as she vented her frustration aloud.

"She did open it actually."

"Oh?" Tryphena stood at attention. "And how did she find it?" There was a nervous energy hidden behind her grin.

"I think the better question is who the sender is and why they sent it?"

"On that note, I am going to have to come clean with you about something..." Triphy clasped her hands together. "I am not employed by the Royal Mail..."

The grey clouds rolled in and intermingled with the white ones as the skies grew darker; a wind gusted and bent all the strands of grass in the meadow beyond the gate which whined in response to the brief gale.

"...Truth be told, I never was..."

I had all sorts of suspicions when she called the first time that there was something off about her, but I am also a man who has obsessive-compulsive disorder and excessive anxiety, so it was easy to dismiss these ideas even when my beloved herself felt she was odd. However, these revelations affirmed what had been previously discerned.

"I think it's time for you to leave then." I stood in front of the closed door and made sure it was shut. I crossed my arms and moving eyes toward the gate. There were enough clowns skulking around my wife, as of late, I wasn't going to take any more chances.

"Do not be alarmed, Mother will explain everything..." Triphy looked back and another woman arrived at the gate and opened it; she looked familiar. The woman had the same shade of hair as Henrietta and Elizabeth along with the same eyes as my beloved. A crimson scarf danced around her neck as she stepped through. Her fair fingers gently pressed the iron gate shut until they made their way upward to the lip of her black hat. A red rose was fixed to the peak of the bonnet and matched the flower fixed to the breast of her crimson bodice. The woman grabbed her dark violet long underskirt as she stepped forward to avoid scuffing it with any dirt

428 K. SCOTT FUCHS

or grass. Her heels clattered against the stone steps; this woman looked like she was from the Victorian era like my beloved, but her deportment, posture, and mannerisms were far too authentic to suggest this was some form of a re-enactment.

"Hello there." The woman curtsied. "I am awfully sorry to trouble you; my daughter has never been one for proper introductions." She removed her hat and let her auburn hair down. "Tryphena, dear..." The woman smiled at her to beckon her to her side. "We don't want to give off the wrong impression." Triphy rolled her eyes in response and obliged. The woman set her steely gaze upon me. "I am the one responsible for the parcel." Her eyes filled with sorrow, darkening as she took them off of me. "You can say, I am responsible for a lot of things."

A small knock came from the turret of the upstairs window. When I looked over my shoulder, I saw Georgiana with her fingers against the glass. She waved down with enormous energy and a huge beaming smile at this strange woman. The woman peered upwards at Georgie and waved back at her with a matching visage; it was as if they were long-lost friends. The woman's disposition grew serious when she focused her attention back upon me. Her blue eyes were filled with a similar sternness and determination that my love exuded when she was focused on any task at hand. There was a striking resemblance between Temperance and this lady.

"Georgiana is a charming girl." The woman adjusted her scarf. She spoke in a non-threatening tone of voice despite knowing my daughter's name which is quite menacing. "I've admired all three of your daughters from a distance. The other two ladies are called Henrietta and Elizabeth, correct?"

I didn't respond. Instinct overruled; I stood vigil, ready for whatever came next. Being a father and husband usurped any form of reason. I was not one for fighting nor would I ever engage in such a thing with a woman no less, it was against everything I stood for.

However, I would do whatever I must do to protect my wife and my daughters who were in our house behind me.

"My middle name is Elizabeth so naturally I have a predilection for the name." She delivered an untimely joke which drew a striking parallel to Temperance. The same puns, the same witty smile, the same dry sense of humour.

"It's Tempie's Christian name." She maintained her smile until her expression went blank. The shift was abrupt which indicated that this unknown visitor didn't want to reveal too much or show too much emotion, though she had failed to do so already. "I recall when she took it." She gleamed for a moment as her eyes watered up.

"Butterscotch!" Temperance called out to me; I could hear her voice behind the door and so could the mysterious woman, as her eyes lit up at the sound of Temperance's voice. Her shoulders tensed her crimson scarf danced in the wind along with her muslin chemise. Though she tried to present herself in a demure manner with refined etiquette, she was too excitable at any notion of my beloved.

"Honey Bee, stay inside, please." I yelled back at her, hoping she would heed my word but soon thereafter, the door opened.

"Who's there?" Temperance poked her head out the door, and the eyes of the stranger grew glassier at the sight of Temperance. Any words she planned to say had evaporated on her red lips. My beloved stared at her and her jaw descended.

Images flashed in front of me: the miniature in the front room; the drawing Georgiana gave me on my birthday; the moment I proposed to Temperance in the park. The significance of the name Elizabeth itself, it all moulded together. But it couldn't be...

"Mother?" Her words were barely audible; it was a whisper that was an inflexion of both nervousness and longing. "Is it truly you?" She took a step out behind me but I nevertheless remained in between her and the two guests on the steps, ready to shield and defend her if anything should happen.

"Oh, my beautiful girl!" Her arms opened. "You've grown into such a remarkable woman." She smiled with an exuberance that was overwhelming. It was then that I realised it was truly Abigail; she glowed in a way at the sight of Temperance that was identical to how my beloved did with Hetta, Bet, or Gee, whenever they did something cute or learned something new or accomplished anything: it was a smile of delight, joy, and pleasure.

Temperance was frozen and mystified, stuck in suspended animation. There was so much going on in her brain and so much to process in a short sprint. All she could do was remain stoic and motionless. She was in shock.

Tryphena smiled at Abigail before fixing her blue eyes back on us. "I take it Perrie wasn't expecting you, Mother..." A smirk formed with a flash of menace as a dash of red sparkled in her eyes at the mention of the antiquarian moniker. My beloved appeared as if she had seen a ghost or perhaps that she was a ghost now being seen.

Triphy's eyes had turned white just like Temperance's did when she controlled electricity; she let out a loud and uncontrollable laugh.

"None have called me Perrie since...." My love's words slurred as her knees buckled, she fell backwards and collapsed into my arms.

"Honey bee..." I stroked her face but she remained unresponsive. "Sweetheart!" I shook her a bit more as I cradled her, but she showed no signs of life.

"Mummy!" The screams of our daughters billowed out of the house as they rushed down the steps toward Temperance, as she was lying motionless in my arms as if her spirit had just fled her.

Don't miss out!

Visit the website below and you can sign up to receive emails whenever K. Scott Fuchs publishes a new book. There's no charge and no obligation.

https://books2read.com/r/B-A-HCTAB-AAXRC

BOOKS 2 READ

Connecting independent readers to independent writers.

Also by K. Scott Fuchs

Six Months in Wigan
Time and Temperance
Poetry From Ryecroft Hall
Mrs. Coleman of Coalbrookdale
Waiting For July
Sycamore Grove
A Day We Met In Lynbrook
The Town Upon A Hill

Watch for more at www.kscottfuchs.com.

About the Author

K. Scott Fuchs is a novelist, published poet, actor, and performer. His debut novel *Time and Temperance* was released in 2023 along with *Six Months in Wigan*, a collection of poetry. He is also the author of *Mrs. Coleman of Coalbrookdale*, (the prequel-sequel to *Time and Temperance*), *Poetry from Ryecroft Hall*, and the forthcoming novel *Sycamore Grove*, the third novel in The Miss Temperance Lee Series.

Please visit **www.kscottfuchs.com** or contact K. Scott Fuchs at **kscottfuchs@gmail.com** to join the mailing list or for any other inquiries related to both novels and poetry releases.

Read more at www.kscottfuchs.com.